The children had been sent to watch the road. Rumor said the Lady meant to break the Rebel movement in Tally province. And here her soldiers came. Closer now. Grim, hard-looking men. Veterans.

"It's them!" the boy gasped. Fear and awe filled his voice. Grudging admiration edged it. "That's the Black Company."

He touched the girl's wrist. "Let's go." They scurried through the weeds.

A shadow lay upon their path. They looked and went pale. Three horsemen stared down at them. The boy gaped. Nobody could have slipped up unheard. "Goblin!"

The small, frog-faced man in the middle grinned. "At your service, laddy-boy."

The boy was terrified. He shouted, "Run!" If his sister could escape. . . .

Goblin made a circular gesture. Pale pink fire tangled his fingers. He made a throwing motion. The boy fell, fighting invisible bonds like a fly caught in a spider's web. His sister whimpered.

"Pick them up," Goblin told his companions. "They should tell an interesting tale."

The second volume of
THE BLACK COMPANY trilogy.

## Tor Books by Glen Cook

*An Ill Fate Marshalling*
*Reap the East Wind*
*The Swordbearer*
*The Tower of Fear*

### The Black Company

*The Black Company* (The First Chronicle)
*Shadows Linger* (The Second Chronicle)
*The White Rose* (The Third Chronicle)
*The Silver Spike*
*Shadow Games* (The First Book of the South)
*Dreams of Steel* (The Second Book of the South)
*Bleak Seasons* (Book One of Glittering Stone)
*She Is the Darkness* (Book Two of Glittering Stone)
*Water Sleeps* (Book Three of Glittering Stone)
*Soldiers Live* (Book Four of Glittering Stone)

### Instrumentalities of the Night

*The Tyranny of the Night*
*Lord of the Silent Kingdom**

*Forthcoming

A TOM DOHERTY ASSOCIATES BOOK
NEW YORK

SHADOWS LINGER



Cover art by Keith Berdak

A Tor Book
Published by Tom Doherty Associates, LLC
175 Fifth Avenue
New York, NY 10010

www.tor.com



ISBN-13: 978-0-812-50842-0
ISBN-10: 0-812-50842-4

First Edition: October 1984

Printed in the United States of America

0 9

# DEDICATION

For David G. Hartwell, without whom there would be neither Sword nor Dread Empire nor Starfishers.

# Chapter One: JUNIPER

All men are born condemned, so the wise say. All suckle the breast of Death.

All bow before that Silent Monarch. That Lord in Shadow lifts a finger. A feather flutters to the earth. There is no reason in His song. The good go young. The wicked prosper. He is king of the Chaos Lords. His breath stills all souls.

We found a city dedicated to His worship, long ago, but so old now it has lost that dedication. The dark majesty of his godhead has frayed, been forgotten by all but those who stand in his shadow. But Juniper faced a more immediate fear, a specter from yesteryear leaking into the present upon a height overlooking the city. And because of that the Black Company went there, to that strange city far beyond the bounds of the Lady's empire. . . . But this is not the beginning. In the beginning we were far away. Only two old friends and a handful of men we would meet later stood nose-to-nose with the shadow.

# Chapter Two: TALLY ROADSIDE

The children's heads popped from the weeds like groundhog heads. They watched the approaching soldiers. The boy whispered, "Must be a thousand of them." The column stretched back and back. The dust it raised drifted up the face of a far hill. The creak and jangle of harness grew ever louder.

The day was hot. The children were sweating. Their thoughts lingered on a nearby brook and a dip in a pool they had found there. But they had been set to watch the road. Rumor said the Lady meant to break the renascent Rebel movement in Tally province.

And here her soldiers came. Closer now. Grim, hard-looking men. Veterans. Easily old enough to have helped create the disaster which had befallen the Rebel six years ago, claiming, among a quarter million men, their father.

"It's them!" the boy gasped. Fear and awe filled his voice. Grudging admiration edged it. "That's the Black Company."

The girl was no student of the enemy. "How do you know?"

The boy indicated a bear of a man on a big roan. He had silvery hair. His bearing said he was accustomed to command. "That's the one they call the Captain. The little black one beside him would be the wizard called One-Eye. See his hat? That's how you tell. The ones behind them must be Elmo and the Lieutenant."

"Are any of the Taken with them?" The girl rose higher, for a better look. "Where are the other famous ones?" She was the younger. The boy, at ten, already considered himself a soldier of the White Rose.

He yanked his sister down. "Stupid! Want them to see you?"

"So what if they do?"

The boy sneered. She had believed their uncle Neat when he had said that the enemy would not harm children. The boy hated his uncle. The man had no guts.

Nobody pledged to the White Rose had any guts. They just played at fighting the Lady. The most daring thing they did was ambush the occasional courier. At least the enemy had courage.

They had seen what they had been sent to see. He touched the girl's wrist. "Let's go." They scurried through the weeds, toward the wooded creek bank.

A shadow lay upon their path. They looked up and went pale. Three horsemen stared down at them. The boy gaped. Nobody could have slipped up unheard. "Goblin!"

The small, frog-faced man in the middle grinned. "At your service, laddy-boy."

The boy was terrified, but his mind remained functional. He shouted, "Run!" If one of them could escape. . . .

Goblin made a circular gesture. Pale pink fire tangled his fingers. He made a throwing motion. The boy fell, fighting invisible bonds like a fly caught in a spider's web. His sister whimpered a dozen feet away.

"Pick them up," Goblin told his companions. "They should tell an interesting tale."

# Chapter Three: JUNIPER: THE IRON LILY

The Lily stands on Floral Lane in the heart of the Buskin, Juniper's worst slum, where the taste of death floats on every tongue and men value life less than they do an hour of warmth or a decent meal. Its front sags against its neighbor to the right, clinging for support like one of its own drunken patrons. Its rear cants in the opposite direction. Its bare wood siding sports leprous patches of grey rot. Its windows are boarded with scraps and chinked with rags. Its roof boasts gaps through which the wind howls and bites when it blows off the Wolander Mountains. There, even on a summer's day, the glaciers twinkle like distant veins of silver.

Sea winds are little better. They bring a chill damp which gnaws the bones and sends ice floes scampering across the harbor.

The shaggy arms of the Wolanders reach seaward, flanking the River Port, forming cupped hands which hold the city and harbor. The city straddles the river, creeping up the heights on both sides.

Wealth rises in Juniper, scrambling up and away from the river. The people of the Buskin, when they lift their eyes from their misery, see the homes of the wealthy above, noses in the air, watching one another across the valley.

Higher still, crowning the ridges, are two castles. On the southern height stands Duretile, hereditary bastion of the Dukes of Juniper. Duretile is in scandalous disrepair. Most every structure in Juniper is.

Below Duretile lies the devotional heart of Juniper, the Enclosure, beneath which lie the Catacombs. There half a hundred generations rest, awaiting the Day of Passage, guarded by the Custodians of the Dead.

On the north ridge stands an incomplete fortress called, simply, the black castle. Its architecture is alien. Grotesque monsters leer from its battlements. Serpents writhe in frozen agonies upon its walls. There are no joints in the obsidian-like material. And the place is growing.

The people of Juniper ignore the castle's existence, its growth. They do not want to know what is happening up there. Seldom do they have time to pause in their struggle for survival to lift their eyes that high.

# Chapter Four:
# TALLY AMBUSH

I drew a seven, spread, discarded a trey, and stared at a lone ace. To my left, Pawnbroker muttered, "That did it. He's down to a rock."

I eyed him curiously. "What makes you say that?"

He drew, cursed, discarded. "You get a face like a corpse when you've got it cold, Croaker. Even your eyes."

Candy drew, cursed, discarded a five. "He's right, Croaker. You get so unreadable you're readable. Come on, Otto."

Otto stared at his hand, then at the pile, as though he could conjure victory from the jaws of defeat. He drew. "Shit." He discarded his draw, a royal card. I showed them my ace and raked in my winnings.

Candy stared over my shoulder while Otto gathered the cards. His eyes were hard and cold. "What?" I asked.

"Our host is working up his courage. Looking for a way to get out and warn them."

I turned. So did the others. One by one the tavern-keeper and his customers dropped their gazes and shrank into themselves. All but the tall, dark man seated alone in shadows near the fireplace. He winked and lifted a mug, as if in salute. I scowled. His response was a smile.

Otto dealt.

"One hundred ninety-three," I said.

Candy frowned. "Damn you, Croaker," he said, without emotion. I had been counting hands. They were perfect ticks of the clocks of our lives as brothers of the Black Company. I had played over ten thousand hands since the battle at Charm. Only the gods themselves know how many I played before I started keeping track.

"Think they got wind of us?" Pawnbroker asked. He was edgy. Waiting does that.

"I don't see how." Candy arrayed his hand with exaggerated care. A dead giveaway. He had something hot. I reexamined mine. Twenty-one. Probably get burned, but the best way to stop him. . . . I went down. "Twenty-one."

Otto sputtered. "You son-of-a-bitch." He laid down a hand strong for going low. But it added to twenty-two because of one royal card. Candy had three nines, an ace and a trey. Grinning, I raked it in again.

"You win this one, we're going to check your sleeves," Pawnbroker grumbled. I collected the cards and started shuffling.

The back door hinges squealed. Everyone froze, stared at the kitchen door. Men stirred beyond it.

"Madle! Where the hell are you?"

The tavern-keeper looked at Candy, agonized. Candy cued him. The taverner called, "Out here, Neat."

Candy whispered, "Keep playing." I started dealing.

A man of forty came from the kitchen. Several others followed. All wore dappled green. They had bows across their backs. Neat said, "They must've got the kids. I don't know how, but. . . ." He saw something in Madle's eyes. "What's the matter?"

We had Madle sufficiently intimidated. He did not give us away.

Staring at my cards, I drew my spring tube. My companions did likewise. Pawnbroker discarded the card he had drawn, a deuce. He usually tries to go low. His play betrayed his nervousness.

Candy snagged the discard and spread an ace-deuce-trey run. He discarded an eight.

One of Neat's companions whined, "I told you we shouldn't send kids." It sounded like breathing life into an old argument.

"I don't need any I-told-you-so," Neat growled. "Madle, I spread the word for a meeting. We'll have to scatter the outfit."

"We don't know nothing for sure, Neat," another green man said. "You know kids."

"You're fooling yourself. The Lady's hounds are on our trail."

The whiner said, "I told you we shouldn't hit those. . . ." He fell silent, realizing, a moment too late, that strangers were present, that the regulars all looked ghastly.

Neat went for his sword.

There were nine of them, if you counted Madle and some customers who got involved. Candy overturned the card table. We tripped the catches on our spring tubes. Four poisoned darts snapped across the common room. We drew swords.

It lasted only seconds.

"Everybody all right?" Candy asked.

"Got a scratch," Otto said. I checked it. Nothing to worry about.

"Back behind the bar, friend," Candy told Madle, whom he had spared. "The rest of you, get this place straightened up. Pawnbroker, watch them. They even think about getting out of line, kill them."

"What do I do with the bodies?"

"Throw them down the well."

I righted the table again, sat down, unfolded a sheet of paper. Sketched upon it was the chain of command of the insurgents in Tally. I blacked out NEAT. It stood at mid-level. "Madle," I said. "Come here."

The barkeep approached with the eagerness of a dog to a whipping.

"Take it easy. You'll get through this all right. If you cooperate. Tell me who those men were."

He hemmed and hawed. Predictably.

"Just names," I said. He looked at the paper, frowning. He could not read. "Madle? Be a tight place to swim, down a well with a bunch of bodies."

He gulped, surveyed the room. I glanced at the man

near the fireplace. He hadn't moved during the encounter. Even now he watched with apparent indifference.

Madle named names.

Some were on my list and some were not. Those that were not I assumed to be spear carriers. Tally had been well and reliably scouted.

The last corpse went out. I gave Madle a small gold piece. He goggled. His customers regarded him with unfriendly eyes. I grinned. "For services rendered."

Madle blanched, stared at the coin. It was a kiss of death. His patrons would think he had helped set the ambush. "Gotcha," I whispered. "Want to get out of this alive?"

He looked at me in fear and hatred. "Who the hell are you guys?" he demanded in a harsh whisper.

"The Black Company, Madle. The Black Company."

I don't know how he managed, but he went even whiter.

# Chapter Five: JUNIPER: MARRON SHED

The day was cold and grey and damp, still, misty, and sullen. Conversation in the Iron Lily consisted of surly monosyllables uttered before a puny fire.

Then the drizzle came, drawing the curtains of the world in tight. Brown and grey shapes hunched dispiritedly along the grubby, muddy street. It was a day ripped full-grown from the womb of despair. Inside the Lily, Marron Shed looked up from his mug-wiping. Keeping the dust off, he called it. Nobody was using his shoddy stoneware because nobody was buying his cheap, sour wine. Nobody could afford it.

The Lily stood on the south side of Floral Lane. Shed's counter faced the doorway, twenty feet deep into the shadows of the common room. A herd of tiny tables, each with its brood of rickety stools, presented a perilous maze for the customer coming out of sunlight. A half-dozen roughly cut support pillars formed additional obstacles. The ceiling beams were too low for a tall man. The boards of the floor were cracked and warped and creaky, and anything spilled ran downhill.

The walls were decorated with old-time odds and ends and curios left by customers which had no meaning for anyone entering today. Marron Shed was too lazy to dust them or take them down.

The common room L-ed around the end of his counter, past the fireplace, near which the best tables stood. Beyond the fireplace, in the deepest shadows, a yard from the kitchen door, lay the base of the stair to the rooming floors.

Into that darksome labyrinth came a small, weasely man. He carried a bundle of wood scraps. "Shed? Can I?"

"Hell. Why not, Asa? We'll all benefit." The fire had dwindled to a bank of grey ash.

Asa scuttled to the fireplace. The group there parted surlily. Asa settled beside Shed's mother. Old June was blind. She could not tell who he was. He placed his bundle before him and started stirring the coals.

"Nothing down to the docks today?" Shed asked.

Asa shook his head. "Nothing came in. Nothing going out. They only had five jobs. Unloading wagons. People were fighting over them."

Shed nodded. Asa was no fighter. Asa was not fond of honest labor, either. "Darling, one draft for Asa." Shed gestured as he spoke. His serving girl picked up the battered mug and took it to the fire.

Shed did not like the little man. He was a sneak, a thief, a liar, a mooch, the sort who would sell his sister for a couple of copper gersh. He was a whiner and complainer and coward. But he had become a project for Shed, who could have used a little charity himself. Asa was one of the homeless Shed let sleep on the common room floor whenever they brought wood for the fire. Letting the homeless have the floor did not put money into the coin box, but it did assure some warmth for June's arthritic bones.

Finding free wood in Juniper in winter was harder than finding work. Shed was amused by Asa's determination to avoid honest employment.

The fire's crackle killed the stillness. Shed put his grimy rag aside. He stood behind his mother, hands to the heat. His fingernails began aching. He hadn't realized how cold he was.

It was going to be a long, cold winter. "Asa, do you have a regular wood source?" Shed could not afford fuel. Nowadays firewood was barged down the Port from far upstream. It was expensive. In his youth. . . .

"No." Asa stared into the flames. Piney smells spread through the Lily. Shed worried about his chimney. Another pine scrap winter, and he hadn't had the chimney swept. A chimney fire could destroy him.

Things had to turn around soon. He was over the edge, in debt to his ears. He was desperate.

"Shed."

He looked to his tables, to his only real paying customer. "Raven?"

"Refill, if you please."

Shed looked for Darling. She had disappeared. He cursed softly. No point yelling. The girl was deaf, needed signs to communicate. An asset, he had thought when Raven had suggested he hire her. Countless secrets were whispered in the Lily. He had thought more whisperers might come if they could speak without fear of being overheard.

Shed bobbed his head, captured Raven's mug. He disliked Raven, partially because Raven was successful at Asa's game. Raven had no visible means of support, yet always had money. Another reason was because Raven was younger, tougher and healthier than the run of the Lily's customers. He was an anomaly. The Lily was on the downhill end of the Buskin, close to the waterfront. It drew all the drunkards, the worn-out whores, the dopers, the derelicts and human flotsam who eddied into that last backwater before the darkness overhauled them. Shed sometimes agonized, fearing his precious Lily was but a final way station.

Raven did not belong. He could afford better. Shed wished he dared throw the man out. Raven made his skin crawl, sitting at his corner table, dead eyes hammering iron spikes of suspicion into anyone who entered the tavern, cleaning his nails endlessly with a knife honed razor-sharp, speaking a few cold, toneless words whenever anyone took a notion to drag Darling upstairs. . . . That baffled Shed. Though there was no obvious connection, Raven protected the girl as though she were his virgin daughter. What the hell was a tavern slut for, anyway?

Shed shuddered, pushed it out of mind. He needed

Raven. Needed every paying guest he could get. He was surviving on prayers.

He delivered the wine. Raven dropped three coins into his palm. One was a silver leva. "Sir?"

"Get some decent firewood in here, Shed. If I wanted to freeze, I'd stay outside."

"Yes, sir!" Shed went to the door, peeked into the street. Latham's wood yard was just a block away.

The drizzle had become an icy rain. The mucky lane was crusting. "Going to snow before dark," he informed no one in particular.

"In or out," Raven growled. "Don't waste what warmth there is."

Shed slid outside. He hoped he could reach Latham's before the cold began to ache.

Shapes loomed out of the icefall. One was a giant. Both hunched forward, rags around their necks to prevent ice from sliding down their backs.

Shed charged back into the Lily. "I'll go out the back way." He signed, "Darling, I'm going out. You haven't seen me since this morning."

"Krage?" the girl signed.

"Krage," Shed admitted. He dashed into the kitchen, snagged his ragged coat off its hook, wriggled into it. He fumbled the door latch twice before he got it loose.

An evil grin with three teeth absent greeted him as he leaned into the cold. Foul breath assaulted his nostrils. A filthy finger gouged his chest. "Going somewhere, Shed?"

"Hi, Red. Just going to see Latham about firewood."

"No, you're not." The finger pushed. Shed fell back till he was in the common room.

Sweating, he asked, "Cup of wine?"

"That's neighborly of you, Shed. Make it three."

"Three?" Shed's voice squeaked.

"Don't tell me you didn't know Krage is on his way."

"I didn't," Shed lied.

Red's snaggle-toothed smirk said he knew Shed was lying.

# Chapter Six: TALLY MIX-UP

You try your damnedest, but something always goes wrong. That's life. If you're smart, you plan for it.

Somehow, somebody got away from Madle's, along about the twenty-fifth Rebel who stumbled into our web, when it really looked like Neat had done us a big favor, summoning the local hierarchy to a conference. Looking backward, it is hard to fix blame. We all did our jobs. But there are limits to how alert you stay under extended stress. The man who disappeared probably spent hours plotting his break. We did not notice his absence for a long time.

Candy figured it out. He threw his cards in at the tail of a hand, said, "We're minus a body, troops. One of those pig farmers. The little guy who *looked* like a pig."

I could see the table from the corner of my eye. I grunted. "You're right. Damn. Should have taken a head count after each trip to the well."

The table was behind Pawnbroker. He did not turn around. He waited a hand, then ambled to Madle's counter and bought a crock of beer. While his rambling distracted the locals, I made rapid signs with my fingers, in deaf-speech. "Better be ready for a raid. They know who we are. I shot my mouth off."

The Rebel would want us bad. The Black Company has earned a widespread reputation as a successful eradicator of the Rebel pestilence, wherever it appears. Though we are not as vicious as reputed, news of our coming strikes terror wherever we go. The Rebel often goes to ground, abandoning his operations, where we appear.

Yet here were four of us, separated from our companions, evidently unaware that we were at risk. They would try. The question at hand was how hard.

We did have cards up our sleeves. We never play fair if we can avoid it. The Company philosophy is to maximize effectiveness while minimizing risk.

The tall, dark man rose, left his shadow, stalked toward the stair to the sleeping rooms. Candy snapped, "Watch him, Otto." Otto hurried after him, looking feeble in the man's wake. The locals watched, wondering.

Pawnbroker used signs to ask, "What now?"

"We wait," Candy said aloud, and with signs added, "Do what we were sent to do."

"Not much fun, being live bait," Pawnbroker signed back. He studied the stair nervously. "Set Otto up with a hand," he suggested.

I looked at Candy. He nodded. "Why not? Give him about seventeen." Otto would go down first time around every time if he had less than twenty. It was a good percentage bet.

I quick figured the cards in my head, and grinned. I could give him seventeen and have enough low cards left to give each of us a hand that would burn him. "Give me those cards."

I hurried through the deck, building hands. "There." Nobody had higher than a five. But Otto's hand had higher cards than the others.

Candy grinned. "Yeah."

Otto did not come back. Pawnbroker said, "I'm going up to check."

"All right," Candy replied. He went and got himself a beer. I eyed the locals. They were getting ideas. I stared at one and shook my head.

Pawnbroker and Otto returned a minute later, preceded by the dark man, who returned to his shadow. Pawnbroker and Otto looked relieved. They settled down to play.

Otto asked, "Who dealt?"

"Candy did," I said. "Your go."

He went down. "Seventeen."

"Heh-heh-heh," I replied. "Burned you. Fifteen."

And Pawnbroker said, "Got you both. Fourteen."

And Candy, "Fourteen. You're hurting, Otto."

He just sat there, numbed, for several seconds. Then he caught on. "You bastards! You stacked it! You don't think I'm going to pay off. . . ."

"Settle down. Joke, son," Candy said. "Joke. It was your deal anyhow." The cards went around and the darkness came. No more insurgents appeared. The locals grew ever more restless. Some worried about their families, about being late. As everywhere else, most Tallylanders are concerned only with their own lives. They don't care whether the White Rose or the Lady is ascendant.

The minority of Rebel sympathizers worried about when the blow might fall. They were afraid of getting caught in the crossfire.

We pretended ignorance of the situation.

Candy signed, "Which ones are dangerous?"

We conferred, selected three men who might become trouble. Candy had Otto bind them to their chairs.

It dawned on the locals that we knew what to expect, that we were prepared. Not looking forward, but prepared.

The raiders waited till midnight. They were more cautious than the Rebel we encountered ordinarily. Maybe our reputation was *too* strong. . . .

They burst in in a rush. We discharged our spring tubes and began swinging swords, retreating to a corner away from the fireplace. The tall man watched indifferently.

There were a lot of Rebels. Far more than we had expected. They kept storming inside, crowding up, getting into one another's ways, climbing over the corpses of their comrades. "Some trap," I gasped. "Must be a hundred of them."

"Yeah," Candy said. "It don't look good." He kicked at a man's groin, cut him when he covered up.

The place was wall-to-wall insurgents, and from the

noise there were a hell of a lot more outside. Somebody didn't want us getting away.

Well, that was the plan.

My nostrils flared. There was an odor in the air, just the faintest off-key touch, subtle under the stink of fear and sweat. "Cover up!" I yelled, and whipped a wad of damp wool from my belt pouch. It stunk worse than a squashed skunk. My companions followed suit.

Somewhere a man screamed. Then another. Voices rose in a hellish chorus. Our enemies surged around, baffled, panicky. Faces twisted in agony. Men fell down in writhing heaps, clawing their noses and throats. I was careful to keep my face in the wool.

The tall, thin man came out of his shadows. Calmly, he began despatching guerrillas with a fourteen-inch, silvery blade. He spared those customers we had not bound to their chairs.

He signed, "It's safe to breathe now."

"Watch the door," Candy told me. He knew I had an aversion to this kind of slaughter. "Otto, you take the kitchen. Me and Pawnbroker will help Silent."

The Rebel outside tried to get us by speeding arrows through the doorway. He had no luck. Then he tried firing the place. Madle suffered paroxysms of rage. Silent, one of the three wizards of the Company, who had been sent into Tally weeks earlier, used his powers to squelch the fire. Angrily, the Rebel prepared for a siege.

"Must have brought every man in the province," I said.

Candy shrugged. He and Pawnbroker were piling corpses into defensive barricades. "They must have set up a base camp near here." Our intelligence about the Tally guerrillas was extensive. The Lady prepares well before she sends us in. But we hadn't been told to expect such strength available at short notice.

Despite our successes, I was scared. There was a big mob outside, and it sounded like more were arriving regularly. Silent, as an ace in the hole, hadn't much more value.

"You send your bird?" I demanded, assuming that had

been the reason for his trip upstairs. He nodded. That provided some relief. But not much.

The tenor changed. They were quieter outside. More arrows zipped through the doorway. It had been ripped off its hinges in the first rush. The bodies heaped in it would not slow the Rebel long. "They're going to come," I told Candy.

"All right." He joined Otto in the kitchen. Pawnbroker joined me. Silent, looking mean and deadly, stationed himself in the center of the common room.

A roar went up outside.

"Here they come!"

We held the main rush, with Silent's help, but others began to batter the window shutters. Then Candy and Otto had to concede the kitchen. Candy killed an overzealous attacker and spun away long enough to bellow, "Where the hell are they, Silent?"

Silent shrugged. He seemed almost indifferent to the proximity of death. He hurled a spell at a man being boosted through a window.

Trumpets brayed in the night. "Ha!" I shouted. "They're coming!" The last gate of the trap had closed.

One question remained. Would the Company close in before our attackers finished us?

More windows gave. Silent could not be everywhere. "To the stair!" Candy shouted. "Fall back to the stair."

We raced for it. Silent called up a noxious fog. It was not the deadly thing he had used before. He could not do that again, now. He hadn't time to prepare.

The stair was easily held. Two men, with Silent behind them, could hold it forever.

The Rebel saw that. He began setting fires. This time Silent could not extinguish all the flames.

# Chapter Seven: JUNIPER: KRAGE

The front door opened. Two men shoved into the Lily, stamped their feet and beat the ice off themselves. Shed scuttled over to help. The bigger man pushed him away. The smaller crossed the room, kicked Asa away from the fire, squatted with his hands extended. Shed's guests stared into the flames, seeing and hearing nothing.

Except Raven, Shed noted. Raven looked interested, and not particularly disturbed.

Shed sweated. Krage finally turned around. "You didn't stop by yesterday, Shed. I missed you."

"I couldn't, Krage. I didn't have anything to bring you. Look in my coin box. You know I'll pay you. I always do. I just need a little time."

"You were late last week, Shed. I was patient. I know you're having problems. But you were late the week before that, too. And the week before that. You're making me look bad. I know you mean it when you say you'll pay me. But what will people think? Eh? Maybe they start thinking it's all right for them to be late, too. Maybe they start thinking they don't have to pay at all."

"Krage, I can't. Look in my box. As soon as business picks up. . . ."

Krage gestured. Red reached behind the counter. "Business is bad everywhere, Shed. I got problems, too. I got expenses. I can't meet mine if you don't meet yours." He ambled around the common room, examining the furnishings. Shed could read his mind. He wanted the Lily. Wanted Shed in a hole so deep he would have to give the place up.

Red handed Shed's box to Krage. Krage made a face. "Business really is bad." He gestured. The big man, Count, seized Shed's elbows from behind. Shed nearly fainted. Krage grinned wickedly. "Pat him down, Red. See if he's holding out." He emptied the coin box. "On account, Shed."

Red found the silver leva Raven had given Shed.

Krage shook his head. "Shed, Shed, you lied to me." Count pressed his elbows together painfully.

"That isn't mine," Shed protested. "That belongs to Raven. He wanted me to buy wood. That's why I was headed for Latham's."

Krage eyed him. Shed knew Krage knew he was telling the truth. He didn't have the guts to lie.

Shed was scared. Krage might bust him up just so he would give up the Lily to buy his life.

What then? He would be without a gersh, and in the street with an old woman to look after.

Shed's mother cursed Krage. Everyone ignored her, including Shed. She was harmless. Darling stood in the kitchen doorway, frozen, one hand fisted before her mouth, eyes full of appeal. She watched Raven more than Krage and Shed.

"What do you want me to break, Krage?" Red asked. Shed cringed. Red enjoyed his work. "You shouldn't hold out on us, Shed. You shouldn't lie to Krage." He unleashed a vicious punch. Shed gagged, tried to fall forward. Count held him upright. Red hit him again.

A soft, cold voice said, "He told the truth. I sent him for wood."

Krage and Red shifted formation. Count did not relax his grip. "Who are you?" Krage demanded.

"Raven. Let him be."

Krage exchanged glances with Red. Red said, "I think maybe you'd better not talk that way to Mister Krage."

Raven's gaze rose. Red's shoulders tightened defensively.

Then, aware of his audience, he stepped over and threw an open-palmed punch.

Raven plucked his hand out of the air, twisted. Red went to his knees, grinding his teeth on a whimper. Raven said, "That was stupid."

Astonished, Krage replied, "Smart is as smart does, mister. Let him go while you're healthy."

Raven smiled for the first time in Shed's recollection. "*That* wasn't smart." There was an audible *pop*. Red screamed.

"Count!" Krage snapped.

Count hurled Shed aside. He was twice Red's size, quick, strong as a mountain, and barely as smart. Nobody survived Count.

A wicked nine-inch dagger appeared in Raven's hand. Count stopped so violently his feet tangled. He fell forward, rolling off the edge of Raven's table.

"Oh, shit," Shed groaned. Somebody was going to get killed. Krage wouldn't put up with this. It would be bad for business.

But as Count rose, Krage said, "Count, help Red." His tone was conversational.

Count obediently turned to Red, who had dragged himself away to nurse his wrist.

"Maybe we had a little misunderstanding here," Krage said. "I'll put it plain, Shed. You've got one week to pay me. The big and the nut both."

"But. . . ."

"No buts, Shed. That's according to terms. Kill somebody. Rob somebody. Sell this dump. But get the money." The or-elses did not have to be explained.

I'll be all right, Shed promised himself. He won't hurt me. I'm too good a customer.

How the hell would he come up with it? He couldn't sell out. Not with winter closing in. The old woman couldn't survive in the street.

Cold air gusted into the Lily as Krage paused at the door. He glared at Raven. Raven did not bother looking back.

"Some wine here, Shed," Raven said. "I seem to have spilled mine."

Shed hustled despite his pain. He could not help fawning. "I thank you, Raven, but you shouldn't have interfered. He'll kill you for that."

Raven shrugged. "Go to the wood-seller before somebody else tries to take my money."

Shed looked at the door. He did not want to go outside. They might be waiting. But then he looked at Raven again. The man was cleaning his nails with that wicked knife. "Right away."

It was snowing now. The street was treacherous. Only a thin white mask covered the mud.

Shed could not help wondering why Raven had intervened. To protect his money? Reasonable. . . . Only, reasonable men stayed quiet around Krage. He would cut your throat if you looked at him wrong.

Raven was new around here. Maybe he did not know about Krage.

He would learn the hard way. His life wasn't worth two gersh anymore.

Raven seemed well-heeled. He wouldn't carry his whole fortune around with him, would he? Maybe he kept part hidden in his room. Maybe enough to pay off Krage. Maybe he could set Raven up. Krage would appreciate that.

"Let's see your money," Latham said when he asked for wood. Shed produced Raven's silver leva. "Ha! Who died this time?"

Shed reddened. An old prostitute had died at the Lily last winter. Shed had rifled her belongings before summoning the Custodians. His mother had lived warm for the rest of the winter. The whole Buskin knew because he had made the mistake of telling Asa.

By custom, the Custodians took the personal possessions of the newly dead. Those and donations supported them and the Catacombs.

"Nobody died. A guest sent me."

"Ha! The day you have a guest who can afford

generosity. . . ." Latham shrugged. "But what do I care? The coin is good. I don't need its provenance. Grab some wood. You're headed that way."

Shed staggered back to the Lily, face burning, ribs aching. Latham hadn't bothered to hide his contempt.

Back home, with the fire taking hold of the good oak, Shed drew two mugs of wine and sat down opposite Raven. "On the house."

Raven stared momentarily, took a sip, maneuvered the mug to an exact spot upon the tabletop. "What do you want?"

"To thank you again."

"There's nothing to thank me for."

"To warn you, then. You didn't take Krage serious enough."

Latham tramped in with an armload of firewood, grumbling because he couldn't get his wagon out. He would be back and forth for a long time.

"Go away, Shed." And, as Shed rose, face hot, Raven snapped, "Wait. You think you owe me? Then someday I'll ask a favor. You do it. Right?"

"Sure, Raven. Anything. Just name it."

"Go sit by the fire, Shed."

Shed squeezed in between Asa and his mother, joining their surly silence. That Raven really was creepy.

The man in question was engaged in a lively exchange of signs with the deaf serving girl.

# Chapter Eight: TALLY: CLOSE-UP

I let the tip of my blade drop to the inn floor. I slumped in exhaustion, coughing weakly in the smoke. I swayed, feebly reached for the support of an overturned table. Reaction was setting in. I had been sure this time was the end. If they hadn't been forced to extinguish the fires themselves. . . .

Elmo crossed the room and threw an arm around me. "You hurt, Croaker? Want me to find One-Eye?"

"Not hurt. Just burned out. Been a long time since I been so scared, Elmo. Thought I was a goner."

He righted a chair with a foot and sat me down. He was my closest friend, a wiry, old hardcase seldom given to moodiness. Wet blood reddened his left sleeve. I tried to stand. "Sit," he ordered. "Pockets can take care of it."

Pockets was my understudy, a kid of twenty-three. The Company is getting older—at least at its core, my contemporaries. Elmo is past fifty. The Captain and Lieutenant straddle that five-zero. I wouldn't see forty again. "Get them all?"

"Enough." Elmo settled on another chair. "One-Eye and Goblin and Silent went after the ones who took off." His voice was vacant. "Half the Rebels in the province, first shot."

"We're getting too old for this." The men began bringing prisoners inside, sifting them for characters who might know something useful. "Ought to leave this stuff to the kids."

"They couldn't handle it." He stared into nothing, at long ago and far away.

"Something wrong?"

He shook his head, then contradicted himself. "What are we doing, Croaker? Isn't there any end to it?"

I waited. He did not go on. He doesn't talk much. Especially not about his feelings. I nudged. "What do you mean?"

"Just goes on and on. Hunting Rebels. No end to the supply. Even back when we worked for the Syndic in Beryl. We hunted dissidents. And before Beryl. . . . Thirty-six years of same old same old. And me never sure I was doing right. Especially now."

It was like Elmo to keep his reservations in abeyance eight years before airing them. "We're in no position to change anything. The Lady won't take kindly to us if we suddenly say we're only going to do thus and so, and none of that."

The Lady's service has not been bad. Though we get the toughest missions, we never have to do the dirty stuff. The regulars get those jobs. Preemptive strikes sometimes, sure. The occasional massacre. But all in the line of business. Militarily necessary. We'd never gotten involved in atrocities. The Captain wouldn't permit that.

"It's not the morality, Croaker. What's moral in war? Superior strength. No. I'm just tired."

"Not an adventure anymore, eh?"

"Stopped being that a long time ago. Turned into a job. Something I do because I don't know anything else."

"Something you do very well." That did not help, but I couldn't think of anything better to say.

The Captain came in, a shambling bear who surveyed the wreckage with a cold eye. He came over. "How many did we get, Croaker?"

"Count's not in yet. Most of their command structure, I'd guess."

He nodded. "You hurt?"

"Worn out. Physically and emotionally. Been a while since I was so scared."

He righted a table, dragged up a chair, produced a case of maps. The Lieutenant joined him. Later, Candy brought Madle over. Somehow, the innkeeper had survived.

"Our friend has some names for you, Croaker."

I spread my paper, scratched out those Madle named.

The company commanders began drafting prisoners for grave-digging detail. Idly, I wondered if they realized they were preparing their own resting places. No Rebel soldier is paroled unless we can enlist him inescapably into the Lady's cause. Madle we enlisted. We gave him a story to explain his survival and eliminated everyone who could deny it. Candy, in a fit of generosity, had the bodies removed from his well.

Silent returned, with Goblin and One-Eye, the two smaller wizards bickering caustically. As usual. I do not recall the argument. It didn't matter. The struggle was all, and it was all decades old.

The Captain gave them a sour look, asked the Lieutenant, "Heart or Tome?" Heart and Tome are the only substantial towns in Tally. There is a king at Heart who is allied with the Lady. She crowned him two years ago, after Whisper slew his predecessor. He is not popular with the Tallylanders. My opinion, never asked, is that she should dispose of him before he does her further harm.

Goblin laid a fire. The morning hours were nippy. He knelt before it, toasting his fingers.

One-Eye poked around behind Madle's counter, found a beer jar miraculously unscathed. He drained it in a single draft, wiped his face, surveyed the room, winked at me.

"Here we go," I murmured.

The Captain glanced up. "Eh?"

"One-Eye and Goblin."

"Oh." He went back to work and did not look up again.

A face formed in the flames before frog-faced little Goblin. He did not see it. His eyes were closed. I looked at One-Eye. His eye was sealed, too, and his face was all pruned, wrinkles atop wrinkles, shadowed by the brim of his floppy hat. The face in the fire took on detail.

"Eh!" It startled me for a moment. Staring my way, it looked like the Lady. Well, like the face the Lady wore the one time I actually saw her. That was during the battle at Charm. She called me in to dredge my mind for suspicions about a conspiracy among the Ten Who Were Taken. . . . A thrill of fear. I have lived with it for years. If ever she questions me again, the Black Company will be short its senior physician and Annalist. I now have knowledge for which she would flatten kingdoms.

The face in the fire extended a tongue like that of a salamander. Goblin squealed. He jumped up clutching a blistered nose.

One-Eye was draining another beer, back to his victim. Goblin scowled, rubbed his nose, seated himself again. One-Eye turned just enough to place him at the corner of his vision. He waited till Goblin began to nod.

This has been going on forever. Both were with the Company before I joined, One-Eye for at least a century. He is *old*, but is as spry as men my age.

Maybe spryer. Lately I've felt the burden of time more and more, all too often dwelling on everything I've missed. I can laugh at peasants and townies chained all their lives to a tiny corner of the earth while I roam its face and see its wonders, but when I go down, there will be no child to carry my name, no family to mourn me save my comrades, no one to remember, no one to raise a marker over my cold bit of ground. Though I have seen great events, I will leave no enduring accomplishment save these Annals.

Such conceit. Writing my own epitaph disguised as Company history.

I am developing a morbid streak. Have to watch that.

One-Eye cupped his hands palms-down on the countertop, murmured, opened them. A nasty spider of fist size stood revealed, wearing a bushy squirrel tail. Never say One-Eye has no sense of humor. It scuttled down to the floor, skipped over to me, grinned up with a One-Eye black face wearing no eye-patch, then zipped toward Goblin.

The essence of sorcery, even for its nonfraudulent practitioners, is misdirection. So with the bushy-tailed spider.

Goblin was not snoozing. He was lying in the weeds. When the spider got close, he whirled and swung a stick of firewood. The spider dodged. Goblin hammered the floor. In vain. His target darted around, chuckling in a One-Eye voice.

The face formed in the flames. Its tongue darted out. The seat of Goblin's trousers began to smoulder.

"I'll be damned," I said.

"What?" the Captain asked, not looking up. He and the Lieutenant had taken opposite ends of an argument over whether Heart or Tome would be the better base of operations.

Somehow, word gets out. Men streamed in for the latest round of the feud. I observed, "I think One-Eye is going to win one."

"Really?" For a moment old grey bear was interested. One-Eye hadn't bested Goblin in years.

Goblin's frog mouth opened in a startled, angry howl. He slapped his bottom with both hands, dancing. "You little snake!" he screamed. "I'll strangle you! I'll cut your heart out and eat it! I'll. . . . I'll. . . ."

Amazing. Utterly amazing. Goblin never gets mad. He gets even. Then One-Eye will put his twisted mind to work again. If Goblin is even, One-Eye figures he's behind.

"Settle that down before it gets out of hand," the Captain said.

Elmo and I got between the antagonists. This thing was disturbing. Goblin's threats were serious. One-Eye had caught him in a bad temper, the first I'd ever seen. "Ease up," I told One-Eye.

He stopped. He, too, smelled trouble.

Several men growled. Some heavy bets were down. Usually, nobody will put a copper on One-Eye. Goblin coming out on top is a sure thing, but this time he looked feeble.

Goblin did not want to quit. Did not want to play the

usual rules, either. He snatched a fallen sword and headed for One-Eye.

I couldn't help grinning. That sword was huge and broken, and Goblin was so small, yet so ferocious, that he seemed a caricature. A bloodthirsty caricature. Elmo couldn't handle him. I signaled for help. Some quick thinker splashed water on Goblin's back. He whirled, cussing, started a deadly spell.

Trouble for sure. A dozen men jumped in. Somebody threw another bucket of water. That cooled Goblin's temper. As we relieved him of the blade, he looked abashed. Defiant, but abashed.

I led him back to the fire and settled beside him. "What's the matter? What happened?" I glimpsed the Captain from the corner of my eye. One-Eye stood before him, drained by a heavy-duty dressing down.

"I don't know, Croaker." Goblin slumped, stared into the fire. "Suddenly everything was too much. This ambush tonight. Same old thing. There's always another province, always more Rebels. They breed like maggots in a cowpie. I'm getting older and older, and I haven't done anything to make a better world. In fact, if you backed off to look at it, we've all made it worse." He shook his head. "That isn't right. Not what I want to say. But I don't know how to say it any better."

"Must be an epidemic."

"What?"

"Nothing. Thinking out loud." Elmo. Myself. Goblin. A lot of the men, judging by their tenor lately. Something was wrong in the Black Company. I had suspicions, but wasn't ready to analyze. Too depressing.

"What we need is a challenge," I suggested. "We haven't stretched ourselves since Charm." Which was a half-truth. An operation which compelled us to become totally involved in staying alive might be a prescription for symptoms, but was no remedy for causes. As a physician, I was not fond of treating symptoms alone. They could recur indefinitely. The disease itself had to be attacked.

"What we need," Goblin said in a voice so soft it

almost vanished in the crackle of the flames, "is a cause we can believe in."

"Yeah," I said. "That, too."

From outside came the startled, outraged cries of prisoners discovering that they were to fill the graves they had dug.

# Chapter Nine: JUNIPER: DEATH PAYS

Shed grew increasingly frightened as the days passed. He had to get some money. Krage was spreading the word. He was to be made an example.

He recognized the tactic. Krage wanted to scare him into signing the Lily over. The place wasn't much, but it was damned sure worth more than he owed. Krage would resell it for several times his investment. Or turn it into whore cribs. And Marron Shed and his mother would be in the streets, with winter's deadly laughter howling in their faces.

Kill somebody, Krage had said. Rob somebody. Shed considered both. He would do anything to keep the Lily and protect his mother.

If he could just get real customers! He got nothing but one-night chiselers and scroungers. He needed residential regulars. But he could not get those without fixing the place up. And that he couldn't do without money.

Asa rolled through the doorway. Pale and frightened, he scuttled to the counter. "Find a wood supply yet?" Shed asked.

The little man shook his head, slid two gersh across the counter. "Give me a drink."

Shed scooped the coins into his box. One did not question money's provenance. It had no memory. He poured a full measure. Asa reached eagerly.

"Oh, no," Shed said. "Tell me about it."

"Come on, Shed. I paid you."

"Sure. And I'll deliver when you tell me why you're so rocky."

"Where's that Raven?"

"Upstairs. Sleeping." Raven had been out all night.

Asa shook a little more. "Give me that, Shed."

"Talk."

"All right. Krage and Red grabbed me. They wanted to know about Raven."

So Shed knew how Asa had come by money. He had tried to sell Raven. "Tell me more."

"They just wanted to know about him."

"What did they want to know?"

"If he ever goes out."

"Why?"

Asa stalled. Shed pulled the mug away. "All right. They had two men watching him. They disappeared. Nobody knows anything. Krage is furious." Shed let him have the wine. He drained it in a single gulp.

Shed glanced toward the stair, shuddered. Maybe he had underestimated Raven. "What did Krage say about me?"

"Sure could use another mug, Shed."

"I'll give you a mug. Over the noggin."

"I don't need you, Shed. I made a connection. I can sleep over to Krage's any time I want."

Shed grunted, made a mask of his face. "You win." He poured wine.

"He's going to put you out of business, Shed. Whatever it takes. He's decided you're in it with Raven." Wicked little smile. "Only he can't figure where you got the guts to buck him."

"I'm not. I don't have anything to do with Raven, Asa. You know that."

Asa enjoyed his moment. "I tried to tell Krage, Shed. He didn't want to hear it."

"Drink your wine and get out, Asa."

"Shed?" The old whine filled Asa's voice.

"You heard me. Out. Back to your new friends. See how long they have a use for you."

"Shed! . . ."

"They'll throw you back into the street, Asa. Right beside me and Mom. Git, you bloodsucker."

Asa downed his wine and fled, shoulders tight against his neck. He had tasted the truth of Shed's words. His association with Krage would be fragile and brief.

Shed tried to warn Raven. Raven ignored him. Shed polished mugs, watched Raven chatter with Darling in the utter silence of sign language, and tried to imagine some way of making a hit in the upper city. Usually he spent these early hours eying Darling and trying to imagine a way to gain access, but lately sheer terror of the street had abolished his customary randiness.

A cry like that of a hog with a cut throat came from upstairs. "Mother!" Shed took the stairs two steps at a time.

His mother stood in the doorway of the big bunkroom, panting. "Mom? What's wrong?"

"There's a dead man in there."

Shed's heart fluttered. He pushed into the room. An old man lay in the bottom right bunk inside the door.

There had been only four bunkroom customers last night. Six gersh a head. The room was six feet wide and twelve long, with twenty-four platforms stacked six high. When the room was full, Shed charged two gersh to sleep leaning on a rope stretched down the middle.

Shed touched the old-timer. His skin was cold. He had been gone for hours.

"Who was he?" old June asked.

"I don't know." Shed probed his ragged clothing. He found four gersh and an iron ring. "Damn!" He could not take that. The Custodians would be suspicious if they found nothing. "We're jinxed. This is our fourth stiff this year."

"It's the customers, son. They have one foot in the Catacombs already."

Shed spat. "I'd better send for the Custodians."

A voice said, "He's waited this long, let him wait a little longer."

Shed whirled. Raven and Darling stood behind his mother. "What?"

"He might be the answer to your problems," Raven said. And immediately Darling began flashing signs so fast Shed could not catch one in twenty. Evidently she was telling Raven not to do something. Raven ignored her.

Old June snapped, "Shed!" Her voice was heavy with admonition.

"Don't worry, Mom. I'll handle it. Go ahead with your work." June was blind, but when her health permitted, she dumped the slops and handled what passed for maid service—mainly dusting beds between guests to kill fleas and lice. When her health confined her to bed, Shed brought in his cousin Wally, a ne'er-do-well like Asa, but with a wife and kids. Shed used him out of pity for the wife.

He headed downstairs. Raven followed, still arguing with Darling. Momentarily, Shed wondered if Raven was diddling her. Be a damned waste of fine womanflesh if someone wasn't.

How could a dead man with four gersh get him out from under Krage? Answer: He could not. Not legitimately.

Raven settled onto his usual stool. He scattered a handful of copper. "Wine. Buy yourself a mug, too."

Shed collected the coins, deposited them in his box. Its contents were pitiful. He wasn't making expenses. He was doomed. His debt to Krage could miraculously be discharged and still he'd be doomed.

He deposited a mug before Raven, seated himself on a stool. He felt old beyond his years, and infinitely weary. "Tell me."

"The old man. Who was he? Who were his people?"

Shed shrugged. "Just somebody who wanted to get out of the cold. The Buskin is full of them."

"So it is."

Shed shuddered at Raven's tone. "Are you proposing what I think?"

"What's that?"

"I don't know. What use is a corpse? I mean, even the Custodians only stuff them in the Catacombs."

"Suppose there was a buyer?"

"I've been supposing that."

"And?"

"What would I have to do?" His voice barely carried across the table. He could imagine no more disgusting crime. Even the least of the city's dead were honored above the living. A corpse was a holy object. The Enclosure was Juniper's epicenter.

"Very little. Late tonight, have the body at the back door. You could do that?"

Shed nodded weakly.

"Good. Finish your wine."

Shed downed it in a gulp. He drew another mug, polished his stoneware industriously. It was a bad dream. It would go away.

The corpse seemed almost weightless, but Shed had difficulty negotiating the stairs. He had drunk too much. He eased through the shadowed common, stepping with exaggerated care. The people clustered near the fireplace looked demonic in the sullen red of the last coals.

One of the old man's feet toppled a pot as Shed entered the kitchen. He froze. Nothing happened. His heartbeat gradually slowed. He kept reminding himself that he was doing this so his mother would not have to freeze on winter streets.

He thumped the door with his knee. It swung inward immediately. A shadow hissed, "Hurry up," and seized the old man's feet, helped Shed heave it into a wagon.

Panting, terrified, Shed croaked, "What now?"

"Go to bed. You get your share in the morning."

Shed's relieved sigh nearly became tears. "How much?" he gasped.

"A third."

"Only a third?"

"I'm taking all the risk. You're safe already."

"All right. How much would it be?"

"The market varies." Raven turned away. Shed closed the door, leaned against it with closed eyes. What had he done?

He built up the fire and went to bed, lay listening to his mother's snores. Had she guessed? Maybe she wouldn't. The Custodians often waited for night. He would tell her she had slept through everything.

He could not sleep. Who knew about the death? If word got out, people would wonder. They would begin to suspect the unsuspectable.

What if Raven got caught? Would the Inquisitors make him talk? Bullock could make a stone sing.

He watched his mother all next morning. She did not speak except in monosyllables, but that was her custom.

Raven appeared shortly after noon. "Tea and a bowl of porridge, Shed." When he paid, he did not shove copper across the counter.

Shed's eye widened. Ten silver leva lay before him. Ten? For one dead old man? That was a third? And Raven had done this before? He must be rich. Shed's palms grew moist. His mind howled after potential crimes.

"Shed?" Raven said softly when he delivered the tea and porridge. "Don't even think about it."

"What?"

"Don't think what you're thinking. *You* would end up in the wagon."

Darling scowled at them from the kitchen doorway. For a moment Raven seemed embarrassed.

Shed slunk into the hostel where Krage held court. From the outside the place was as crummy as the Lily. Timidly, he looked for Count, tried to ignore Asa. Count would not torment him for fun. "Count, I need to see Krage."

Count opened big brown cow eyes. "Why?"

"I brought him some money. On account."

Count heaved himself upright. "All right. Wait here." He stalked off.

Asa sidled up. "Where'd you get the money, Shed?"

"Where do you get yours, Asa?" Asa did not answer.

"It isn't polite to ask. Mind your own business or stay away from me."

"Shed, I thought we were friends."

"I tried to be friends, Asa. I even let you have a place to sleep. And as soon as you hooked up with Krage. . . ."

A shadow crossed Asa's face. "I'm sorry, Shed. You know me. I don't think so fast. I do dumb things."

Shed snorted. So Asa had come to the inevitable conclusion: Krage would dump him once he settled with Raven.

Shed was tempted to betray Raven. The man had to have a fortune hidden. But he was afraid of a thousand things, and his guest stood at the top of the list.

Asa said, "I found a way to get deadwood from the Enclosure." His face brightened in pathetic appeal. "Mostly pine, but it's wood."

"The Enclosure?"

"It's not illegal, Shed. It keeps the Enclosure cleaned up."

Shed scowled righteously.

"Shed, it's less wrong than going through somebody's. . . ."

Shed controlled his anger. He needed allies inside the enemy camp. "Firewood could be like money, Asa. No provenance."

Asa smiled fawningly. "Thanks, Shed."

Count called, "Shed."

Shed shook as he crossed the room. Krage's men smirked.

This wouldn't work. Krage wouldn't listen. He was going to throw his money away.

"Count says you've got something to give me on account," Krage said.

"Uhm." Krage's den could have been ripped whole from a mansion high up the wall of the valley. Shed was stunned.

"Stop gawking and get on with it. You'd better not give me a handful of copper and beg for an extension, either. Picked a warm doorway yet? Your payments are a joke, Shed."

"No joke, Mr. Krage. Honest. I can pay over half of it."

Krage's eyebrows rose. "Interesting." Shed laid nine silver leva before him. "Very interesting." He fixed Shed with a penetrating stare.

Shed stammered, "That's over half, counting interest. I hoped maybe seeing as how that would put me ahead. . . ."

"Quiet." Shed shut up. "You think I should forget what happened?"

"That wasn't my fault, Mr. Krage. I didn't tell him to. . . . You don't know what Raven is like."

"Shut up." Krage stared at the coins. "Maybe something can be arranged. I know you didn't put him up to it. You don't have the guts."

Shed stared at the floor, unable to deny his cowardice.

"Okay, Shed. You're a regular client. Back to the regular schedule." He eyed the money. "You're ahead three weeks, looks like."

"Thank you, Mr. Krage. Really. You don't know how much this means. . . ."

"Shut up. I know exactly what it means. Get out. Start getting another payment together. This is your last reprieve."

"Yes, sir." Shed retreated. Count opened the door.

"Shed! I may want something sometime. A favor for a favor. Understand?"

"Yes, sir."

"All right. Go."

Shed left, a sinking feeling replacing relief. Krage would make him help get Raven. He almost wept as he tramped homeward. It never got any better. He was always in a trap.

# Chapter Ten: TALLY TURNAROUND

Tome was typical of towns we had garrisoned recently. Small, dirty, boring. One wondered why the Lady bothered. What use were these remote provinces? Did she insist they bend the knee merely to puff her ego? There was nothing here worth having, unless it was power over the natives.

Even they viewed their country with a certain contempt.

The presence of the Black Company strained the resources of the area. Within a week the Captain started talking about shifting a company to Heart and billeting smaller units in the villages. Our patrols seldom encountered the Rebel, even when our wizards helped hunt. The engagement at Madle's had all but eliminated the infestation.

The Lady's spies told us the few committed Rebels left had fled into Tambor, an even bleaker kingdom to the northeast. I supposed Tambor would be our next mission.

I was scribbling away at these Annals one day, when I decided I needed an estimate of the mileage we'd covered in our progression eastward. I was appalled to learn the truth. Tome was two thousand miles east of Charm! Far beyond the bounds of the empire as it had existed six years ago. The great bloody conquests of the Taken Whisper had established a border arc just this side of the Plain of Fear. I ran down the line of city-states forming that forgotten frontier. Frost and Ade, Thud and Barns, and Rust, where the Rebel had defied the Lady successfully for years.

Huge cities all, formidable, and the last such we had seen. I still shuddered, recalling the Plain of Fear.

We crossed it under the aegis of Whisper and Feather, two of the Taken, the Lady's black apprentices, both sorceresses orders of magnitude above our three puny wizards. Even so, and traveling with entire armies of the Lady's regulars, we suffered there. It is a hostile, bitter land where none of the normal rules apply. Rocks speak and whales fly. Coral grows in the desert. Trees walk. And the inhabitants are the strangest of all. . . . But that is neither here nor there. Just a nightmare from the past. A nightmare that haunts me still, when the screams of Cougar and Fleet come echoing down the corridors of time, and once again I can do nothing to save them.

"What's the trouble?" Elmo asked, slipping the map from beneath my fingers, cocking his head sideways. "Look like you saw a ghost."

"Just remembering the Plain of Fear."

"Oh. Yeah. Well, buck up. Have a beer." He slapped my back. "Hey! Kingpin! Where the hell you been?" He charged away, in pursuit of the Company's leading malingerer.

One-Eye arrived a moment later, startling me. "How's Goblin?" he asked softly. There had been no intercourse between them since Madle's. He eyed the map. "The Empty Hills? Interesting name."

"Also called the Hollow Hills. He's all right. Why don't you check him out?"

"What the hell for? He was the one who acted the ass. Can't take a little joke. . . ."

"Your jokes get a bit rough, One-Eye."

"Yeah. Maybe. Tell you what. You come with me."

"Got to prepare my reading." One night a month the Captain expects me to exhort the troops with a reading from the Annals. So we'll know where we came from, so we'll recall our ancestors in the outfit. Once that meant a lot. The Black Company. Last of the Free Companies of Khatovar. All brethren. Tight. Great esprit. Us against the world, and let the world watch out. But the something that had manifested itself in Goblin's behavior, in the low-grade depression of Elmo and others, was affecting everybody. The pieces were coming unglued.

I had to pick a good reading. From a time when the Company had its back against the wall and survived only by clinging to its traditional virtues. There have been many such moments in four hundred years. I wanted one recorded by one of the more inspired Annalists, one with the fire of a White Rose revivalist speaking to potential recruits. Maybe I needed a series, one that I could read several nights running.

"Crap," One-Eye said. "You know those books by heart. Always got your nose in them. Anyway, you could fake the whole thing and nobody would know the difference."

"Probably. And nobody would care if I did. It's going sour, old-timer. Right. Let's go see Goblin."

Maybe the Annals needed a rereading on a different level. Maybe I was treating symptoms. The Annals have a certain mystic quality, for me. Maybe I could identify the disease by immersing myself, hunting something between the lines.

Goblin and Silent were playing no-hands mumbletypeg. I'll say this for our three spook-pushers: They aren't great, but they keep their talents polished. Goblin was ahead on points. He was in a good mood. He even nodded to One-Eye.

So. It was over. The stopper could be put into the bottle. One-Eye just had to say the right thing.

To my amazement, he even apologized. By sign, Silent suggested we get out and let them conclude their peace in private. Each had an overabundance of pride.

We stepped outside. As we often did when no one could intercept our signs, we discussed old times. He, too, was privy to the secret for which the Lady would obliterate nations.

Half a dozen others suspected once, and had forgotten. We knew, and would never forget. Those others, if put to the question, would leave the Lady with serious doubts.

We two, never. We *knew* the identity of the Lady's most potent enemy—and for six years we had done nothing to apprise her of the fact that that enemy even existed as more than a Rebel fantasy.

The Rebel tends to a streak of superstition. He loves prophets and prophecies and grand, dramatic foretellings of victories to come. It was pursuit of a prophecy which led him into the trap at Charm, nearly causing his extinction. He regained his balance afterward by convincing himself that he was the victim of false prophets and prophecies, laid upon him by villains trickier than he. In that conviction he could go on, and believe more impossible things.

The funny thing was, he lied to himself with the truth. I was, perhaps, the only person outside the Lady's inner circle who knew he had been guided into the jaws of death. Only, the enemy who had done the guiding was not the Lady, as he believed. That enemy was an evil greater still, the Dominator, the Lady's one-time spouse, whom she had betrayed and left buried but alive in a grave in the Great Forest north of a far city called Oar. From that grave he had reached out, subtly, and twisted the minds of men high in Rebel circles, bending them to his will, hoping to use them to drag the Lady down and bring about his own resurrection. He failed, though he had help from several of the original Taken in his scheme.

If he knew of my existence, I must be high on his list. He lay up there still, scheming, maybe hating me, for I helped betray the Taken helping him. . . . Scary, that. The Lady was medicine bad enough. The Dominator, though, was the body of which her evil was but a shadow. Or so the legend goes. I sometimes wonder why, if that is true, she walks the earth and he lies restless in the grave.

I have done a good deal of research since discovering the power of the thing in the north, probing little-known histories. Scaring myself each time. The Domination, an era when the Dominator actually ruled, smelled like an era of hell on earth. It seemed a miracle that the White Rose had put him down. A pity she could not have destroyed him. And all his minions, including the Lady. The world would not be in the straits it is today.

I wonder when the honeymoon will end. The Lady hasn't been that terrible. When will she relax, and give the darkness within her free rein, reviving the terror of the past?

I also wonder about the villainies attributed to the Domination. History, inevitably, is recorded by self-serving victors.

A scream came from Goblin's quarters. Silent and I stared at one another a moment, then rushed inside.

I honestly expected one of them to be bleeding his life out on the floor. I did not expect to find Goblin having a fit while One-Eye desperately strove to keep him from hurting himself. "Somebody made contact," One-Eye gasped. "Help me. It's strong."

I gaped. Contact. We hadn't had a direct communication since the desperately swift campaigns when the Rebel was closing in on Charm, years ago. Since then, the Lady and Taken have been content to communicate through messengers.

The fit lasted only seconds. That was customary. Then Goblin relaxed, whimpering. It would be several minutes before he recovered enough to relay the message. We three looked at one another with card-playing faces, frightened inside. I said, "Somebody ought to tell the Captain."

"Yeah," One-Eye said. He made no move to go. Neither did Silent.

"All right. I'm elected." I went. I found the Captain doing what he does best. He had his feet up on his worktable, was snoring. I wakened him, told him.

He sighed. "Find the Lieutenant." He went to his map cases. I asked a couple questions he ignored, took the hint and got out.

He had expected something like this? There was a crisis in the area? How could Charm have heard first?

Silly, worrying before I heard what Goblin had to say.

The Lieutenant seemed no more surprised than the Captain. "Something up?" I asked.

"Maybe. A courier letter came after you and Candy left for Tally. Said we might be called west. This could be it."

"West? Really?"

"Yeah." Such dense sarcasm he put into the word!

Stupid. If we chose Charm as the customary demarcation point between east and west, Tally lay two thousand plus miles away. Three months' travel under perfect conditions. The country between was anything but perfect. In places roads just didn't exist. I thought six months sounded too optimistic.

But I was worrying before the fact again. I had to wait and see.

It turned out to be something even the Captain and Lieutenant hadn't anticipated.

We waited in trepidation while Goblin pulled himself together. The Captain had his map case open, sketching a tentative route to Frost. He grumbled because all westbound traffic had to cross the Plain of Fear. Goblin cleared his throat.

Tension mounted. He did not lift his eyes. The news had to be unpleasant. He squeaked, "We've been recalled. That was the Lady. She seemed disturbed. The first leg goes to Frost. One of the Taken will meet us there. He'll take us on to the Barrowland."

The others frowned, exchanged puzzled looks. I muttered, "Shit. Holy Shit."

"What is it, Croaker?" the Captain asked.

They didn't know. They paid no attention to historical things. "That's where the Dominator is buried. Where they all were buried, back when. It's in the forest north of Oar." We'd been to Oar seven years ago. It was not a friendly city.

"Oar!" the Captain yelled. "Oar! That's twenty-five hundred miles!"

"Add another hundred or two to the Barrowland."

He stared at the maps. "Great. Just great. That means not just the Plain of Fear but the Empty Hills and the Windy Country too. Just fandamntastic great. I suppose we've got to get there next week?"

Goblin shook his head. "She didn't seem rushed, Captain. Just upset and wanting us headed the right way."

"She give you any whys or wherefores?"

Goblin smirked. Did the Lady ever? Hell, no.

"Just like that," the Captain muttered. "Out of the blue. Orders to hike halfway around the world. I love it." He told the Lieutenant to begin preparations for movement.

It was bad news, mad news, insanity squared, but not as bad as he made out. He had been preparing since receiving the courier letter. It wasn't that hard to get rolling. The trouble was, nobody wanted to roll.

The west was far nicer than anything we'd known out here, but not so great anybody wanted to walk that far.

Surely she could have summoned a closer unit?

We are the victims of our own competence. She always wants us where the going threatens to become toughest. She knows we will do the best job.

Damn and double damn.

# Chapter Eleven: JUNIPER: NIGHT WORK

Shed had given Krage only nine of ten leva. The coin he held back bought firewood, wine, and beer to replenish his stocks. Then other creditors caught wind of his prosperity. A slight upturn in business did him no good. He met his next payment to Krage by borrowing from a moneylender named Gilbert.

He found himself wishing somebody would die. Another ten leva would put him in striking distance of getting through the winter.

It was a hard one, that winter. Nothing moved in the harbor. There was no work in the Buskin. Shed's only bit of good fortune was Asa. Asa brought wood whenever he got away from Krage, in a pathetic effort to buy a friend.

Asa arrived with a load. Privately, he said, "Better watch out, Shed. Krage heard about you borrowing from Gilbert." Shed went grey. "He's got a buyer for the Lily lined up. They're rounding up girls already."

Shed nodded. The whoremasters recruited desperate women this time of year. By the time summer brought its sailors, they were broken to their trade.

"The bastard. Made me think he'd given me a break. I should have known better. This way he gets my money *and* my place. The bastard."

"Well, I warned you."

"Yeah. Thanks, Asa."

Shed's next due date came on like a juggernaut. Gilbert

refused him another loan. Smaller creditors besieged the Lily. Krage was aiming them Shed's way.

He took Raven a complimentary drink. "May I sit?"

A hint of a smile crossed Raven's lips. "It's your place." And: "You haven't been friendly lately, Shed."

"I'm nervous," Shed lied. Raven irritated his conscience. "Worried about my debts."

Raven saw through the excuse. "You thought maybe I could help?"

Shed almost groaned. "Yes."

Raven laughed softly. Shed thought he detected a note of triumph. "All right, Shed. Tonight?"

Shed pictured his mother being carted off by the Custodians. He swallowed his self-disgust. "Yeah."

"All right. But this time you're a helper, not a partner." Shed swallowed and nodded. "Put the old woman to bed, then come back downstairs. Understand?"

"Yes," Shed whispered.

"Good. Now go away. You irritate me."

"Yes, sir." Shed retreated. He couldn't look anyone in the eye the rest of that day.

A bitter wind howled down the Port valley, freckled with flakes of snow. Shed huddled miserably, the wagon seat a bar of ice beneath him. The weather was worsening. "Why tonight?" he grumbled.

"Best time." Raven's teeth chattered. "We're not likely to be seen." He turned into Chandler's Lane, off which innumerable narrow alleyways ran. "Good hunting territory here. In this weather they crawl back in the alleys and die like flies."

Shed shivered. He was too old for this. But that was why he was here. So he wouldn't have to face the weather every night.

Raven stopped the wagon. "Check that passageway."

Shed's feet started aching the instant he put weight on them. Good. At least he felt something. They weren't frozen.

There was little light in the alley. He searched more by

feel than sight. He found one lump under an overhang, but it stirred and muttered. He ran.

He reached the wagon as Raven dumped something into the bed. Shed averted his eyes. The boy couldn't have been more than twelve. Raven concealed the body with straw. "That's one. Night like this, we ought to find a load."

Shed choked his protests, resumed his seat. He thought about his mother. She wouldn't last one night in this.

Next alley he found his first corpse. The old man had fallen and frozen because he couldn't get up again. Aching in his soul, Shed dragged the body to the wagon.

"Going to be a good night," Raven observed. "No competition. The Custodians won't come out in this." Softly: "I hope we can make the hill."

Later, after they had moved to the waterfront and each had found another corpse, Shed asked, "Why're *you* doing this?"

"I need money, too. Got a long way to travel. This way I get a lot, fast, without much risk."

Shed thought the risks far greater than Raven would admit. They could be torn apart. "You're not from Juniper, are you?"

"From the south. A shipwrecked sailor."

Shed did not believe it. Raven's accent was not at all right for that, mild though it was. He hadn't the nerve to call the man a liar, though, and press for the truth.

The conversation continued by fits and starts. Shed didn't uncover anything more of Raven's background or motives.

"Go that way," Raven told him. "I'll check over here. Last stop, Shed. I'm done in."

Shed nodded. He wanted to get the night over. To his disgust, he had begun seeing the street people as objects, and he hated them for dying in such damned inconvenient places.

He heard a soft call, turned back quickly. Raven had one. That was enough. He ran to the wagon.

Raven was on the seat, waiting. Shed scrambled up,

huddled, tucked his face away from the wind. Raven kicked the mules into motion.

The wagon was halfway across the bridge over the Port when Shed heard a moan. "What?" One of the bodies was moving! "Oh. Oh, shit, Raven. . . ."

"He's going to die anyway."

Shed huddled back down, stared at the buildings on the north bank. He wanted to argue, wanted to fight, wanted to do anything to deny his part in this atrocity.

He looked up an hour later and recognized nothing. A few large houses flanked the road, widely spaced, their windows dark. "Where are we?"

"Almost there. Half an hour, unless the road is too icy."

Shed imagined the wagon sliding into a ditch. What then? Abandon everything and hope the rig couldn't be traced? Fear replaced loathing.

Then he realized where they were. There wasn't anything up here but that accursed black castle. "Raven. . . ."

"What's the matter?"

"You're head for the black castle."

"Where'd you think we were going?"

"People live there?"

"Yes. What's your problem?"

Raven was a foreigner. He couldn't understand how the black castle affected Juniper. People who got too close disappeared. Juniper preferred to pretend that the place did not exist.

Shed stammered out his fears. Raven shrugged. "Shows your ignorance."

Shed saw the castle's dark shape through the snow. The fall was lighter on the ridge, but the wind was more fierce. Resigned, he muttered, "Let's get it over with."

The shape resolved into battlements, spires, towers. Not a light shown anywhere. Raven halted before a tall gate, went forward on foot. He banged a heavy knocker. Shed huddled, hoping there would be no response.

The gate opened immediately. Raven scrambled onto the wagon's seat. "Get up, mules."

"You're not going inside?"

"Why not?"

"Hey. No way. No."

"Shut up, Shed. You want your money, you help unload."

Shed stifled a whimper. He hadn't bargained for this.

Raven drove through the gate, turned right, halted beneath a broad arch. A single lantern battled the darkness clotting the passageway. Raven swung down. Shed followed, his nerves shrieking. They dragged the bodies out of the wagon and swung them onto stone slabs nearby. Then Raven said, "Get back on the wagon. Keep your mouth shut."

The one body stirred. Shed grunted. Raven pinched his leg savagely. "Shut up."

A shadowy shape appeared. It was tall, thin, clad in loose black pantaloons and a hooded shirt. It examined each body briefly, seemed pleased. It faced Raven. Shed glimpsed a face all of sharp angles and shadows, lustrous, olive, cold, with a pair of softly luminous eyes.

"Thirty. Thirty. Forty. Thirty. Seventy," it said.

Raven countered, "Thirty. Thirty. Fifty. Thirty. One hundred."

"Forty. Eighty."

"Forty-five. Ninety."

"Forty. Ninety."

"Done."

They were dickering! Raven was not interested in quibbling over the old people. The tall being would not advance his offer for the youth. But the dying man was negotiable.

Shed watched the tall being count out coins at the feet of the corpses. That was a damned fortune! Two hundred twenty pieces of silver! With that he could tear the Lily down and build a new place. He could get out of the Buskin altogether.

Raven scooped the coins into his coat pocket. He gave Shed five.

"That's all?"

"Isn't that a good night's work?"

It was a good month's work, and then some. But to get only five of. . . .

"Last time we were partners," Raven said, swinging onto the driver's seat. "Maybe we will be again. But tonight you're a hired hand. Understand?" There was a hard edge to his voice. Shed nodded, beset by new fears.

Raven backed the wagon. Shed felt a sudden chill. That archway was hot as hell. He shuddered, feeling the hunger of the thing watching them.

Dark, glassy, jointless stone slid past. "My god!" He could see into the wall. He saw bones, fragments of bones, bodies, pieces of bodies, all suspended as if floating in the night. As Raven turned toward the gate, he saw a staring face. "What kind of place is this?"

"I don't know, Shed. I don't want to know. All I care is, they pay good money. I need it. I have a long way to go."

# Chapter Twelve: THE BARROWLAND

The Taken called the Limper met the Company at Frost. We'd spent a hundred and forty-six days on the march. They were long days and hard, grinding, men and animals going on more by habit than desire. An outfit in good shape, like ours, is capable of covering fifty or even a hundred miles in a day, pushing hell out of it, but not day after week after month, upon incredibly miserable roads. A smart commander does not push on a long march. The days add up, each leaving its residue of fatigue, till men begin collapsing if the pace is too desperate.

Considering the territories we crossed, we made damned good time. Between Tome and Frost lie mountains where we were lucky to make five miles a day, deserts we had to wander in search of water, rivers that took days to cross using makeshift rafts. We were fortunate to reach Frost having lost only two men.

The Captain shone with a glow of accomplishment—till the military governor summoned him.

He assembled the officers and senior noncoms when he returned. "Bad news," he told us. "The Lady is sending the Limper to lead us across the Plain of Fear. Us and the caravan we'll escort."

Our response was surly. There was bad blood between the Company and the Limper. Elmo asked, "How soon will we leave, sir?" We needed rest. None had been promised, of course, and the Lady and the Taken seem unconscious of human frailties, but still. . . .

"No time specified. Don't get lazy. He's not here now, but he could turn up tomorrow."

Sure. With the flying carpets the Taken use, they can turn up anywhere within days. I muttered, "Let's hope other business keeps him away a while."

I did not want to encounter him again. We had done him wrong, frequently, way back. Before Charm we worked closely with a Taken called Soulcatcher. Catcher used us in several schemes to discredit Limper, both out of old enmity and because Catcher was secretly working on behalf of the Dominator. The Lady was taken in. She nearly destroyed the Limper, but rehabilitated him instead, and brought him back for the final battle.

Way, way back, when the Domination was aborning, centuries before the foundation of the Lady's empire, the Dominator overpowered his greatest rivals and compelled them into his service. He accumulated ten villains that way, soon known as the Ten Who Were Taken. When the White Rose raised the world against the Dominator's wickedness, the Ten were buried with him. She could destroy none of them outright.

Centuries of peace sapped the will of the world to guard itself. A curious wizard tried to contact the Lady. The Lady manipulated him, effected her release. The Ten rose with her. Within a generation she and they forged a new dark empire. Within two they were embattled with the Rebel, whose prophets agreed the White Rose would be reincarnated to lead them to a final victory.

For a while it looked like they would win. Our armies collapsed. Provinces fell. Taken feuded and destroyed one another. Nine of the Ten perished. The Lady managed to Take three Rebel chieftains to replace a portion of her losses: Feather, Journey, and Whisper—likely the best general since the White Rose. She gave us a terrible time before her Taking.

The Rebel prophets were correct in their prophecies, except about the last battle. They expected a reincarnated

White Rose to lead them. She did not. They did not find her in time.

She was alive then. But she was living on our side of the battleline, unaware of what she was. I learned who she was. It is that knowledge which makes my life worthless should I be put to the question.

"Croaker!" the Captain snapped. "Wake up!" Everybody looked at me, wondering how I could daydream through whatever he'd said.

"What?"

"You didn't hear me?"

"No, sir."

He glowered his best bear glower. "Listen up, then. Be ready to travel by carpet when the Taken arrive. Fifty pounds of gear is your limit."

Carpet? Taken? What the hell? I looked around. Some of the men grinned. Some pitied me. Carpet flight? "What for?"

Patiently, the Captain explained, "The Lady wants ten men sent to help Whisper and Feather in the Barrowland. Doing what I don't know. You're one of the ones she picked."

Flutter of fear. "Why me?" It was rough, back when I was her pet.

"Maybe she still loves you. After all these years."

"Captain. . . ."

"Because she said so, Croaker."

"I guess that's good enough. Sure can't argue with it. Who else?"

"Pay attention and you'd know these things. Worry about it later. We have other fish to fry now."

Whisper came to Frost before the Limper. I found myself tossing a pack aboard her flying carpet. Fifty pounds. The rest I had left with One-Eye and Silent.

The carpet was a carpet only by courtesy, because tradition calls it that. Actually, it is a piece of heavy fabric stretched on a wooden frame a foot high when grounded. My fellow passengers were Elmo, who would command our team, and Kingpin. Kingpin is a lazy bastard, but he swings a mean blade.

Our gear, and another hundred pounds belonging to men who would follow us later, rested at the center of the carpet. Shaking, Elmo and Kingpin tied themselves in place at the carpet's two rear corners. My spot was the left front. Whisper sat at the right. We were heavily bundled, almost to immobility. We would be flying fast and high, Whisper said. The temperature upstairs would be low.

I shook as much as Elmo and Kingpin, though I had been aboard carpets before. I loved the view and dreaded the anticipation of falling that came with flight. I also dreaded the Plain of Fear, where strange, fell things cruise the upper air.

Whisper queried, "You all use the latrine? It's going to be a long flight." She did not mention us voiding ourselves in fear, which some men do up there. Her voice was cool and melodious, like those of the women who populate your last dream before waking. Her appearance belied that voice. She looked every bit the tough old campaigner she was. She eyed me, evidently recalling our previous encounter in the Forest of Cloud.

Raven and I had lain in wait where she was expected to meet the Limper and lead him over to the Rebel side. The ambush was successful. Raven took the Limper. I captured Whisper. Soulcatcher and the Lady came and finished up. Whisper became the first new Taken since the Domination.

She winked.

Taut fabric smacked my butt. We went up fast.

Crossing the Plain of Fear was faster by air, but still harrowing. Windwhales quartered across our path. We zipped around them. They were too slow to keep pace. Turquoise manta things rose from their backs, flapped clumsily, caught updrafts, rose above us, then dived past like plunging eagles, challenging our presence in their airspace. We could not outrun them, but outclimbed them easily. However, we could not climb higher than the windwhales. So high and the air becomes too rare for human beings. The whales could rise another mile, becoming diving platforms for the mantas.

There were other flying things, smaller and less dangerous, but determinedly obnoxious. Nevertheless, we got through. When a manta did attack, Whisper defeated it with her thaumaturgic craft.

To do so, she gave up control of the carpet. We fell, out of control, till she drove the manta away. I got through without losing my breakfast, but just barely. I never asked Elmo and Kingpin, figuring they might not want their dignity betrayed.

Whisper would not attack first. That is the prime rule for surviving the Plain of Fear. Don't hit first. If you do, you buy more than a duel. Every monster out there will go after you.

We crossed without harm, as carpets usually do, and raced on, all day long, into the night. We turned north. The air became cooler. Whisper dropped to lower altitudes and slower speeds. Morning found us over Forsberg, where the Company had served when new in the Lady's service. Elmo and I gawked over the side.

Once I pointed, shouted, "There's Deal." We had held that fortress briefly. Then Elmo pointed the other way. There lay Oar, where we had pulled some fine, bloody tricks on the Rebel, and earned the enmity of the Limper. Whisper flew so low we could distinguish faces in the streets. Oar looked no more friendly than it had eight years ago.

We passed on, rolled along above the treetops of the Great Forest, ancient and virgin wilderness from which the White Rose had conducted her campaigns against the Dominator. Whisper slowed around noon. We drifted down into a wide sprawl that once had been cleared land. A cluster of mounds in its middle betrayed the handiwork of man, though now the barrows are scarcely recognizable.

Whisper landed in the street of a town that was mostly ruin. I presumed it to be the town occupied by the Eternal Guard, whose task it is to prevent tampering with the

Barrowland. They were effective till betrayed by apathy elsewhere.

It took the Resurrectionists three hundred seventy years to open the Barrowland, and then they did not get what they wanted. The Lady returned, with the Taken, but the Dominator remained chained.

The Lady obliterated the Resurrectionist movement root and branch. Some reward, eh?

A handful of men left a building still in good repair. I eavesdropped on their exchange with Whisper, understood a few words. "Recall your Forsberger?" I asked Elmo, while trying to shake the stiffness out of my muscles.

"It'll come back. Want to give Kingpin a look? He don't seem right."

He wasn't bad off. Just scared. Took a while to convince him we were back on the ground.

The locals, descendants of the Guards who had watched the Barrowland for centuries, showed us to our quarters. The town was being restored. We were the forerunners of a horde of new blood.

Goblin and two of our best soldiers came in on Whisper's next flight, three days later. They said the Company had left Frost. I asked if it looked like the Limper was holding a grudge.

"Not that I could see," Goblin said. "But that don't mean anything."

No, it didn't.

The last four men arrived three days later. Whisper moved into our barracks. We formed a sort of bodyguard cum police force. Besides protecting her, we were supposed to help make sure unauthorized persons did not get near the Barrowland.

The Taken called Feather appeared, bringing her own bodyguard. Specialists determined to investigate the Barrowland came up with a battalion of laborers hired in Oar. The laborers cleared the trash and brush, up to the Barrowland proper. Entry there, without appropriate protection, meant a slow, painful death. The protective spells the White Rose left hadn't faded with the Lady's resurrection. And she had added her own. I guess she is terrified he will break loose.

The Taken Journey arrived, bringing troops of his own. He established outposts in the Great Forest. The Taken took turns making airborne patrols. We minions watched one another as closely as we watched the rest of the world.

Something big was afoot. Nobody was saying so, but that much was obvious. The Lady definitely anticipated a breakout attempt.

I spent my free time reviewing the Guard's records, especially for the period when Bomanz lived here. He spent forty years in the garrison town, disguised as an antique digger, before he tried to contact the Lady and unintentionally freed her. He interested me. But there was little to dig out, and that little was colored.

Once I'd had his personal papers, having stumbled onto them shortly before Whisper's Taking. But I passed them on to our then mentor Soulcatcher for transportation to the Tower. Soulcatcher kept them for her own reasons, and they fell into my hands again, during the battle at Charm, as the Lady and I pursued the renegade Taken. I didn't mention the papers to anyone but a friend, Raven. The Raven, who deserted to protect a child he believed to be the reincarnation of the White Rose. When I got a chance to pick up the papers from where I hid them, they were gone. I guess Raven took them with him.

I often wonder what became of him. His declared intent was to flee so far no one could find him again. He did not care about politics. He just wanted to protect a child he loved. He was capable of doing anything to protect Darling. I guess he thought the papers might turn into insurance someday.

In the Guard headquarters there are a dozen landscapes painted by past members of the garrison. Most portray the Barrowland. It was magnificent in its day.

It had consisted of a central Great Barrow on a north-south axis, containing the Dominator and his Lady. Surrounding the Great Barrow was a star of earth raised above the plain, outlined by a deep, water-filled moat. At the points of that star stood lesser barrows containing five of The Ten Who Were Taken. A circle rising above the star connected its inward points, and there, at each, stood another barrow containing another Taken. Every barrow was surrounded by spells and fetishes. Within the inner ring, around the Great Barrow, were rank on rank of additional defenses. The last was a dragon curled around the Great Barrow, its tail in its mouth. A later painting by an eyewitness shows the dragon belching fire on the countryside the night of the Lady's resurrection. Bomanz is walking into the fire.

He was caught between Resurrectionists and the Lady, all of whom were manipulating him. His accident was their premeditated event.

The records say his wife survived. She said he went into the Barrowland to stop what was happening. No one believed her at the time. She claimed he carried the Lady's true name and wanted to reach her with it before she could wriggle free.

Silent, One-Eye and Goblin will tell you the direst fear of any sorcerer is that knowledge of his true name will fall to some outsider. Bomanz's wife claimed the Lady's was encoded in papers her husband possessed. Papers that vanished that night. Papers that I recovered decades later. What Raven snatched may contain the only lever capable of dumping the empire.

Back to the Barrowland in its youth. Impressive construction. Its weather faces were sheathed in limestone. The moat was broad and blue. The surrounding countryside was park-like. . . . But fear of the Dominator faded, and so did appropriations. A later painting, contemporary with Bomanz, shows the countryside gone to seed, the limestone facings in disrepair, and the moat becoming a swamp. Today you can't tell where the moat was. The limestone has disappeared beneath brush. The elevations and barrows are nothing but humps. That part of the Great Barrow where the Dominator lies remains in fair shape, though it, too, is heavily overgrown. Some of the fetishes anchoring the spells keeping his friends away still stand, but weather has devoured their features.

The edge of the Barrowland is now marked by stakes trailing red flags, put there when the Lady announced she was sending outsiders to investigate. The Guards themselves, having lived there always, need no markers to warn them off.

I enjoyed my month and a half there. I indulged my curiosities, and found Feather and Whisper remarkably accessible. That hadn't been true of the old Taken. Too, the commander of the Guard, called the Monitor, bragged up his command's past, which stretches back as far as the Company's. We swapped lies and tales over many a gallon of beer.

During the fifth week someone discovered something. We peons were not told what. But the Taken got excited. Whisper started lifting in more of the Company. The reinforcements told harrowing fables about the Plain of Fear and the Empty Hills. The Company was at Lords now, only five hundred miles distant.

At the end of the sixth week Whisper assembled us and announced another move. "The Lady wants me to take some of you out west. A force of twenty-five. Elmo, you'll be in command. Feather and I, some experts, and several language specialists will join you. Yes, Croaker. You're on the list. She wouldn't deny her favorite amateur historian, would she?"

A thrill of fear. I didn't want her getting interested again.

"Where're we headed?" Elmo asked. Professional to the core, the son-of-a-bitch. Not a single complaint.

"A city called Juniper. Way beyond the western bounds of the empire. It's connected with the Barrowland somehow. It's a ways north, too. Expect it to be cold and prepare accordingly."

Juniper? Never heard of it. Neither had anyone else. Not even the Monitor. I scrounged through his maps till I found one showing the western coast. Juniper *was* way up north, near where the ice persists all year long. It was a big city. I wondered how it could exist there, where it should be frozen all the time. I asked Whisper. She seemed to know something about the place. She said Juniper benefits from an ocean current that brings warm water north. She said the city is very strange—according to Feather, who'd actually been there.

I approached Feather next, only hours before our departure. She couldn't tell me much more, except that Juniper is the demense of a Duke Zimerlan, and he appealed to the Lady a year ago (just a while before the Captain's courier letter would have left Charm) for help solving a local problem. That someone had approached the Lady, when the world's desire is to keep her far away, argued that we faced interesting times. I wondered about the connection with the Barrowland.

The negative was that Juniper was so far away. I was pleased that I would be there when the Captain learned he was expected to head there after resting in Oar, though.

Could be I'd hear his howl of outrage even from that far. I knew he wouldn't be happy.

# Chapter Thirteen: JUNIPER: THE ENCLOSURE

Shed slept badly for weeks. He dreamt of black glass walls and a man who hadn't been dead. Twice Raven asked him to join a night hunt. Twice he refused. Raven did not press, though they both knew Shed would jump if he insisted.

Shed prayed that Raven would get rich and disappear. He remained a constant irritant to the conscience.

Damnit, why didn't Krage go after him?

Shed couldn't figure why Raven remained unperturbed by Krage. The man was neither a fool nor stupid. The alternative, that he wasn't scared, made no sense. Not to a Marron Shed.

Asa remained on Krage's payroll, but visited regularly, bringing firewood. By the wagonload, sometimes. "What're you up to?" Shed demanded one day.

"Trying to build credit," Asa admitted. "Krage's guys don't like me much."

"Hardly anybody does, Asa."

"They might try something nasty. . . ."

"Want a place to hide when they turn on you, eh? What're you doing for Krage? Why is he bothering with you?"

Asa hemmed and hawed. Shed pushed. Here was a man he could bully. "I watch Raven, Shed. I report what he does."

Shed snorted. Krage was using Asa because he was

expendable. He'd had two men disappear early on. Shed thought he knew where they were.

Sudden fear. Suppose Asa reported Raven's night adventures? Suppose he'd seen Shed. . . .

Impossible. Asa couldn't have kept quiet. Asa spent his life looking for leverage.

"You've been spending a lot lately, Asa. Where are you getting the money?"

Asa turned pale. He looked around, gobbled a few times. "The wood, Shed. Selling the wood."

"You're a liar, Asa. Where're you getting it?"

"Shed, you don't ask questions like that."

"Maybe not. But I need money bad. I owe Krage. I almost had him paid off. Then he started buying my little debts from everybody else. That damned Gilbert! . . . I need to get ahead enough so I don't have to borrow again."

The black castle. Two hundred twenty pieces of silver. How he had been tempted to attack Raven. And Raven just smiled into the wind, knowing exactly what he was thinking. "Where're you getting that money, Asa?"

"Where did you get the money you paid Krage? Huh? People are wondering, Shed. You don't come up with that kind of money overnight. Not you. You tell me and I'll tell you."

Shed backed down. Asa beamed in triumph.

"You little snake. Get out before I lose my temper."

Asa fled. He looked back once, face knotted thoughtfully. Damnit, Shed thought. Made him suspicious. He ground his rag into a tacky mug.

"What was that?"

Shed spun. Raven had come to the counter. His look brooked no crap. Shed gave him the gist.

"So Krage hasn't quit."

"You don't know him or you wouldn't ask. It's you or him, Raven."

"Then it has to be him, doesn't it?"

Shed gaped.

"A suggestion, Shed. Follow your friend when he goes

wood-gathering.'' Raven returned to his seat. He spoke to Darling animatedly, in sign, which he blocked from Shed's view. The set of the girl's shoulders said she was against whatever it was he was proposing. Ten minutes later he left the Lily. Each afternoon he went out for a few hours. Shed suspected he was testing Krage's watchers.

Darling leaned against the door frame, watching the street. Shed watched her, his gaze sliding up and down her frame. Raven's, he thought. They're thick. I don't dare.

But she was such a fine looking thing, tall, lean of leg, ready for a man. . . . He was a fool. He did not need to get caught in that trap, too. He had troubles enough.

''I think today would be good for it,'' Raven said as Shed delivered his breakfast.

''Eh? Good for what?''

''For a hike up the hill to watch friend Asa.''

''Oh. No. I can't. Got nobody to watch the place.'' Back by the counter, Darling bent to pick something off the floor. Shed's eyes widened and his heart fluttered. He had to do something. Visit a whore, or something. Or get hurt. But he couldn't afford to pay for it. ''Darling couldn't handle it alone.''

''Your cousin Wally has stood in for you before.''

Caught off balance, Shed could not marshall his excuses quickly. And Darling was driving him to distraction. She had to start wearing something that concealed the shape of her behind better. ''Uh. . . . He couldn't deal with Darling. Doesn't know the signs.''

Raven's face darkened slightly. ''Give her the day off. Get that girl Lisa you used when Darling was sick.''

Lisa, Shed thought. Another hot one. ''I only use Lisa when I'm here to watch her.'' A hot one not attached. ''She'll steal me blinder than my mother. . . .''

''Shed!''

''Eh?''

"Get Wally and Lisa here; then go keep an eye on Asa. I'll make sure they don't carry off the family silver."

"But. . . ."

Raven slapped a palm on the tabletop. "I said go!"

The day was clear and bright and, for winter, warm. Shed picked up Asa's trail outside Krage's establishment.

Asa rented a wagon. Shed was amazed. In winter stable-keepers demanded huge deposits. Draft animals slaughtered and eaten had no provenance. He thought it a miracle anyone trusted Asa with a team.

Asa went directly to the Enclosure. Shed stalked along behind, keeping his head down, confident Asa would not suspect him even if he looked back. The streets were crowded.

Asa left the wagon in a public grove across a lane running alongside the wall which girdled the Enclosure. It was one of many similar groves where Juniper's citizenry gathered for the Spring and Autumn Rites for the Dead. The wagon could not be seen from the lane.

Shed squatted in shadow and bush and watched Asa dash to the Enclosure wall. Somebody ought to clear that brush away, Shed thought. It made the wall look tacky. For that matter, the wall needed repairing. Shed crossed and found a gap through which a man could duck-walk. He crept through. Asa was crossing an open meadow, hurrying uphill toward a stand of pines.

The inner face of the wall was brush-masked, too. Scores of bundles of wood lay among the bushes. Asa had more industry than Shed had suspected. Hanging around Krage's gang had changed him. They had him scared for sure.

Asa entered the pines. Shed puffed after him. Ahead, Asa sounded like a cow pushing through the underbrush.

The whole Enclosure was tacky. In Shed's boyhood it had been park-like, a fit waiting place for those who had gone before. Now it had the threadbare look that characterized the rest of Juniper.

Shed crept toward hammering racket. What was Asa doing, making so much noise?

He was cutting wood from a fallen tree, stacking the pieces in neat bundles. Shed could not picture the little man orderly, either. What a difference terror made.

An hour later Shed was ready to give up. He was cold and hungry and stiff. He had wasted half a day. Asa was doing nothing remarkable. But he persevered. He had a time investment to recoup. And an irritable Raven awaiting his report.

Asa worked hard. When not chopping, he hustled bundles down to his wagon. Shed was impressed.

He stayed, watched, and told himself he was a fool. This was going nowhere.

Then Asa became furtive. He collected his tools and concealed them, looked around warily. This is it, Shed thought.

Asa took off uphill. Shed puffed after him. His stiff muscles protested every step. Asa traveled more than a mile through lengthening shadows. Shed almost lost him. A clinking brought him back to the track.

The little man was using flint and steel. He crouched over a supply of torches wrapped in an oilskin, taken from hiding. He got a brand burning, hastened into some brush. A moment later he clambered over some rocks beyond, disappeared. Shed gave it a minute, then followed. He slid round the boulder where he had seen Asa last. Beyond lay a crack in the earth just big enough to admit a man.

"My god," Shed whispered. "He's found a way into the Catacombs. He's looting the dead."

"I came straight back," Shed gasped. Raven was amused by his distress. "I knew Asa was foul, but I never dreamed he'd commit sacrilege."

Raven smiled.

"Aren't you disgusted?"

"No. Why are *you*? He didn't steal any bodies."

Shed came within a hair's breadth of assaulting him. He *was* worse than Asa.

"He making out at it?"

"Not as well as you. The Custodians take all the burial gifts except passage urns." Every corpse in the Catacombs was accompanied by a small, sealed urn, usually fixed on a chain around the body's neck. The Custodians did not touch the few coins in those. When the Day of Passage came, the Boatmen would demand payment for passage to Paradise.

"All those souls stranded," Shed murmured. He explained.

Raven looked baffled. "How can anybody with an ounce of brains believe that crap? Dead is dead. Be quiet, Shed. Just answer questions. How many bodies in the Catacombs?"

"Who knows? They've been putting them away since. . . . Hell, for a thousand years. Maybe there's millions."

"Must have them stacked like cordwood."

Shed wondered about that. The Catacombs were vast, but a thousand years' worth of cadavers from a city Juniper's size would make a hell of a pile. He looked at Raven. Damn the man. "It's Asa's racket. Let's not try."

"Why not?"

"Too dangerous."

"Your friend hasn't suffered."

"He's smalltime. If he gets greedy, he'll get killed. There are Guardians down there. Monsters."

"Describe them."

"I can't."

"Can't or won't?"

"Can't. All they tell you is that they're there."

"I see." Raven rose. "This needs investigating. Don't discuss it. Especially not with Asa."

"Oh, no." Panicked, Asa would do something stupid.

Word drifted in off the street. Krage had sent his two best men after Raven. They had disappeared. Three more had vanished since. Krage himself had been injured by an unknown assailant. He had survived only because of Count's immense strength. Count wasn't expected to live.

Shed was terrified. Krage was neither reasonable nor rational. He asked Raven to move out. Raven stared at him in contempt. ''Look, I don't want him killing you here,'' Shed said.

''Bad for business?''

''For my health, maybe. He's *got* to kill you now. People will stop being scared of him if he doesn't.''

''He won't learn, eh? A damned city of fools.''

Asa boiled through the doorway. ''Shed, I got to talk to you.'' He was scared. ''Krage thinks I turned him over to Raven. He's after me. You got to hide me, Shed.''

''Like hell.'' The trap was closing. Two of them here. Krage would kill him for sure, would dump his mother into the street.

''Shed, I kept you in wood all winter. I kept Krage off your back.''

''Oh, sure. So I should get killed, too?''

''You owe me, Shed. I never told nobody how you go out at night with Raven. Maybe Krage would want to know that, huh?''

Shed grabbed Asa's hands and yanked him forward, against the counter. As if cued, Raven stepped up behind the little man. Shed glimpsed a knife. Raven pricked Asa's back, whispered, ''Let's go to my room.''

Asa went pallid. Shed forced a smile. ''Yeah.'' He released Asa, took a stoneware bottle from beneath the counter. ''I want to talk to you, Asa.'' He collected three mugs.

Shed went up last, intensely aware of his mother's blind stare. How much had she heard? How much had she guessed? She had been cool lately. His shame had come between them. He no longer felt deserving of her respect.

He clouted his conscience. I did it for her!

Raven's room had the only door left on the upper floors. Raven held it for Asa and Shed. ''Sit,'' he told Asa, indicating his cot. Asa sat. He looked scared enough to wet himself.

Raven's room was as Spartan as his dress. It betrayed no hint of wealth.

"I invest it, Shed," Raven said, wearing a mocking smile. "In shipping. Pour the wine." He began cleaning his nails with a knife.

Asa downed his wine before Shed finished pouring the rest. "Fill him up," Raven said. He sipped his own wine. "Shed, why have you been giving me that sour cat's piss when you had this?"

"Nobody gets it without asking. It costs more."

"I'll take this from now on." Raven locked gazes with Asa, tapped his own cheek with his knife blade.

No, Raven wouldn't have to live frugally. The body business would be lucrative. He invested? In shipping? Odd the way he said that. Where the money went might be as interesting as whence it came.

"You threatened my friend," Raven said. "Oh. Excuse me, Shed. A misstatement. It's partner, not friend. Partners don't have to like each other. Little man. You have something to say for yourself?"

Shed shuddered. Damn Raven. He'd said that so Asa would spread it around. Bastard was taking control of his life. Nibbling away at it like a mouse slowly destroying a head of cheese.

"Honest, Mr. Raven. I didn't mean nothing. I was scared. Krage thinks I tipped you. I got to hide, and Shed's scared to put me up. I was just trying to get him to. . . ."

"Shut up. Shed, I thought he was your friend."

"I just did him some favors. I felt sorry for him."

"You'd shelter him from weather, but not from enemies. You're a real gutless wonder, Shed. Maybe I made a mistake. I was going to make you a full partner. Going to give you the whole business eventually. Thought I'd do you a favor. But you're a yellow-dog creep. Without the guts to deny it." He whirled. "Talk, little man. Tell me about Krage. Tell me about the Enclosure."

Asa went white. He didn't open up till Raven threatened to call the Custodians.

* * *

Shed's knees racketed off one another. The hilt of his butcher knife was sweat-moist and slippery. He could not have used the blade, but Asa was too scared to see that. He just squeaked at his team and started rolling. Raven followed them in his own wagon. Shed glanced across the valley. The black castle brooded on the northern skyline, casting its dread shadow across Juniper.

Why was it there? Where had it come from? He rejected the questions. Best to ignore it.

How had he gotten into this? He feared the worst. Raven had no sensibilities.

They left the wagons in the grove, entered the Enclosure. Raven examined Asa's wood stash. "Move these bundles to the wagons. Stack them alongside for now."

"You can't take my wood," Asa protested.

"Shut up." Raven pushed a bundle through the wall. "You first, Shed. Little man, I'll hunt you down if you run off."

They had moved a dozen bundles when Asa whispered, "Shed, one of Krage's goons is watching us." He was about to panic.

Raven was not displeased with the news. "You two go get bundles from the woods."

Asa protested. Raven glared. Asa headed uphill. "How does he know?" he whined at Shed. "He never followed me. I'm sure of that."

Shed shrugged. "Maybe he's a sorcerer. He always knows what I'm thinking."

Raven was gone when they returned. Shed looked around, nervously decided, "Let's get another load."

Raven was waiting next trip. "Take those bundles to Asa's wagon."

"An object lesson," Shed said, pointing into the wagon. Blood ran across the floorboards, seeping from under a pile of wood. "See what kind of man he is?"

"Up the hill now," Raven ordered when they returned. "Lead off, Asa. Collect your tools and torches to start."

Suspicion nagged Shed as he watched Raven build a

litter. But no. Even Raven wouldn't stoop that low. Would he?

They stood looking down into the dark mouth of the underworld. "You first, Asa," Raven said. Reluctantly, Asa descended. "You're next, Shed."

"Have a heart, Raven."

"Get moving."

Shed moved. Raven came down behind him.

The Catacombs had a carnal smell, but weaker than Shed had anticipated. A draft stirred Asa's torch.

"Stop," Raven said. He took the brand, examined the gap through which they had entered, nodded, passed the torch back. "Lead on."

The cavern widened and joined a larger cave. Asa halted halfway across. Shed stopped, too. He was surrounded by bones. Bones on the cave floor, bones on racks on the walls, skeletons hanging from hooks. Loose bones in tumbles and piles, all mixed together. Skeletons sleeping amidst the clutter. Bones still within shreds of burial raiment. Skulls leering from wooden pegs on the far wall, empty eyes sinister in the torchlight. A passage urn shared each peg.

There were mummified bodies, too, though only a few. Only the rich demanded mummification. Here riches meant nothing. They were heaped with all the rest.

Asa volunteered, "This is a real old place. The Custodians don't come here anymore, unless maybe to get rid of loose bones. The whole cave is filled up up that way, like they just pushed them out of the way."

"Let's look," Raven said.

Asa was right. The cavern narrowed and its ceiling descended. The passageway was choked with bones. Shed noted the absence of skulls and urns.

Raven chuckled. "Your Custodians aren't as passionate about the dead as you thought, Shed."

"The chambers you see during Spring and Autumn Rites aren't like this," Shed admitted.

"I don't guess anybody cares about the old ones anymore," Asa said.

"Let's go back," Raven suggested. As they walked, he observed, "We all end up here. Rich or poor, weak or strong." He kicked a mummy. "But the rich stay in better shape. Asa, what's down the other way?"

"I only ever went about a hundred yards. More of the same." He was trying to open a passage urn.

Raven grunted, took an urn, opened it, dumped several coins onto his hand. He held them near the torch. "Uhm. How did you explain their age, Asa?"

"Money has no provenance," Shed said.

Asa nodded. "And I made out like I'd found a buried treasure."

"I see. Lead on."

Soon Asa said, "This is as far as I ever went."

"Keep going."

They wandered till even Raven responded to the oppression of the cavern. "Enough. Back to the surface." Once up top, he said, "Get the tools. Damn. I'd hoped for better."

Soon they were back with a spade and ropes. "Shed, dig a hole over there. Asa, hang on to this end of the rope. When I yell, start pulling." Raven descended into the Catacombs.

Asa remained rooted, as instructed. Shed dug. After a while, Asa asked, "Shed, what's he doing?"

"You don't know? I thought you knew everything he did."

"I just told Krage that. I couldn't keep up with him all night."

Shed grimaced, turned another spadeful of earth. He could guess how Asa worked. By sleeping somewhere most of the time. Spying would have interfered with wood-gathering and grave-robbing.

Shed was relieved. Asa didn't know what he and Raven had done. But he would before long.

He looked inside himself and found little self-disgust. Damn! He was accustomed to these crimes already. Raven was making him over in his own image.

Raven shouted. Asa hauled away. He called, "Shed, give me a hand. I can't get this by myself."

Resigned, Shed joined him. Their catch was exactly what he expected, a mummy sliding out of the darkness like some denizen of the deeps of yesteryear. He averted his gaze. "Get his feet, Asa."

Asa gagged. "My God, Shed. My God. What are you doing?"

"Be quiet and do what you're told. That's the best way. Get his feet."

They moved the body into the brush near Shed's pit. A passage urn rolled out of a bundle tied upon its chest. The bundle contained another two dozen urns. So. The hole was for burying empty urns. Why didn't Raven fill his pockets down there?

"Let's get out of here, Shed," Asa whined.

"Back to your rope." Urns took time to empty. And Raven had two men up top with little to do but think. So. They were busy-work. And an incentive, of course. Two dozen urns with each cadaver would build up quite a pile.

"Shed. . . ."

"Where you going to run to, Asa?" The day was clear and unseasonably warm, but it was still winter. There was no way out of Juniper. "He'd find you. Go back to your rope. You're in it now, like it or not." Shed resumed digging.

Raven sent up six mummies. Each carried its bundle of urns. Then Raven returned. He studied Asa's ashen face, Shed's resignation. "Your turn, Shed."

Shed gulped, opened his mouth, swallowed his protest, slunk toward the hole. He lingered over it, a hair's breadth from rebellion.

"Move it, Shed. We don't have forever."

Marron Shed went down among the dead.

It seemed he was in the Catacombs forever, numbly selecting cadavers, collecting urns, dragging his grisly booty to the rope. His mind had entered another reality. This was the dream, the nightmare. At first he did not understand when Raven called for him to come up.

He clambered into gathering dusk. "Is that enough? Can we go now?"

"No," Raven replied. "We've got sixteen. I figure we can get thirty on the wagons."

"Oh. Okay."

"You haul up," Raven said. "Asa and I will go down."

Shed hauled. In the silvery light of a three-quarters moon the dead faces seemed accusing. He swallowed his loathing and placed each with the others, then emptied urns.

He was tempted to take the money and run. He stayed more out of greed than fear of Raven. He was a partner this time. Thirty bodies at thirty leva meant nine hundred leva to share out. Even if he took the small cut, he would be richer than he'd ever dreamed.

What was that? Not Raven's order to haul away. It sounded like someone screaming. . . . He nearly ran. He did go to pieces momentarily. Raven's bellowing brought him together. The man's cold, calm contempt had vanished.

Shed heaved. This one was heavy. He grunted, strained. . . . Raven came scrambling up. His clothing was torn. A bloody gash marked one cheek. His knife was red. He whirled, grabbed the rope. "Pull!" he shouted. "Damn you, pull!"

Asa came out a moment later, tied to the rope. "What happened? My God, what happened?" Asa was breathing, and that was about it.

"Something jumped us. It tore him up before I could kill it."

"A Guardian. I warned you. Get another torch. Let's see how bad he is." Raven just sat there panting, flustered. Shed got the torch, lighted it.

Asa's wounds were not as bad as he had feared. There was a lot of blood, and Asa was in shock, but he wasn't dying. "We ought to get out of here, Raven. Before the Custodians come."

Raven recovered his composure. "No. There was only one. I killed it. We're in this now. Let's get it done right."

"What about Asa?"

"I don't know. Let's get to work."

"Raven, I'm exhausted."

"You're going to get a lot tireder before we're done. Come on. Let's get the mess cleaned up."

They moved the bodies to the wagons, then the tools, then carted Asa down. As they worked the litter through the wall, Shed asked, "What should we do with him?"

Raven looked at him as though he were a moron. "What do you think, Shed?"

"But. . . ."

"It doesn't much matter now, does it?"

"I guess not." But it did matter. Asa wasn't much, but Shed knew him. He was no friend, but they had helped one another out. . . . "No. Can't do it, Raven. He can make it. If I was sure he was checking out, yeah. Okay. No body, no questions. But I can't kill him."

"Well. A little spirit after all. How are you going to keep him quiet? He's the kind who gets throats cut with loose talk."

"I'll handle him."

"Whatever you say, partner. It's your neck."

The night was well along when they reached the black castle. Raven went in first. Shed followed closely. They pulled into the same passage as before. The drill was the same. After they laid out the bodies, a tall, lean creature went down the line. "Ten. Ten. Thirty. Ten. Ten." And so forth.

Raven protested vigorously. The only offers above ten were for the men who had followed them to the Enclosure and for Asa, who remained in his wagon.

The tall being faced Raven. "These have been dead too long. They have little value. Take them back if you're not satisfied."

"All right. All right. Let's have it."

The being counted out coins. Raven pocketed six of each ten. He handed the rest to Shed. As he did so, he told the tall being, "This man is my partner. He may come alone."

The tall figure inclined its head, took something from within its clothing, handed it to Shed. It was a silver pendant in the form of serpents entwined.

"Wear that if you come up alone," Raven said. "That's your safe-conduct." Under his icy stare Shed slipped the pendant into a pocket already filled with silver.

He ran the arithmetic. One hundred twelve leva as his share. It would have taken him half a decade to accumulate that much honestly. He was rich! Damn him, he was rich! He could do anything he wanted. No more debts. No more Krage killing him slowly. No more gruel every meal. Turn the Lily into something decent. Maybe find a place where his mother would have proper care. Women. All the women he could handle.

As he turned his wagon, he glimpsed a high chunk of wall that hadn't been there last visit. A face stared out. It was the face of the man he and Raven had brought in alive. Its eyes watched him.

# Chapter Fourteen: JUNIPER: DURETILE

Whisper delivered us to a broken-down castle named Duretile. It overlooks Juniper in general and the Enclosure in specific. For a week we had no contact with our hosts. We had no language in common. Then we were graced with the presence of a thug named Bullock who spoke the languages of the Jewel Cities.

Bullock was some kind of enforcer for the local religion. Which I could not figure out at all. It looks like a death cult at first. Look again and you find death or the dead not worshipped but revered, with bodies fanatically preserved against some millennial revival. The whole character of Juniper is shaped by this, except for the Buskin, where life has so many concerns more vital than the welfare of the dead.

I took an instant dislike to Bullock. He struck me as violence-prone and sadistic, a policeman who would solve his cases with a truncheon. He would survive when the Lady annexed Juniper. Her military governors have a need for his ilk.

I expected annexation to occur within days of the Captain's arrival. We'd have it scoped out before he got here. One word from Charm would do it. I saw no indication the Duke's people could stop it.

As soon as Feather and Whisper had all our people in, including translators, Bullock, the Duke himself, and a man named Hargadon, who was senior Custodian of the Dead—

meaning he ran the Catacombs where bodies were stored—they led us into the bitter cold atop Duretile's north wall. The Duke extended an arm. "That fortress over there is why I asked for help."

I looked at it and shuddered. There was something creepy about the place.

"We call it the black castle," he said. "It's been there for centuries." And then he gave us a chunk almost too big to swallow. "It started out as a little black rock lying beside a dead man. The man who found them tried to pick the rock up. He died. And the rock started growing. It's been growing ever since. Our ancestors experimented on it. They attacked it. Nothing harmed it. Anybody who touched it died. For the sake of their sanity, they decided to ignore it."

I shaded my eyes, stared at the castle. Not that unusual, from Duretile, except it was black and gave me the creeps.

The Duke continued, "For centuries it hardly grew. It's only a few generations since it stopped looking like a rock." He got a haunted look. "They say there are things living inside there."

I smiled. What did he expect? A fortress exists to surround something, whether built or grown.

Hargadon assumed the narrative. He had been in his job too long. He'd developed an official's pompous style. "For the last several years it's grown damned fast. The Custodial Office became concerned when we heard rumors—out of the Buskin, so unreliable to be sure—saying the creatures inside were buying cadavers. The accuracy of those rumors remains a source of heated debate within the Office. However, no one can deny that we're not getting enough corpses out of the Buskin these days. Our street patrols collect fewer than they did ten years ago. Times are leaner now. The street poor are more numerous. More should be expiring of exposure."

A real sweetheart, this Hargadon. He sounded like a manufacturer whining because his profit margin was down.

He continued, "It's been hypothesized that the castle may soon be beyond a need to purchase bodies—if it is at all. I'm not convinced.'' Came down squarely on both sides of a question, too. That's my boy. ''Its occupants may become numerous enough to come take what they want.''

Elmo asked, ''You think people are selling bodies, why don't you grab them and make them talk?''

Time for the policeman to enter his bit. Bullock said, ''We can't catch them.'' He had a but-if-they'd-let-me-do-it-my-way tone. ''It's happening down in the Buskin, you see. It's another world down there. You don't find out much if you're an outsider.''

Whisper and Feather stood a bit apart, examining the black castle. Their faces were grim.

The Duke wanted something for nothing. In essence, he wanted to stop worrying about that fortress. He said we could do whatever it took to eliminate his worry. Only we'd have to do it his way. Like he wanted us to stay inside Duretile while *his* men and Hargadon's acted as our eyes, ears and hands. He was afraid of repercussions our presence could cause if known.

A few Rebel fugitives had come to Juniper after their defeat at Charm. The Lady was known here, though little considered. The Duke feared the refugees would incite trouble if he was suspected of collaborating.

In some ways he was an ideal overlord. All he wanted from his people was to be left alone. He was willing to grant the same favor.

So, for a while, we stayed tucked away—till Whisper became irritated by the quality of information we were given.

It was filtered. Sanitized, it was useless. She cornered the Duke and *told* him her men would be going out with his.

He actually stood up to her for a few minutes. The battle was bitter. She threatened to pull out, leaving him twisting in the wind. Pure bluff. She and Feather were intensely interested in the black castle. Armed force could not have levered them out of Juniper.

The Duke subdued, she turned on the Custodians. Bullock was stubbornly jealous of his prerogatives. I do not know how she brought him around. He never was gracious about it.

I became his companion on investigative jaunts, mainly because I learned the language quickly. Nobody down below paid me any mind.

Him they did. He was a walking terror. People crossed the street to avoid him. I guess he had a bad reputation.

Then came news which miraculously cleared the obstacles the Duke and Custodians had dumped in our path.

"You hear?" Elmo asked. "Somebody broke into their precious Catacombs. Bullock is smoking. His boss is having a shit hemorrhage."

I tried to digest that, could not. "More detail, if you please." Elmo tends to abbreviate.

"During the winter they let poor people get away with sneaking into the Enclosure. To collect deadwood for firewood. Somebody got in who decided to take more. Found a way into the Catacombs. Three or four men."

"I still don't get the whole picture, Elmo." He enjoys being coaxed.

"All right. All right. They got inside and stole all the passage urns they could lay hands on. Took them out, emptied them, and buried them in a pit. They also lifted a bunch of old-time mummies. I never seen such moaning and carrying on. You better back off your scheme for getting into the Catacombs."

I had mentioned a desire to see what went on down there. The whole setup was so alien I wanted a closer look. Preferably unchaperoned. "Think they'd get overwrought, eh?"

"Overwrought isn't the half. Bullock is talking bad. I'd hate to be those guys and get caught by him."

"Yeah? I'd better check this out."

Bullock was in Duretile at the time, coordinating his work with that of the Duke's incompetent secret police.

Those guys were a joke. They were practically celebrities, and not a one had the guts to go down into the Buskin, where really interesting things happened.

There is a Buskin in every city, though the name varies. It is a slum so bad the police dare go in only in force. Law there is haphazard at best, mostly enforced by self-proclaimed magistrates supported by toughs they recruit themselves. It is a very subjective justice they mete, likely to be swift, savage, unforgiving, and directed by graft.

I caught up with Bullock, told him, "Till this latest business is cleaned up, I stick like your leg." He scowled. His heavy cheeks reddened. "Orders," I lied, faking an apologetic tone.

"Yeah? All right. Come on."

"Where you headed?"

"The Buskin. Thing like this had to come out of the Buskin. I'm going to track it down." He had guts, for all his other failings. Nothing intimidated him.

I wanted to see the Buskin. He might be the best guide available. I'd heard he went there often, without interference. His reputation was that nasty. A good shadow to walk in.

"Now?" I asked.

"Now." He led me out into the cold and down the hill. He did not ride. One of his little affectations. He never rode. He set a brisk pace, as a man will who is accustomed to getting things done afoot.

"What're we going to look for?" I asked.

"Old coins. The chamber they defiled goes back several centuries. If somebody spent a lot of old money in the last couple days, we might get a line on our men."

I frowned. "I don't know spending patterns here. Places I've been, though, people can hang on to a family horde for ages, then have one black sheep up and spend it all. A few old coins might not mean anything."

"We're looking for a flood, not a few. For a man who spent a fistful. There were three or four men involved. Odds are good one of them is a fool." Bullock had a good grasp of the stupid side of human nature. Maybe because he was close to it himself. Meow.

"We'll be real nice doing the tracing," he told me, as though he expected me to hammer people in outrage. His values were the only ones he could imagine. "The man we want will run when he hears me asking questions."

"We chase him?"

"Just enough so he keeps moving. Maybe he'll lead us somewhere. I know several bosses down there who could've engineered this. If one of them did, I want his balls on a platter."

He spoke in a fever, like a crusader. Did he have some special grievance against the crime lords of the slum? I asked.

"Yeah. I came out of the Buskin. A tough kid who got lucky and got on with the Custodians. My dad wasn't lucky. Tried to buck a protection gang. He paid, and they didn't protect him from another gang in the same racket. He said he wasn't going to put out good money for something he wasn't getting. They cut his throat. I was one of the Custodians who picked him up. They stood around laughing and cracking jokes. The ones responsible."

"Ever settle them up?" I asked, certain of the answer.

"Yeah. Brought them into the Catacombs, too." He glanced at the black castle, half obscured by mists drifting across the far slope. "If I'd heard the rumors about that place, maybe I'd have. . . . No, I wouldn't."

I didn't think so myself. Bullock was a fanatic of sorts. He'd never break the rules of the profession that had brought him out of the Buskin, unless he could advance its cause by so doing.

"Think we'll start right at the waterfront," he told me. "Work our way up the hill. Tavern to tavern, whorehouse to whorehouse. Maybe hint that there's a reward floating around." He ground one fist into another, a man restraining anger. There was a lot of that bottled up inside him. Someday he would blow up good.

We'd gotten an early start. I saw more taverns, cathouses, and reeking dives than I'd passed through in a dozen years. And in every one Bullock's advent engendered a sudden, frightened hush and a promise of dutiful cooperation.

But promises were all we got. We could find no trace of

any old money, except a few coins that had been around too long to be the booty we sought.

Bullock was not discouraged. "Something will turn up," he said. "Times are tough. Just take a little patience." He looked thoughtful. "Might just put some of your boys down here. They aren't known, and they look tough enough to make it."

"They are." I smiled, mentally assembling a team including Elmo, Goblin, Pawnbroker, Kingpin, and a few others. Be great if Raven were still with the Company and could go in with them. They would be running the Buskin inside six months. Which gave me an idea to take up with Whisper.

If we wanted to know what was happening, we should take charge of the Buskin. We could bring in One-Eye. The little wizard was a gangster born. Stand out some, though. I hadn't seen another black face since we'd crossed the Sea of Torments.

"Had an idea?" Bullock asked, about to enter a place called the Iron Lily. "You look like your brain is smoking."

"Maybe. On something down the line. If it gets tougher than we expect."

The Iron Lily looked like every other place we'd been, only more so. The guy who ran it cringed. He didn't know nothing, hadn't heard nothing, and promised to scream for Bullock if anybody so much as spent a single gersh struck before the accession of the present Duke. Every word bullshit. I was glad to get out of there. I was afraid the place would collapse on me before he finished kissing Bullock's ass.

"Got an idea," Bullock said. "Moneylenders."

Took me a second to catch it and to see where the idea had come from. The guy in the tavern, whining about his debts. "Good thinking." A man in the snares of a moneylender would do anything to wriggle away.

"This is Krage's territory. He's one of the nastiest. Let's drop in."

No fear in the man. His confidence in the power of his office was so strong he dared walk into a den of cutthroats without blinking an eye. I faked it good, but I was scared. The villain had his own army, and it was jumpy.

We found out why in a moment. Our man had come up on the short end of somebody in the last couple days. He was down on his back, mummified in bandages.

Bullock chuckled. "Customers getting frisky, Krage? Or did one of your boys try to promote himself?"

Krage eyed us from a face of stone. "I help you with something, Inquisitor?"

"Probably not. You'd lie to me if the truth would save your soul, you bloodsucker."

"Flattery will get you nowhere. What do you want, you parasite?"

Tough boy, this Krage. Struck from the same mold as Bullock, but he had drifted into a socially less honored profession. Not much to choose between them, I thought. Priest and moneylender. And that was what Krage was saying.

"Cute. I'm looking for a guy."

"No shit."

"He's got a lot of old money. Cajian period coinage."

"Am I supposed to know him?"

Bullock shrugged. "Maybe he owes somebody."

"Money's got no provenance down here, Bullock."

Bullock told me: "A proverb of the Buskin." He faced Krage. "This money does. This money better, let's say. This is a big one, Krage. Not a little let's-look-around-and-make-a-show. Not some bump-and-run. We're going the route. Anybody covers on it, they go down with this boy. You remember Bullock said it."

For a second Bullock made an impression. The message got through. Then Krage blank-faced us again. "You're sniffing up the wrong tree, Inquisitor."

"Just telling you so you'd know."

"What did this guy do?"

"Hit somebody who don't take hitting."

Krage's eyebrows rose. He looked puzzled. He could think of no one who fit that description. "Who?"

"Uhn-uh. Just don't let your boys take any old money

without you checking the source and getting back to me. Hear?''

''Said your piece, Inquisitor?''

''Yeah.''

''Shouldn't you better be going, then?''

We went. I didn't know the rules of the game, so didn't know how the locals would score the exchange. I rated it too close to call.

Outside, I asked, ''Would he have told us if he'd been paid in old coin?''

''No. Not until he looked into it, at least. But he hasn't seen any old money.''

I wondered why he thought that. I didn't ask. These were his people. ''He might know something. Thought I saw a glint in his eye a couple times.''

''Maybe. Maybe not. Let him stew.''

''Maybe if you'd told him why. . . .''

''No! That doesn't get out. Not even a rumor. If people thought we couldn't protect their dead or them after they kick off, all hell would break loose.'' He made a downward gesture with one hand. ''Juniper like that. Crunch.'' We walked on. He muttered, ''All hell would break loose.'' And after another half-block: ''That's why we've got to get these guys. Not so much to punish them. To shut them up.''

''I see.'' We strolled back the direction we had come, planning to resume tavern-hopping and to see a moneylender named Gilbert when we reached his territory. ''Hey?''

Bullock stopped. ''What?''

I shook my head. ''Nothing. Thought I saw a ghost. Guy down the street. . . . Walked like somebody I used to know.''

''Maybe it was.''

''Nah. Long ago and far away. Long dead now. Just because I was thinking about him a little bit ago.''

''I figure we got time for half a dozen more visits. Then we head uphill. Don't want to hang around here after dark.''

I looked at him, one eyebrow raised.

"Hell, man, it gets dangerous down here when the sun goes down." He chuckled and gave me one of his rare smiles. It was the genuine article.

For one moment then, I liked him.

# Chapter Fifteen: JUNIPER: DEATH OF A GANGSTER

Shed had long, violent arguments with his mother. She never accused him directly, but she left little doubt she suspected him of hideous crimes.

He and Raven took turns nursing Asa.

Then it was time to face Krage. He did not want to go. He was afraid Krage might have lumped him with Raven and Asa. But if he didn't go, Krage would come to him. And Krage was looking for people to hurt. . . . Shaky, Shed trudged up the frozen street. Snow fell in lazy, fat flakes.

One of Krage's men ushered him into the presence. There was no sign of Count, but word was out that the big man was recovering. Too damned stupid to die, Shed thought.

"Ah, Shed," Krage said from the deeps of a huge chair. "How are you?"

"Cold. How're you keeping?" Krage worried him when he was affable.

"Be all right." Krage plucked at his bandages. "Close call. I was lucky. Come to make your payment?"

"How much do I owe, all told? You buying up my debts, I couldn't keep track."

"You can pay out?" Krage's eyes narrowed.

"I don't know. I have ten leva."

Krage sighed dramatically. "You got enough. Didn't think you had it in you, Shed. Well. You win some and you lose some. It's eight and some change."

Shed counted out nine coins. Krage made change. "You've had a run of luck this winter, Shed."

"Sure have."

"You seen Asa?" Krage's voice tautened.

"Not since three days ago. Why?"

"Nothing important. We're even, Shed. But it's time I collected that favor. Raven. I want him."

"Krage, I don't want to tell you your business, but that's one man you'd better leave alone. He's crazy. He's nasty and he's tough. He'd as soon kill you as say hi. I don't mean no disrespect, but he acts like you're a big joke."

"The joke will be on him, Shed." Krage dragged himself out of his chair, wincing. He grabbed his wound. "The joke will be on him."

"Maybe next time he won't let *you* get away, Krage."

Fear crossed Krage's features. "Shed, it's him or me. If I don't kill him, my business will fall apart."

"Where will it be if he kills you?"

Again that flicker of fear. "I don't have any choice. Be ready when I need you, Shed. Soon now."

Shed bobbed his head and retreated. He ought to get out of the Buskin, he thought. He could afford it. But where would he go? Krage could find him anywhere in Juniper. Running didn't appeal, anyway. The Lily was home. He had to weather this. One or the other would die, and either way he would be off the hook.

He was in the middle now. He hated Krage. Krage had humiliated him for years, keeping him in debt, stealing food from his mouth with ridiculous interest rates. On the other hand, Raven could connect him with the black castle and crimes in the Enclosure.

The Custodians were on the hunt, looking for somebody spending a lot of old money. Little had been said publicly, but Bullock being on the case told Shed just how seriously they were taking the case up the hill. He'd nearly had a stroke when Bullock walked into the Lily.

What had become of the passage money? Shed hadn't

seen any of it. He supposed Raven still had it. He and Raven were partners now. . . .

"What did Krage say?" Raven asked when Shed reached the Lily.

"Wants me to help kill you."

"I thought so. Shed, it's late in the season. It's time to send Krage up the hill. Which way are you leaning, partner? Him or me?"

"I. . . . Uh. . . ."

"In the long run you're better off getting rid of Krage. He'd find a way to get the Lily eventually."

True, Shed reflected. "All right. What do we do?"

"Tomorrow, go tell him you think I've been selling bodies. That you think Asa was my partner. That you think I did Asa in. Asa was your friend and you're upset. It'll all be just near enough reality to confuse him. . . . What's the matter?"

Always a trap. Raven was right. Krage would believe the story. But Shed had hoped for a less direct role. If Raven screwed up, Marron Shed would be found in a gutter with his throat cut.

"Nothing."

"All right. Night after tomorrow night, I'll go out. You run to tell Krage. I'll let his men track me. Krage will want to be in at the kill. I'll ambush him."

"You did that before, didn't you?"

"He'll come anyway. He's stupid."

Shed swallowed. "That isn't a plan that does much for my nerves."

"Your nerves aren't my problem, Shed. They're yours. *You* lost them. Only you can find them again."

Krage bought Shed's story. He was ecstatic because Raven was such a villain. "If I didn't want him myself, I'd yell for the Custodians. You did good, Shed. I should have suspected Asa. He never brought no news worth hearing."

Shed whined, "Who would buy bodies, Krage?"

Krage grinned. "Don't worry your ugly head. Let me

know next time he goes on one of his jaunts. We'll rig up a little surprise."

Next night Shed reported according to plan. And suffered all the disappointment he expected of life. Krage insisted he join the hunt.

"What good would I be, Krage? I'm not even armed. And he's one tough nut. You won't take him without a fight."

"I don't expect to. You're coming along just in case."

"In case?"

"In case there's a trap in this and I want to lay hands on you fast."

Shed shuddered, whined, "I done right by you. Don't I always do right by you?"

"You always do what a coward would. Which is why I don't trust you. Anybody can scare you. And you had all that money. It occurs to me you might be in the racket with Raven."

Shed went cold. Krage donned his coat. "Let's go, Shed. Stay right beside me. You try to wander off, I'll kill you."

Shed started shaking. He was dead. All he had gone through to get Krage off his back. . . . It wasn't fair. It just wasn't fair. Nothing ever worked for him. He stumbled into the street, wondering what he could do and knowing there was no escape. Tears froze on his cheeks.

No exit. If he fled, Krage would be warned. If he did not, Krage would kill him when Raven sprang his ambush. What was his mother going to do?

He had to *do* something. Had to find some guts, make a decision, *act*. He couldn't surrender to fate and hope for luck. That meant the Catacombs or black castle before dawn.

He had lied to Krage. He had a butcher knife up his left sleeve. He had put it there out of sheer bravado. Krage hadn't searched him. Old Shed armed? Ha! Not likely. He might get himself hurt.

Old Shed did go armed sometimes, but he never advertised the fact. The knife did wonders for his confidence.

He could tell himself he would use it, and he'd believe the lie long enough to get by, but in any tight spot he would let fate run its course.

His fate was sealed. . . . Unless he whipped it heads-up, no holds barred.

How?

Krage's men were amused by his terror. There were six of them. . . . Then there were seven . . . and eight, as those tracking Raven reported in. Could he hope to beat those odds? Raven himself didn't stand a chance.

*You are a dead man*, a tiny voice whispered, over and over. *Dead man. Dead man.*

"He's working his way down Chandler's," a shadow reported. "Going into all the little alleyways."

Krage asked Shed, "Think he'll find anything this late in the winter? The weaklings have all died."

Shed shrugged. "I wouldn't know." He rubbed his left arm against his side. The knife's presence helped, but not much.

His terror peaked and began to recede. His mind cooled to an unemotional numbness. Fear in abeyance, he tried to find the unseen exit.

Again someone loomed out of the darkness, reported they were a hundred feet from Raven's wagon. Raven had gone into an alley ten minutes ago. He hadn't come out.

"He spot you?" Krage growled.

"I don't think so. But you never know."

Krage eyed Shed. "Shed, would he abandon his team and wagon?"

"How would I know?" Shed squeaked. "Maybe he found something."

"Let's take a look." They moved to the alley, one of countless dead-end breezeways opening off Chandler's Lane. Krage stared into the darkness, head canted slightly. "Quiet as the Catacombs. Check it out, Luke."

"Boss?"

"Take it easy, Luke. Old Shed is going to be right behind you. Won't you, Shed?"

"Krage. . . ."

"Move out!"

Shed shambled forward. Luke advanced cautiously, wicked knife probing the darkness. Shed tried to talk to him. "Shut up!" he snarled. "Don't you have a weapon?"

"No," Shed lied. He glanced back. It was just the two of them.

They reached the dead end. No Raven. "I'll be damned," Luke said. "How did he get out?"

"I don't know. Let's find out." This might be his chance.

"Here we go," Luke said. "He climbed this down-spout."

Shed's guts knotted. His throat tightened. "Give it a try. Maybe we can follow him."

"Yeah." Luke started up.

Shed didn't think about it. The butcher knife materialized in his hand. His hand slammed forward. Luke arched back, dropped. Shed jumped on him, jammed a palm against his mouth, held on for the minute it took him to die. He backed away, unable to believe he'd done it.

"What's going on back there?" Krage demanded.

"Can't find anything," Shed yelled. He dragged Luke against a wall, buried him under trash and snow, ran to the down-spout.

Krage's approach made a marvelous incentive. He grunted, strained, popped a muscle, reached the roof. It consisted of a skirt two feet wide set at a shallow angle, then twelve feet rising at forty-five degrees, above which the roof was flat. Shed leaned against the steep slate, panting, still unable to believe that he had killed a man. He heard voices below, began moving sideways.

Someone snarled, "They're gone, Krage. No Raven. No Luke and no Shed, either."

"That bastard. I knew he was setting me up."

"Why did Luke go with him, then?"

"Hell, I don't know. Don't stand there. Look around. They got out of here somehow."

"Hey. Over here. Somebody went up this spout. Maybe they're after Raven."

"Climb the damned thing. Find out. Luke! Shed!"

"Over here," a voice called. Shed froze. What the hell? Raven? Had to be Raven.

He inched along, trying to fake himself into believing there wasn't thirty-five feet of nothing behind his heels. He reached a ridged corner where he could clamber up to the flat top.

"Over here. I think we got him cornered."

"Get up there, you bastards!" Krage raged.

Lying motionless on the cold, icy tar, Shed watched two shadows appear on the skirt and begin easing toward the voice. A squeal of metal and vicious cursing proclaimed the fate of a third climber. "Twisted my ankle, Krage," the man complained.

"Come on," Krage growled. "We'll find another way up."

*Run while you got the chance*, Shed thought. *Go home and hole up till it's over*. But he could not. He slid down to the skirt and crept after Krage's men.

Someone cried out, scrabbled for a hold, plunged into the darkness between buildings. Krage shouted. Nobody answered.

Shed crossed to the roof next door. It was flat and forested with chimneys. "Raven?" he called softly. "It's me. Shed." He touched the knife in his sleeve, still unable to believe that he'd used it.

A shape materialized. Shed settled into a sitting position, arms around his knees. "What now?" he asked.

"What're you doing here?"

"Krage dragged me along. I was supposed to be the first one dead if it was a trap." He told Raven what he had done.

"Damn! You've got guts after all."

"He backed me into a corner. What now?"

"The odds are getting better. Let me think about it."

Krage shouted out in Chandler's Lane. Raven yelled back, "Over here! We're right behind him." He told Shed: "I don't know how long I can fool him. I was going to pick them off one at a time. I didn't know he'd bring an army."

"My nerves are shot," Shed said. Heights were another of the thousand things that terrified him.

"Hang on. It's a long way from over." Raven yelled, "Cut him off, why don't you?" He took off. "Come on, Shed."

Shed could not keep up. He wasn't as nimble as Raven.

A shape loomed out of the darkness. He squeaked.

"That you, Shed?" It was one of Krage's men. Shed's heartbeat doubled.

"Yeah. You seen Raven?"

"No. Where's Luke?"

"Damnit, he was headed right at you. How could you miss him? Look here." Shed indicated disturbances in traces of snow.

"Look, man, I didn't see him. Don't come on at me like you was Krage. I'll kick your ass up around your ears."

"All right. All right. Calm down. I'm scared and I want to get it over. Luke fell off. Back there. Slipped on some ice or something. Be careful."

"I heard. Sounded like Milt, though. I'd have sworn it was Milt. This is stupid. He can pick us off up here. We ought to back off and try something else."

"Uhn-uh. I want him now. I don't want him tracking me down tomorrow." Shed was amazed. How easily the lies came! Silently, he cursed the man because he wouldn't turn his back. "You got an extra knife or something?"

"You? Use a knife? Come on. Stick with me, Shed. I'll look out for you."

"Sure. Look, the trail goes that way. Let's get it done."

The man turned to examine Raven's tracks. Shed drew his knife and hit him hard. The man let out a yell, twisted. The knife broke. Shed almost pitched off the roof. His victim did. People shouted questions. Krage and his men all seemed to be on the rooftops now.

When Shed stopped shaking, he started moving again, trying to recall the layout of the neighborhood. He wanted to get down and head home. Raven could finish this insanity.

Shed ran into Krage on the next roof. "Krage!" he whined. "God! Let me out of here! He'll kill us all!"

"I'll kill you, Shed. It was a trap, wasn't it?"

"Krage, no!" What could he do? He didn't have the butcher knife now. Fake. Whine and fake. "Krage, you got to get out of here. He already got Luke and Milt and somebody else. He would've gotten me when he got Luke, except he fell down and I got away—only he caught up again when I was talking to one of your guys right over there. They got fighting, and one of them went off the edge; I don't know which, but I bet it wasn't Raven. We got to get down from here, on account of we can't tell who we're running into so we got to be careful. I could have had him this last time, only I didn't have a weapon and we didn't know it wasn't one of our own guys coming. Raven don't have that problem. Anybody he sees he knows is an enemy, so he don't have to be so careful. . . ."

"Shut up, Shed."

Krage was buying it. Shed talked a little louder, hoping Raven would hear, come, and finish it.

There was a cry across the rooftops. "That's Teskus," Krage growled. "That's four. Right?"

Shed bobbed his head. "That we know about. Maybe there's only you and me now. Krage, we should get out of here before he finds us."

"Might be something to what you say, Shed. Might be. We shouldn't have come up here. Come on."

Shed followed, keeping up the chatter. "It was Luke's idea. He thought he'd make points with you. See, we saw him at the top of this drain-spout and he didn't see us, so Luke said why don't we go after him and get him, and old Krage will. . . ."

"Shut up, Shed. For God's sake, shut up. Your voice sickens me."

"Yes, sir, Mr. Krage. Only I can't. I'm so scared. . . ."

"If you don't, I'll shut you up permanent. You won't have to worry about Raven."

Shed stopped talking. He had pushed as far as he dared.

Krage halted a short time later. "We'll set an ambush near his wagon. He'll come back for it, won't he?"

"I expect so, Mr. Krage. But what good will I be? I mean, I don't have a weapon, and wouldn't know how to use one if I did."

"Shut up. You're right. You're not much good, Shed. But I think you'll do fine as a distraction. You get his attention. Talk to him. I'll hit him from behind."

"Krage. . . ."

"Shut up." Krage rolled over the side of the building, clung to the parapet while getting a solid foothold. Shed leaned forward. Three storeys to the ground.

He kicked Krage's fingers. Krage cursed, scrabbled for a fresh hold, missed, dropped, yelled, hit with a muted thump. Shed watched his vague shape twitch, become still.

"I did it again." He started shaking. "Can't stay here. His men might find me." He swung over the parapet and monkeyed down the side of the building, more afraid of being caught than of falling.

Krage was still breathing. In fact, he was conscious but paralyzed. "You were right, Krage. It was a trap. You shouldn't have pushed me. You made me hate you more than I was scared of you." He looked around. It wasn't as late as he had thought. The rooftop hunt hadn't lasted long. Where was Raven, anyway?

Somebody had to clean up. He grabbed Krage, dragged him toward Raven's wagon. Krage squealed. For a moment Shed was afraid someone would investigate. No one did. This was the Buskin.

Krage screamed when Shed hoisted him into the wagon. "Comfy, Krage?"

He retrieved Luke next, then went seeking other bodies. He found another three. None were Raven. He muttered, "If he doesn't show in a half hour, I'll take them up myself and the hell with him." Then: "What's come over you, Marron Shed? Letting this go to your head? So you found some guts. So what? That don't make you no Raven."

Someone was coming. He snatched a booty dagger, faded into a shadow.

Raven tumbled a body into the wagon. "How the hell?"

"I collected them," Shed explained.

"Who are they?"

"Krage and his men."

"I thought he ran for it. Figured I had to go through it all again. What happened?"

Shed explained. Raven shook his head in disbelief. "You? Shed?"

"I guess there's only so much they can scare you."

"True. But I never thought you'd figure it out. Shed, you amaze me. Disappoint me, too, some. I wanted Krage myself."

"That's him making the noise. He's got a broken back or something. Kill him if you want."

"He's worth more alive."

Shed nodded. Poor Krage. "Where are the rest of them?"

"There's one on the roof. Guess the other one got away."

"Damn. That means it's not over."

"We can get him later."

"Meanwhile, he goes and gets the others and we have them all after us."

"You think they'd risk their lives to avenge Krage? No way. They'll be fighting among themselves. Trying to take over. Wait here. I'll get the other one."

"Hurry up," Shed said. The reaction was catching up. He had survived. The old Shed was coming back, dragging all his hysteria with him.

Coming down from the castle, with pink and purple strands of dawn smearing the gaps between the Wolanders, Shed asked, "Why is he screaming?"

The tall being had laughed and paid a hundred twenty leva for Krage. His shrieks could still be heard.

"I don't know. Don't look back, Shed. Do what you have to and move on." And, a moment later: "I'm glad it's over."

"Over? What do you mean?"

"That was my last visit." Raven patted his pocket. "I have enough."

"Me, too. I'm out of debt. I can refurbish the Lily, set my mother up in her own place, and have plenty to make it next winter, no matter what business is like. I'm going to forget that castle exists."

"I don't think so, Shed. You want to get away from it, better come with me. It'll always be calling when you want some fast money."

"I couldn't leave. I have to look out for my mother."

"All right. I warned you." Then Raven asked, "What about Asa? He's going to be a problem. The Custodians are going to keep looking till they find the people who raided the Catacombs. He's the weak link."

"I can handle Asa."

"I hope so, Shed. I hope so."

Krage's disappearance was the talk of the Buskin. Shed played a baffled role, claiming he knew nothing, despite rumors to the contrary. His story held up. He was Shed the coward. The one man who knew differently did not contradict him.

The hard part was facing his mother. Old June said nothing, but her blind stare was accusing. She made him feel evil, an infidel, and disowned in the secret reaches of her mind. The gap had become unbridgable.

# Chapter Sixteen: JUNIPER: NASTY SURPRISE

Bullock looked me up next time he wanted to go downhill. Maybe he just wanted company. He had no local friends.

"What's up?" I asked when he barged into my tiny office cum dispensary.

"Get your coat. Buskin time again."

His eagerness excited me for no reason other than that I was bored with Duretile. I pitied my comrades. They hadn't yet had a chance to get out. The place was a drudge.

So away we went, and going down the hill, past the Enclosure, I asked, "Why all the excitement?"

He replied, "Not really excitement. Not even anything to do with us, probably. Remember that sweetheart of a moneylender?"

"In the bandages?"

"Yeah. Krage. He's vanished. Him and half of his boys. Seems he took a crack at the guy who cut him. And hasn't been seen since."

I frowned. That did not seem remarkable. Gangsters are always disappearing, then popping up again.

"Over there." Bullock pointed to some brush along the Enclosure wall. "That's where our men got inside." He indicated a stand of trees across the way. "Parked their wagons there. We've got a witness who saw those. Filled with wood, he says. Come on. I'll show you." He pushed into the brush, dropped to hands and knees. I followed, grumbling because I was getting wet. The north wind did nothing to improve matters.

The interior of the Enclosure was seedier than its exterior. Bullock showed me several dozen bundles of wood found in the brush near the breach.

"Looks like they were moving a lot."

"I figure they needed a lot to cover the bodies. Cut it up there." He indicated trees above us, back toward Duretile. The castle stood limned against streamers of cloud, a grey stone rockpile one earth tremor short of collapse.

I examined the bundles. Bullock's associates had dragged them out and stacked them, which may not have been smart detective work. Looked to me like they had been cut and bundled over a period of weeks. Some ends were more weathered than others. I mentioned that to Bullock.

"I noticed. Way I figure, somebody was getting wood regular. They found the Catacombs by accident. That's when they got greedy."

"Uhm." I considered the woodpile. "Figure they were selling it?"

"No. That we know. Nobody has been selling Enclosure wood. Probably a family or a group of neighbors using the wood themselves."

"You check on wagon rentals?"

"How stupid do you think people are? Rent a wagon for a raid on the Catacombs?"

I shrugged. "We're counting on one of them being stupid, aren't we?"

He admitted, "You're right. It should be checked. But it's hard when I'm the only one who has guts enough to do legwork in the Buskin. I'm hoping we get lucky somewhere else. If I have to, I'll cover it. When there's nothing more pressing."

"I see the place where they got in?" I asked.

He wanted to tell me no. Instead, he said, "It's a fair hike. Use up an hour. I'd rather go sniff around this Krage thing while it's hot."

I shrugged. "Some other time, then."

We got down into Krage's territory and started rambling.

Bullock still had a few contacts left from his boyhood. Coaxed properly, with a few gersh, they would talk. I was not allowed to sit in. I spent the time sipping beer in a tavern where they alternately fawned over my money and acted like I had the plague. When asked, I did not deny being an Inquisitor.

Bullock joined me. "Maybe we don't have anything after all. There's all kinds of rumors. One says his own men did him in. One says it was his competition. He's a little pushy with his neighbors." He accepted a mug of wine on the house, something I hadn't seen him do before. I put it down to preoccupation.

"There's one angle we can check. He was obsessed about getting some foreigner who made a fool of him in public. There's some say the same foreigner was the man who cut him up." He took out a list and began to peruse it. "Not going to be a lot there for us, I expect. The night Krage disappeared there was a lot of whoop and holler. Not a single eyewitness, of course." He grinned. "Ear-witnesses say it was a running battle. That makes me favor the palace revolution theory."

"What have you got there?"

"A list of people who were maybe getting wood out of the Enclosure. Some might have seen each other. I was thinking I might find something interesting if I compared their stories." He waved for more wine. This time he paid, and covered the first mug, too, though the house would have forgiven him payment. I got the impression Juniper's people were used to giving Custodians anything they wanted. Bullock simply had a sense of ethics, at least where the people of the Buskin were concerned. He would not make their lives harder than they already were.

I could not help liking him on some levels.

"You're not going to pursue the Krage thing, then?"

"Oh, yeah. Of course. The bodies are missing. But that's not unusual. Probably turn up across the river in a couple days, if they're dead. Or screaming for blood if they're not." He tapped a name on his list. "This guy hangs around the same place. Maybe I'll talk to this guy Raven while I'm there."

I felt the blood drain from my face. "Who?"

He looked at me strangely. I forced myself to relax, to look casual. His eyebrows dropped. "Guy named Raven. The foreigner who was supposed to be feuding with Krage. Hangs out the same place as this one guy on my wood-gatherer's list. Maybe I'll ask him a few questions."

"Raven. Unusual name. What do you know about him?"

"Just that he's a foreigner and supposed to be bad news. Been around a couple years. Typical drifter. Hangs out with the Crater crowd."

The Crater crowd were the Rebel refugees who had established themselves in Juniper.

"Do me a favor? It's a long shot, but this guy could be the ghost I was talking about the other day. Stand off a ways. Pretend you never heard the name. But get me a physical description. And find out if he's got anybody with him."

Bullock frowned. He didn't like it. "Is it important?"

"I don't know. It could be."

"All right."

"Keep the whole thing under your hat if you can."

"This guy means something to you, eh?"

"If he's the guy I knew, that I thought was dead, yeah. Him and me got business."

He smiled. "Personal?"

I nodded. I was feeling my way now. This was touchy. If this was my Raven, I had to go careful. I didn't dare let him get caught in the coils of our operation. He knew too damned much. He could get half the Company officers and noncoms put to the question. And made dead.

I decided Bullock would respond best if I kept it mysterious, with Raven an old enemy by implication. Somebody I would do most anything to jump in the dark, but not somebody important in any other way.

"I got you," he said. He looked at me somewhat differently, as though glad to discover I wasn't different after all.

Hell, I'm not. But I like to pretend I am, most of the time. I told him, "I'm going back to Duretile. Got to talk to a couple buddies."

"Can you find your way?"

"I can. Let me know what you find out."

"Will do."

We separated. I went up the hill as fast as forty-year-old legs would carry me.

I got Elmo and Goblin off where nobody could overhear us. "We maybe got a problem, friends."

"Like what?" Goblin wanted to know. He had been aching for me to talk from the minute I rounded him up. I guess I looked a little ragged around the fringes.

"There's a guy named Raven operating down in the Buskin. The other day, when I was down there with Bullock, I thought I saw a guy who looked like our Raven from a distance, but I shrugged it off then."

They quick got as nervous as me. "You sure it's him?" Elmo asked.

"No. Not yet. I got the hell out of there the minute I heard the name Raven. Let Bullock think he's an old enemy I want to stick a knife in. He's going to ask around for me while he's doing his own business. Get me a description. See if Darling is with him. I'm probably off in the wild blue yonder, but I wanted you guys to know. In case."

"What if it is him?" Elmo said. "What do we do then?"

"I don't know. It could be big trouble. If Whisper had some reason to get interested, like because he hangs around with the Rebel refugees here. . . . Well, you know."

Goblin mused, "Seems Silent said Raven was going to run so far nobody would ever find him again."

"So maybe he thought he'd run far enough. This is damned near the end of the world." Which, in part, was why I was so nervous. This was the kind of place I could picture Raven having gone to ground. As far from the Lady as you could get without learning to walk on water.

"Seems to me," Elmo said, "we ought to make sure

before we panic. Then decide what to do. This might be the time to put our guys into the Buskin."

"That's what I was thinking. I already got a plan in front of Whisper, for something else. Let's tell her we're going with that, and have the guys watch for Raven."

"Who?" Elmo asked. "Raven would recognize anybody who knows him."

"Not true. Use guys who joined up at Charm. Send Pawnbroker just to make sure. He's not likely to remember the new guys. There were so many of them. If you want somebody reliable to run the thing, and back them up, use Goblin. Park him where he can stay out of sight but keep his hands on the reins."

"What do you think, Goblin?" he asked.

Goblin smiled nervously. "Give me something to do, anyway. I'm going out of my skull up here. These people are weird."

Elmo chuckled. "Missing One-Eye?"

"Almost."

"All right," I said. "You'll need a guide. That'll have to be me. I don't want Bullock getting his nose any deeper into this. But they think I'm one of his men down there. You'll have to follow me from a distance. And try not to look like what you are. Don't make it hard on yourselves."

Elmo stretched. "I'll get Kingpin and Pawnbroker now. You take them down and show them a place. One can come back for the others. Go ahead and scope it out with Goblin." He left.

And so it went. Goblin and the six soldiers took rooms not far from the moneylender Krage's headquarters. Up on the hill I pretended it was all for the cause.

I waited.

# Chapter Seventeen: JUNIPER: TRAVEL PLANS

Shed caught Asa trying to sneak out. "What the hell is this?"

"I need to get out, Shed. I'm going crazy up there."

"Yeah? You want to know something, Asa? The Inquisitors are looking for you. Bullock himself was in here the other day, and he asked for you by name." Shed was stretching the facts slightly. Bullock's interest had not been intense. But it had to have something to do with the Catacombs. Bullock and his sidekick were in the Buskin almost every day, asking, asking, asking questions. He didn't need Asa meeting Bullock face-to-face. Asa would either panic or crumble under questioning. Either way, Marron Shed would get into the heat damned fast. "Asa, if they catch you, we're all dead."

"Why?"

"You were spending those old coins. They're looking for somebody with a lot of old money."

"Damn that Raven!"

"What?"

"He gave me the passage money. As my share. I'm rich. And now you tell me I can't spend it without getting grabbed."

"He probably figured you'd hold off till the excitement died down. He'd be gone by then."

"Gone?"

"He's leaving as soon as the harbor opens."

"Where's he headed?"

"South somewhere. He won't talk about it."

"So what do I do? Keep scrambling for a living? Damn it, Shed, that's not fair."

"Look on the bright side, Asa. Nobody wants to kill you anymore."

"So? Now Bullock is after me. Maybe I could have made a deal with Krage. Bullock don't deal. It ain't fair! All my life. . . ."

Shed did not listen. He sang the same song all too often.

"What can I do, Shed?"

"I don't know. Stay holed up, I guess." He had a glimmer of a notion. "How about you get out of Juniper for a while?"

"Yeah. You might have something. That money would spend just fine somewhere else, wouldn't it?"

"I don't know. I've never traveled."

"Get Raven up here when he shows up."

"Asa. . . ."

"Hey, Shed, come on. It won't hurt to ask. All he can do is say no."

"Whatever you want, Asa. I hate to see you go."

"Sure you do, Shed. Sure you do." As Shed ducked out the doorway, Asa called, "Wait a second."

"Yeah?"

"Uh. . . . It's kind of hard. I never did thank you."

"Thank me for what?"

"You saved my life. You brought me back, didn't you?"

Shed shrugged, nodded. "No big thing, Asa."

"Sure it is, Shed. And I'll remember it. I owe you the big one."

Shed went downstairs before he could be embarrassed further. He discovered that Raven had returned. The man was in one of his animated discussions with Darling. Arguing again. They had to be lovers. Damn it all. He waited till Raven noticed him watching. "Asa wants to see you. I think he wants to go with you when you leave."

Raven chuckled. "That would solve your problem, wouldn't it?"

Shed did not deny that he would be more comfortable with Asa out of Juniper. "What do you think?"

"Not a bad idea, actually. Asa isn't much, but I need men. I have a hold on him. And him being gone would help cover my backtrail."

"Take him with my blessing."

Raven started upstairs. Shed said, "Wait." He didn't know how to approach this, because he didn't know if it was important. But he'd better tell Raven. "Bullock's been hanging around the Buskin a lot lately. Him and a sidekick."

"So?"

"So maybe he's closer than we think. For one thing, he was in here looking for Asa. For another, he's been asking about you."

Raven's face went empty. "About me? How so?"

"On the quiet. My cousin Wally's wife Sal? Her brother is married to one of Bullock's cousins. Anyway, Bullock still knows people down here, from when before he got on the Custodians. He helps them out sometimes, so some of them tell him things he wants to know. . . ."

"I get the picture. Get to the point."

"Bullock was asking about you. Who you are, where you come from, who your friends are—things like that."

"Why?"

Shed could only shrug.

"All right. Thanks. I'll check it out."

# Chapter Eighteen: JUNIPER: BLOWING SMOKE

Goblin stood across the street, leaning against a building, staring intently. I frowned angrily. What the hell was he doing on the street? Bullock might recognize him and realize we were playing games.

Obviously, he wanted to tell me something.

Bullock was about to enter another of countless dives. I told him, "Got to see a man about a horse in the alley."

"Yeah." He went inside. I slipped into the alley and made water. Goblin joined me there. "What is it?" I asked.

"What it is, Croaker, is it's him. Raven. Our Raven. Not only him, but Darling. She's a barmaid in a place called the Iron Lily."

"Holy shit," I murmured.

"Raven lives there. They're doing a show like they don't know each other that well. But Raven looks out for her."

"Damnit! It had to be, didn't it? What do we do now?"

"Maybe bend over and kiss our asses good-bye. The bastard could be smack in the middle of the body-selling racket. Everything we found could add up that way."

"How come you could find that when Bullock couldn't?"

"I got resources Bullock doesn't."

I nodded. He did. Sometimes it's handy, having a wizard around. Sometimes it's not, if it's one of those bitches up in Duretile. "Hurry it up," I said. "He'll wonder where I am."

"Raven has his own wagon and team. Keeps it way across town. Usually only takes it out late at night." I nodded. We'd already determined that body-runners worked the night shift. "But. . . ." he said, "and you're going to love this but, Croaker. He took it out in the daytime, once, a while back. Coincidentally, the day somebody hit the Catacombs."

"Oh boy."

"I looked that wagon over, Croaker. There was blood in it. Fairly fresh. I date it about when that moneylender and his pals disappeared."

"Oh boy. Shit. We're in for it now. Better get. Going to have to think of a story for Bullock now."

"Later."

"Yeah."

At that moment I was ready to give up. Despair overwhelmed me. That damned fool Raven—I knew exactly what he was doing. Getting together a fat bunch of running money by selling bodies and plundering graves. His conscience wouldn't bother him. In his part of the world, such things were of much less consequence. And he had a cause: Darling.

I couldn't get away from Bullock. I wanted desperately to run to Elmo, but I had to trudge hither and yon asking questions.

I looked up the northern slope, at the black castle, and thought of it as the fortress Raven had built.

I was going off the deep end. I told myself that. The evidence wasn't yet conclusive. . . . But it was. Enough. My employers did not wait on legal niceties or absolute evidence.

Elmo was rattled, too. "We could kill him. No risk him giving anything away then."

"Really, Elmo!"

"I didn't mean it. But you know I'd do it if the choice got narrow enough."

"Yeah." We all would. Or we'd try. Raven might not let us. He was the toughest son-of-a-bitch I'd ever known. "If you ask me, we ought to find him and just tell him to get the hell out of Juniper."

Elmo gave me a disgusted look. "Haven't you been paying attention? Right now the only way in or out is the one we took. The harbor is frozen. The passes are snowed in. You think we could get Whisper to fly some civilian out for us?"

"Civilians. Goblin says Darling is still with him."

Elmo looked thoughtful. I started to say something else. He waved a hand for silence. I waited. He finally asked, "What would he do if he saw you? If he's been hanging around with the Crater bunch?"

I clicked my tongue. "Yeah. I didn't think of that. Let me go check something."

I hunted Bullock up. "You or the Duke got somebody inside the Crater bunch?"

He looked puzzled. "Maybe? Why?"

"Let's have a sit-down with them. An idea. It might help us break our thing here."

He looked at me a long moment. Maybe he was sharper than he pretended. "All right. Not that they would've learned much. The only reason they haven't run our guys off is we don't bother them. They just get together and talk about the old days. They don't have any fight left."

"Let's give it a look anyway. Maybe they're less innocent than they look."

"Give me a half-hour."

I did. And when that time was up, he and I sat down with two secret policemen. He and I took turns asking questions, each coming from his own private slant.

Neither knew Raven, at least not by that name. That was a relief. But there was something there, and Bullock sensed it immediately. He hung on till he had something to chew.

"I'm going to my boss," I told him. "She'll want to know about this." I had come up with a diversion. It seemed it would suit Bullock.

He said, "I'll take it up with Hargadon. Didn't occur to me this might be foreigners. Political. That could be why the money didn't show up. Maybe they're selling bodies, too."

"Rebellions do take money," I observed.

We moved next evening, at Whisper's insistence, over the objections of the Duke, but with the support of the chief Custodian. The Duke still did not want us seen. The Custodians didn't give a damn. They just wanted to salvage their reputation.

Elmo came slinking through the evening shadows. "Ready here?" he whispered.

I glanced at the four men with me. "Ready." Every Company man in Juniper was there, with the Duke's secret police and a dozen of Bullock's men. I'd thought his job silly, but even so had been astonished to discover how few men his office actually employed. All but one were there. The one was legitimately sick.

Elmo made a sound like a cow mooing, repeated three times.

The one-time Rebels were all together for their regular confab. I snickered, thinking of the surprise they were going to get. They thought they were safe from the Lady by fifteen hundred miles and seven years.

It took less than a minute. No one was injured. They just looked at us dumbly, arms hanging slack. Then one even recognized us, and groaned, "The Black Company. In Juniper."

Then another: "It's over. It's the end. She's really won."

They didn't seem to care much. Some, in fact, looked relieved.

We pulled it off so smoothly there was hardly any notice from the neighbors. The slickest raid I'd ever seen. We marched them up to Duretile, and Whisper and Feather went to work.

I just hoped one of them wouldn't know too much.

I'd made a long bet, hoping Raven would not have told them who Darling was. If he had, I'd pulled the roof down instead of misdirecting attention.

I did not hear from Whisper, so I guessed I'd won.

# Chapter Nineteen: JUNIPER: FEAR

Raven slammed through the door of the Lily. Shed looked up, startled. Raven leaned against the door frame, panting. He looked like he'd just stared his death in the face. Shed put his rag aside and hurried over, a stoneware bottle in hand.

"What happened?"

Raven stared over his shoulder, at Darling, who was waiting on Shed's lone paying customer. He shook his head, took several deep breaths, shuddered.

He was scared! By all that was holy, the man was terrified! Shed was aghast. What could have gotten him into this state? Even the black castle did not shake him.

"Raven. Come over here and sit." He took Raven's arm. The man followed docilely. Shed caught Darling's eye, signed for two mugs and another stoneware bottle.

Darling took one look at Raven and forgot her customer. She was there with mugs and bottle in seconds, her fingers flashing at Raven.

Raven did not see.

"Raven!" Shed said in a sharp whisper. "Snap out of it, man! What the hell happened?"

Raven's eyes focused. He looked at Shed, at Darling, at the wine. He tossed off a mug in one gulp, slapped it down. Darling poured again.

Her customer protested at being abandoned.

"Get it yourself," Shed told him.

The man became abusive.

"Go to hell, then," Shed said. "Raven, talk. Are we in trouble?"

"Uh. . . . No. Not we, Shed. Me." He shuddered like a dog coming out of water, faced Darling. His fingers started talking.

Shed caught most of it.

Raven told her to pack. They had to run again.

Darling wanted to know why.

Because they've found us, Raven told her.

Who? Darling asked.

The Company. They're here. In Juniper.

Darling did not seem distressed. She denied the possibility.

The Company? Shed thought. What the hell was this?

They are here, Raven insisted. I went to the meeting. I was late. Lucky. I got there after it started. The Duke's men. The Custodians. And the Company. I saw Croaker and Elmo and Goblin. I heard them call each other by name. I heard them mention Whisper and Feather. The Company is in Juniper, and the Taken are with them. We have to go.

Shed had no idea what in hell this was about. Who were these people? Why was Raven scared? "How you going to run anywhere, Raven? You can't get out of town. The harbor's still frozen."

Raven looked at him as if he were a heretic.

"Settle down, Raven. Use your head. I don't know what the hell is going on, but I can tell you this. Right now you're acting more like Marron Shed than like Raven. Old Shed is the guy who panics. Remember?"

Raven managed a feeble grin. "You're right. Yeah. Raven uses his brain." He snickered sourly. "Thanks, Shed."

"What happened?"

"Let's just say the past came back. A past I didn't expect to see again. Tell me about this sidekick you said Bullock's been pulling around lately. Word I've heard, Bullock is a loner."

Shed described the man, though he could not recall him

well. His attention had been on Bullock. Darling positioned herself so she could read his lips. She formed a word with hers.

Raven nodded. "Croaker."

Shed shivered. The name sounded sinister when Raven translated it. "He some kind of hired killer?"

Raven laughed softly. "No. Actually, he's a physician. Halfway competent, too. But he has other talents. Like being crafty enough to come around looking for me in Bullock's shadow. Who would pay attention to him? They'd be too worried about the damned Inquisitor."

Darling flashed signs. She went too fast for Shed, but he thought she was admonishing Raven, telling him Croaker was his friend and would not be hunting him. It was coincidence that their paths had crossed.

"Not coincidence at all," Raven countered, both aloud and by sign. "If they aren't hunting me, why are they in Juniper? Why are two of the Taken here?"

Again Darling responded too fast for Shed to catch everything. She seemed to be arguing that if someone called the Lady had gotten to this Croaker or another someone called Silent, Croaker would not be here.

Raven stared at her a good fifteen seconds, still as stone. He downed another mug of wine. Then he said, "You're right. Absolutely right. If they were looking for me, they would have had me. And you. The Taken themselves would have been all over us. So. Coincidence, after all. But coincidence or not, the Lady's top thugs are in Juniper. And they're looking for something. What? Why?"

This was the old Raven. Cool and hard and thinking.

Darling flashed, Black castle.

Shed's humor vanished. Raven looked at the girl for several seconds, glanced in the general direction of the black castle. Then he looked at Darling again. "Why?"

Darling shrugged. She flashed, There is nothing else about Juniper that would bring Her here.

Raven thought a few minutes more. Then he turned to Shed. "Shed, have I made you rich? Have I gotten your ass far enough out of trouble?"

"Sure, Raven."

"Your turn to give me a hand, then. Some very powerful enemies of mine are in Juniper. They're working with the Custodians and the Duke, and are probably here because of the black castle. If they spot me, I'm in trouble."

Marron Shed had a full belly. He had a warm place to sleep. His mother was safe. He had no debts and no immediate threats hanging over his head. The man opposite him was responsible. Also responsible for saddling him with an agonized conscience, but that he could forgive. "Ask. I'll do what I can."

"You'll be helping yourself, too, if they're looking into the castle. You, me, and Asa. We made a mistake, raiding the Catacombs. Never mind. I want you to find out whatever you can about what's going on in Duretile. If you need bribe money, tell me. I'll cover it."

Puzzled, Shed said, "Sure. Can't you tell me a little more?"

"Not till I know a little more. Darling, get your stuff together. We have to disappear."

For the first time, Shed protested. "Hey! What're you doing? How am I supposed to run this place without her?"

"Get that girl Lisa in here. Get your cousin. I don't care. We have to disappear."

Shed frowned.

Raven said, "They want her more than they want me."

"She's just a kid."

"Shed."

"Yes, sir. How do I get in touch, sir?"

"You don't. I'll get in touch with you. Darling, go. Those are Taken up there."

"What're Taken?" Shed asked.

"If you have gods, Shed, pray that you never find out. Pray hard." And, when Darling returned with her meager belongings, Raven said, "I think you ought to reconsider leaving Juniper with me. Things are going to start happening around here, and you won't like them."

"I have to take care of my mother."

"Think about it anyway, Shed. I know what I'm talking about. I used to work for those people."

# Chapter Twenty: JUNIPER: SHADOW TALK

Raven vanished on us. Even Goblin could find no trace. Feather and Whisper worked on our prisoners till each was drained, and got nothing on our old friend. I concluded that Raven had used an assumed name when dealing with them.

Why hadn't he used one down in the Buskin? Folly? Pride? As I recall, Raven had too much of that.

Raven was not his real name, any more than Croaker is mine. But that was the name we knew him by the year he served with us. None of us, unless maybe the Captain, knew his real one. He had been a man of substance once, in Opal. That I knew. He and the Limper became bitter enemies when the Limper used his wife and her lovers to do him out of his rights and titles. That I knew. But not who he was before he became a soldier of the Black Company.

I dreaded telling the Captain what we had found. He was fond of Raven. Like brothers, the two of them. The Captain, I think, was hurt when Raven deserted. He would be hurt more deeply when he learned what his friend had done in Juniper.

Whisper called us in to announce the results of the interrogations. She said roughly, "We did not exactly score a triumph, gentlemen. All but a couple of those men were dabblers. We knocked the fight out of them at Charm. But we did learn that the black castle *has* been buying corpses. Its denizens even buy live bodies. Two of our captives have sold to them. Raising money for the Rebel.''

The idea of trading in corpses was repellent, but not especially wicked. I wondered what use the black castle people had for them.

Whisper continued, ''They were not responsible for the raid on the Catacombs. In fact, they are of no interest to us. We're turning them over to the Custodians to do with as they please. You gentlemen will now go out into the city and resume digging.''

''Excuse me, ma'am?'' Elmo said.

''Somewhere in Juniper there is someone who is feeding the black castle. Find him. The Lady wants him.''

Raven, I thought. Had to be Raven. Just had to be. We had to find that son-of-a-bitch, yes. And get him out of town or dead.

You have to understand what the Company means. For us, it is father, mother, family. We are men with nothing else. Raven getting caught would kill the family, figuratively and literally. The Lady would disband what remained of the outfit after she'd mauled us for not turning Raven in back when.

I told Whisper: ''It might help if we knew what we're dealing with. It's hard to take something serious when nobody tells you anything. What's the point of the exercise? That castle is damned bizarre, I grant you. But why should we care?''

Whisper seemed to think about it. For several seconds her eyes were blank. She had taken the matter to higher authority. She was in communion with the Lady. When she returned, she said, ''The black castle has its roots in the Barrowland.''

That got our attention. I croaked, ''What?''

''The black castle is the Dominator's escape hole. When it reaches a certain size and certain set of circumstances, the creatures who live there, who are his creatures, heart and soul, will conjur him out of the Great Barrow. Here.''

Several men snorted in disbelief. It did seem far-fetched, for all the weirdness and sorceries we have seen.

Whisper said, "He foresaw his defeat by the White Rose, though not his betrayal by the Lady. Even before the Domination fell, he started preparing his return. He sent a faithful follower here with the seed of the black castle. Something went wrong. He never planned to spend so long waiting. Maybe he did not know of Juniper's preoccupation with preserving the dead. What are they waiting for? A ship that will carry them to paradise?"

"Roughly," I agreed. "I studied it, but the whole business is still monkey chatter to me. Go on. The Dominator is going to pop out on us here?"

"Not if we can stop him. But we may have gotten here too late. This man. If we don't take him soon, it *will* be too late. The portal is almost ready to open."

I looked at Elmo. He looked at me. Oh boy, I thought. If Raven knew what he was doing. . . . I still couldn't get upset. He did it for Darling. He couldn't have known he was doing the Dominator's work. He had that much conscience. He would have found another way. . . . What the hell was he going to do with so much money?

We had to find him. That was all there was to it. Whatever we did from now on, our main goal, for the sake of the Company, had to be to warn him off.

I glanced at Elmo. He agreed. From this moment forward we would be fighting for the survival of the outfit.

Somewhere, somehow, Raven must have smelled trouble. Goblin looked under every rock in the Buskin, watched every alley, practically lived in the Iron Lily, and still found a big bunch of nothing. Time ground past. Warmer weather threatened. And we became ever more panicky.

# Chapter Twenty-One: JUNIPER

Raven departed soon after the outer channel opened. Shed went down to say good-bye—and only then discovered the nature of Raven's shipping investment. He had had a ship built and crewed. A whole new ship, and as big a vessel as Shed had seen. "No wonder he needed a fortune," he mused. How many bodies to build that?

He returned to the Lily numbed. He poured himself some wine, sat staring into nothing. "That Raven was a man of vision," he mumbled. "Glad he's gone, though. Asa, too. Maybe things can get back to normal."

Shed bought a cottage near the Enclosure. He installed his mother with a staff of three. It was a relief to be rid of her evil, blind stare.

He had workmen into the Lily every day. They interfered with business, but business remained good. The harbor was busy. There was work for anyone who wanted it.

Shed could not handle prosperity. He hared after every impulse he had known during his impoverishment. He bought fine clothing he dared not wear. He went places frequented only by the wealthy. And he bought the attentions of beautiful women.

Women cost a lot when you pretended to be somebody off the high slope.

One day Shed went to his secret cash box and found it

empty. All that money gone? Where? The improvements on the Lily weren't finished. He owed the workmen. He owed the people caring for his mother. Damn! Was he back where he started?

Hardly. He had his profits.

He scampered downstairs, to his business cash box, opened it, sighed in relief. He'd done all his spending out of the box upstairs.

But something was wrong. There wasn't anywhere near enough in the box. . . . "Hey, Wally."

His cousin looked at him, gulped, raced out the door. Baffled, Shed hurried outside, saw Wally vanish into an alley. Then the truth hit him. "Damn you!" he yelled. "Damn you, you damned thief!" He went back in and tried to figure where he stood.

An hour later he told the workmen to knock off. He left his new girl Lisa in charge, started the rounds of his suppliers.

Wally had screwed him good. He had bought on credit and pocketed monies payable. Shed covered his debts as he went, growing increasingly alarmed as his reserves dwindled. Down to little more than copper, he returned to the Lily and started an inventory.

At least Wally hadn't sold what he had bought on credit. The Lily was well-stocked.

Only what was he going to do about his mother?

The house was paid for. That was a plus. But the old girl needed her servants to survive. And he couldn't pay their wages. But he didn't want her back in the Lily. He could sell all those clothes. He'd spent a fortune on them and couldn't wear them. He did some figuring. Yes. Sell the clothes and he could support his mother till next summer.

No more clothes. No more women. No more improvements on the Lily. . . . Maybe Wally hadn't spent it all.

Finding Wally was not difficult. He returned to his family after two days in hiding. He thought Shed would endure the loss. He didn't know he was dealing with a new Shed.

Shed stormed to his cousin's tiny one-room apartment, kicked the door in. "Wally!"

Wally squealed. His children and wife and mother all screeched questions. Shed ignored them. "Wally, I want it back! Every damned copper!"

Wally's wife got in his way. "Calm down, Marron. What's the matter?"

"Wally!" Wally cowered in a corner. "Out of my way, Sal. He stole damned near a hundred leva." Shed grabbed his cousin and dragged him out the doorway. "I want it back."

"Shed. . . ."

Shed shoved him. He staggered backward, tripped, rolled down a flight of stairs. Shed charged after him, hurled him down another flight.

"Shed, please. . . ."

"Where's the money, Wally? I want the money."

"I don't have it, Shed. I spent it. Honest. The kids had to have clothes. We had to eat. I couldn't help it, Shed. You had so much. . . . You're family, Shed. You're supposed to help."

Shed shoved him into the street, kicked him in the groin, dragged him upright, started slapping. "Where is it, Wally? You couldn't have spent that much. Hell, your kids are wearing rags. I paid you enough to handle that. Because you were family. I want the money you stole." As he raged, Shed drove his cousin toward the Lily.

Wally whined and begged, refusing to tell the truth. Shed guessed he had stolen upward of fifty leva, enough to have completed the renovation of the Lily. This hadn't been petty pilfering. He hurled blows in an angry rain.

He herded Wally around behind the Lily, away from prying eyes. "Now I get nasty, Wally."

"Shed, please. . . ."

"You stole from me and you're lying about it. I could forgive you for doing it for your family. But you didn't. Tell me. Or give it back." He punched Wally hard.

The pain in his hands, from hitting the man, sapped his rage. But then Wally broke. "I lost it gambling. I know I was stupid. But I was so sure I was going to win. They took me. They let me think I was going to win big, then took me, and the only way out was to steal. They would have killed me. I borrowed from Gilbert after I told him how good you were doing. . . ."

"Lost it? Gambling? Borrowed from Gilbert?" Shed muttered. Gilbert had moved in on Krage's territories. He was a bad as his predecessor. "How could you be so stupid?" The rage took him again. He snatched a board off a scrap pile left for kindling. He hit Wally hard. And hit him again. His cousin went down, stopped trying to fend off the blows.

Shed froze, suddenly coldly rational. Wally wasn't moving. "Wally? Wally? Hey, Wally. Say something."

Wally did not respond.

Shed's stomach knotted. He tossed the board into the pile. "Have to get that inside before people cart it off." He gripped his cousin's shoulder. "Come on, Wally. I won't hit you anymore."

Wally did not move.

"Oh, shit," Shed muttered. "I killed him." This tore it. What now? There wasn't much justice in the Buskin, but what there was was quick and rough. They would hang him sure.

He whirled, looking for witnesses. He saw no one. His mind flew in a hundred directions. There was a way out. No body, no proof that murder had been done. But he'd never gone up that hill alone.

Hastily, he dragged Wally to the scrap pile and covered him. The amulet he needed to get into the black castle. Where was it? He dashed into the Lily, roared upstairs, found the amulet, examined it. Definitely serpents intertwined. The workmanship was amazingly detailed. Tiny jewels formed the eyes of the snakes. They sparkled menacingly in the afternoon sun.

He stuffed the amulet into his pocket. "Shed, get yourself together. Panic and you're dead."

How long before Sal yelled for the law? A few days, surely. Plenty of time.

Raven had left him his wagon and team. He hadn't thought to keep paying the stable-keeper. Had the man sold them? If so, he was in trouble.

He cleaned out his coin boxes, left the Lily in Lisa's care.

The stable-keeper hadn't sold off, but the mules were looking lean. Shed cursed him.

"I should feed them at my own expense, mister?"

Shed cursed him some more and paid what was owed. He said, "Feed them. And have them hitched and ready at the tenth hour."

Shed remained panicky all afternoon. Somebody might find Wally. But no lawman came stamping in. Soon after dark he stole away to the stable.

He spent the journey alternately being terrified and wondering how much Wally would bring. And how much he could get for his wagon and team. He hadn't factored them into his earlier calculations.

He ought to help Wally's family. He had to. It was the decent thing. . . . He was acquiring too many dependents.

Then he was facing the dark gate. The castle, with all its monstrous decoration, was terrible, but it didn't seem to have grown since last he had been there. He knocked as Raven had done, his heart in his throat. He gripped his amulet in his left hand.

What was taking them so long? He hammered again. The gate jumped open, startling him. He fled to his wagon, got the mules moving.

He entered exactly as Raven had done, ignoring everything but his driving. He halted in the same place, climbed down, dragged Wally out.

No one came for several minutes. He grew ever more nervous, wishing he'd had the sense to come armed. What guarantee did he have that they wouldn't turn on him? That silly amulet?

Something moved. He gasped.

The creature that stepped out of the shadow was short and wide and radiated an air of contempt. It never looked at him. Its examination of the cadaver was detailed. It was being difficult, like some petty official with a helpless citizen momentarily in his power. Shed knew how to handle that. Stubborn patience and refusal to become irritated. He stood motionless, waiting.

The creature finally placed twenty-five pieces of silver near Wally's feet.

Shed grimaced, but collected the cash. He returned to his seat, backed the wagon, got the team aligned with the gate. Only then did he register his protest. "That was a prime corpse. Next time you'll do better, or there won't be a time after that. Git up." Out the gate he went, amazed at his temerity.

Going down the hill he sang. He felt great. Except for a fading guilt about Wally—the bastard had earned it—he was at peace with his world. He was free and safe, out of debt, and now had money in reserve. He returned his team to its stable, wakened the stable-keeper, paid four months in advance. "Take good care of my animals," he admonished.

A representative of the precinct Magistrate showed up next day. He had questions about Wally's disappearance. Sal had reported the fight.

Shed admitted it. "I kicked the shit out of him. But I don't know what happened to him. He just took off. I would've run, too, if I had somebody that mad at me."

"What was the fight about?"

Shed played the role of a man who didn't want to get anybody in trouble. Finally, he admitted, "He worked for me. He stole money to pay back money he borrowed to pay gambling debts. Check with my suppliers. They'll tell how he bought on credit. He told me he was paying cash."

"How much was involved?"

"Can't say exactly," Shed replied. "More than fifty leva. My whole profit for the summer, and then some."

The questioner whistled. "I don't blame you for getting pissed."

"Yeah. I wouldn't have begrudged him money to help

his family. He's got a whole mob to take care of. But to lose it gambling. . . . Damn, I was hot. I borrowed to fix this place up. The payments are rough. I probably won't make it through the winter now, because that bastard couldn't resist a game. I may still break his neck."

It was a good act. Shed pulled it off.

"You want to register a formal complaint?"

Shed played reluctant. "He's family. My cousin."

"I'd break my own father's back if he did that to me."

"Yeah. All right. I'll register it. But don't go hanging him right away. Maybe he can work it out or something. Hell, maybe he's still got some he can pay back. He could have lied about losing it all. He lied about a lot of things." Shed shook his head. "He worked for us on-and-off since my father ran this place. I never thought he'd do anything like that."

"You know how it is. You get too far into debt and the vultures start closing in, you'll do anything to save your ass. You don't worry about tomorrow. We see it all the time."

Shed nodded. He knew how it was.

After the Magistrate's man departed, Shed told Lisa: "I'm going out." He wanted one last fling before he settled in to the dreary business of managing the Lily.

He bought the most skilled, most beautiful woman he could find. She cost, but she was worth every copper. He returned to the Lily wishing he could live that way all the time. He dreamed about the woman that night.

Lisa wakened him early. "There's a man here who wants to see you."

"Who is he?"

"He didn't say."

Cursing, Shed rolled out. He did nothing to hide his nakedness. More than once he had hinted that Lisa should include more than barmaid's chores in her duties. She was not cooperating. He had to find a handle. . . . He'd better look out. He was getting obsessed with sex. That could give somebody a handle.

He descended to the common room. Lisa indicated a

man. He was no one Shed knew. "You wanted to see me?"

"You got someplace private?"

A hard case. Now what? He did not owe anyone. He did not have any enemies. "What's your business?"

"Let's talk about your cousin. The one who didn't disappear the way people think."

Shed's stomach knotted. He concealed his distress. "I don't understand."

"Suppose somebody saw what happened?"

"Come into the kitchen."

Shed's visitor peeped back through the kitchen door. "Thought the split-tail might try to listen in." Then he gave Shed an accurate account of Wally's death.

"Where did you get that fairy tale?"

"I saw it."

"In a pipe dream, maybe."

"You're cooler than I heard. Here's the way it goes, friend. I have a trick memory. Sometimes I forget. Depends on how I'm treated."

"Ah. I begin to see the light. This is about hush money."

"There you go."

Shed's thoughts scurried like frightened mice. He couldn't *afford* hush money. He had to find another way out. But he couldn't do anything right now. He was too confused. He needed time to get himself together. "How much?"

"A leva a week would buy a first-class case of amnesia."

Shed goggled. He sputtered. He choked back his protest.

The extortionist made a what-can-I-do? gesture. "I have problems too. I got expenses. A leva a week. Or take your chances."

The black castle flickered through Shed's thoughts. Low cunning grabbed it, turned it over, looked at the possibilities. Murder did not bother him anymore.

But not now. Not here. "How do I pay you?"

The man grinned. "Just hand me a leva."

Shed brought his coin box into the kitchen. "You'll have to take copper. I don't have any silver."

The man's smile grew broader. He was pleased. Why?

The man left. Shed said, "Lisa, I have a job for you. Worth a bonus. Follow that man. Find out where he goes." He gave her five gersh. "Another five when you get back, if it's worth it."

Lisa zipped out in a whirl of skirts.

"He wandered around a lot," Lisa reported. "Like he was killing time. Then he headed down by the Sailmakers'. To see that one-eyed moneylender."

"Gilbert?"

"Yeah. Gilbert."

"Thank you," Shed said thoughtfully. "Thanks a bunch. That casts light on the problem."

"Five gersh worth?"

"Sure. You're a good girl." He made a suggestive offer as he counted.

"I don't need money that bad, Mr. Shed."

He retreated to his kitchen, began preparing supper. So Gilbert was behind the extortionist. Did Gilbert want him financially pressed? Why?

The Lily. Why else? The renovations made the place that much more attractive a steal.

So. Assume Gilbert was opening a campaign to snatch the Lily. He had to fight. But this time nobody could help him. He was on his own.

Three days later Shed visited an acquaintance who operated on the nether edge of the Buskin. For a consideration he received a name. He visited the man attached, and left him with two pieces of silver.

Back at the Lily, he asked Lisa to tell her favorite customers that Gilbert was trying to force them out by spreading lies and making threats. He wanted the Magistrate suspicious of accusations leveled against him later.

The morning of the next payoff, Shed told Lisa, "I'll be gone all day. Anybody comes looking for me, tell them to come back after supper."

"The man I followed?"

"Him especially."

At first Shed just roamed, killing time. His nerve worsened with time. Something would go wrong. Gilbert would come back rough. . . . But he wouldn't dare, would he? That would tarnish his reputation. Shed's rumors had him on the defensive now. People would make their loans elsewhere if he pressed.

Shed found himself a woman. She cost too much, but she made him forget. For a while. He returned to the Lily at sunset. "He came by?" he asked Lisa.

"Be back, too. He looked put out. I don't think he's going to be nice, Mr. Shed."

"That's the way it goes. I'll be out back working on the woodpile." Shed glanced at a customer he'd never before seen. The man nodded, departed through the front door.

Shed chopped wood by lanternlight. Now and again he searched the shadows, saw nothing. He prayed nothing would go wrong.

The extortionist stormed out the kitchen doorway. "You trying to duck me, Shed? You know what happens if you mess with me?"

"Duck you? What do you mean? I'm right here."

"You weren't this afternoon. Now that girl of yours gives me a hard way to go, trying to steer me away. I like to had to pound her before she'd tell me where you were."

Very creative. Shed wondered how much Lisa suspected. "Save the dramatics. You want your money. I want your ugly face away from my place. Let's get on with it."

The extortionist looked puzzled. "You talking tough? They told me you were the biggest coward in the Buskin."

"Who told you? You working for somebody? This not a freelance play?"

The man's eyes narrowed as he realized his mistake.

Shed produced a handful of copper. He counted, counted, counted again, put a few coins away. "Hold out your hands."

The extortionist extended cupped hands.

Shed had not expected it to be this easy. He dumped the coins, grabbed the man's wrists.

"Hey! What the hell?"

A hand clamped over the man's mouth. A face appeared over his shoulder, mouth stretched in a grimace of effort. The extortionist rose to his toes, arching backward. His eyes widened in fear and pain, then rolled up. He slumped forward.

"All right. Perfect. Get out of here," Shed said.

Hastening footsteps faded quickly.

Shed dragged the body into shadow, quickly covered it with wood scraps, then dropped to hands and knees and began collecting coins. He found all but two.

"What are you doing, Mr. Shed?"

He jumped. "What're *you* doing?"

"I came to see if you were all right."

"I'm fine. We had an argument. He knocked some coins out of my hand. I can't find them all."

"Need help?"

"Mind the counter, girl. Or they'll steal us blind."

"Oh. Sure." She ducked back inside.

Shed gave it up a few minutes later. He would search again tomorrow.

He got antsy waiting for closing time. Lisa was too curious. He was afraid she would look for the missing coins and find the body. He did not want her disappearance on his conscience, too.

Two minutes after he closed, he was out his back door and heading for his wagon and team.

The tall being was back on duty. He paid Shed thirty pieces of silver. As he was maneuvering to leave, though, the thing demanded, "Why do you come so seldom?"

"I'm not as skilled as my partner."

"What has become of him? We have missed him."

"He's out of town."

Shed could have sworn he heard the thing chuckle as he went out the gate.

# Chapter Twenty-Two: JUNIPER: RUNNING SCARED

A long time had passed and nothing had happened. The Taken were not pleased. Neither was Elmo. He dragged me into his quarters. "Were the hell did Raven go, Croaker?"

"I don't know," I told him. As if he were the only one disturbed. I was scared and getting more so by the day.

"I want to know. Soon."

"Look, man. Goblin's done everything but torture people trying to pick up his trail. He flat vanished. He got wind of us somehow."

"How? Will you tell me how? We've been here half our lives, it seems like. And nobody else down there has noticed. Why should Raven be any different?"

"Because we were around looking for him. He must have spotted one of us."

"If he did, I want to know that. You hike on down there and light a fire under Goblin's ass. Hear?"

"Right. Whatever you say, boss." Though he commanded the advance party, technically I outranked Elmo. But I was not about to press for prerogatives at the moment. There was too much tension in the air.

There was stress throughout Duretile, and I did not understand most of it. I remained on the periphery of the Taken's study of the black castle. Just another messenger boy, a foot-slogger bringing in data from the city. I hadn't the slightest notion what they had discovered by direct examination. Or even if they were studying the castle directly. They could be lying back, afraid they would alert the Dominator to their presence.

One of the men located me in Elmo's quarters. "Whisper wants you, Croaker."

I jumped a foot. Guilty conscience. "What for?" I had not seen her for weeks.

"You'll have to go see. She didn't say." He sneered, hoping he would see an officer in the soup. He figured I was in trouble.

He figured that; so did I. I dawdled as much as I dared, but eventually had to present myself. Whisper glared at me as I entered. "You people haven't found a damned thing down there. What are you doing? Dogging it? Taking a vacation? Well, say something."

"I. . . ."

"Do you know the black castle stopped growing after our raid on the Crater group? No? Why not? You're supposed to be finding out these things."

"None of the prisoners accounted for the. . . ."

"I know that. I know none of them knew who the main body supplier was. But that supplier must have known them. He packed up. There have been just two bodies delivered since. The latest just last night. Why didn't you know that? Why have you got people in the Buskin? They seem incapable of learning anything."

Oh, she was in a mood. I said, "Is the deadline close or something? The way I understood it, we wouldn't be in trouble if only a few bodies were delivered."

"True. As far as it goes. But we've reached a point where a handful might make all the difference."

I bit my lower lip, tried to look properly chastised, and waited.

She told me: "The Lady is pressing. She's *very* nervous. She wants something to happen up here."

So. As always, the shit rolls downhill. The normal course would be for me to go out and tromp on somebody below me.

"Half the problem is, we don't know what's going on.

If you claim you know what the castle is, how it's growing and so forth, how come you don't go over and kick it down? Or turn it into grape preserves or something?"

"It's not that simple."

It never is. I tend to overlook political ramifications. I am not politically minded.

"Maybe once the rest of your company gets here. The city will have to be controlled. The Duke and his incompetents couldn't manage that."

I stood there looking expectant. Sometimes that will con people into telling you more than they plan.

"The city will go up in flames if it's not buttoned up tight when the truth comes out. Why do you think the Custodians are so determined to keep the Catacombs thing hushed? Several thousand citizens have relatives who went into that monstrosity. That's a lot of people who'll get very irate about the souls of loved ones being lost."

"I see." I did a little. It took a certain willing suspension of reason, though.

"We're going at this from a different angle," she told me. "I'm taking charge of your investigations. Report to me daily. I'll decide what you're going to do, and how. Understand?"

"Yes, ma'am." Only too well. It was going to get that much more difficult to keep her and Raven apart.

"The first thing you'll do is set a watch on the castle. And if that doesn't shake something loose, I'll send Feather down there. Understand?"

"Yes, ma'am." Again, only too well.

I wondered if Whisper suspected we were working at cross-purposes.

"You can leave. I'll expect you back tomorrow. With something to report."

"Yes, ma'am."

I went straight back to Elmo, fuming. He should have faced her, not me. Just because I'd sort of taken over. . . .

I was with Elmo barely long enough to tell him what had happened when a messenger came from Bullock. He wanted to see me right away.

Bullock was another problem. I'd become convinced he was smarter than he put on, and was almost as sure that he suspected we were up to more than we admitted.

I eased into his cubicle in the secret police headquarters. "What's up?"

"I've made a little headway on the Catacombs raid. Result of pure stubborn footwork."

"Well?" I felt pretty curt about then, and he raised an eyebrow. "Just had a face-to-face with my boss," I told him, which was as near an apology as I cared to come. "What have you got?"

"A name."

I waited. Like Elmo, Bullock liked to be coaxed. I was in no mood to play that game.

"I followed up your notion about rented wagons. Turned up the name Asa. A wood-gatherer named Asa was, probably, working through the hole I showed you. A man named Asa spent a number of old coins, but before the raid on the Catacombs. A man named Asa worked for Krage before he and his men disappeared. Everywhere I go, it's Asa-this or Asa-that."

"Anything to connect him with the black castle?"

"No. I don't think he's a principal in anything. But he must know something."

I thought back. Bullock had mentioned this name once before, referring to a man who hung around the same place as Raven. Maybe there was a connection. Maybe I ought to find this Asa before anybody else did.

"I'm headed down to the Buskin," I said. "Direct orders from her holiness. I'll have Goblin round the guy up."

Bullock scowled. There had been some ill will when he found out that we had put men into the Buskin without consulting him. "All right. But don't play any more fast shuffle with me, eh? Your people and mine aren't after the same things, but that's no reason to undermine each other, eh?"

"You're right. We're just used to doing things different. I'll see you when I get back."

"I'd appreciate that." He eyed me in a way that said he did not trust me anymore. If ever he had. I left thinking the Company and I were into it deep. Trouble on every hand. Juggling with too many balls in the air. Only we were juggling knives with poisoned edges.

I hustled on down and looked up Goblin, told him about our escalating troubles. He was no happier than Elmo or I.

# Chapter Twenty-Three: JUNIPER: INTERROGATION

Shed had no more trouble with extortionists. Somebody did tell the Magistrate that he had killed Wally. The Magistrate did not believe it, or did not care.

Then Bullock's sidekick turned up. Shed nearly dropped a valuable piece of crockery. He had felt safe from that. The only people who knew anything were far away. He clamped down on his nerves and guilt, went to the man's table. "How may we serve you, Reverend Sir?"

"Bring me a meal and your best wine, landlord."

Shed lifted an eyebrow. "Sir?"

"I'll pay. Nobody in the Buskin can afford to give away meals."

"Ain't it the truth, sir. Ain't it the truth."

When Shed returned with the wine, the Inquisitor observed, "You seem to be doing well, landlord."

Shed snorted. "We live on the edge, Reverend Sir. On the ragged edge. One bad week would destroy me. I spend every winter borrowing from one moneylender to pay another. This summer was good, though. I found a partner. I was able to fix a few things. That made the place more attractive. Probably my last dying gasp before it gets away." He donned his sourest face.

The Inquisitor nodded. "Leave the bottle. Let the Brotherhood contribute to your prosperity."

"I'll ask no profit, Reverend Sir."

"Why be foolish? Charge me the same as anyone else."

Shed mentally upped the tab twenty percent over normal. He was glad to be rid of the bottle. Raven had left him stuck with several.

When Shed delivered the meal, the Inquisitor suggested, "Bring a mug and join me."

Shed's nerves twisted as tight as a bowstring. Something was wrong. They had caught on. "As you wish, Reverend Sir." He dragged over and collected his own mug. It was dusty. He had not done much drinking lately, afraid his tongue would wag.

"Sit down. And wipe the scowl off your face. You haven't done anything. Have you? I don't even know your name."

"Shed, Reverend Sir. Marron Shed. The Iron Lily has been in my family for three generations."

"Admirable. A place with tradition. Tradition is falling by the wayside nowadays."

"As you say, Reverend Sir."

"I guess our reputation has preceded me. Won't you calm down?"

"How may I help you, Reverend Sir?"

"I'm looking for a man named Asa. I hear he was a regular here."

"So he was, sir," Shed admitted. "I knew him well. A lazy wastrel. Hated honest work. Never a copper to his name, either. Yet he was a friend, after his fashion, and generous in his way. I let him sleep on the common room floor during the winter, because in the days of my hardship he never failed to bring wood for the fire."

The Inquisitor nodded. Shed decided to tell most of the truth. He could not hurt Asa. Asa was beyond the reach of the Custodians.

"Do you know where he acquired the wood?"

Shed pretended acute embarrassment. "He collected it in the Enclosure, Reverend Sir. I debated with myself about using it. It wasn't against the law. But it seemed reprehensible anyway."

The Inquisitor smiled and nodded. "No failing on your

part, Marron Shed. The Brotherhood doesn't discourage gleaning. It keeps the Enclosure from becoming too seedy."

"Why are you looking for Asa, then?"

"I understand he worked for a man named Krage."

"Sort of. For a while. He thought he was king of the Buskin when Krage took him on. Strutting and bragging. But it didn't last."

"So I heard. It's the timing of their falling-out that intrigues me."

"Sir?"

"Krage and some of his friends disappeared. So did Asa, about the same time. And all of them vanished soon after somebody got into the Catacombs and looted several thousand passage urns."

Shed tried to look properly horrified. "Krage and Asa did that?"

"Possibly. This Asa started spending old money after he began gleaning in the Enclosure. Our investigations suggest he was petty at his grandest. We think he pilfered a few urns each time he gathered wood. Krage may have found out and decided to plunder in a big way. Their falling-out may have been over that. Assuming Asa had any conscience."

"Possibly, sir. I understood it to be a squabble over a guest of mine. A man named Raven. Krage wanted to kill him. He hired Asa to spy on him. Asa told me that himself. Krage decided he wasn't doing his job. He never did anything right. Anyway, he never did anything very well. But that doesn't invalidate your theory. Asa could have been lying. Probably was. He lied a lot."

"What was the relationship between Asa and Raven?"

"There wasn't any."

"Where is Raven now?"

"He left Juniper right after the ice broke up in the harbor."

The Inquisitor seemed both startled and pleased. "What became of Krage?"

"Nobody knows, Reverend Sir. It's one of the great

mysteries of the Buskin. One day he was there; the next he wasn't. There were all kinds of rumors."

"Could he have left Juniper, too?"

"Maybe. Some people think so. Whatever, he didn't tell anybody. The people who worked for him don't know anything, either."

"Or so they say. Could he have looted enough from the Catacombs to make it worthwhile to leave Juniper?"

Shed puzzled that question. It sounded treacherous. "I don't. . . . I don't understand what you're asking, sir."

"Uhm. Shed, thousands of the dead were violated. Most were put away at a time when the wealthy were very generous. We suspect a sum of gold may have been involved."

Shed gaped. He hadn't seen any gold. The man was lying. Why? Laying traps?

"It was a major plundering operation. We'd very much like to ask Asa some questions."

"I can imagine." Shed bit his lip. He thought hard. "Sir, I can't tell you what became of Krage. But I think Asa took ship for the south." He went into a long song-and-dance about how Asa had come to him after falling out with Krage, begging to be hidden. One day he had gone out, returned later badly wounded, had hidden upstairs for a while, then had vanished. Shed claimed to have seen him from a distance only, on the docks, the day the first ships sailed for the South. "I never got close enough to talk, but he looked like he was going somewhere. He had a couple bundles with him."

"Do you recall what ship?"

"Sir?"

"What ship did he take?"

"I didn't actually see him board a ship, sir. I just assumed he did. He might still be around. Only I figure he would have gotten in touch if he was. He always came to me when he was in trouble. I guess he's in trouble now, eh?"

"Maybe. The evidence isn't conclusive. But I'm morally convinced he was in on the looting. You didn't see Krage on the dock, did you?''

"No, sir. It was crowded. Everybody always goes down to see the first ships off. It's like a holiday." Was the Inquisitor buying it? Damn. He had to. An Inquisitor wasn't somebody you got off your back by selling him into the black castle.

The Inquisitor shook his head wearily. "I was afraid you'd tell me a story like that. Damn it. You leave me no choice."

Shed's heart leapt into his throat. Crazy ideas swarmed through his head. Hit the Inquisitor, grab the coin box, make a run for it.

"I hate to travel, Shed. But it looks like either Bullock or I will have to go after those people. Guess who'll get stuck?"

Relief swamped Shed. "Go after them, Reverend Sir? But the law down there doesn't recognize the Brotherhood's right. . . ."

"Won't be easy, will it? The barbarians just don't understand us." He poured some wine, stared into it for a long while. Finally, he said, "Thank you, Marron Shed. You've been very helpful."

Shed hoped that was a dismissal. He rose. "Anything else, Reverend Sir?"

"Wish me luck."

"Of course, sir. A prayer for your mission this very evening."

The Inquisitor nodded. "Thank you." He resumed staring into his mug.

He left a fine tip. But Shed was uneasy when he pocketed it. The Inquisitors had a reputation for doggedness. Suppose they caught up with Asa?

# Chapter Twenty-Four: JUNIPER: SHADOW DANCING

"I think I was pretty slick," I told Goblin.

"You should have seen that Shed," Pawnbroker cackled. "A chicken sweating like a pig and lying like a dog. A one-man barnyard."

"Was he really lying?" I mused. "He didn't say anything that conflicted with what we know."

"What did you learn?" Goblin asked.

"I think he was lying," Pawnbroker insisted. "Maybe by not telling everything he knew, but he was lying. He was into it somehow."

"You keep hanging around the Lily, then. Keep an eye on him."

"What did you learn?" Goblin demanded.

Elmo came in. "How'd it go?"

"Great," I said. "I found out what happened to Raven."

"What?" he and Goblin both demanded.

"He left town. By ship. The first day the harbor was open."

"Darling, too?" Goblin asked.

"You see her around? What do you think?"

Pawnbroker mused, "Bet that Asa went with him. Old Shed said they both left the first day."

"Could be. I was proud of myself, catching him with that. Looks to me, now, like this Shed is our only outside loose end. He's the only one who knows what happened to them. No Shed, nobody to maybe tell Bullock or the Taken anything.''

Elmo frowned. The suggestion was more in keeping with his style than mine. He thought I'd put it forward seriously. ''I don't know. Sounds too simple. Anyway, we're starting to get noticed down there, aren't we?''

Goblin nodded. ''We're supposed to be sailors who missed our ship, but people are comparing notes, trying to figure us out. If Shed got killed, there might be enough fuss to get Bullock wondering. If he gets wondering, sooner or later the news would get back to the Taken. I figure we ought to save heroic measures for heroic circumstances.''

Pawnbroker agreed. ''That Shed's got something to hide. I know that in my guts. Croaker told him about the raid on the Catacombs. He hardly blinked. Anybody else would have whooped off and spread the news like the plague.''

''Kingpin still watching him?'' I asked.

''Him and Sharkey and Tickle are taking turns. He ain't going to be able to poot without we know about it.''

''Good. Keep it that way. But don't mess with him. We just want to keep him away from Bullock and the Taken.'' I faded away into my thoughts.

''What?'' Elmo finally asked.

''I had an idea while I was talking to Shed. Bullock is our main risk, right? And we know he'll stick like a bulldog once he gets on a trail. And he's on the trail of this Asa character. So why don't we con him into going south after this Asa?''

''I don't know,'' Elmo muttered. ''He might find him.''

''What's he want him for? Questioning about a raid on the Catacombs. What kind of cooperation is he going to get someplace else? Not much. Way I hear it, the cities down the coast think Juniper is a bad joke. Anyway, we just want to buy a little time. And if he does catch up with Asa, I figure he catches up with Raven, too. Ain't nobody going to bring Raven back. Not if he thinks the Taken are after Darling. They tangle, I'll put my money on Raven. Cut out the only source of info. Temporarily or permanently. See what I mean? And if he does kill Raven, then Raven can't talk."

"How you going to talk Bullock into it?" Elmo asked. "It's dumb, Croaker. He's not going to go haring off after some minor suspect."

"Yes, he will. You remember, when we came here, he had to translate? How do you figure he learned the language of the Jewel Cities? I asked him. He spent three years there looking for a guy who wasn't any more important than Asa."

Goblin said, "This mess gets crazier every day. We got so many cons and lies going I can't keep track of them anymore. I don't think we better do anything except cover our asses till the Captain gets here."

I often had a feeling we were making things worse. But I could see no exit, other than to keep coping and hoping.

"Best way out," Elmo observed laconically, "would be to kill everybody who knows anything, then all of us fall on our swords."

"Sounds a little extreme," Goblin opined. "But if you want to go first, I'm right behind you."

"I've got to report in to Whisper," I said. "Anybody got any brilliant ideas what I should tell her?"

Nobody did. I went, dreading the encounter. I was sure guilt smouldered in my eyes whenever I faced her. I resented Elmo because he did not have to endure her daily fits of ire.

Bullock was almost too easy. He was packing almost before I finished handing him my line of bull. He wanted that Asa bad.

I wondered if he knew something we did not. Or if he'd just worked up an obsession with the mystery of the invaded Catacombs.

Whisper was more of a problem.

She told me: "I want you to send somebody with him." I had had to tell her something, so had told her most of the truth. I figured the chances of anybody tracking Asa and Raven were nil. But. . . . She seemed a little too interested, too. Perhaps she knew more than she pretended. She was, after all, one of the Taken.

Elmo picked three men, put Kingpin in charge, and told him to stick a knife in Bullock if he looked like needing it.

The Captain and Company were, I was told, in the Wolander Mountains a hundred miles from Juniper. They faced a slow passage through tough passes, but I began to anticipate their arrival. Once the Old Man showed, the weight would be off Elmo and me. ''Hurry,'' I muttered, and returned to tangling our skein of deceits.

# Chapter Twenty-Five: JUNIPER: LOVERS

Marron Shed fell in love. In love in the worst possible way—with a woman far younger, who had tastes far beyond his means. He charged into the affair with all the reserve of a bull in rut, disdaining consequences, squandering his cash reserve as though it came from a bottomless box. His boxes dried up. Two weeks after he met Sue, he made a loan with Gilbert, the moneylender. Another loan followed that, then another. Within a month he had gone into debt farther than he had been during the winter.

And he did not care. The woman made him happy, and that was that. Compounding his negative attributes was a tendency toward willful stupidity and an unconscious confidence that money could be no problem ever again.

Wally's wife Sal visited the Lily one morning, grim and slightly ashamed. "Marron," she said, "can we talk?"

"What's the matter?"

"You were going to help with rent and stuff."

"Sure. So what's the problem?"

"Well, I don't want to sound ungrateful or like I have any right to expect you to support us, but our landlord is threatening to throw us out on account of the rent hasn't been paid for two weeks. We can't get work on account of nobody is putting out any sewing right now."

"The rent isn't paid? But I saw him just the other day. . . ." It hadn't been just the other day. He had forgotten. His mother, too. Her servants' salaries would be due in a few days. Not to mention Lisa's. "Oh my," he said. "I'm sorry. I forgot. I'll take care of it."

"Shed, you've been good to us. You didn't have to be. I don't like seeing you get into this kind of mess."

"What kind of mess?"

"With that woman. She's trying to destroy you."

He was too puzzled to become angry. "Sue? Why? How?"

"Give her up. It'll hurt less if you break it off. Everybody knows what she's doing."

"What's she doing?" Shed's voice was plaintive.

"Never mind. I said more than I should already. If there's ever anything we can do for you, let us know."

"I will. I will," he promised. He went upstairs, to his hidden cash box, and found it barren.

There was not a gersh in the place, upstairs or down. What was going on? "Lisa. Where's all the money?"

"I hid it."

"What?"

"I hid it. The way you're carrying on, you're going to lose this place. You have a legitimate expense, tell me. I'll cover it."

Shed goggled. He sputtered. "Who the hell do you think you are, girl?"

"The girl who's going to keep you in business in spite of yourself. The girl who's going to stop you from being a complete fool with Gilbert's woman."

"Gilbert's?"

"Yes. What did you think was going on?"

"Get out," Shed snapped. "You don't work here anymore."

Lisa shrugged. "If that's what you want."

"Where's the money?"

"Sorry. Come see me when you get your common sense back."

Shed raged around the common room. His customers clapped, egging him on. He threatened. He cajoled. Nothing worked. Lisa remained adamant. "It's my family!" he protested.

"You go prove that woman isn't Gilbert's whore. Then I'll give you the money and walk."

"I'll do that."

"What if I'm right?"

"You're not. I know her."

"You don't know shit. You're infatuated. What if I'm right?"

He was incapable of entertaining the possibility. "I don't care."

"All right. If I'm right, I want to run things here. You let me get us out of debt."

Shed bobbed his head once and stormed out. He was not risking anything. She was wrong.

What was her game? She was acting like a partner or something. Like his mother had, after his father died and before she lost her sight. Treating him like he did not have twice her experience of business and the world.

He wandered for half an hour. When he came up from his melancholy, he saw he was near Sailmakers' Hall. Hell. He was there; he'd just go see Gilbert. Make a loan so he could see Sue that night. Little bitch Lisa could hide his money, maybe, but she couldn't keep him away from Gilbert.

Half a block later he began to suffer conscience pangs. Too many people depended upon him. He shouldn't make his financial situation worse.

"Damned woman," he muttered. "Shouldn't talk to me that way. Now she's got me doubting everybody." He leaned against a wall and fought his conscience. Sometimes lust pulled ahead, sometimes the urge toward responsibility. He ached for Sue. . . . He should not need money if she really loved him. . . .

"What?" he said aloud. He looked again. His eyes had not deceived him. That was Sue stepping into Gilbert's place.

His stomach sank like a falling rock. "No. She couldn't. . . . There must be an explanation."

But his traitor mind started cataloguing little oddities about their relationship, particularly mauling her penchant for spending. A low-grade anger simmered over the fire of his hurt. He slipped across the street, hurried into the alley leading behind Gilbert's place. Gilbert's office was in the back. It had an alley window. Shed did not expect that to be open. He did hope to sneak a peek.

The window was not open, but he could hear. And the sounds of lovemaking in no way approximated what he *wanted* to hear.

He considered killing himself on the spot. Considered killing himself on Sue's doorstep. Considered a dozen other dramatic protests. And knew none would move either of these villains.

They began talking. Their chatter soon killed Shed's hold-out doubts. The name Marron Shed came up.

"He's ready," the woman said. "I've taken him as far as I can. Maybe one more loan before he starts remembering his family."

"Do it, then. I want him wrapped up. Make the hill steep, then grease it. He got away from Krage."

Shed shook with anger.

"How far down do you have him?"

"Eighteen leva, and nearly another ten in interest."

"I can work him for another five."

"Do it. I have a buyer hot to go."

Shed left. He wandered the Buskin for hours. He looked so grim people crossed the street. There is no vengeance as terrible as the vengeance a coward plots in the dark of his heart.

Late that afternoon Shed strolled into Gilbert's office, all emotion locked back in the shadows he had discovered the night he had run with Krage's hunters. "I need fifteen leva, Gilbert. In a hurry."

Gilbert was startled. His one eye opened wide. "Fifteen? What the hell for?"

"I've set up a sweet deal, but I have to close it tonight. I'll go a couple extra points if you want."

"Shed, you're into me big now. I'm worried about you covering that."

"This deal goes off and I can clear it all."

Gilbert stared. ''What's up, Shed?''

''Up?''

''You're awful sure of yourself.''

Shed told the lie that hurt most. ''I'm going to get married, Gilbert. Going to ask the lady tonight. I want to close this deal so I can make the Lily over into a decent place for her.''

''Well,'' Gilbert breathed. ''Well, well, well. Marron Shed getting married. Interesting. All right, Shed. It's not good business, but I'll take a chance. Fifteen, you said?''

''Thank you, Mr. Gilbert. I'm really grateful. . . .''

''You sure you can meet the payments?''

''I'll have you ten leva before the end of the week. Guaranteed. And with Sue helping out at the Lily, I'll have no problem clearing enough to cover the rest.''

Gilbert controlled a thin smile. ''Then you won't mind putting up collateral more valuable than your word?''

''Sir?''

''I want a lien on the Iron Lily.''

Shed pretended to think hard. Finally: ''All right. She's worth the risk.''

Gilbert smiled the smile of a hungry stoat, but managed to look worried at the same time. ''Wait here. I'll have a note drawn up and get the money.''

Shed smiled nastily as Gilbert departed.

# Chapter Twenty-Six: JUNIPER: LOVERS' PARTING

Shed pulled his rig into the alleyway behind Sue's place, raced around front, pounded on the door. It was a class place for the Buskin. A man guarded the entrance from within. Eight women lived there, each in her own apartment. Each in the same business as Sue. Each commanding a substantial premium for her time.

"Hello, Mr. Shed," the door guard said. "Go on up. She's expecting you."

Shed tipped him, something he hadn't done before. The man became obsequious. Shed ignored him, mounted the stair.

Now came the difficult part. Playing cow-eyed lover when he was no longer blind. But he would fool her, just as she had fooled him.

She answered the door, radiantly beautiful. Shed's heart climbed into his throat. He shoved something into her hand. "This is for you."

"Oh, Marron, you shouldn't have." But, if he hadn't, he would not have gotten past her door. "What a strange necklace. Are these serpents?"

"Real silver," he said. "And rubies. It caught my fancy. Ugly, but the craftsmanship is superb."

"I think it's gorgeous, Marron. How much did it cost?"

"Too much," Shed replied, smiling sardonically. "I couldn't tell you. More than I should have paid for anything."

Sue did not press. "Come here, Marron." She must have had orders to play him carefully. Usually she gave him a hard time before surrendering. She began disrobing.

Shed went. He took her rough, something he had not done before. Then he took her again. When it was over, she asked, "What's gotten into you?"

"I have a big surprise for you. A big surprise. I know you'll love it. Can you sneak out without anyone knowing?"

"Of course. But why?"

"That's the surprise. Will you do it? You won't be disappointed, I promise."

"I don't understand."

"Just do it. Slip out a few minutes after I leave. Meet me in the alley. I want to take you somewhere and show you something. Be sure to wear the necklace."

"What are you up to?" She seemed amused, not suspicious.

Good, Shed thought. He finished dressing. "No answers now, darling. This will be the biggest surprise of your life. I don't want to spoil it." He headed for the door.

"Five minutes?" she called.

"Don't make me wait. I'm a bear when I have to wait. And don't forget the necklace."

"I won't, dear."

Shed waited nearly fifteen minutes. He grew impatient, but was certain greed would bring Sue out. The hook was set. She was playing with him.

"Marron?" Her voice was soft and musical. His heart twisted. How could he do this?

"Here, love." She came to him. He enfolded her in his arms.

"Now, now. Enough of that. I want my surprise. I can hardly wait."

Shed took a deep breath. Do it! he yelled inside. "I'll help you up." She turned. *Now!* But his hands were made of lead.

"Come on, Marron."

He swung. Sue slammed into the wagon, a mewl the

only sound she made. He hit her again as she bounced back. She sagged. He took a gag from the wagon, forced it into her mouth before she could scream, then tied her hands quickly. She began kicking when he went for her ankles. He kicked her back, nearly let anger carry him away.

She quit fighting. He finished binding her, then propped her on the wagon seat. In the darkness they looked like man and wife about some late business.

He did not speak till they were across the Port. "You're probably wondering what's going on, darling."

Sue grunted. She was pale and frightened. He retrieved his amulet. While he was at it, he stripped her of jewelry and valuables.

"Sue, I loved you. I really did. I would have done anything for you. When you kill a love like that, you turn it into a big hatred." At least twenty leva worth of jewelry, he guessed. How many men had she destroyed? "Working for Gilbert like that. Trying to steal the Lily. Anything else I could have forgiven. Anything."

He talked all the way up the hill. It distracted her till the black castle loomed so large it could no longer be overlooked. Then her eyes got huge. She began to shake, to stink as she lost all control.

"Yes, darling," Shed said, voice pleasantly rational, conversational. "Yes. The black castle. You were going to deliver me to the mercy of *your* friends. You made a bet and lost. Now I deliver you to *mine*." He halted, climbed down, went to the gate. It opened immediately.

The tall being met him, wringing spidery hands. "Good," it said. "Very good. Your partner never brought healthy game."

Shed's guts knotted. He wanted to change his mind. He only wanted to hurt and humiliate Sue. . . . But it was too late. He could not turn back. "I'm sorry, Sue. You shouldn't have done it. You and Gilbert. His turn will come. Marron Shed isn't what everybody thinks."

A whining noise came from behind Sue's gag. Shed

turned away. He had to get out. He faced the tall creature. It began counting coins directly into his hand.

As always, Shed did not barter. In fact, he did not look at the money, just kept stuffing his pockets. His attention was on the darkness behind the creature.

More of its kind were back there, hissing, jostling. Shed recognized the short one he'd dealt with once.

The tall being stopped counting. Absently, Shed put the coins into a pocket, returned to his wagon. The things in shadow swept forward, seized Sue, began ripping her clothing. One yanked the gag out of her mouth. Shed started packing his rig.

''For God's sake, Marron. Don't leave me.''

''It's done, woman. It's done.'' He snapped his traces. ''Back up, mules.''

She started screaming as he turned toward the gate. He did not look. He did not want to know. ''Keep moving, mules.''

''Come again soon, Marron Shed,'' the tall creature called after him.

# Chapter Twenty-Seven: JUNIPER: BANISHED

The summons from Whisper caught me unprepared. It was too early for the daily report. I'd barely finished breakfast. I knew it meant trouble.

I was not disappointed.

The Taken prowled like a caged animal, radiating tension and anger. I went inside by the numbers, stood at a perfect attention, giving no excuse for the picking of nits—in case whatever it was was not my fault.

She ignored me for several minutes, working off energy. Then she seated herself, stared at her hands thoughtfully.

Her gaze rose. And she was in complete control. She actually smiled. Had she been as beautiful as the Lady, that smile would have melted granite. But she was what she was, a scarred old campaigner, so a smile only ameliorated the grimness of her face.

"How were the men disposed last night?" she asked.

Baffled, I responded, "Excuse me? You mean their temper?"

"Where were they stationed?"

"Oh." That was properly Elmo's province, but I knew better than to say so. The Taken do not tolerate excuses, sound though they may be. "The three men on the ship south with Bullock, looking for that man Asa." I worried about her having sent them. When I do not understand the motives of the Taken, I get paranoid. "Five down in the Buskin pretending to be foreign sailors. Three more down there watching people we've found especially interesting. I'd have to double-check with Elmo to be positive, but at least four more were in other parts of the city, trying to pick up something of interest. The rest of us were here in the castle, off duty. Wait. One man would have been down in the Duke's secret police office, and two would have been at the Enclosure, hanging around with the Custodians. I was with the Inquisitors most of the night, picking their brains. We're scattered pretty thin right now. I'll be glad when the Captain gets here. We've got too much going for the available manpower. The occupation planning is way behind."

She sighed, rose, resumed pacing. "My fault as much as anyone's, I suppose." She looked out a window for a long time. Then she beckoned. I joined her.

She indicated the black castle. "Just whiskers short. They're trying to open the way for the Dominator already. It's not yet time, but they're getting hurried. Maybe they've sensed our interest."

This Juniper business was like some giant, tentacled sea beast from a sailor's lie. No matter where we turned or what we did, we got deeper into trouble. By working at cross-purposes with the Taken, trying to cover an increasingly more obvious trail, we were complicating their efforts to deal with the peril of the black castle. If we did cover well, we just might make it possible for the Dominator to emerge into an unprepared world.

I did not want that horror upon my conscience.

Though I fear I tend not to record it that way, we were embroiled in substantial moral quandaries. We are not accustomed to such problems. The lot of the mercenary does not require much moralizing or making of moral decisions. Essentially, the mercenary sets morality aside, or at best reorders the customary structures to fit the needs of his way of life. The great issues become how well he does his job, how faithfully he carries out his commission, how well he adheres to a standard demanding unswerving loyalties to his comrades. He dehumanizes the world outside the bounds of his outfit. Then anything he does, or witnesses, becomes of minor significance as long as its brunt is borne outside the Company.

We had drifted into a trap where we might have to face the biggest choice in the Company's history. We might have to betray four centuries of Company mythos on behalf of the greater whole.

I knew I could not permit the Dominator to restore himself, if that turned out to be the only way we could keep the Lady from finding out about Darling and Raven.

Yet. . . . The Lady was not much better. We served her, and, till lately, well and faithfully, obliterating the Rebel wherever we found him, but I don't think many of us were indifferent to what she was. She was less evil than the Dominator only because she was less determined about it, more patient in her drive for total and absolute control.

That presented me with another quandary. Was I capable of sacrificing Darling to prevent the Dominator's return? If that became the price?

"You seem very thoughtful," Whisper said.

"Uhm. There're too many angles to this business. The Custodians. The Duke. Us. Bullock, who has axes of his own to grind." I had told her about Bullock's Buskin origins, feeding her seemingly irrelevant information to complicate and distract her thinking.

She pointed again. "Didn't I suggest a close watch be kept on that place?"

"Yes, ma'am. We did for a while, too. But nothing ever happened, and then we were told to do some other things. . . ." I broke off, quaking with a sudden nasty suspicion.

She read my face. "Yes. Last night. And this delivery was still alive."

"Oh boy," I murmured. "Who did it? You know?"

"We just sensed the consequent changes. They tried to open the way. They weren't strong enough yet, but they came very close."

She began to prowl. Mentally, I ticked off the roster for the Buskin last night. I was going to ask some very pointed questions.

"I consulted the Lady directly. She's very worried. Her orders are to let ancillary business slide. We're to prevent any more bodies reaching the castle. Yes, the rest of your Company will be here soon. From six to ten days. And there is much to be done to prepare for their arrival. But, as you observed, there is too much to do and too few to do it. Let your Captain cope when he arrives. The black castle must be isolated."

"Why not fly some men in?"

"The Lady has forbidden that."

I tried to look perplexed. "Buy why?" I had a sweating, fearful suspicion that I knew.

Whisper shrugged. "Because she doesn't want you wasting time making hellos and briefing newcomers. Go see what can be done about isolating the castle."

"Yes, ma'am."

I departed, thinking it had gone both better and worse than I had anticipated. Better, because she did not throw one of her screaming rages. Worse, because she had in effect announced that we who were here already were suspect, that we might have succumbed to a moral infection the Lady did not want communicated to our brethren.

Scary.

"Yeah," Elmo said when I told him. He did not need it explained. "Which means we got to make contact with the Old Man."

"Messenger?"

"What else? Who can we break loose and cover?"

"One of the men from the Buskin."

Elmo nodded. "I'll handle that. You go ahead and figure how to isolate the castle with the manpower we have."

"Why don't you go scout the castle? I want to find out what those guys were doing last night."

"That's neither here nor there now, Croaker. I'm taking over. Not saying you done a bad job, just you didn't get it done. Which is my fault, really. I'm the soldier."

"Being a soldier won't make any difference, Elmo. This isn't soldier's work. It's spy stuff. And spies need time to worm into the fabric of a society. We haven't had enough of that."

"Time is up now. Isn't that what you said?"

"I guess," I admitted. "All right. I'll scout the castle. But you find out what went on down there last night. Especially around that placed called the Iron Lily. It keeps turning up, just like that guy Asa."

All the while we talked, Elmo was changing. Now he looked like a sailor down on his luck, too old to ship, but still tough enough for dirty work. He would fit right in down in the Buskin. I told him so.

"Yeah. Let's get moving. And don't plan on getting much sleep till the Captain gets here."

We looked at one another, not saying what lay in the backs of our minds. If the Taken did not want us in touch with our brethren, what might they do when the Company hove in sight, coming out of the Wolanders?

Up close, the black castle was both intriguing and unsettling. I took a horse over, circled the place several times, even flipped a cheerful wave at the one movement I detected atop its glassy ramparts.

There was some difficult ground behind it—steep, rocky, overgrown with scraggly, thorny brush which had a sagey odor. Nobody lugging a corpse would reach the fortress from that direction. The ground was better along the ridgeline to east and west, but even there an approach was improbable. Men of the sort who sold corpses would do things the easy way. That meant using the road which ran from the Port River waterfront, through the scatter of merchant class houses on the middle slopes, and just kept on to the castle gate. Someone had followed that course often, for wheel ruts ran from the end of the road to the castle.

My problem was, there was no place a squad could lie in wait without being seen from the castle wall. It took me till dusk to finalize my plan.

I found an abandoned house a ways down the slope and a little upriver. I would conceal my squad there and post sentries down the road, in the populated area. They could run a message to the rest of us if they saw anything suspicious. We could hustle up and across the slope to intercept potential body-sellers. Wagons would be slow enough to allow us the time needed.

Old Croaker is a brilliant strategist. Yes, sir. I had my troops in place and everything set by midnight. And had two false alarms before breakfast. I learned the embarrassing way that there was legitimate night traffic past my sentry post.

I sat in the old house with my team, alternately playing tonk and worrying, and on rare occasions napping. And wondering a lot about what was happening down in the Buskin and across the valley in Duretile.

I prayed Elmo could keep his fingers on all the strings.

# Chapter Twenty-Eight: JUNIPER: LISA

Shed spent an entire day lying in his room, staring at the ceiling, hating himself. He had sunk as low as a man could. There was no deed too foul for him anymore, and nothing more he could do to blacken his soul. A million-leva passage fee could not buy him aboard on Passage Day. His name had to be written in the Black Book with those of the greatest villains.

"Mr. Shed?" Lisa said from the doorway next morning, as he was contemplating another day of ceiling study and self-pity. "Mr. Shed?"

"Yeah?"

"Bo and Lana are here."

Bo and Lana, with a daughter, were his mother's servants. "What do they want?"

"Their accounts settled for the month, I expect."

"Oh." He got up.

Lisa stopped him at the head of the stair. "I was right about Sue, wasn't I?"

"You were."

"I'm sorry. I wouldn't have said anything if we could have afforded it."

"We? What do you mean, we? Oh, hell. Never mind. Forget about it. I don't want to hear about it anymore."

"Whatever you say. But I'm going to hold you to your promise."

"What promise?"

"To let me manage the Lily."

"Oh. All right." At that moment he did not care. He collected the monthly accounting from the servants. He had chosen them well. They were not cheating him. He suggested they deserved a small bonus.

He returned upstairs for the money. Lisa watched him go, perplexed. He realized his mistake too late. Now she wondered why he had money today when he'd had none yesterday. He located his dirty clothing, emptied his pockets onto his bed. And gasped.

"Oh, damn! Damn," he muttered. "What the hell am I going to do with three gold pieces?"

There was silver, too, and even a fistful of copper, but. . . . It was a gyp! A fortune he could not spend. Juniper law made it illegal for commoners to hold minted gold. Even incoming foreigners had to exchange theirs for silver—though foreign silver was as welcome as local. Lucky, too, for the black castle mintage was a decidedly odd coinage, though in the standard weights.

How could he get rid of the gold? Sell it to some ship captain headed south? That was the usual procedure. He slipped it into his most secret hiding place, with the amulet from the black castle. A useless fortune. He assessed the remainder. Twenty-eight pieces of silver, plus several leva in copper. Enough to take care of his mother and Sal. Way short of enough to pry Gilbert off his back. "Still be in the damned money trap," he whined.

He recalled Sue's jewelry, smiled nastily, muttered, "I'll do it." He pocketed everything, returned to the ground floor, paid his mother's servants, told Lisa, "I'm going out for a while."

First he made sure Wally's family was cared for, then ambled down toward Gilbert's place. No one seemed to be around. Gilbert was not like Krage, in that he felt he needed an army on hand, but he did have his bonebreakers. They were all away. But someone was in Gilbert's office because lamplight illuminated the curtains. He smiled thoughtfully, then hustled back to the Lily.

He went to a table back in the shadows, near where

Raven used to sit. A couple of foreign sailors were seated there. Tough merchandise if he'd ever seen it. They'd been around for some time. They said they and their friends, who came and went, had missed their ship. They were waiting for another. Shed could not recall having heard the name of their home port.

"You men like to pick up some easy money?" he asked.

"Who doesn't?" one responded.

And the other, "What you got in mind?"

"I have a little problem. I've got to do some business with a man. He's liable to get vicious."

"Want some back-up, eh?"

Shed nodded.

The other sailor looked at him narrowly. "Who is he?"

"Name's Gilbert. A moneylender. You heard of him?"

"Yeah."

"I was just past his place. Don't look like there's anybody there but him."

The men exchanged glances. The taller said, "Tell you what. Let me go get a friend of ours."

"I can't afford a whole army."

"Hey, no problem. You two work out what you'd pay two of us; he'll come along free. Just feel more comfortable having him with us."

"Tough?"

Both men grinned. One winked at the other. "Yeah. Like you wouldn't believe."

"Then get him."

One man left. Shed dickered with the other. Lisa watched from across the room, eyes narrow and hard. Shed decided she was getting too much into his business too fast.

The third man was a frog-faced character barely five feet tall. Shed frowned at him. His fetcher reminded, "He's tough. Remember?"

"Yeah? All right. Let's go." He felt a hundred percent better with three men accompanying him, though he had no real assurance they would help if Gilbert started something.

There were a couple of thugs in the front room when Shed arrived. He told them: "I want to see Gilbert."

"Suppose he don't want to see you?" It was standard tough-guy game-playing. Shed did not know how to respond. One of his companions saved him the worry.

"He don't got much choice, does he? Unless that fat's all muscle in disguise." He produced a knife, began cleaning his nails. The deed was so reminiscent of Raven that Shed was startled.

"He's back in the office." The fat thug exchanged a look with his companion. Shed figured one would run for help.

He started moving. His frog-faced companion said, "I'll just stay out here."

Shed pushed into Gilbert's office. The moneylender had a sack of leva on his desk, was weighing coins one at a time on a fine scale, sorting out those that had been clipped. He looked up angrily. "What the hell is this?"

"Couple of friends wanted to stop by with me and watch how you do business."

"I don't like what this says about our relationship, Shed. It says you don't trust me."

Shed shrugged. "There's some nasty rumors out there. About you and Sue working on me. To do me out of the Lily."

"Sue, eh? Where is she, Shed?"

"There is a connection, eh?" Shed let his face fall. "Damn you. That's why she turned me down. You villain. Now she won't even see me. That ape at the door keeps telling me she isn't there. You arrange that, Mister Gilbert? You know, I don't like you much."

Gilbert gave the lot of them a nasty one-eyed stare. For a moment he seemed to consider his chances. Then the small man ambled in, leaned against the wall, his wide mouth wrinkled into a sneer.

Gilbert said, "You come to talk or to do business? If it's business, get at it. I want these creeps out of here. They'll give the neighborhood a bad name."

Shed produced a leather bag. "You have the bad name,

Gilbert. I hear people saying they won't do business with you anymore. They don't think it's right you should try to screw people out of their property."

"Shut up and give me some money, Shed. You just want to whine, get out."

"Sure talks tough for being down four to one," one of the men remarked. A companion admonished him in another language. Gilbert glared in a way that said he was memorizing faces. The little man grinned and beckoned with one finger. Gilbert decided it could wait.

Shed counted coins. Gilbert's eyes widened as the stack grew. Shed said, "Told you I was working on a deal." He tossed in Sue's jewelry.

One of his companions picked up a bracelet, examined it. "How much do you owe this character?"

Gilbert snapped a figure, which Shed suspected to be inflated.

The sailor observed, "You're shorting yourself, Shed."

"I just want quit of this jackal's lien on my place."

Gilbert stared at the jewelry, pallid, stiff. He licked his lips and reached for a ring. His hand shook.

Shed was both fearful and filled with malicious glee. Gilbert knew the ring. Now maybe he would be a little nervous about messing with Marron Shed. Or he might decide to cut a few throats. Gilbert had some of the same ego problems Krage had had.

"This should more than cover everything, Mr. Gilbert. The big, too. Even with the extra points. Let's have my lien back."

Dully, Gilbert retrieved that from a box on a nearby shelf. His eyes never left the ring.

Shed destroyed the lien immediately. "Don't I still owe you a little something, though, Mr. Gilbert? Yes, I think so. Well, I'll do my best to see you get everything you've got coming."

Gilbert squinted angrily. Shed thought he saw a hint of fear, too. That pleased him. Nobody was ever afraid of Marron Shed, except maybe Asa, who did not count.

Best make his exit, before he stretched his luck. "Thank you, Mr. Gilbert. See you again soon."

Passing through the outer room, he was astonished to find Gilbert's men snoring. The frog-faced man grinned. Outside, Shed paid his guardians. "He wasn't as much trouble as I expected."

"You had us with you," the little man said. "Let's go to your place and have a beer."

One of the others observed, "He looked like he was in shock."

The little man asked, "How'd you ever get that far into a moneylender, anyway?"

"A skirt. I thought I was going to marry her. She was just taking me for my money. I finally woke up."

His companions shook their heads. One said, "Women. Got to watch them, buddy. They'll pick your bones."

"I learned my lesson. Hey. Drinks on the house. I've got some wine I used to keep for a special customer. He left town, so I'm stuck with it."

"That bad, eh?"

"No. That good. Nobody can afford it."

Shed spent his entire evening sipping wine, even after the sailors decided they had business elsewhere. He broke into a grin each time he recalled Gilbert's reaction to the ring. "Got to be careful now," he muttered. "He's as crazy as Krage."

In time the good feeling departed. Fear took over. He'd face anything Gilbert did alone, and he was still very much the same old Shed under the patina left by Raven and a few deals since.

"Ought to haul the bastard up the hill," he muttered into his mug. Then: "Damn! I'm as bad as Raven. Worse. Raven never delivered them alive. Wonder what that bastard is doing now, with his fancy ship and slick young slot?"

He got himself very, very drunk and very, very filled with self-pity.

The last guest went to his bunk. The last outsider went home. Shed sat there nursing his wine and glowering at

Lisa, angry with her for no reason he could define. Her body, he thought. Ripe. But she wouldn't. Too good for him. And her pushiness lately. Yeah.

She studied him as she cleaned up. Efficient little witch. Better even than Darling, who had worked hard but hadn't the economy of movement Lisa had. Maybe she *did* deserve to manage the place. He hadn't done such a great job.

He found her seated opposite him. He glowered. She did not retreat. A hard lass, too. Wouldn't bluff. Didn't scare. Tough Buskin bitch. Be trouble someday.

"What's the matter, Mr. Shed?"

"Nothing."

"I hear you paid Gilbert off. On a loan you took on this place. How could you take a loan on the Lily? It's been in your family for ages."

"Don't give me that sentimental crap. You don't believe it."

"Where did you get the money?"

"Maybe you shouldn't be so nosy. Maybe nosiness could be bad for your health." He was talking surly and tough but not meaning what he said.

"You've been acting strange lately."

"I was in love."

"That wasn't it. What happened to that, anyway? I hear Sue disappeared. Gilbert says you did her in."

"Did what? I was over to her place today."

"You see her?"

"No. The door guard said she wasn't home. Which means she didn't want to see me. Probably had somebody else up there."

"Maybe it meant she wasn't home."

Shed snorted. "I told you I don't want to talk about her anymore. Understand?"

"Sure. Tell me where you got the money."

Shed glared. "Why?"

"Because if there's more, I want a chunk. I don't want to spend my life in the Buskin. I'll do whatever it takes to get out."

Shed smirked.

She misunderstood. "This job is just to keep body and soul together till I find something."

"A million people have thought that, Lisa. And they've frozen to death in Buskin alleys."

"Some make it. I don't intend to fail. Where did you get the money, Mr. Shed?" She went for a bottle of the good wine. Vaguely, Shed thought it must be about gone.

He told her about his silent partner.

"That's a crock. I've been here long enough to know that."

"Better believe it, girl." He giggled. "You keep pushing and you're liable to meet him. You won't like him, I guarantee." He recalled the tall creature telling him to hurry back.

"What happened to Sue?"

Shed tried to rise. His limbs were limp. He fell back into his seat. "I'm drunk. Drunker than I thought. Getting out of shape." Lisa nodded gravely. "I loved her. I really loved her. She shouldn't ought to have done that. I would have treated her like a queen. Would have gone into hell for her. Almost did." He chuckled. "Went in with her. . . . Oops."

"Would you do that for me, Mr. Shed?"

"What?"

"You're always trying to get me. What's it worth?"

Shed leered. "Don't know. Can't tell till I've tried you."

"You don't have anything to give me, old man."

"Know where to get it, though."

"Where?"

Shed just sat there grinning, a bit of drool trailing from one corner of his mouth.

"I give up. You win. Come on. I'll help you get up the stairs before I go home."

The climb was an epic. Shed was one drink short of passing out. When they reached his room, he just toppled into bed. "Thanks," he mumbled. "What're you doing?"

"You have to get undressed."

"Guess so." He made no effort to help. "What're you doing now? Why're you grabbing me like that?"

"You want me, don't you?" A moment later she was in the bed with him, rubbing her nakedness against his. He was too drunk to make anything of the situation. He held her, and became maudlin, spouting his trials. She played to it.

# Chapter Twenty-Nine: JUNIPER: PAYOFF

Shed sat up so suddenly his head twisted around. Somebody started beating drums inside. He rolled to the edge of the bed and was noisily sick. And then became sick in another way. With terror.

"I told her. I told her the whole damned thing." He tried to jump up. He had to get out of Juniper before the Inquisitors came. He had gold. A foreign captain might take him south. He could catch up with Raven and Asa. . . . He settled onto the cot, too miserable to act. "I'm dying," he muttered. "If there's a hell, this is what it's going to be like."

*Had* he told her? He thought so. And for nothing. He had gotten nothing. "Marron Shed, you were born to lose. When will you ever learn?"

He rose once more, cautiously, and fumbled through his hiding place. The gold was there. Maybe he hadn't told her everything. He considered the amulet. Lisa could follow the trail blazed by Sue. If she hadn't told anybody yet. But she would be wary, wouldn't she? Be hard to catch her off guard. Even assuming he could find her.

"My head! Gods! I can't think." There was a sudden racket downstairs. "Damn," he muttered. "She left the place unlocked. They'll steal everything." Tears rolled down his cheeks. Such an end he had come to. Maybe that was Bullock and his thugs knocking around down there.

Best to meet his fate. Cursing, he eased into his clothing, began the long journey downstairs.

"Good morning, Mr. Shed," Lisa called brightly. "What will you have for breakfast?"

He stared, gulped, finally stumbled to a table, sat there with his head in his hands, ignoring the amused stare of one of his companions of the Gilbert adventure.

"A little hung over, Mr. Shed?" Lisa asked.

"Yes." His own voice sounded thunderous.

"I'll mix you something my father taught me to make. He's a master drunkard, you know."

Shed nodded weakly. Even that proved painful. Lisa's father was one reason he had hired her. She needed all the help she could get. Another of his charities gone sour.

She returned with something so foul even a sorcerer would not have touched it. "Drink fast. It goes down easier that way."

"I can imagine." Half praying it would poison him, he gulped the malodorous concoction. After gasping for breath, he murmured, "When are they coming? How long do I have?"

"Who, Mr. Shed?"

"The Inquisitors. The law. Whoever you called."

"Why would they come here?"

Painfully, he raised his gaze to meet hers.

She whispered, "I told you I'll do anything to get out of the Buskin. This is the chance I've been looking for. We're partners now, Mr. Shed. Fifty-fifty."

Shed buried his head in his hands and groaned. It would never end. Not till it devoured him. He cast curses on Raven and all his house.

The common room was empty. The door was closed. "First we have to take care of Gilbert," Lisa said.

Shed bobbed his head, refused to look up.

"That was stupid, giving him jewelry he would recognize. He'll kill you if we don't kill him first."

Again Shed bobbed his head. Why me? he whined to himself. What have I done to deserve this?

"And don't you think you can get rid of me the way you did Sue and that blackmailer. My father has a letter he'll take to Bullock if I disappear."

"You're too smart for your own good." And: "It won't be long till winter."

"Yes. But we won't do it Raven's way. Too risky and too much work. We'll get charitable. Let all the derelicts in. One or two can disappear every night."

"You're talking murder!"

"Who'll care? Nobody. They'll be better off themselves. Call it mercy."

"How can anybody so young be so heartless?"

"You don't prosper in the Buskin if you have a heart, Mr. Shed. We'll fix a place where the outside cold will keep them till we get a wagonload. We can take them up maybe once a week."

"Winter is. . . ."

"Is going to be my last season in the Buskin."

"I won't do it."

"Yes, you will. Or you'll hear from Bullock. You don't have a choice. You have a partner."

"God, deliver me from evil."

"Are you less evil than me? You killed five people."

"Four," he protested weakly.

"You think Sue is still alive? You're splitting hairs. Any way you look at it, you're guilty of murder. You're a murderer so dumb about money he doesn't have a gersh to his name. So stupid he keeps getting tangled with Sues and Gilberts. Mr. Shed, they only execute you once."

How to argue with sociopathic reasoning? Lisa was the heart of Lisa's universe. Other people existed only to be exploited.

"There are some others we should think about after Gilbert. That man of Krage's who got away. He knows there was something strange about the bodies not turning up. He hasn't talked or it would be all over the Buskin. But someday he might. And there's the man you hired to help you with the blackmailer."

She sounded like a general plan
ning murder wholesale. How could
"I want no more blood on my hand
"How much choice do you have?"
He could not deny that Gilbert's death
the equation of his survival. And after Gilb
Before she destroyed him. She would let her own
sometime.

What about that letter? Damn. Maybe her father had to go first. . . . The trap was vast and had no apparent exits.

"This could be my only chance to get out, Mr. Shed. You'd better believe I'm going to grab it."

Shed shook his lethargy, leaned forward, stared into the fireplace. His own survival came first. Gilbert had to go. That was definite.

What about the black castle? Had he told her about the amulet? He could not recall. He had to imply the existence of a special passkey, else she might try to kill and sell *him*. He would become a danger to her once they implemented her plan. Yes. For sure. She would try to rid herself of him once she made her connection with the things in the castle. So add another to his must-kill list.

Damn. Raven had done the smart thing, the only thing possible. Had taken the only exit. Leaving Juniper was the only way out.

"Going to have to follow him," he muttered. "There isn't any choice."

"What?"

"Just muttering, girl. You win. Let's get to work on Gilbert."

"Good. Stay sober and get up early tomorrow. You'll need to watch the Lily while I check something out."

"All right."

"Time you pulled your own weight again, anyway."

"Probably so."

Lisa eyed him suspiciously. "Good night, Mr. Shed."

* * *

Shed: "It's set up. He'll meet me at my place ght. Alone. You bring your wagon. I'll make sure my ad isn't around."

"I hear Gilbert won't go anywhere without a bodyguard now."

"He will tonight. He's supposed to pay me ten leva to help get control of the Lily. I let him think he's going to get something else, too."

Shed's stomach growled. "What if he catches on?"

"There's two of us and one of him. How did such a chicken-shit manage everything you have?"

He had dealt with the lesser fear. But he kept that thought to himself. There was no point giving Lisa more handles than she had. It was time to find handles on her. "Aren't you scared of anything, child?"

"Poverty. Especially of being old and poor. I get the grey shakes whenever I see the Custodians haul some poor old stiff out of an alley."

"Yeah. That I can understand." Shed smiled thinly. That was a beginning.

Shed stopped the wagon, glanced at the window of a downstairs rear apartment. No candle burning there. Lisa hadn't yet arrived. He snapped the traces, rolled on. Gilbert might have scouts out. He was not stupid.

Shed pulled around a kink in the alleyway, strolled back pretending to be a drunk. Before long someone lighted a candle in the apartment. Heart hammering, Shed slunk to the rear door.

It was unlocked. As promised. Maybe Gilbert *was* stupid. Gently, he eased inside. His stomach was a mess of knots. His hands shook. A scream lay coiled in his throat.

This was not the Marron Shed who had fought Krage and his troops. That Shed had been trapped and fighting for his life. He had had no time to think himself into a panic. This Shed did. He was convinced he would foul up.

The apartment consisted of two tiny rooms. The first, behind the door, was dark and empty. Shed moved through carefully, eased to a ragged curtain. A man murmured beyond the doorway. Shed peeked.

Gilbert had disrobed and was resting a knee on a bedraggled excuse of a bed. Lisa was in it, covers pulled to her neck, pretending second thoughts. Gilbert's withered, wrinkled, blue-veined old body contrasted bizarrely with her youth.

Gilbert was angry.

Shed cursed mutely. He wished Lisa would stop playing games. Always she had to do more than go directly to her goal. She had to manipulate along the way, just to satisfy something within herself.

He wanted to get it over.

Lisa pretended surrender, made room for Gilbert beside her.

The plan was for Shed to strike once Lisa enwrapped Gilbert in arms and legs. He decided to play a game of his own. He let it wait. He stood there grinning while her face betrayed her thoughts, while Gilbert sated himself upon her.

Finally, Shed moved in.

Three quick, quiet steps. He looped a garotte around Gilbert's skinny neck, leaned back. Lisa tightened her grip. How small and mortal the moneylender appeared. How unlike a man feared by half the Buskin.

Gilbert struggled, but could not escape.

Shed thought it would never end. He hadn't realized it took so long to strangle a man. Finally, he stepped back. His shakes threatened to overcome him.

"Get him off!" Lisa squealed.

Shed rolled the corpse aside. "Get dressed. Come on. Let's get out of here. He might have some men hanging around. I'll get the wagon." He swept to the door, peeped into the alleyway. Nobody around. He recovered the wagon fast.

"Come on!" he snapped when he returned and found Lisa still undressed. "Let's get him out of here."

She could not tear herself away.

Shed shoved clothing into her arms, slapped her bare behind. "Get moving, damn it."

She dressed slowly. Shed fluttered to the door, checked the alley. Still no one around. He scooted back to the body, hustled it to the wagon and covered it with a tarp. Funny how they seemed lighter when they were dead.

Back inside: "Will you come on? I'll drag you out the way you are."

The threat had no effect. Shed grabbed her hand, dragged her out the door. "Up." He hoisted her onto the seat, jumped up himself.

He flicked the traces. The mules plodded forward. Once he crossed the Port River bridge, they knew where they were headed and needed little guidance. Idly, he wondered how many times they had made the journey.

The wagon was halfway up the hill before he calmed down enough to study Lisa. She seemed to be in shock. Suddenly, murder was not just talk. She had helped kill. Her neck was in a noose. "Not as easy as you thought, eh?"

"I didn't know it would be like that. I was holding him. I felt the life go out. It. . . . It wasn't what I expected."

"And you want to make a career of it. I'll tell you something. I'm not killing my customers. You want it done that way, you do it yourself."

She tried a feeble threat.

"You don't have any power over me anymore. Go to the Inquisitors. They'll take you to a truth-sayer. Partner."

Lisa shivered. Shed held his tongue till they neared the black castle. "Let's not play games anymore." He was considering selling her along with Gilbert, but decided he could not muster the hatred, anger or downright meanness to do it.

He stopped the mules. "You stay here. Don't get off the wagon no matter what. Understand?"

"Yes." Lisa's voice was small and distant. Terrified, he thought.

He knocked on the black gate. It swung inward. He resumed his seat and drove inside, stepped down, swung Gilbert onto a stone slab. The tall creature came forth, examined the body, looked at Lisa.

"Not this one," Shed said. "She's a new partner."

The creature nodded. "Thirty."

"Done."

"We need more bodies, Marron Shed. Many bodies. Our work is nearing completion. We grow eager to finish."

Shed shuddered at its tone. "There'll be more soon."

"Good. Very good. You shall be rewarded richly."

Shed shuddered again, looked around. The thing asked, "You seek the woman? She has not yet become one with the portal." It snapped long, yellow fingers.

Feet scuffed in the darkness. Shadows came forth. They held the arms of a naked Sue. Shed swallowed hard. She had been used badly. She had lost weight, and her skin was colorless where not marked with bruises or abrasions. One of the creatures raised her chin, made her look at Shed. Her eyes were hollow and vacant. "The walking dead," he whispered.

"Is the revenge sweet enough?" the tall creature asked.

"Take her away! I don't want to see her."

The tall being snapped its fingers. Its compatriots retreated into the shadows.

"My money!" Shed snarled.

Chuckling, the being counted coins at Gilbert's feet. Shed scooped them into his pocket. The being said, "Bring us more live ones, Marron Shed. We have many uses for live ones."

A scream echoed from the darkness. Shed thought he heard his name called.

"She recognized you, friend."

A whimper crawled out of Shed's throat. He vaulted onto the wagon seat, snarled at his mules.

The tall creature eyed Lisa with unmistakable meaning. Lisa read it. "Let's get out of here, Mr. Shed. Please?"

"Git up, mules." The wagon creaked and groaned and seemed to take forever getting through the gate. Screams continued echoing from somewhere deep inside the castle.

Outside, Lisa looked at Shed with a decidedly odd expression. Shed thought he detected relief, fear, and a little loathing. Relief seemed foremost. She sensed how vulnerable she had been. Shed smiled enigmatically, nodded, and said nothing. Like Raven, he recalled.

He grinned. Like Raven.

Let her think. Let her worry.

The mules halted. ''Eh?''

Men materialized out of the darkness. They held naked weapons. Military-type weapons.

A voice said, ''I'll be damned. It's the innkeeper.''

# Chapter Thirty: JUNIPER: MORE TROUBLE

Otto rolled in out of the night. "Hey! Croaker! We got a customer."

I folded my hand but did not throw the cards in. "You sure?" I was damned tired of false alarms.

Otto looked sheepish. "Yeah. For sure."

Something was wrong here. "Where is he? Let's have all of it."

"They're going to make it inside."

"They?"

"Man and a woman. We didn't think they were anything to worry about till they were past the last house and still headed uphill. It was too late to stop them then."

I slapped my hand down. I was pissed. There would be hell to pay in the morning. Whisper had had it up to her chin with me already. This might be her excuse to park me in the Catacombs. Permanently. The Taken are not patient.

"Let's go," I said in as calm a voice as I could manage, while glaring a hole through Otto. He made sure he stayed out of reach. He knew I was not pleased. Knew I was in a tight place with the Taken. He did not want to give me any excuse to wrap my hands around his neck. "I'm going to cut some throats if this gets screwed up again." We all grabbed weapons and rushed into the night.

We had our place picked, in brush two hundred yards

below the castle gate. I got the men into position just as somebody started screaming inside.

"Sounds bad," one of the men said.

"Keep it down," I snapped. Cold crept my spine. It did sound bad.

It went on and on and on. Then I heard the muted jangle of harness and the creak of wheels improperly greased. Then the voices of people talking softly.

We jumped out of the brush. One of the men opened the eye of a lantern. "I'll be damned!" I said. "It's the innkeeper."

The man sagged. The woman stared at us, eyes widening. Then she sprang off the wagon and ran.

"Get her, Otto. And heaven help you if you don't. Crake, drag this bastard down. Walleye, take the wagon around to the house. The rest of us will cut across."

The man Shed did not struggle, so I detailed another two men to help Otto. He and the woman were crashing through the brush. She was headed toward a small precipice. She should corner herself there.

We led Shed to the old house. Once in the light, he became more deflated, more resigned. He said nothing. Most captives resist detention somehow, if only by denying that there is any reason to detain them. Shed looked like a man who thought he was overdue for the worst.

"Sit," I said, and indicated a chair at the table where we had played cards. I took another, turned it, parked myself with forearms atop its back and chin upon my forearms. "We've got you dead, Shed."

He just stared at the tabletop, a man without hope.

"Anything to say?"

"There's nothing to be said, is there?"

"Oh, I think there's a whole lot. You've got your ass in a sling for sure, but you're not dead yet. You maybe could talk your way out of this."

His eyes widened slightly, then emptied again. He did not believe me.

"I'm not an Inquisitor, Shed."

His eyes flickered with momentary life.

"It's true. I followed Bullock around because he knew the Buskin. My job had very little to do with his. I couldn't care less about the Catacombs raid. I do care about the black castle, because it's a disaster in the making, but not as much as I care about you. Because of a man named Raven."

"One of your men called you Croaker. Raven was scared to death of somebody named Croaker that he saw one night when the Duke's men grabbed some of his friends."

So. He'd witnessed our raid. Damn, but I had cut it close to the wind that time.

"I'm that Croaker. And I want to know everything you know about Raven and Darling. And everything about anybody else who knows anything."

The slightest hint of defiance crossed his face.

"A lot of folks are looking for you, Shed. Bullock isn't the only one. My boss wants you, too. And she's worse trouble than he is. You wouldn't like her at all. And she'll get you if you don't do this right."

I would rather have given him to Bullock. Bullock wasn't interested in our problems with the Taken. But Bullock was out of town.

"There's Asa, too. I want to know everything you haven't told me about him." I heard the woman cursing in the distance, carrying on like Otto and the guys were trying to rape her. I knew better. They hadn't the nerve after having screwed up once already tonight. "Who's the slot?"

"My barmaid. She. . . ." And his story boiled out. Once he started, there was no stopping him.

I had a notion how to wriggle out of a potentially embarrassing situation. "Shut him up." One of the men clamped a hand over Shed's mouth. "Here's what we're going to do, Shed. Assuming you want out of this alive."

He waited.

"The people I work for will know a body was delivered tonight. They'll expect me to catch whoever did it. I'll have to give them someone. That could be you, the girl, or both of you. *You* know some things I don't want the Taken to find out. One way I can avoid handing you over is having you turn up dead. I can make that real if I have to. Or you can fake it for me. Let the slot see you looking like you've been wrecked. You follow?"

Shaking, he replied, "I think so."

"I want to know everything."

"The girl. . . ."

I held up a hand, listened. The uproar was close. "She won't come back from her meeting with the Taken. There's no reason we couldn't turn you loose once we're done doing what we have to do."

He did not believe me. He had committed crimes he believed deserved the harshest punishment, and he expected it.

"We're the Black Company, Shed. Juniper is going to get to know that real well soon. Including the fact that we keep our promises. But that's not important to you. Right now you want to stay alive long enough to get a break. That means you'd damned well better fake being dead, and do it better than any stiff you ever hauled up the hill."

"All right."

"Take him over by the fire and make him look like he's had it rough."

The men knew what to do. They sort of scattered Shed around without actually hurting him. I tossed a few things around to make it look like there had been a fight, and finished just in time.

The girl came sailing through the doorway, propelled by Otto's fist. She looked the worse for wear. So did Otto and the men I'd sent to help. "Wildcat, eh?"

Otto tried to grin. Blood leaked from the corner of his mouth. "Ain't the half of it, Croaker." He kicked the girl's feet from under her. "What happened to the guy?"

"Got a little feisty. I stuck a knife in him."

"I see."

We stared at the girl. She stared back, the fire gone. Each few seconds she glanced at Shed, looked back more subdued.

"Yep. You're in a heap of trouble, sweetheart."

She gave us the song-and-dance I'd expected from Shed. We ignored it, knowing it was bullshit. Otto cleaned up, then bound her hands and ankles. He parked her in a chair. I made sure it faced away from Shed. The poor bastard had to breathe.

I sat down opposite the girl and began to question her. Shed said he had told her almost everything. I wanted to know if she knew anything about Raven that could give him or us away.

I got no chance to find out.

There was a great rush of air around the house. A roar like a tornado passing. A crack like thunder.

Otto said it all. "Oh shit! Taken."

The door blew inward. I rose, stomach twisting, heart hammering. Feather came in looking like she'd just walked through a burning building. Wisps of smoke rose from her smouldering apparel.

"What the hell?" I asked.

"The castle. I got too close. They almost knocked me out of the sky. What have you got?"

I told my story quickly, not omitting the fact that we had allowed a corpse to get past. I indicated Shed. "One dead, trying to fight questioning. But this one is healthy." I indicated the girl.

Feather moved close to the girl. She had taken a real blast out there. I did not feel the aura of great power rigidly constrained that one usually senses in the presence of the Taken. And she did not sense the life still throbbing in Marron Shed. "So young." She lifted the girl's chin. "Oh. What eyes. Fire and steel. The Lady will love this one."

"We keep the watch?" I asked, assuming she would confiscate the prisoner.

"Of course. There may be others." She faced me. "No more will get through. The margin is too narrow. Whisper will forgive the latest. But the next is your doom."

"Yes, ma'am. Only it's hard to do and not attract the attention of the locals. We can't just go set up a roadblock."

"Why not?"

I explained. She had scouted the black castle and knew the lay of the land. "You're right. For the moment. But your Company will be here soon. There'll be no need for secrecy then."

"Yes, ma'am."

Feather took the girl's hand. "Come," she said.

I was amazed at how docilely our hellcat followed Feather. I went outside and watched Feather's battered carpet rise and hurry toward Duretile. One despairing cry floated in its wake.

I found Shed in the doorway when I turned to go inside. I wanted to smack him for that, but controlled myself.

"Who was *that*?" he asked. "'*What* was that?"

"Feather. One of the Taken. One of my bosses."

"Sorceress?"

"One of the greatest. Go sit. Let's talk. I need to know exactly what that girl knows about Raven and Darling."

Intense questioning convinced me that Lisa did not know enough to arouse Whisper's suspicions. Unless she connected the name Raven with the man who had helped capture her years ago.

I continued grilling Shed till first light. He practically begged to tell every filthy detail of his story. He had a big need to confess. Over coming days, when I sneaked down to the Buskin, he revealed everything recorded where he appears as the focal character. I do not think I have met many men who disgusted me more. Nastier men, yes. I have encountered scores. Greater villains come by the battalion. Shed's leavening of self-pity and cowardice reduced him from those categories to an essentially pathetic level.

Poor dolt. He was born to be used.

And yet. . . . There was one guttering spark in Marron Shed, reflected in his relationships with his mother, Raven, Asa, Lisa, Sal, and Darling, that he noted but did not recognize himself. He had a hidden streak of charity and decency. It was the gradual growth of that spark, with its eventual impact upon the Black Company, which makes me feel obligated to record all the earlier noxious details about that frightened little man.

The morning following his capture, I rode into the city in Shed's wagon and allowed him to open the Iron Lily as usual. During the morning I got Elmo and Goblin in for a conference. Shed was unsettled when he discovered that we all knew one another. Only through sheer luck had he not been taken earlier.

Poor fellow. The grilling never ceased. Poor us. He could not tell us everything we wanted to know.

"What are we going to do about the girl's father?" Elmo asked.

"If there is a letter, we've got to grab it," I replied. "We can't have anybody stirring up more problems. Goblin, you take care of the papa. He's even a little suspicious, see he has a heart attack."

Sourly, Goblin nodded. He asked Shed for the father's whereabouts, departed. And returned within half an hour. "A great tragedy. He didn't have a letter. She was bluffing. But he did know too much that would come out under questioning. This business is beginning to get to me. Hunting Rebels was cleaner. You knew who was who and where you stood."

"I'd better get back up the hill. The Taken might not be understanding about me being down here. Elmo, better keep somebody in Shed's pocket."

"Right. Pawnbroker lives there from now on. That clown takes a crap, he's holding his hand."

Goblin looked remote and thoughtful. "Raven buying a ship. Imagine that. What do you figure he was going to do?"

"I think he wanted to head straight out to sea," I said. "I hear there're islands out there, way out. Maybe another continent. A guy could hide pretty good out there."

I went back up the hill and loafed for two days, except to slip off and get everything I could out of Shed. Not a damned thing happened. Nobody else tried to make a delivery. I guess Shed was the only fool in the body business.

Sometimes I looked at those grim black battlements and wondered. They had taken a crack at Feather. Somebody in there knew the Taken meant trouble. How long before they realized they had been cut off and did something to get the meat supply moving again?

# Chapter Thirty-One: JUNIPER: THE RETURN

Shed was still rattled two days after his capture. Each time he looked across the common room and saw one of those Black Company bastards, he started falling apart again. He was living on borrowed time. He was not sure what use they had for him, but he was sure that when he was used up, they would dump him with the garbage. Some of his babysitters clearly thought him trash. He could not refute their viewpoint in his own mind.

He was behind his counter, washing mugs, when Asa walked through the door. He dropped a mug.

Asa met his eye for only an instant, sidled around the L and headed upstairs. Shed took a deep breath and followed. The man called Pawnbroker was a step behind when he reached the head of the stair, moving as silent as death. He had a knife ready for business.

Shed stepped into what had been Raven's room. Pawnbroker remained outside. "What the hell are you doing here, Asa? The Inquisitors are after you. About that Catacombs business. Bullock himself went south looking for you."

"Easy, Shed. I know. He caught up with us. It got hairy. We left him cut up, but he'll mend. And he'll come back looking for you. I came to warn you. You've got to get out of Juniper."

"Oh, no," Shed said softly. Another tooth in the jaws of fate. "Been considering that anyway." That would not tell Pawnbroker anything he could not guess for himself. "Things have gotten rotten here. I've started looking for a buyer." Not true, but he would before day's end.

For some reason Asa's return restored his heart. Maybe just because he felt he had an ally, somebody who shared his troubles.

Most of the story poured out. Pawnbroker did not take exception. He did not make an appearance.

Asa had changed. He did not seem shocked. Shed asked why not.

"Because I spent so much time with Raven. He told me stories that would curl your hair. About the days before he came to Juniper."

"How is he?"

"Dead."

"Dead?" Shed gasped.

"What?" Pawnbroker bulled through the doorway. "Did you say Raven was dead?"

Asa looked at Pawnbroker, at Shed, at Pawnbroker again. "Shed, you bastard. . . ."

"You shut up, Asa," Shed snapped. "You haven't got the faintest what's happened while you were gone. Pawnbroker is a friend. Sort of."

"Pawnbroker, eh? Like from the Black Company?"

Pawnbroker's eyebrows rose. "Raven been talking?"

"He had some tales about the old days."

"Uh-huh. Right, buddy. That's me. Let's get back to Raven being dead."

Asa looked at Shed. Shed nodded. "Tell us."

"Okay. I don't really know what happened. We were clearing out after our mix-up with Bullock. Running. His hired thugs caught us by surprise. We're hiding in some woods outside of town when all of a sudden he starts screaming and jumping around. It don't make no sense to me." Asa shook his head. His face was pale and sweaty.

"Go on," Shed urged gently.

"Shed, I don't know."

"What?" Pawnbroker demanded.

"I don't know. I didn't hang around."

Shed grimaced. That was the Asa he knew.

"You're a real buddy, fellow," Pawnbroker said.

"Look. . . ."

Shed motioned for silence.

Asa said, "Shed, you've got to get out of Juniper. Fast. Any day a ship could bring a letter from Bullock."

"But. . . ."

"It's better down there than we thought, Shed. You got money; you're all right. They don't care about the Catacombs. Think it was a big joke on the Custodians. That's how Bullock found us. Everybody was laughing about the raid. There was even some guys talking about getting up an expedition to come clean them out."

"How did anybody find out about the Catacombs, Asa? Only you and Raven knew."

Asa looked abashed.

"Yeah. Thought so. Had to brag, didn't you?" He was confused and frightened and starting to take it out on Asa. He did not know what to do. He had to get out of Juniper, like Asa said. But how to give his watchdogs the slip? Especially when they knew he had to try?

"There's a ship at the Tulwar dock that leaves for Meadenval in the morning, Shed. I had the Captain hold passage for two. Should I tell him you'll be there, too?"

Pawnbroker stepped into position to block the doorway. "Neither one of you will be there. Some friends of mine want to talk to you."

"Shed, what is this?" Panic edged Asa's voice.

Shed looked at Pawnbroker. The mercenary nodded. Shed poured out most everything. Asa did not understand. Shed did not himself, because his chaperones had not told him everything, so there was some sense missing from the picture he had.

Pawnbroker was alone at the Lily. Shed suggested, "How about I go get Goblin?"

Pawnbroker smiled. "How about we just wait?"

"But. . . ."

"Somebody will turn up. We'll wait. Let's go downstairs.

You." He indicated Asa with his blade. "Don't get any funny ideas."

Shed said, "Be careful, Asa. These are the guys Raven was scared of."

"I will. I heard enough from Raven."

"That's a pity, too," Pawnbroker said. "Croaker and Elmo aren't going to like that. Down, gents. Shed, just go on about your business."

"Somebody's liable to recognize Asa," Shed warned.

"We'll take a chance. Git." Pawnbroker stood aside and allowed both men to pass. Downstairs, he seated Asa at the shadowiest table and joined him, cleaning his nails with his knife. Asa watched in fascination. Seeing ghosts, Shed figured.

He could get away now if he wanted to sacrifice Asa. They wanted Asa more than they wanted him. If he just headed out through the kitchen, Pawnbroker would not come after him.

His sister-in-law came from the kitchen, a platter balanced on each hand. "When you get a minute, Sal." And when she got the minute: "You think you and the kids could run the place for me for a few weeks?"

"Sure. Why?" She looked puzzled. But she glanced quickly into the shadows.

"I might have to go somewhere for a while. I'd feel better if I knew somebody in the family was running the place. I don't really trust Lisa."

"You haven't heard from her yet?"

"No. You'd have thought she'd turn up when her father died, wouldn't you?"

"Maybe she's shacked up somewhere and hasn't heard yet." Sal did not sound convinced. In fact, Shed suspected, she thought he had something to do with the disappearance. Way too many people had disappeared around him. He was afraid she would do her sums and decide he had had something to do with Wally disappearing, too.

"There's one rumor I heard said she got arrested. Keep an eye out for Mom. She's got good people taking care of her, but they need supervising."

"Where are you going, Marron?"

"I don't know yet." He was afraid it might be just a way up the hill, to the Enclosure. If not that, then certainly somewhere, away from everything that had happened here. Away from these merciless men and their even less merciful employers. Have to talk to Asa about the Taken. Maybe Raven had told him something.

He wished he could get a moment with Asa to plan something. The two of them making a break. But not on the Tulwar ship. Asa had mentioned that, damn him. Some other ship, headed south.

What had become of Raven's big new vessel? And Darling?

He went over to the table. "Asa. What happened to Darling?"

Asa reddened. He stared at his folded hands. "I don't know, Shed. Honest. I panicked. I just ran for the first ship headed north."

Shed walked away, shaking his head in disgust. Leaving the girl alone like that. Asa hadn't changed much after all.

The one called Goblin came through the door. He began to beam at Asa before Pawnbroker said anything. "My, my, my, my, my," he said. "Is this who I think it is, Pawn?"

"You got it. The infamous Asa himself, home from the wars. And does he have stories to tell."

Goblin seated himself opposite Asa. He wore a big frog grin. "Such as?"

"Mainly, he claims Raven is dead."

Goblin's smile vanished. In an eye's blink he became deadly serious. He made Asa tell his story again while staring into a mug of wine. When he finally looked up, he was subdued. "Better talk this over with Elmo and Croaker. Good job, Pawnbroker. I'll take him. Keep your eye on friend Shed."

Shed winced. In the back of his head had lain the small hope that both would leave with Asa.

His mind was made up. He would flee at the first

opportunity. Get south, change his name, use his gold pieces to buy into an inn, behave himself so thoroughly nobody would notice him ever again.

Asa showed a spark of rebellion. "Who the hell do you guys think you are? Suppose I don't want to go anywhere?"

Goblin smiled nastily, muttered something under his breath. Dark brown smoke drifted out of his mug, illuminated by a bloody inner glow. Goblin stared at Asa. Asa stared at the mug, unnerved.

The smoke coalesced, formed a small, headlike shape. Points began glowing where eyes might be. Goblin said, "My little friend *wants* you to argue. He feeds on pain. And he hasn't eaten for a long time. I've had to keep a low profile in Juniper."

Asa's eyes kept getting bigger. So did Shed's. Sorcery! He had sensed it in the thing called the Taken, but that had not upset him much. It had been removed, not experienced. Something that had happened to Lisa, out of sight. But this. . . .

It was a minor sorcery, to be sure. Some slight trick. But it was sorcery in a city which saw none other than that involved in the slow growth of the black castle. The dark arts hadn't gained any following in Juniper.

"All right," Asa said. "All right." His voice was high and thin and squeaky, and he was trying to push his chair back. Pawnbroker prevented him.

Goblin grinned. "I see Raven mentioned Goblin. Good. You'll behave. Come along."

Pawnbroker released Asa's chair. The little man followed Goblin docilely.

Shed sidled over and looked into Goblin's mug. Nothing. He frowned. Pawnbroker grinned. "Cute trick, eh?"

"Yeah." Shed took the mug to his sink. When Pawnbroker was not looking, he dropped it into the trash. He was more scared than ever. How did he get away from a sorcerer?

His head filled with tales he had heard from southern sailors. Bad business, wizards were.

He wanted to weep.

# Chapter Thirty-Two: JUNIPER: VISITORS

Goblin brought me the man Asa, and insisted we wait for Elmo before questioning him. He had sent someone to dig Elmo out of Duretile, where he was trying to placate Whisper. Whisper was getting goosed by the Lady regular and taking it out on anyone handy.

Goblin was unsettled by what he had learned. He did not play the usual game and try to make me guess what was going on. He blurted, "Asa says him and Raven had a run-in with Bullock. Raven is dead. He lit out. Darling is on her own down there."

Excitement? Better believe it. I was ready to put the little man to the question, then and there. But I controlled myself.

Elmo was a while showing up. Goblin and I got damned antsy before he did, while Asa worked himself up for a stroke.

The wait proved worthwhile. Elmo did not come alone.

The first hint was a faint but sour odor that seemed to come from the fireplace, where I'd had a small fire lighted. Just in case, you know. With a few iron rods set by, ready to be heated, so Asa could look them over and think, and maybe convince himself he ought not to leave anything out.

"What's that smell?" somebody asked. "Croaker, you let that cat in again?"

"I kicked him out after he sprayed my boots," I said.

"Like halfway down the hill. Maybe he got the firewood before he left."

The odor grew stronger. It wasn't really obnoxious, just mildly irritating. We took turns examining the firewood. Nothing.

I was in the middle of a third search for the source when the fire caught my eye. For a second I saw a face in the flames.

My heart nearly stopped. For half a minute I was in a panic, nothing but the face's presence having registered. I considered every evil that could happen: Taken watching, the Lady watching, the things from the black castle, maybe the Dominator himself peeking through our fire. . . . Then something calm, back in the far marches of mind, reiterated something I hadn't noticed because I had no reason to expect it. The face in the flames had had only one eye.

"One-Eye," I said without thinking. "That little bastard is in Juniper."

Goblin spun toward me, eyes wide. He sniffed the air. His famous grin split his face. "You're right, Croaker. Absolutely right. That stink is the little skunk himself. Should have recognized it straight off."

I glanced at the fire. The face did not reappear.

Goblin mused, "What would be a suitable welcome?"

"Figure the Captain sent him?"

"Probably. Be logical to send him or Silent ahead."

"Do me a favor, Goblin."

"What?"

"Don't give him no special welcome."

Goblin looked deflated. It had been a long time. He did not want to miss an opportunity to refresh his acquaintance with One-Eye with a flash and a bang.

"Look," I said. "He's here on the sneak. We don't want the Taken to know. Why give them anything to sniff out?"

Bad choice of words. The smell was about to drive us outside.

"Yeah," Goblin grumbled. "Wish the Captain had sent

Silent. I was all worked up for this. Had him the biggest surprise of his life."

"So get him later. Meantime, why not clear this smell out? Why not get his goat by just ignoring him?"

He thought about it. His eyes gleamed. "Yeah," he said, and I knew he had shaped my suggestion to his own warped sense of humor.

A fist hammered on the door. It startled me even though I was expecting it. One of the men let Elmo in.

One-Eye came in behind Elmo, grinning like a little black mongoose about to eat snake. We paid him no heed. Because the Captain came in behind him.

The Captain! The last man I expected to reach Juniper before the Company itself.

"Sir?" I blurted. "What the hell are *you* doing here?"

He lumbered to the fire, extended his hands. Summer had begun to fade, but it was not that cold. He was as bear-like as ever, though he had lost weight and aged. It had been a hard march indeed.

"Stork," he replied.

I frowned, looked at Elmo. Elmo shrugged, said, "I sent Stork with the message."

The Captain expanded, "Stork didn't make any sense. What's this about Raven?"

Raven, of course, had been his closest friend before deserting. I began to get a glimmer.

I indicated Asa. "This guy was in the thick of it from the beginning. Been Raven's sidekick. He says Raven is dead, down. . . . What's the name of that place, Asa?"

Asa stared at the Captain and One-Eye and swallowed about six times without being able to say anything. I told the Captain, "Raven told stories about us that turned his hair grey."

"Let's hear the story," the Captain said. He was looking at Asa.

So Asa told his tale for the third time, while Goblin hovered, listening for the clunk of untruth. He ignored One-Eye in the most masterful show of ignoring I've ever seen. And all for nought.

The Captain dropped Asa completely the moment he finished his tale. A matter of style, I think. He wanted the information to percolate before he trotted it out for reexamination. He had me review everything I had experienced since arriving in Juniper. I presumed he had gotten Elmo's story already.

I finished. He observed, "You're too suspicious of the Taken. The Limper has been with us all along. He doesn't act like there's anything up." If anyone had a cause for malice toward us, the Limper did.

"Nevertheless," I said, "there're wheels within wheels within wheels with the Lady and the Taken. Maybe they didn't tell him anything because they figured he couldn't keep it secret."

"Maybe," the Captain admitted. He shuffled around, occasionally gave Asa a puzzled look. "Whatever, let's not get Whisper wondering any more than she is. Play it close. Pretend you're not suspicious. Do your job. One-Eye and his boys will be around to back you up."

Sure, I thought. Against the Taken? "If the Limper is with the Company, how did you get away? If he knows you're gone, the word will be out to the Lady, won't it?"

"He shouldn't find out. We haven't spoken in months. He stays to himself. Bored, I think."

"What about the Barrowland?" I was primed to find out everything that had happened during the Company's long trek, for I had nothing in the Annals concerning the majority of my comrades. But it was not yet time to exhume details. Just to feel for high points.

"We never saw it," the Captain said. "According to the Limper, Journey and the Lady are working that end. We can expect a major move as soon as we have Juniper under control."

"We haven't done squat to prepare," I said. "The Taken kept us busy fussing about the black castle."

"Ugly place, isn't it?" He looked us over. "I think you might've gotten more done had you not been so paranoid."

"Sir?"

"Most of your trail-covering strikes me as needless and

a waste of time. The problem was Raven's, not yours. And he solved it in typical fashion. Without help." He glared at Asa. "In fact, the problem seems solved for all time."

He had not been here and had not felt the pressures, but I did not mention that. Instead, I asked, "Goblin, you figure Asa is telling the truth?"

Warily, Goblin nodded.

"How about you, One-Eye? You catch any false notes?"

The little black man responded with a cautious negative.

"Asa. Raven should have had a bunch of papers with him. He ever mention them?"

Asa looked puzzled. He shook his head.

"He have a trunk or something that he wouldn't let anybody near?"

Asa seemed baffled by the direction my questions had taken. The others did too. Only Silent knew about those papers. Silent, and maybe Whisper, who had possessed them once herself.

"Asa? Anything he treated unusually?"

A light dawned in the little man's mind. "There was a crate. About the size of a coffin. I remember making a joke about it. He said something cryptic about it being somebody's ticket to the grave."

I grinned. The papers still existed. "What did he do with that crate down there?"

"I don't know."

"Asa. . . ."

"Honest. I only saw it a couple times on the ship. I never thought anything about it."

"What are you getting at, Croaker?" the Captain asked.

"I have a theory. Just based on what I know about Raven and Asa."

Everyone frowned.

"Generally, what we know about Asa suggests he's a character Raven wouldn't take up with on a bet. He's chicken. Unreliable. Too talkative. But Raven *did* take up with him. Took him south and made him part of the team. Why? Maybe that don't bother you guys, but it does me."

"I don't follow you," the Captain said.

"Suppose Raven wanted to disappear so people wouldn't even bother looking for him? He tried to vanish once, by coming to Juniper. But we turned up. Looking for him, he thought. So what next? How about he dies? In front of a witness. People don't hunt for dead men."

Elmo interrupted. "You saying he staged his death and used Asa to report it so nobody would come looking?"

"I'm saying we ought to consider the possibility."

The Captain's sole response was a thoughtful, "Uhm."

Goblin said, "But Asa did see him die."

"Maybe. And maybe he only thinks he did."

We all looked at Asa. He cowered. The Captain said, "Take him through his story again, One-Eye. Step-by-step."

For two hours One-Eye dragged the little man through again and again. And we could not spot one flaw. Asa insisted he had seen Raven die, devoured from within by something snake-like. And the more my theory sprung leaks, the more I was sure it was valid.

"My case depends on Raven's character," I insisted, when everybody ganged up on me. "There's the crate, and there's Darling. Her and a damned expensive ship that he, for godsakes, had built. He left a trail going out of here, and he knew it. Why sail a few hundred miles and tie up to a dock when somebody is going to come looking? Why leave Shed alive behind you, to tell about you being in on the raid on the Catacombs? And there's no way in hell he'd leave Darling twisting in the wind. Not for a minute. He would have had arrangements made for her. You know that." My arguments were beginning to sound a little strained to me, too. I was in the position of a priest trying to sell religion. "But Asa says they just left her hanging around some inn. I tell you, Raven had a plan. I bet, if you went down there now, you'd find Darling gone without a trace. And if the ship is still there, that crate wouldn't be aboard."

"What is this with the crate?" One-Eye demanded. I ignored him.

"I think you have too much imagination, Croaker," the

Captain said. "But, on the other hand, Raven is crafty enough to pull something like that. Soon as I can spring you, figure on going down to check."

"If Raven's crafty enough, how about the Taken being villainous enough to try something against us?"

"We'll cross that bridge when we come to it." He faced One-Eye. "I want you and Goblin to save the games. Understand? Too much clowning around and the Taken will get curious. Croaker. Hang on to this Asa character. You'll want him to show you where Raven died. I'm heading back to the outfit. Elmo. Come ride with me part way."

So. A little private business. Bet it had to do with my suspicions about the Taken. After a while you get so used to some people you can almost read their minds.

# Chapter Thirty-Three: JUNIPER: THE ENCOUNTER

Things changed after the Captain's visit. The men became more alert. Elmo's influence waxed while mine waned. A less wishy-washy, more inflexible tone characterized the Company deputation. Every man became ready to move at an instant's notice.

Communications improved dramatically while time available for sleep declined painfully. None of us were ever out of touch more than two hours. And Elmo found excuses to get everyone but himself out of Duretile, into places where the Taken would have trouble finding them. Asa became my ward out on the black castle slope.

Tension mounted. I felt like one of a flock of chickens poised to scatter the moment a fox landed among us. I tried to bleed off my shakiness by updating the Annals. I had let them slide sadly, seldom having done more than keep notes.

When the tension became too much for me, I walked uphill to stare at the black castle.

It was an intentional risk-taking, like that of a child who crawls out a tree branch overhanging a deadly fall. The closer I approached the castle, the more narrow my concentration. At two hundred yards all other cares vanished. I felt the dread of that place down to my ankle bones and the shallows of my soul. At two hundred yards I felt what it meant to have the shadow of the Dominator overhanging the world. I felt what the Lady felt when she considered her husband's potential resurrection. Every emotion became edged with a hint of despair.

In a way, the black castle was more than a gateway through which the world's great old evil might reappear. It was a concretization of metaphorical concepts, and a living symbol. It did things a great cathedral does. Like a cathedral, it was far more than an edifice.

I could stare at its obsidian walls and grotesque decoration, recall Shed's stories, and never avoid dipping into the cesspool of my own soul, never avoid searching myself for the essential decency shelved through most of my adult life. That castle was, if you like, a moral landmark.If you had a brain. If you had any sensitivity at all.

There were times when One-Eye, Goblin, Elmo or another of the men accompanied me. Not one of them went away untouched. They could stand there with me, talking trivialities about its construction or, weightily, about its significance in the Company's future, and all the while something would be happening inside.

I do not believe in evil absolute. I have recounted that philosophy in specific elsewhere in the Annals, and it affects my every observation throughout my tenure as Annalist. I believe in our side and theirs, with the good and evil decided after the fact, by those who survive. Among men you seldom find the good with one standard and the shadow with another. In our war with the Rebel, eight and nine years ago, we served the side perceived as the shadow. Yet we saw far more wickedness practiced by the adherents of the White Rose than by those of the Lady. The villains of the piece were at least straightforward.

The world knows where it stands with the Lady. It is the Rebel whose ideals and morals conflict with fact, becoming as changeable as the weather and as flexible as a snake.

But I digress. The black castle has that effect. Makes you amble off into all the byways and cul-de-sacs and false trails you have laid down during your life. It makes you reassess. Makes you *want* to take a stand somewhere, even if on the black side. Leaves you impatient with your own malleable morality.

I suspect that is why Juniper decided to pretend the place did not exist. It is an absolute demanding absolutes in a world with a preference for relatives.

Darling was in my thoughts often while I stood below those black, glossy walls, for she was the castle's antipode when I was up there. The white pole, and absolute in opposition to what the black castle symbolized. I had not been much in her presence since realizing what she was, but I could recall being morally unnerved by her, too. I wondered how she would affect me now, after having had years to grow.

From what Shed said, she did not reek the way the castle did. His main interest in her had been hustling her upstairs. And Raven had not been driven into puritanical channels. If anything, he had slipped farther into the darkness—though for the highest of motives.

Possibly there was a message there. An observation upon means to ends. Here was Raven who had acted with the pragmatic amorality of a prince of Hell, all so he could save the child who represented the best hope of the world against the Lady and the Dominator.

Oh, 'twould be marvelous if the world and its moral questions were like some game board, with plain black players and white, and fixed rules, and nary a shade of grey.

Even Asa and Shed could be made to feel the aura of the castle if you took them up during the daytime and made them stand there looking at those fell walls.

Shed especially.

Shed had achieved a position where he could afford conscience and uncertainty. I mean, he had none of the financial troubles that had plagued him earlier, and no prospect of digging himself a hole with us watching him, so he could reflect upon his place in things and become disgusted with himself. More than once I took him up and watched as that deep spark of hidden decency flared, twisted him upon a rack of inner torment.

* * *

I do not know how Elmo did it. Maybe he went without sleep for a few weeks. But when the Company came down out of the Wolanders, he had an occupation plan prepared. It was crude, to be sure, but better than any of us expected.

I was in the Buskin, at Shed's Iron Lily, when the first rumors raged down the waterfront and stirred one of the most massive states of confusion I've ever seen. Shed's wood-seller neighbor swept into the Lily, announced, "There's an army coming down out of the pass! Foreigners! Thousands of them! They say. . . ."

During the following hour a dozen patrons brought the news. Each time the army was larger and its purpose more obscure. Nobody knew what the Company wanted. Various witnesses assigned motives according to their own fears. Few came anywhere near the mark.

Though the men were weary after so long a march, they spread through the city quickly, the larger units guided by Elmo's men. Candy brought a reinforced company into the Buskin. The worst slums are always the first site of rebellion, we've found. There were few violent confrontations. Juniper's citizens were taken by surprise and had no idea what to fight about anyway. Most just turned out to watch.

I got myself back up to my squad. This was the time the Taken would do their deed. If they planned anything.

Nothing happened. As I might have guessed, knowing that men from our forerunner party were guiding the new arrivals. Indeed, nobody got in touch with me, up there, for another two days. By then the city was pacified. Every key point was in our hands. Every state building, every arsenal, every strong point, even the Custodians' headquarters in the Enclosure. And life went on as usual. What little trouble there was came when Rebel refugees tried to start an uprising, accurately accusing the Duke of having brought the Lady to Juniper.

The people of Juniper didn't much care.

There were problems in the Buskin, though. Elmo wanted to straighten the slum out. Some of the slum dwellers didn't want to be straightened. He used Candy's company forcefully, cracking the organizations of the crime bosses. I did not see the necessity, but wiser heads feared the gangs could become the focus of future resistance. Anything with that potential had to be squashed immediately. I think there was a hope the move would win popular favor, too.

Elmo brought the Lieutenant to my hillside shack the third day after the Company's arrival. "How goes it?" I asked. The Lieutenant had aged terribly since I had seen him last. The passage westward had been grim.

"City's secure," he said. "Stinking dump, isn't it?"

"Better believe. It's all snake's belly. What's up?"

Elmo said, "He needs a look at the target."

I lifted an eyebrow.

The Lieutenant said, "The Limper says we're going to take this place. I don't know how soon. Captain wants me to look it over."

"Fun times tomorrow," I muttered. "Ain't going to grab it on the sneak." I donned my coat. It was chilly up on the slopes. Elmo and One-Eye tagged along when I took the Lieutenant up. He eyeballed the castle, deep in thought. Finally, he said, "I don't like it. Not even a little bit." He felt the cold dread of the place.

"I got a man who's been inside," I said. "But don't let the Taken know. He's supposed to be dead."

"What can he tell me?"

"Not much. He's only been there at night, in a court behind the gate."

"Uhm. The Taken have a girl up at Duretile, too. I talked to her. She couldn't tell me nothing. Only in there once, and was too scared to look around."

"She's still alive?"

"Yeah. That's the one you caught? Yeah. She's alive. Lady's orders, apparently. Nasty little witch. Let's hike around it."

We got onto the far slope, where the going was rough, to the accompaniment of constant crabbing by One-Eye. The Lieutenant stated the obvious. "No getting at it from here. Not without help from the Taken."

"Going to take a big lot of help to get at it from any direction."

He looked me a question.

I told him about Feather's troubles the night we took Shed and his barmaid.

"Anything since?"

"Nope. Not before, either. My man who's been inside never saw anything extraordinary, either. But, dammit, the thing connects with the Barrowland. It's got the Dominator behind it. You *know* it's not going to be a pushover. They know there's trouble out here."

One-Eye made a squeaking sound. "What?" the Lieutenant snapped.

One-Eye pointed. We all looked up the wall, which loomed a good sixty feet above us. I did not see anything. Neither did the Lieutenant. "What?" he asked again.

"Something was watching us. Nasty-looking critter."

"I saw it too," Elmo volunteered. "Long, skinny, yellowish guy with eyes like a snake."

I considered the wall. "How could you tell from here?"

Elmo shivered and shrugged. "I could. And I didn't like it. Looked like he wanted to bite me." We dragged on through brush and over boulders, keeping one eye on the castle, the other on the down slope. Elmo muttered, "Hungry eyes. That's what they were."

We reached the ridgeline west of the castle. The Lieutenant paused. "How close can you get?"

I shrugged. "I haven't had the balls to fina out."

The Lieutenant moved here, there, as if sighting on something. "Let's bring up some prisoners and find out."

I sucked spittle between my teeth, then said, "You won't get the locals anywhere near the place."

"Think not? How about in exchange for a pardon? Candy's rounded up half the villains in the Buskin. Got a regular anti-crime crusade going. He gets three complaints about somebody, he nabs them."

"Sounds a little simple," I said. We were moving around for a look at the castle gate. By simple I meant simplistic, not easy.

The Lieutenant chuckled. Months of hardship had not sapped his bizarre sense of humor. "Simple minds respond to simple answers. A few months of Candy's reforms and the Duke will be a hero."

I understood the reasoning. Juniper was a lawless city, ruled by regional strongmen. There were hordes of Sheds who lived in terror, continuously victimized. Anyone who lessened the terror would win their affection. Adequately developed, that affection would survive later excesses.

I wondered, though, if the support of weaklings was worth much. Or if, should we successfully infect them with courage, we might not be creating trouble for ourselves later. Take away daily domestic oppression and they might imagine oppression on our part.

I have seen it before. Little people have to hate, have to blame someone for their own inadequacies.

But that was not the problem of the moment. The moment demanded immediate, vigorous, violent attention.

The castle gate popped open as we came in line. A half-dozen wild beings in black rushed us. A fog of lethargy settled upon me, and I found fear fading the moment it sparked into existence. By the time they were halfway to us, all I wanted was to lie down.

Pain filled my limbs. My head ached. Cramps knotted my stomach. The lethargy vanished.

One-Eye was doing strange things, dancing, yelping like a wolf pup, throwing his hands around like wounded birds. His big, weird hat flew off and tumbled with the breeze, downhill, till it became tangled in the brush. Between yelps he snapped, "Do something, you idiots! I can't hold them forever."

*Shang!* Elmo's sword cleared its scabbard. The Lieutenant's did the same. I was carrying nothing but a long dagger. I whipped it out and joined the rush. The castle creatures stood frozen, surprise in their ophidian eyes. The Lieutenant reached them first, stopped, wound up, took a mighty two-handed swing.

He lugs a hanger that is damned near an executioner's sword. A blow like that would have severed the necks of three men. It did not remove the head of his victim, though it did bite deep. Blood sprayed the three of us.

Elmo went with a thrust, as did I. His sword drove a foot into his victim. My dagger felt like it had hit soft wood. It sank but three inches into my victim. Probably not deeply enough to reach anything vital.

I yanked my blade free, poked around in my medical knowledge for a better killing point. Elmo kicked his victim in the chest to get his weapon free.

The Lieutenant had the best weapon and approach. He hacked another neck while we diddled around.

Then One-Eye lost it. The eyes of the castle creatures came alive. Pure fiery venom burned there. I feared the two not yet harmed would swarm all over us. But the Lieutenant threw a wild stroke and they retreated. The one I had wounded staggered after them. He fell before he reached the gate. He kept crawling. The gate closed in his face.

"So," the Lieutenant said. "There's a few lads we don't have to face later. My commendation, One-Eye." He spoke calmly enough, but his voice was up in the squeak range. His hands shook. It had been close. We would not have survived had One-Eye not come along. "I think I've seen enough for today. Let's hike."

Ninety percent of me wanted to run as fast as I could. Ten percent stuck to business. "Let's drag one of these bastards along," it croaked out of a mouth dry with fear.

"What the hell for?" Elmo demanded.

"So I can carve it up and see what it is."

"Yeah." The Lieutenant squatted and grabbed a body under the arms. It struggled feebly. Shuddering, I took hold of booted feet and hoisted. The creature folded in the middle.

"Hell with that," the Lieutenant said. He dropped his end, joined me. "You pull that leg. I'll pull this one."

We pulled. The body slid sideways. We started bickering about who should do what.

"You guys want to stop crapping around?" One-Eye snarled. He stabbed a wrinkled black finger. I looked back. Creatures had appeared on the battlements. I felt an increase in the dread the castle inspired.

"Something's happening," I said, and headed downhill, never letting go of the body. The Lieutenant came along. Our burden took a beating going through the rock and brush.

*Wham!* Something hit the slope like the stamp of a giant's foot. I felt like a roach fleeing a man who hated cockroaches and had his stomping boots on. There was another stamp, more earth-shaking.

"Oh, shit," Elmo said. He came past me, arms and legs pumping. One-Eye was right behind him, flying low, gaining ground. Neither offered to help.

A third thump, and a fourth, about equally spaced in time, each closer than the last. The last sent chunks of stone and dead brush arcing overhead.

Fifty yards down-slope One-Eye halted, whirled, did one of his magic things. A chunk of pale blue fire exploded in his upraised hands, went roaring up the hill, moaning past me less than a foot away. The Lieutenant and I passed One-Eye. A fifth giant stomp spattered our backs with shards of rock and brush.

One-Eye let out a mad howl and ran again. He yelled, "That was my best shot. Better dump that clown and scatter." He pulled away, bounding like a hare fleeing hounds.

A scream filled the valley of the Port. A pair of dots came hurtling over from the southern slope, almost too fast for the eye to follow. They passed over with a hollow, deep roar, and boomed like a god's drum behind us. I was not sure, but it seemed the dots were connected.

Another pair appeared, revolving about a common center. I got a better look. Yes, they were connected. They roared. They boomed. I glanced back. The face of the black castle had vanished behind a wall of color like paint thrown against, then running down, a pane of glass to which it would not adhere.

"Taken are on the job," the Lieutenant panted. His eyes were wild, but he clung to his side of our burden.

The damned creature got hung up. Panicky, we hacked

its clothing free from a thorn bush. I kept looking up, expecting something to come down and smash us all over the slope.

Another pair of balls arrived, spraying color. They did no obvious harm, but kept the castle occupied.

We freed our booty, hurried on.

A different sort of dot pair came, dropping from high above. I pointed. "Feather and Whisper." The Taken plunged toward the black castle, preceded by a high-pitched shriek. Fire enveloped the castle wall. Obsidian seemed to melt and run like candle wax, shifting the already grotesque decorations into forms even more bizarre. The Taken pulled out, gained altitude, came around for another pass. In the interim another pair of dots screamed across the Port valley and painted the planes of the air. It would have been a great show if I had not been so damned busy getting away.

The slope resounded to the stamp of an invisible giant. A circle fifteen feet across and five deep appeared above us. Sticks and stones flew. It missed by only a dozen feet. The impact knocked us down. A line of like imprints marched back up the slope.

Mighty though that blow was, it was less forceful than its predecessors.

Feather and Whisper swooped again, and again the face of the black castle melted, ran, shifted form. Then thunder racked the air. *Bam-bam!* Both Taken vanished in clouds of smoke. They wobbled out, fighting for control of their carpets. Both smouldered the way Feather had the night we captured Shed. They fought for altitude.

The castle turned its entire attention to them. The Lieutenant and I made our escape.

# Chapter Thirty-Four: JUNIPER: FLIGHT

The Lily shuddered several times.

Shed was doing mugs and wondering which of his customers were Black Company. The shaking made him nervous. Then a shriek flashed overhead, rising, then falling as it whipped away north. A moment later the earth shivered again, strong enough to rattle crockery. He rushed into the street. One small, cunning part of him kept watching his customers, trying to determine who was watching him. His chance of escape had lessened drastically with the advent of the Company. He no longer knew who was who. They all knew him.

He hit the street as a second shriek came from the direction of the Enclosure. He followed pointing hands. A pair of balls joined by a cord whipped away to the north. Seconds later all Juniper was illuminated by a particolored glare.

"The black castle!" people said. "They hit the black castle."

Shed could see it from his street. It had vanished behind a curtain of color. Terror gripped his heart. He could not understand it. He was safe down here. Wasn't he?

Wasn't he? The Company had great wizards supporting it. They would not let the castle do anything. . . . A mighty hammer blow threw stuff around the north slope. He could not see what was happening, but instantly sensed that the castle had struck at someone. Possibly that Croaker, who was up there keeping the place isolated. Maybe the castle was trying to open the road.

Crowd yammer directed his attention to two dots dropping from the blue. Fire enveloped the castle. Obsidian shifted form, writhing, then found its normal shape again. The flying attackers soared, turned. Another pair of balls hurtled in, apparently thrown from Duretile. And down came the carpet riders.

Shed knew who they were and what was happening, and he was terrified. Around him, the Buskin, taken unawares, went berserk.

He retained the presence of mind to consider his own position. Here, there, members of the Black Company were running for battle stations. Squads formed up, hurried off. Pairs of soldiers took stations apparently assigned against times when rioting and looting looked possible. Nowhere did Shed see anyone identifiable as his babysitter.

He slipped back inside the Lily, upstairs, into his room, dug into his secret place. He stuffed gold and silver into his pockets, dithered over his amulet, then hung it around his neck, under his clothing. He scanned the room once, saw nothing else he wanted to take, hurried back downstairs. There was no one in the common room but Sal, who stood at the door watching the display on the north slope. He'd never seen her more homebody and calm.

"Sal."

"Marron? Is it time?"

"Yes. I'm leaving twenty leva in the box. You'll do fine as long as the soldiers keep coming in."

"Is that up there what's been going on?"

"That's where it's been headed. It'll probably get worse. They're here to destroy the castle. If they can."

"Where are you going?"

"I don't know." He honestly did not. "Wouldn't tell you if I did. They would find out from you."

"When will you be back?"

"Maybe never. Certainly not before they pull out." He doubted the Company ever would. Or, if it did, it would be replaced. Its Lady seemed the type not to turn loose of anything.

He gave Sal a peck on the cheek. "Take care. And don't short yourself or the kids. If Lisa turns up, tell her she's fired. If Wally does, tell him I forgive him."

He headed for the back door. The flash and roar on the slope continued. At one point there was a howling which fluttered toward Duretile, but it broke up somewhere over the Enclosure. He put his head down and his collar up and followed alleyways toward the waterfront.

Only twice did he encounter patrols. Neither boasted a man who knew him. The first ignored him. The corporal commanding the second told him to get his ass off the street and went on.

From Wharf Street he could see the black castle once more, through the masts and stays of countless ships. It seemed to have gotten the worst of the exchange, which had died away. Thick, black smoke boiled out of the fortress, an oily column leaning a few degrees and rising thousands of feet, then spreading in a dark haze. On the slopes below the castle there was a twinkling and seething, an anthill-like suggestion of movement. He supposed the Company was hurrying into action.

The waterfront was in a frenzy. The channel boasted a dozen vessels heading out. Every other foreign ship was preparing to sail. The river itself seemed strangely disturbed and choppy.

Shed tried three ships before he found one where money talked loudly enough to be heard. He paid ten leva to a piratical purser and found himself a spot where he would not be seen from shore.

Nevertheless, as the crew were casting off, the man called Pawnbroker came racing along the pier with a squad of soldiers, shouting at the ship's master to hold fast.

The ship's master made an obscene gesture, told them where they could go, and began drifting with the current. There were too few tugs for the number of ships moving out.

For his defiance the skipper got an arrow through the

throat. Astonished sailors and officers stood frozen, aghast. Arrows stormed aboard, killed more than a dozen men, including the mate and boatswain. Shed cowered in his hiding place, gripped by a terror deeper than any he had known before.

He had known they were hard men, men who did not play games. He had not realized just how hard they were, how savage they could be. The Duke's men would have thrown up their hands in despair and wandered away cursing. They would not have massacred anyone.

The arrows kept coming, in a light patter, till the vessel was out of range.

Only then did Shed peep out and watch the city dwindle slowly. Oh, slowly, did it drift away.

To his surprise none of the sailors were angry with him. They were angry, true, but had not made a connection between the attack and their last-minute passenger.

Safe, he thought, elated. That lasted till he began to wonder where he was bound and what he would do once he got there.

A sailor called, "Sir, they're coming after us in a launch." Shed's heart dropped to his ankles. He looked and saw a small ship pulling out, trying to put on sail. Men in Black Company uniform abused the crew, hurrying them.

He got back into hiding. After the mauling these men had taken, there was no doubt they would surrender him rather than suffer more. If they realized he was what Pawnbroker wanted.

How had the man picked up his trail?

Sorcery. Of course. Had to be.

Did that mean they could find him anywhere?

# Chapter Thirty-Five: JUNIPER: BAD NEWS

The fuss was over. It had been a dramatic display while it lasted, though not as impressive as some I've seen. The battle on the Stair of Tear. The fighting around Charm. This was all flash and show, more rattling to Juniper's people than to us or the denizens of the black castle. They did us no harm. The worst they suffered was the direct deaths outside their gate. The fire inside did no real harm. Or so the Taken reported.

Grimy, Whisper grounded her carpet outside my headquarters, trundled inside looking the worse for wear but unharmed. "What started it?" she asked.

The Lieutenant explained.

"They're getting frightened," she said. "Maybe desperate. Were they trying to scare you off or take you prisoner?"

"Definitely prisoner," I said. "They hit us with some kind of sleepy spell before they came after us." One-Eye supported me with a nod.

"Why were they unsuccessful?"

"One-Eye broke the spell. Turned it around on them. We killed three."

"Ah! No wonder they were upset. You brought one down with you?"

"I thought we could understand them better if I cut one up to see how he was made."

Whisper did one of her mental fades, communing with

the mistress of us all. She returned. "A good idea. But Feather and I will do the cutting. Where is the corpse? I'll take it to Duretile now."

I indicated the body. It was in plain sight. She had two men carry it to her carpet. I muttered, "Don't damn trust us to do anything anymore." Whisper heard me. She did not comment.

Once the body was loaded, she told the Lieutenant, "Begin your preliminary siegework immediately. A circumvallation. Limper will support you. It's likely the Dominator's creatures will try to break out or take prisoners, or both. Don't permit it. A dozen captives would allow them to open the pathway. You would find yourself facing the Dominator. He would not be kind."

"No shit." The Lieutenant is a tough guy's tough guy when it suits him. In those moments not even the Lady could intimidate him. "Why don't you clear out? Tend to your job and let me tend to mine."

His remarks didn't fit the moment, but he was fed up with Taken in general. He had been on the march with the Limper for months, and the Limper fancied himself a commander. He gave the Lieutenant and Captain both a bellyful. And maybe that was the source of the friction between the Company and Taken. The Captain had his limits, too, though he was more diplomatic than the Lieutenant. He would ignore orders that did not suit him.

I went out to watch the circumvallation of the black castle. Drafts of laborers arrived from the Buskin, shovels over their shoulders and terror in their eyes. Our men put down their tools and assumed guardianship and supervisory roles. Occasionally the black castle sputtered, making a feeble attempt to interfere, like a volcano muttering to itself after its energy has been spent. The locals sometimes scattered and had to be rounded up. We lost a lot of good will won earlier.

A sheepish yet angry Pawnbroker came looking for me, gravity accentuated by the afternoon sunlight. I eased away and went to meet him. "What's the bad news?"

"That damned Shed. Made a run for it in the confusion."

"Confusion?"

"The city went crazy when the Taken started sniping at the castle. We lost track of Shed. By the time Goblin found him, he was on a ship headed for Meadenvil. I tried to keep it from pulling out, but they wouldn't stop. I shot them up, then grabbed a boat and went after them, but I couldn't catch up."

After cursing Pawnbroker, and stifling an urge to strangle him, I sat down to think. "What's the matter with him, Pawn? What's he afraid of?"

"Everything, Croaker. His own shadow. I reckon he figured we were going to kill him. Goblin says it was more than that, but you know how he loves to complicate stuff."

"Like what?"

"Goblin says he wants to make a clean break with the old Shed. Fear of us was the motivation he needed to get moving."

"Clean break?"

"You know. Like from guilt about everything he did. And from reprisals by the Inquisitors. Bullock knows he was in on the Catacombs raid. Bullock would jump on him as soon as he got back."

I stared down at the shadowed harbor. Ships were getting under way still. The waterfront looked naked. If outsiders kept running, we would become very unpopular. Juniper depended heavily on trade.

"You find Elmo. Tell him. Say I think you ought to go after Shed. Find Kingpin and those guys and bring them back. Check on Darling and Bullock while you're at it."

He looked like a man condemned, but did not protest. He had several screw-ups to his credit. Being separated from his comrades was a cheap penalty to pay. "Right," he said, and hustled off.

I returned to the task at hand.

Disorganization resolved itself as the troops formed the locals into work crews. The earth was flying. First a good deep trench so the creatures from the castle would have trouble getting out, then a palisade behind that.

One of the Taken remained airborne, circling high above, watching the castle.

Wagons began coming up from the city, carrying timber and rubble. Down there other work crews were demolishing buildings for materials. Though they were structures unfit for occupation and long overdue for replacement, they housed people who were not going to love us for destroying their homes.

One-Eye and a sergeant named Shaky took a large labor draft around the castle, down to the roughest slope, and began a mine designed to drop part of the castle wall down the steep slope. They did nothing to conceal their purpose. Wasn't much point trying. The things we faced had the power to knife through any subterfuge.

Actually managing to breech the wall would be a tough job. It might take weeks, even with One-Eye helping. The miners would have to cut through many yards of solid rock.

The project was one of several feints the Lieutenant would employ, though the way he plans a siege, one day's feint can become another's main thrust. Drawing on a manpower pool like Juniper, he could exercise every option.

I felt a certain pride, watching the siege take shape. I have been with the Company a long time. Never had we undertaken so ambitious a project. Never had we been given the wherewithal. I wandered around till I found the Lieutenant. "What's the plan here, anyway?" Nobody ever told me anything.

"Just nail them down so they can't get out. Then the Taken will jump all over them."

I grunted. Basic and simple. I expected it would get more complicated. The creatures inside would fight. I suspect the Dominator was lying restless, shaping a counterstroke.

Must be hell to be buried alive, able to do nothing but wish and hope at minions far beyond direct control. Such impotence would destroy me in a matter of hours.

I told the Lieutenant about Shed's escape. He did not

get excited. Shed meant little to him. He did not know about Raven and Darling. To him, Raven was a deserter and Darling his camp follower. Nothing special. I wanted him to know about Shed so he would mention it to the Captain. The Captain might want to take action more vigorous than my recommendation to Elmo.

I stayed with the Lieutenant a while, he watching the work crews, I watching a wagon train come uphill. This one should be bringing supper. "Getting damned tired of cold meals," I muttered.

"Tell you what you ought to do, Croaker. You ought to get married and settle down."

"Sure," I replied, more sarcastically than I felt. "Right after you."

"No, really. This might be the place to do it. Set yourself up in practice, catering to the rich. That Duke's family, say. Then, when your girlfriend gets here, you pop the question and you're all set."

Daggers of ice drove into my soul, twisting. I croaked, "Girlfriend?"

He grinned. "Sure. Nobody told you? She's coming out for the big show. Going to run it personally. Be your big chance."

My big chance. But for what?

He was talking about the Lady, of course. It had been years, but still they rode me about some romantic stories I wrote before I actually met the Lady. They always ride anybody about anything they know will get their goat. All part of the game. All part of the brotherhood.

I bet the son-of-a-bitch had been boiling with the news since first he heard it, waiting to spring in on me.

The Lady. Coming to Juniper.

I considered deserting for real. While there was a ship or two left to get away.

# Chapter Thirty-Six: JUNIPER: FIREWORKS

The castle lulled us. Let us think we could slam the door without a squawk. For two days the labor crews ripped at the north ridge, gouging out a good deep trench, getting up much of the needed stockade, hammering out a nice beginning of a mine. Then they let us in on their displeasure.

It was a little bit chaotic and a whole lot hairy, and in retrospect, it seems it may not have started as what it became.

It was a moonless night, but labor crews were working by firelight, torchlight, lanternlight. The Lieutenant had wooden towers going up each hundred feet where the trench and palisade were complete, and nearby them small ballistae for mounting atop them. A waste of time, I thought. What value mundane siege equipment against minions of the Dominator? But the Lieutenant was our siege specialist. He was determined to do things properly, by the numbers, even if the ballistae never were used. They had to be available.

Sharp-eyed Company members were in the towers nearing completion, trying to see into the castle. One detected movement at the gate. Instead of raising a fuss, he sent a message down. The Lieutenant went up. He decided that someone had left the castle and slipped around to One-Eye's side. He had drums sounded, trumpets blown, and fire arrows shot into the air.

The alarm wakened me. I rushed up to see what was happening. For a while there was nothing to see.

On the far slope One-Eye and Shaky stood to arms. Their workers panicked. Many were killed or crippled trying to flee across the brushy, rocky, steep slope. A minority had sense enough to stand fast.

The castle folks wanted to make a quick strike and catch some of One-Eye's workers, drag them inside, and complete whatever rites were necessary to bring the Dominator through. Once they were discovered, their strategy shifted. The men in the towers yelled that more were coming out. The Lieutenant ordered harassing fire. He had a couple of small trebuchets chuck balls of burning brush into the area near the gate. And he sent men to find Goblin and Silent, figuring they could do more than he to provide needed illumination.

Goblin was down in the Buskin. It would take him an hour to respond. I had no idea where Silent might be. I had not seen him, though he had been in Juniper a week.

The Lieutenant had signal fires lighted to warn watchers on Duretile's walls that we had a situation.

The Taken above finally came down to investigate. It proved to be the Limper. His first act was to take a handful of javelins, do something to them, then cast them to earth from above. They became pillars of chartreuse light between trench and castle.

On the far slope One-Eye provided his own illumination by spinning spiderwebs of violet and hanging their corners on the breeze. They quickly betrayed the approach of a half-dozen shapes in black. Arrows and javelins flew.

The creatures suffered several casualties before they took exception. Light blazed, then faded into a shimmer which surrounded each. They attacked.

Other shapes appeared atop the castle wall. They hurled objects down-slope. The size of a man's head, they bounded toward the minehead. One-Eye did something to alter their course. Only one escaped him. It left a trail of unconscious soldiers and workers.

The castle creatures had, evidently, planned for every

possibility but One-Eye. They were able to give the Limper hell, but did nothing about One-Eye at all.

He shielded his men and made them fight toe-to-toe when the castle creatures closed. Most of his men were killed, but they wiped out their attackers.

By then the castle creatures were mounting a sortie against the trench and wall, directly toward where I stood watching. I recall being more puzzled than fearful.

How many were there? Shed had given the impression the castle was practically untenanted. But a good twenty-five of them, attacking with wizardry backing them, made the trench and wall almost pointless.

They came out the gate. And something came over the castle wall, vast and bladder-like. It hit the ground, bounded twice, mashed down on the trench and palisade, crushing one and filling the other. The sortie streaked for the opening. Those creatures could *move*.

The Limper came down out of the night, shrieking with the fury of his descent, glowing ever more brightly as he dropped. The glow peeled off in flakes the size of maple seeds, which fluttered in his wake, spinning and twisting earthward, eating into whatever they contacted. Four or five attackers went down.

The Lieutenant launched a hasty counterattack, finished several of the injured, then had to retreat. Several of the creatures dragged fallen soldiers toward the castle. The others came on.

Without a heroic bone in my body, I picked up my heels and headed across the slope. And a wise move that proved.

The air crackled and sparked and opened like a window. Something poured through from somewhere else. The slope froze so cold and so fast the air itself turned to ice. The air around me rushed into the affected area, and it too froze. The cold took most of the castle creatures, enveloping them in frost. A random javelin struck one. The creature shattered, turning to powder and small shards. Men hurled whatever missiles were available, destroying the others.

The opening closed after only a few seconds. The relative warmth of the world sapped the bitter cold. Fogs boiled up, concealed the area for several minutes. When they cleared, no trace of the creatures could be found.

Meantime, three untouched creatures raced down the road toward Juniper. Elmo and an entire platoon raged in pursuit. Above, the Limper passed the apex of a climb and descended for a strike upon the fortress. As another band of creatures came out.

They grabbed up whatever bodies they could and hurried back. Limper adjusted his descent and hit them. Half went down. The others dragged at least a dozen dead men inside.

A pair of those flying balls came shrieking across from Duretile and impacted the castle wall, hurling up a shield of color. Another carpet dropped behind Limper. It released something which plunged into the black castle. There was a flash so brilliant it blinded people for miles around. I was facing away at the moment, but, even so, fifteen seconds passed before my vision recovered enough to show me the fortress afire.

This was not the shifting fire we had seen earlier. This was more like a conflagration actually consuming the stuff of the fortress itself. Strange screams came from inside. They set chills crawling my spine. They were screams not of pain but of rage. Creatures appeared on the battlements, flailing away with what looked like cats-o'-nine-tails, extinguishing the flames. Wherever the flames had burned, the fortress was visibly diminished.

A steady stream of ball pairs howled across the valley. I do not see that they contributed anything, yet I'm sure there was purpose behind them.

A third carpet dropped while Limper and the other were climbing. This one trailed a cloud of dust. Wherever the dust touched, it had an effect like Limper's maple seeds, only generalized. Exposed castle creatures shrieked in agony. Several seemed to melt. The others abandoned the walls.

Events proceeded in like fashion for quite a while, with the black castle appearing to get the worst of it. Yet they had gotten those bodies inside, and I suspected that meant trouble.

Sometime during all this Asa made a getaway. I was unaware of it. So was everyone else, till hours later, when Pawnbroker spotted him going into the Iron Lily. But Pawnbroker was a good distance away, and the Lily was doing a booming business despite the hour, with everyone who could gathered for drinks while watching the fury on the north ridge. Pawnbroker lost him in the mob. I expect Asa spoke to Shed's sister-in-law and learned that he, too, had escaped. We never had time to interview her.

Meantime, the Lieutenant was getting things under control. He had the casualties cleared away from the break in the circumvallation. He moved ballistae into position to fire into any further break-out attempt. He had pit traps dug. He sent laborers around to replace those One-Eye had lost.

The Taken continued their harassment of the castle, though at a more leisurely pace. They had shot their best bolts early.

The occasional pair of balls howled over from Duretile. I later learned that Silent was throwing them, having been taught by the Taken.

The worst of it seemed over. Except for the three escapees Elmo was hunting, we had contained the thing. The Limper peeled off to join the hunt for the three. Whisper returned to Duretile to refurbish her store of nasty tricks. Feather patrolled above the castle, dipping down occasionally when its denizens came out to battle the last consuming flames. Relative peace had returned.

Nobody rested, though. Bodies had been hauled inside. We all wondered if they had gleaned enough to bring the Dominator through.

But they were up to something else in there.

A group of creatures appeared on the wall, setting up a device pointing down-slope. Feather dove.

*Bam!* Smoke boiled around her, illuminated from within. She came out wobbling. *Bam!* And *bam!* again. And thrice more still. And after the last she could no longer hold it. She was afire, a comet arcing up, out, away, and down into the city. A violent explosion occurred where she hit. In moments a savage conflagration raged upon the waterfront. The fire spread swiftly among the tightly packed tenements.

Whisper was out of Duretile and hitting the black castle in minutes, with the vicious dust that melted and the fire that burned the stuff of the fortress itself. There was an intensity to her flying that betrayed her anger over Feather's fall.

The Limper, meantime, broke off hunting escapees to help fight the fire in the Buskin. With his aid it was controlled within hours. Without him the entire district might have burned.

Elmo got two of the fugitives. The third vanished utterly. When the hunt resumed with the help of the Taken, no trace could be found.

Whisper maintained her attack till she exhausted her resources. That came well after sunrise. The fortress looked more like a giant hunk of slag than a castle, yet she had not overcome it. One-Eye, when he came around seeking more tools, told me there was plenty of activity inside.

# Chapter Thirty-Seven: JUNIPER: THE CALM

I caught a two-hour nap. The Lieutenant allowed half the troops and workers the same, then the other half. When I wakened, I found few changes, except that the Captain had sent Pockets over to establish a field hospital. Pockets had been down in the Buskin, trying to win friends with free medical attention. I looked in, found only a handful of patients and the situation under control, went on to check the siegework.

The Lieutenant had repaired the gap in the palisade and trench. He had extended both, intending to take them all the way around, despite the difficulty of the nether slope. New, heavier missile weapons were under construction.

He was not content to rely upon the Taken to reduce the place. He did not trust them to do the necessary.

Sometime during my brief sleep, drafts of Candy's prisoners came up. But the Lieutenant did not permit the civilians to leave. He put them to gathering earth while he scoped out a site for building a ramp.

I suggested, "You'd better get some sleep."

"Need to ride herd," he said. He had a vision. His talent had gone unused for years. He wanted this. I suspect he found the Taken an irritation, despite the formidable nature of the black castle.

"It's your show," I said. "But you won't be much good if they hit back and you're too exhausted to think straight."

We were communicating on a level outside words. Weariness had us all fragmented and choppy, neither our thoughts nor actions nor speech moving logically or linearly. He nodded curtly. "You're right." He surveyed the slope. "Seems to be clicking. I'll go down to the hospital. Have somebody get me if something happens."

The hospital tent was the nearest place out of the sun. It was a bright, clear, intense day, promising to be unseasonably warm. I looked forward to that. I was tired of shivering. "Will do."

He was right about things running smoothly. They usually do once the men know what has to be done.

From the viewpoint of the Limper, who again had the air patrol, the slope must have looked like an overturned anthill. Six hundred Company troops were supervising the efforts of ten times as many men from the city. The road uphill carried so much traffic it was being destroyed. Despite the night's excitement and their lack of sleep, I found the men in excellent spirits.

They had been on the march so long, doing nothing else, that they had developed a big store of violent energy. It was pouring out now. They worked with an eagerness which infected the locals. Those seemed pleased to participate in a task which required the concerted efforts of thousands. Some of the more thoughtful mentioned that Juniper had mounted no major communal effort in generations. One man suggested that that was why the city had gone to seed. He believed the Black Company and its attack on the black castle would be great medicine for a moribund body politic.

That, however, was not a majority opinion. Candy's prisoners, especially, resented being used as a labor force. They represented a strong potential for trouble.

I have been told I always look at the dark underbelly of tomorrow. Possibly. You're less likely to be disappointed that way.

The excitement I expected did not materialize for days. The castle creatures seemed to have pulled their hole in after them. We eased the pace slightly, ceased working as if everything had to be done before tomorrow.

The Lieutenant completed the circumvallation, including the back slope, looping around One-Eye's excavation. He then broke the front wall and began building his ramp. He did not use many mantlets, for he designed it to provide its own shielding. It rose steeply at our end, with steps constructed of stone from demolished buildings. The work crews downtown were now pulling down structures ruined in the fire following Feather's crash. There were more materials than could be used in the siege. Candy's outfit was salvaging the best to use in new housing planned for the cleared sites.

The ramp would rise till it overtopped the castle by twenty feet, then it would descend to the wall. The work went faster than I expected. So did One-Eye's project. He found a combination of spells which turned stone soft enough to be worked easily. He soon reached a point beneath the castle.

Then he ran into the material that looked like obsidian. And could go no farther. So he started spreading out.

The Captain himself came over. I had been wondering what he was doing. I asked.

"Finding ways to keep people busy," he said. He shambled around erratically. If we did not pay attention, we found ourselves wandering off after he made some sudden turn and went to inspect something apparently trivial. "Damned Whisper is turning me into a military governor."

"Uhm?"

"What, Croaker?"

"I'm the Annalist, remember? Got to get this all down somewhere."

He frowned, eyeballed a barrel of water set aside for animals. Water was a problem. A lot had to be hauled to augment the little we caught during the occasional shower. "She has me running the city. Doing what the Duke and city fathers should." He kicked a rock and said nothing more till it stopped rolling. "Guess I'm coping. Isn't anybody in town who isn't working. Aren't getting paid anything but keep, but they're working. Even got people lined up with projects they want done as long as we're making people work. The Custodians are driving me crazy. Can't tell them all their clean-ups may be pointless."

I caught an odd note in that. It underscored a feeling I'd had already, that he was depressed about what was happening. "Why's that?"

He glanced around. No natives were within earshot. "Just a guess, mind. Nobody's put it in words. But I think the Lady plans to loot the Catacombs."

"People aren't going to like that."

"I know. You know; I know; even Whisper and Limper know. But we don't give the orders. There's talk about how the Lady is short of money."

In all the years we'd been in her service we'd never missed a payday. The Lady played that straight. The troops got paid, be they mercenaries or regulars. I suspect the various outfits could tolerate a few delays. It's almost a tradition for commanders to screw their troops occasionally.

Most of us didn't much care about money, anyway. We tended toward inexpensive and limited tastes. I suppose attitudes would shift if we had to do without, though.

"Too many men under arms on too many frontiers," the Captain mused. "Too much expansion too fast for too long. The empire can't take the strain. The effort in the Barrowland ate up her reserves. And it's still going. If she whips the Dominator, look for things to change."

"Maybe we made a mistake, eh?"

"Made a lot. Which one are you talking about?"

"Coming north, over the Sea of Torments."

"Yes. I've known that for years."

"And?"

"And we can't get out. Not yet. Someday, maybe, when our orders take us back to the Jewel Cities, or somewhere where we could leave the empire and still find ourselves in a civilized country." There was an almost bottomless yearning in his voice. "The longer I spend in the north, the less I want to end my days here, Croaker. Put that in your Annals."

I had him talking, a rare occurrence. I merely grunted, hoping he would continue filling the silence. He did.

"We're running with the darkness, Croaker. I know that don't make no never-mind, really. Logically. We're the Black Company. We're not good or evil. We're just soldiers with swords for sale. But I'm tired of having our work turned to wicked ends. If this looting thing happens, I may step aside. Raven had the right idea back at Charm. He got the hell out."

I then set forth a notion that had been in the back of my mind for years. One I'd never taken seriously, knowing it quixotic. "That doesn't contribute anything, Captain. We also have the option of going the other way."

"Eh?" He came back from whatever faraway place ruled him and really looked at me. "Don't be silly, Croaker. That's a fool's game. The Lady squashes anybody who tries." He ground a heel into the earth. "Like a bug."

"Yeah." It *was* a silly idea, on several levels, not the least of which was that the other side could not afford us. I could not picture us in the Rebel role anyway. The majority of Rebels were idiots, fools or ambitious types hoping to grab a chunk of what the Lady had. Darling was the outstanding exception, and she was more symbol than substance, and a secret symbol at that.

"Eight years since the comet was in the sky," the Captain said. "You know the legends. She won't fall till the Great Comet is up there. You want to try surviving twenty-nine years on the run from the Taken? No, Croaker. Even if our hearts were with the White Rose, we couldn't make that choice. That's suicide. Getting out of the empire is the way."

"She'd come after us."

"Why? Why shouldn't she be satisfied with what she's had of us these ten years? We're no threat to her."

But we were. We very much were, if only because we knew of the existence of the reincarnation of the White Rose. And I was sure that, once we left the empire, either Silent or I would spill that secret.

Of course, the Lady did not know that we knew.

"This chatter is an exercise in futility," the Captain said. "I'd rather not talk about it."

"As you wish. Tell me what we're going to do here."

"The Lady is coming in tonight. Whisper says we'll begin the assault as soon as the auspices are right."

I glanced at the black castle.

"No," he said. "It won't be easy. It may not be possible, even with the Lady helping."

"If she asks about me, tell her I'm dead. Or something," I said.

That won a smile. "But, Croaker, she's your. . . ."

"Raven," I snapped. "I know things about him that could get us all killed. So does Silent. Get him out of Duretile before she gets here. Neither one of us dares face the Eye."

"For that, neither do I. Because I know you know something. We're going to have to take our chances, Croaker."

"Right. So don't put notions into her head."

"I expect she's forgotten you long since, Croaker. You're just another soldier."

# Chapter Thirty-Eight: JUNIPER: THE STORM

The Lady hadn't forgotten me. Not even a little. Shortly after midnight a grim Elmo rousted me out. "Whisper is here. Wants you, Croaker."

"Eh?" I hadn't done anything to arouse her ire. Not for weeks.

"They want you over to Duretile. *She* wants you. Whisper is here to take you back."

Ever seen a grown man faint? I haven't. But I came close. I may have come close to having a stroke, too. My blood pressure must have soared. For two minutes I was vertiginous and unable to think. My heart pounded. My guts ached with fear. I *knew* she was going to drag me in for a session with the Eye, which sees every secret buried in a man's mind. And yet I could do nothing to evade her. It was too late to run. I wished I had been aboard the ship to Meadenvil with Pawnbroker.

Like a man walking to the gallows, I went out to Whisper's carpet, settled myself behind her, and dwindled into my thoughts as we rose and rushed through the chill night toward Duretile.

As we passed over the Port, Whisper called back, "You must have made quite an impression back when, physician. You were the first person she asked about when she got here."

I found enough presence of mind to ask, "Why?"

"I suspect because she wants her story recorded again. As she did during the battle at Charm."

I looked up from my hands, startled. How had she known that? I'd always pictured the Taken and Lady as uncommunicative among themselves.

What she said was true. During the battle at Charm the Lady had dragged me around with her so the events of the day would be recorded as they happened. And she did not demand special treatment. In fact, she insisted I write stuff as I saw it. There was just the faintest whiff of a hint that she expected to be toppled sometime, and, once she was, expected maltreatment by historians. She wanted a neutral record to exist. I hadn't thought about that for years. It was one of the more curious anomalies I'd noted about her. She did not care what people thought of her, but was frightened that the record would be bastardized to suit someone else's ends.

The tiniest spark of hope rose from that. Maybe she *did* want a record kept. Maybe I *could* get through this. If I could remain nimble enough to avoid the Eye.

The Captain met us when we landed on Duretile's northern wall. A glance at the carpets there told me all the Taken were on hand. Even Journey, whom I had expected to remain in the Barrowland. But Journey would have a grudge to soothe. Feather had been his wife.

A second glance told me the Captain was silently apologetic about my situation, that there were things he wanted to say but dared not. I fed him a tiny shrug, hoped we would get a moment later. We did not. Whisper led me from the wall directly into the Lady's presence.

She hadn't changed an iota since I had seen her last. The rest of us had aged terribly, but she remained twenty forever, radiantly gorgeous with stunning black hair and eyes into which a man could fall and die. She was, as always, such a focal point of glamor that she could not be physically described. A detailed description would be pointless anyway, as what I saw was not the true Lady. The Lady who looked like that hadn't existed for four centuries, if ever.

She rose and came to greet me, a hand extended. I could not tear my eyes away. She rewarded me with the slightly mocking smile I recalled so well, as though we shared a secret. I touched her hand lightly, and was astonished to find it warm. Away from her, when she vanished from mind except as a distant object of dread, like an earthquake, I could think of her only as cold, dead, and deadly. More on the order of a lethal zombie than a living, breathing, even possibly vulnerable person.

She smiled a second time and invited me to take a seat. I did so, feeling grotesquely out of place amidst a company which included all but one of the great evils of the world. And the Dominator was there in spirit, casting his cold shadow.

I was not there to contribute, that became obvious. The Captain and Lieutenant did the talking for the Company. The Duke and Custodian Hargadon were there, too, but contributed little more than I. The Taken carried the discussion, questioning the Captain and Lieutenant. Only once was I addressed, and that by the Captain, who inquired as to my readiness to treat casualties from the fighting.

The meeting had only one point so far as I was concerned. The assault was set for dawn, day after the one coming up. It would continue till the black castle was destroyed or we lost our capacity to attack.

"The place is a hole in the bottom of the ship of empire," the Lady said. "It has to be plugged or we all drown." She entertained no protests from the Duke or Hargadon, both of whom regretted asking her for help. The Duke was now impotent within his own domain, and Hargadon little better. The Custodian suspected he would be out of work entirely, once the threat of the castle ended. Few of the Company and none of the Taken had been at any pains to conceal their disdain for Juniper's odd religion. Having spent a lot of time among the people, I could say they took it only as seriously as the Inquisitors, Custodians and a few fanatics made them.

I hoped she went slow if she intended changes, though.

Like so slow the Company would be headed elsewhere before she started. You mess with people's religion and you mess with fire. Even people who don't much give a damn. Religion is something that gets hammered in early, and never really goes away. And has powers to move which go beyond anything rational.

Morning after the day coming up. Total war. All-out effort to eradicate the black castle. Every resource of the Lady, Taken, Company and Juniper to be bent to that end, for as long as it took.

Morning after the day coming up. But it did not work that way. Nobody told the Dominator he was supposed to wait.

He got in the first strike six hours before jump-off, while most of the troops and all the civilian laborers were asleep. While the only Taken patrolling was Journey, who was the least of the Lady's henchmen.

It began when one of those bladder-like things bounced over the wall and filled the gap remaining in the Lieutenant's ramp. At least a hundred creatures stormed out of the castle and crossed.

Journey was alert. He had sensed a strangeness in the castle and was watching for trouble. He came down fast and drenched those attackers with the dust that melted.

*Bam! Bam-bam-bam!* The castle hit him the way it had hit his one-time wife. He fishtailed through the air, evading the worst, but caught the edge of every crack, and went down smouldering, his carpet destroyed.

The banging wakened me. It wakened the entire camp, for it started the same time as the alarms and drowned them entirely.

I charged out of the hospital, saw the castle creatures boiling down the steps of the Lieutenant's ramp. Journey hadn't stopped more than a handful. They were enveloped by that protective glow One-Eye had encountered once before. They spread out, sprinting through a storm of missiles from the men who had the watch. A few more fell, but not many. They began extinguishing lights, I suppose because their eyes were more suited to darkness than ours.

Men were running everywhere, dragging their clothing on as they rushed toward or away from the enemy. The laborers panicked and greatly hampered the Company's response. Many were killed by our men, vexed at finding them in the way.

The Lieutenant charged through the chaos bellowing orders. First he got his batteries of heavy weapons manned and trained on the steps. He sent messengers everywhere, ordering every ballista, catapult, mangonel and trebuchet moved to a position where it could fire on the ramp. That baffled me only till the first castle creature headed home with a body under each arm. A storm of missiles hit him, tore the bodies to shreds, battered him to a pulp, and nearly buried him.

The Lieutenant had trebuchets throw cannisters of oil which smashed on the steps and caught fire when flaming balls were thrown after them. He kept the oil and fire flying. The castle creatures would not run through the flames.

So much for my thinking the Lieutenant was wasting time building useless engines.

The man knew his job. He was good. His preparation and quick response were more valuable than anything done by the Lady or Taken that night. He held the line in the critical minutes.

A mad battle began the moment the creatures realized they were cut off. They promptly attacked, trying to reach the engines. The Lieutenant signaled his under-officers and brought the bulk of his available manpower to bear. He had to. Those creatures were more than a match for any two soldiers, and they benefited from the protective glow as well.

Here, there, a brave citizen of Juniper grabbed a fallen weapon and jumped into the struggle. Most paid the ultimate price, but their sacrifice helped keep the enemy away from the engines.

It was obvious to everyone that if the creatures escaped

with many bodies, our cause was lost. We'd soon be face-to-face with their master himself.

The ball pairs began coming over from Duretile, splashing the night with terrible color. Then Taken dropped from the night, Limper and Whisper each depositing an egg which hatched the fire that fed on the stuff of the castle. Limper dodged several attacks from the castle, swooped around, brought his carpet to ground near my hospital, where we were swamped by customers already. I had to retreat there to do the job for which I was paid. I kept the uphill tent flaps open so I could watch.

Limper left his aerial steed, marched uphill with a long, black sword that glimmered evilly in the light from the burning fortress. He radiated a glow not unlike that protecting the castle creatures. His, however, was far more puissant than theirs, as he demonstrated when he pushed through the press and attacked them. Their weapons could not reach him. His sliced through them as though they were made of lard.

The creatures, by that time, had slaughtered at least five hundred men. The majority were workers, but the Company had taken a terrible beating, too. And that beating went on even after the Limper turned the tide, for he could engage but one creature at a time. Our people strove to keep the enemy contained till the Limper could get to them.

They responded by trying to swamp the Limper, which they managed with some success, fifteen or twenty piling on and keeping him pinned by sheer body weight. The Lieutenant shifted the fire of the engines temporarily, pounded that seething pile till it broke up and the Limper regained his feet.

That ploy having failed, a band of the creatures clotted up and tried to break out to the west. I don't know whether they planned to escape entirely or meant to swing around and strike from behind. The dozen who made it through encountered Whisper, and a heavy fall of the melting dust. The dust killed a half-dozen workers for every castle creature, but it stopped the charge. Only five creatures survived it.

Those five immediately encountered the portal from elsewhere that expelled the cold breath of the infinite. They all perished.

Whisper, meantime, was scrambling for altitude. A drum-roll procession of bangs pursued her up the sky. She was a better flyer than Journey, but even so could not evade injury. Down she came, eventually touching down beyond the fortress.

Within the castle itself creatures were out with the cats-o'-nine-tails, extinguishing the fires started by Whisper and the Limper. The structure had begun to look pathetic, so much of its substance had been consumed. Gone was the dark, dreadful grace of weeks before. It was one big, dark, glassy lump, and it seemed impossible that creatures could survive inside it, yet they did, and continued the fight. A handful came out on the ramp and did something which gnawed black chunks out of the Lieutenant's conflagration. All the creatures on the slope ran for home, not a one forgetting to scoop up at least one body.

The ice door opened again, its breath dumping on the steps. The fires died instantly. A score of the creatures died too, hammered to powder by the Lieutenant's missiles.

The things inside took a tack I had anticipated fearfully since I had seen Feather crash. They turned their booming spell on the slope.

If it wasn't the thing that had pursued the Lieutenant, Elmo, One-Eye and me that day, it was a close cousin. There wasn't much flash or smoke when they used it on the slope, but huge holes appeared, often with bloody pulp smashed into their bottoms.

All this happened so swiftly, so dramatically, that nobody really had time to think. I don't doubt that even the Company would have run had events been stretched out enough to allow thinking time. As it was, in their confusion, the men had a chance only to pursue roles for which they had been preparing since reaching Juniper. They stood their ground and, too often, died.

The Limper scampered around the slope like an insane chicken, cackling and hunting creatures who hadn't died on the steps. There were a score of those, most surrounded by angry soldiers. Some of the creatures were slain by their own side, for those knots made tempting targets for the booming spell.

Teams of creatures appeared on the ramparts, assembling devices like the one we'd seen them try to use before. This time there was no Taken above to drop and give them hell.

Not till fool Journey came rushing past the hospital, looking cruelly battered, and stole the Limper's carpet.

It had been my notion that one Taken could not use another's vehicle. Not so, apparently, for Journey got the thing aloft and dove upon the castle again, dumping dust and another fire egg. The castle knocked him down again, and despite the tumult, I heard the Limper howling and cursing him for it.

Ever see how a child draws a straight line? None too straight. Something as shaky as a child's hand scribbled a wobbly line from Duretile to the black castle. It hung against the night like an improbable clothesline, wriggling, of indeterminate color, irridescent. Its tip threw sparks off the obsidian material, like the meeting of flint and steel magnified ten thousand times, generating an actinic glare too intense to view directly. The entire slope was bathed in wild bluish light.

I put aside my instruments and stepped out to better observe, for down in my gut I knew the Lady anchored the nether end of that scrawl, having entered the lists for the first time. She was the big one, the most powerful, and if the castle could be reduced at all, hers was the might that would do it.

The Lieutenant must have been distracted. For a few seconds his fires dwindled. A half-dozen castle creatures went up the steps, dragging two and three corpses apiece. A rush of their compatriots came out to meet the Limper, who was in hot pursuit. My guess is they got twelve bodies inside. Some might not have lost the spark of life entirely.

Chunks flew from the castle where the Lady's line touched, each blazing with that brilliant light. Thin cracks, in crimson, appeared against the black, spreading slowly. The creatures assembling the devices retreated, were replaced by others trying to lessen the effects of the Lady's attack. They had no luck. Several were knocked down by missiles from the Lieutenant's batteries.

The Limper reached the head of the stairs and stood limned against the glow of a section of castle still afire, sword raised high. A giant runt, if you will pardon the contradiction. He is a tiny thing, yet stood huge at that moment. He bellowed, "Follow me!" and charged down the ramp.

To my everlasting amazement, men followed him. Hundreds of men. I saw Elmo and the remnants of his company go roaring up, across, and disappear. Even scores of gutsy citizens decided to take part.

Part of the story of Marron Shed had come out recently, without names or such, but with heavy emphasis on how much wealth he and Raven had garnered. Obviously, the story had been planted against this moment, when a storm of manpower would be needed to subdue the castle. In ensuing minutes the call of wealth led many a man from the Buskin up those steps.

Down on the far side of the castle Whisper reached One-Eye's camp. One-Eye and his men, of course, had stood to arms, but had taken part in nothing yet. His mine operation had stalled once he was certain there was no way to get around or to breech the substance of the castle.

Whisper brought one of those eggs of fire, planted it against the obsidian exposed by One-Eye's mine. She set it off and let it gnaw at the fortress's underbelly.

That, I learned later, had been in the plan for some time. She had done some fancy flying to bring her crippled carpet down near One-Eye so she could carry it out.

Seeing the men pour into the castle, seeing the walls abandoned and being broken up by the Lady, seeing fires burning unchecked, I decided the battle was ours and was all over but the crying. I went back into the hospital and resumed cutting and stitching, setting and just plain shaking my head over men for whom there was nothing I could do. I wished One-Eye weren't on the far side of the ridge. He'd always been my principal assistant, and I missed him. While I could not denigrate Pockets' skill, he did not have One-Eye's talent. Often there was a man beyond my help who could be saved with a little magic.

A whoop and howl told me Journey was back, home from his latest crash and rushing his enemies once more. And not far behind him came those elements of the Company which had been stationed in the Buskin. The Lieutenant met Candy and prevented him from rushing over the ramp. Instead, he manned the perimeter and began rounding up those laborers who could be found still close to the action. He started putting things back together.

The *bam!* weapon had continued pounding away all along. Now it began to falter. The Lieutenant loudly cursed the fact that there were no carpets to drop fire eggs.

There *was* one. The Lady's. And I was sure she knew the situation. But she did not abandon her rope of irridescent light. She must have felt it to be more important.

Down in the mine the fire gnawed through the bottom of the fortress. A hole slowly expanded. One-Eye says there is very little heat associated with those flames. The moment Whisper considered it opportune, she led his force into the fortress.

One-Eye says he really considered going, but had a bad feeling about it. He watched the mob charge in, workers and all, then hiked around to our side. He joined me in the hospital and updated me as he worked.

Moments after he arrived, the backside of the castle collapsed. The whole earth rumbled. A long roar rolled down the thousand feet of the back slope. Very dramatic, but to little effect. The castle creatures were not inconvenienced at all.

Parts of the forewall were falling too, broken by the Lady's incessant attack.

Company members continued to arrive, accompanied by frightened formations of the Duke's men and even some Custodians rigged out as soldiers. The Lieutenant fed them into his lines. He allowed no one else to enter the castle.

Strange lights and fires, fell howls and noises, and terrible, terrible odors came out of that place. I don't know what happened in there. Maybe I never will. I gather that hardly anyone came back.

A strange, deep-throated, almost inaudible moaning began. It had me shuddering before I noted it consciously. It climbed in pitch with extreme deliberation, in volume much more rapidly. Soon it shook the whole ridge. It came from everywhere at once. After a while it seemed to have meaning, like speech incredibly slowed. I could detect a rhythm, like words stretched over minutes.

One thought. One thought alone. The Dominator. He was coming through.

For an instant I thought I could interpret the words. "Ardath, you bitch." But that went away, chased by fear.

Goblin appeared at the hospital, looked us over, and seemed relieved to find One-Eye there. He said nothing, and I got no chance to ask what he had been up to recently. He returned to the night, parting with a wave.

Silent appeared a few minutes later, looking grim. Silent, my partner in guilty knowledge, whom I had not seen in more than a year, whom I had missed during my visit to Duretile. He looked taller, leaner and bleaker than ever. He nodded, began talking rapidly in deaf speech. "There is a ship on the waterfront flying a red banner. Go there immediately."

"What?"

"Go to the ship with the red banner immediately. Stop only to inform others of the old Company. These are orders from the Captain. They are not to be disobeyed."

"One-Eye. . . ."

"I caught it, Croaker," he said. "What the hell, hey, Silent?"

Silent signed, "There will be trouble with the Taken. This ship will sail to Meadenvil, where loose ends must be tied off. Those who know too much must disappear. Come. We just gather the old brothers and go.''

There weren't many old brothers around. One-Eye and I hurried around telling everyone we could find, and in fifteen minutes a crowd of us were headed toward the Port River bridge, one as baffled as another. I kept looking back. Elmo was inside the castle. Elmo, who was my best friend. Elmo, who might be taken by the Taken. . . .

# Chapter Thirty-Nine: ON THE RUN

Ninety-six men reported aboard, as ordered. A dozen were men for whom the order had not been meant, but who could not be sent away. Missing were a hundred brothers from the old days, before we crossed the Sea of Torments. Some had died on the slopes. Some were inside the castle. Some we hadn't been able to find. But none of the missing were men who had dangerous knowledge, except Elmo and the Captain.

I was there. Silent, One-Eye and Goblin were there. The Lieutenant was there, more baffled than anyone else. Candy, Otto, Hagop. . . . The list goes on and on. They were all there.

But Elmo wasn't, and the old man wasn't, and there was a threat of mutiny when Silent passed the word to put out without them. "Orders," was all he would say, and that in the finger speech many of the men could not follow, though we had been using it for years. It was a legacy Darling had left the Company, a mode of communication useful on the hunt or battlefield.

The moment the ship was under way, Silent produced a sealed letter marked with the Captain's sign. Silent took the officers present into the cabin of the ship's master. He instructed me to read the letter aloud.

"You were right about the Taken, Croaker," I read. "They do suspect, and they do intend to move against the Company. I have done what I can to circumvent them by hiring a ship to take my most endangered brothers to safety. I will not be able to join you, as my absence would alert the Taken. Do not dawdle. I do not expect to last long once they discover your desertion. As you and Goblin can attest, no man hides from the Lady's Eye.

"I do not know that flight will present much hope. They will hunt you, for they will get things from me unless I am quick on my feet. I know enough to set them on the trail. . . ."

The Lieutenant interrupted. "What the hell is going on?" He knew there were secrets some of us shared, to which he was not privy. "I'd say we're past playing games and keeping things from each other."

I looked at Silent, said, "I think we should tell everybody, just so there's a chance the knowledge won't die."

Silent nodded.

"Lieutenant, Darling is the White Rose."

"What? But. . . ."

"Yes. Silent and I have known since the battle at Charm. Raven figured it out first. That's why he deserted. He wanted to get her as far from the Lady as he could. You know how much he loved her. I think a few others guessed too."

The announcement did not cause a stir. Only the Lieutenant was surprised. The others had suspected.

The Captain's letter hadn't much more to say. Farewells. A suggestion we elect the Lieutenant to replace him. And a final, private word to me.

"Circumstances seem to have dictated a shift to the option you mentioned, Croaker. Unless you can outrun the Taken back to the South." I could hear the sardonic chuckle that went with the comment.

One-Eye wanted to know what had become of the Company treasure chest. Way, way back in our service to the Lady we had grabbed off a fortune in coin and gems. It had traveled with us through the years, through good times and bad—our final, secret insurance against tomorrow.

Silent told us it was up in Duretile with the old man. There had been no chance to get it out.

One-Eye broke down and wept. That chest meant more to him than all vicissitudes past, present or promised.

Goblin got down on him. Sparks flew. The Lieutenant was about to take a hand when someone shoved through the door. "You guys better come topside and see this." He was gone before we could find out what he meant.

We hurried up to the main deck.

The ship was a good two miles down the Port, riding the current and tide. But the glow from the black castle illuminated both us and Juniper as brightly as a cloudy day.

The castle formed the base of a fountain of fire reaching miles into the sky. A vast figure twisted in the flames. Its lips moved. Long, slow words echoed down the Port. "Ardath. You bitch."

I had been right.

The figure's hand rose slowly, lazily, pointed toward Duretile.

"They got enough bodies inside," Goblin squeaked. "The old bastard is coming through."

The men watched in rapt awe. So did I, able only to think we were lucky to escape in time. At the moment I felt nothing for the men we had left behind. I could think only of myself.

"There," somebody said softly. "Oh, look there."

A ball of light formed on Duretile's wall. It swelled rapidly, shedding many colors. It was gorgeous, like a giant moon of stained glass rotating slowly. It was at least two hundred yards in diameter when it separated from Duretile and drifted toward the black castle. The figure there reached, grabbed at the globe, was unable to affect it.

I giggled.

"What's so damned funny?" the Lieutenant demanded.

"Just thinking how the people of Juniper must feel, looking up at that. They've never seen sorcery."

The stained glass ball rolled over and over. For a moment it presented a side I hadn't noticed before. A side that was a face. The Lady's face. Those great glassy eyes stared right into me, hurting. Without thinking I said, "I didn't betray you. You betrayed me."

Swear to the gods there was some form of communication. Something in the eyes said *she* had heard, and was pained by the accusation. Then the face rolled away, and I did not see it again.

The globe drifted into the fountain of fire. It vanished there. I thought I heard the long, slow voice say, "I have you, Ardath."

"There. Look there," the same man said, and we turned to Duretile. And upon the wall where the Lady had begun moving toward her husband there was another light. For a while I could not make out what was happening. It came our way, faltering, rising, falling.

"That's the Lady's carpet," Silent signed. "I have seen it before."

"But who? . . ." There was no one left who could fly one. The Taken were all over at the black castle.

The thing began to move faster, converting rickety up-and-down into ever-increasing velocity. It came our way, faster and faster, dropping lower and lower.

"Somebody who doesn't know what they're doing," One-Eye opined. "Somebody who is going to get killed if. . . ."

It came directly toward us, now not more than fifty feet off the water. The ship had begun the long turn which would take her around the last headland to the open sea. I said, "Maybe it was sent to hit us. Like a missile. To keep us from getting away."

"No," One-Eye said. "Carpets are too precious. Too hard to create and maintain. And the Lady's is the only one left. Destroy it and even she would have to walk home."

The carpet was down to thirty feet, swelling rapidly, sending an audible murmur ahead. It must have been traveling a hundred fifty miles an hour.

Then it was on us, ripping through the rigging, brushing a mast, and spinning on to impact on the sound half a mile away. A gout of spray arose. The carpet skipped like a flat stone, hit again, bounced again, and smashed into the face of a cliff. The spell energies ruling the carpet degenerated in a violet flash.

And not a word was spoken by any member of the Company. For as that carpet had torn through the rigging, we had glimpsed the face of its rider.

The Captain.

Who knows what he was doing? Trying to join us? Probably. I suspect he went to the wall planning to disable the carpet so it could not be used to pursue us. Maybe he planned to throw himself off the wall afterward, to avoid being questioned later. And maybe he had seen the carpet in action often enough to have been tempted by the idea of using it himself.

No matter. He had succeeded. The carpet would not be used to chase us. He would not be exposed to the Eye.

But he had failed his personal goal. He had died in the North.

His flight and death distracted us while the ship moved down the channel till both Juniper and the north ridge dropped behind the headland. The fire over the black castle continued, its terrible flames extinguishing the stars, but it shrank slowly. Oncoming dawn lessened its brilliance. And when one great shriek rolled across the world, announcing someone's defeat, we were unable to determine who had won.

For us the answer did not matter. We would be hunted by either the Lady or her long-buried spouse.

We reached the sea and turned south, with sailors still cursing as they replaced lines torn by the Captain's passage. We of the Company remained very silent, scattered about the deck, alone with our thoughts. And only then did I begin to worry for comrades left behind.

We held a long service two days out. We mourned everyone left behind, but the Captain especially. Every survivor took a moment to eulogize him. He had been head of the family, patriarch, father to us all.

# Chapter Forty: MEADENVIL: PATHFINDING

Fair weather and good winds carried us to Meadenvil in good time. The ship's master was pleased. He had been well-paid beforehand for his trouble, but was eager to shed a manifest of such vile temper. We had not been the best of passengers. One-Eye was terrified of the sea, a grand victim of seasickness, and insisted everyone else be as scared and sick as he. He and Goblin never let up on one another, though the Lieutenant threatened to throw the pair of them to the sharks. The Lieutenant was in such a foul temper himself that they took him half seriously.

In accordance with the Captain's wishes, we elected the Lieutenant our commander and Candy to become second. That position should have fallen to Elmo. . . . We did not call the Lieutenant Captain. That seemed silly with the outfit so diminished. There weren't enough of us left to make a good street gang.

Last of the Free Companies of Khatovar. Four centuries of brotherhood and tradition reduced to this. A band on the run. It did not make sense. Did not seem right. The great deeds of our forebrethren deserved better of their successors.

The treasure chest was lost, but the Annals themselves had, somehow, found their way aboard. I expect Silent brought them. For him they were almost as important as for me. The night before we entered Meadenvil harbor, I read to the troops, from the Book of Woeg, which chronicled the Company's history after its defeat and near destruction in the fighting along the Bake, in Norssele. Only a hundred four men survived that time, and the Company had come back.

They were not ready for it. The pain was too fresh. I gave it up halfway through.

Fresh. Meadenvil was refreshing. A real city, not a colorless berg like Juniper. We left the ship with little but our arms and what wealth we'd carried in Juniper. People watched us fearfully, and there was no little trepidation on our part, too, for we were not strong enough to make a show if the local Prince took exception to our presence. The three wizards were our greatest asset. The Lieutenant and Candy had hopes of using them to pull something that would provide the wherewithal to move on, aboard another ship, with further hopes of returning to lands we knew on the southern shore of the Sea of Torments. To do that, though, meant an eventual overland journey at least partly through lands belonging to the Lady. I thought we would be wiser to move down the coast, confuse our trail, and hook on with someone out here, at least till the Lady's armies closed in. As they would someday.

The Lady. I kept thinking of the Lady. It was all too likely that her armies now owed allegiance to the Dominator.

We located both Pawnbroker and Kingpin within hours of going ashore. Pawnbroker had arrived only two days before us, having faced unfavorable seas and winds during his journey. The Lieutenant started on Kingpin immediately.

"Where the hell you been, boy?" It was a sure thing Kingpin had turned his assignment into an extended vacation. He was that sort. "You were supposed to come back when . . ."

"Couldn't, sir. We're witnesses in a murder case. Can't leave town till after the trial."

"Murder case?"

"Sure. Raven's dead. Pawn says you know that. Well, we fixed it so that Bullock guy took the rap. Only we've got to hang around and get him hanged."

"Where is he?" I asked.

"In jail."

The Lieutenant reamed him good, cussing and fussing while passersby nervously eyed the hard guys abusing each other in a variety of mystery tongues.

I suggested, "We ought to get off the street. Keep a low profile. We got trouble enough without attracting attention. Lieutenant, if you don't mind, I'd like a chat with Kingpin. Maybe these other guys can show you places to hole up. King, come with me. You, too." I indicated Silent, Goblin and One-Eye.

"Where we going?" Kingpin asked.

"You pick it. Someplace where we can talk. Serious like."

"Right." He led the way, setting a brisk pace, wanting to put distance between himself and the Lieutenant. "That really true? What happened up there? The Captain dead and everything?"

"Too damned true."

He shook his head, awed by the idea of the Company having been destroyed. Finally, he asked, "What do you want to know, Croaker?"

"Just everything you found out since you been here. Especially about Raven. But also about that guy Asa. And the tavern-keeper."

"Shed? I saw him the other day. At least I think I did. Didn't realize it was him till later. He was dressed different. Yeah. Pawn told me he got away. The Asa guy, too. Him I think I know where to find. The Shed guy, though. . . . Well, if you really want him, you'll have to start looking where I thought I saw him."

"He see you?"

That idea caught Kingpin by surprise. Apparently, it hadn't occurred to him to wonder. He isn't the brightest fellow sometimes. "I don't think so."

We went into a tavern favored by foreign sailors. The customers were a polyglot lot and as ragged as we were. They spoke a dozen languages. We settled in at a table, used the language of the Jewel Cities. Kingpin did not speak it well, but understood it. I doubted that anyone else there could follow our discussion.

"Raven," I said. "That's what I want to know about, Kingpin."

He told us a story which matched Asa's closely, the edges being about as uneven as you would expect from someone who hadn't been an eyewitness.

"You still think he faked it?" One-Eye asked.

"Yeah. It's half hunch, but I think he did. Maybe when we go look the place over, I'll change my mind. There a way you guys could tell if he's in town?"

They put their heads together, returned a negative opinion. "Not without we had something that belonged to him to start with," Goblin opined. "We don't got that."

"Kingpin. What about Darling? What about Raven's ship?"

"Huh?"

"What happened to Darling after Raven supposedly died? What happened to his ship?"

"I don't know about Darling. The ship is tied up down at its dock."

We exchanged glances around the table. I said, "That ship gets visited if we have to fight our way aboard. Those papers I told you about. Asa couldn't account for them. I want them to turn up. They're the only thing we got that can get the Lady off our back."

"If there is a Lady," One-Eye said. "Won't be much pumpkin if the Dominator broke through."

"Don't even think that." For no sound reason I had convinced myself that the Lady had won. Mostly, it was wishful thinking, I'm sure. "Kingpin, we're going to visit that ship tonight. What about Darling?"

"Like I said. I don't know."

"You were supposed to look out for her."

"Yeah. But she kind of vanished."

"Vanished? How?"

"Not how, Croaker," One-Eye said, in response to vigorous signing from Silent. "How is irrelevant now. When."

"All right. When, Kingpin?"

"I don't know. Nobody's seen her since the night before Raven died."

"Bingo," Goblin said in a soft, awed voice. "Damn your eyes, Croaker, your instincts were right."

"What?" Kingpin asked.

"There's no way she would have disappeared beforehand unless she knew something was going to happen."

"Kingpin," I said, "did you go look at the place they were staying? Inside, I mean."

"Yeah. Somebody got there before me."

"What?"

"The place was cleaned out. I asked the innkeeper. He said they didn't move out. They was paid up for another month. That sounded to me like somebody knew about Raven getting croaked and decided to clean his place out. I figured it was that Asa. He disappeared right after."

"What did you do then?"

"What? I figured you guys didn't want Bullock back in Juniper, so we got him charged with Raven's murder. There was plenty of witnesses besides us saw them fighting. Enough to maybe convince a court we really saw what we said."

"You do anything to trace Darling?"

Kingpin had nothing to say. He stared at his hands. The rest of us exchanged irritated glances. Goblin muttered, "I told Elmo it was dumb to send him."

I guess it was. In minutes we had come up with several loose ends overlooked by Kingpin.

"How come you're so damned worried about it, anyway, Croaker?" Kingpin demanded. "I mean, it all looks like a big so-what to me."

"Look, King. Like it or not, when the Taken turned on us, we got pushed over to the other side. We're White Rose now. Whether we want it or not. They're going to come after us. The only thing the Rebel has going is the White Rose. Right?"

"If there is a White Rose."

"There is. Darling is the White Rose."

"Come on, Croaker. She's a deaf-mute."

One-Eye observed, "She's also a magical null-point."

"Eh?"

"Magic won't work around her. We noticed that clean back at Charm. And if she follows true for her sort, the null will get stronger as she gets older."

I recalled noting oddities about Darling during the battle of Charm, but hadn't made anything of it then. "What are you talking about?"

"I told you. Some people are negatives. Instead of having a talent for sorcery, they go the other way. It won't work around them. And when you think about it, that's the only way the White Rose makes sense. How could a deaf and dumb kid grow up to challenge the Lady or Dominator on their own ground? I'll bet the original White Rose didn't."

I didn't know. There had been nothing in the histories about her powers or their noteworthy absence. "This makes it more important to find her."

One-Eye nodded.

Kingpin looked baffled. It was easy to fuddle King, I decided. I explained. "If magic won't work around her, we've got to find her and stay close. Then the Taken won't be able to hurt us."

One-Eye said, "Don't forget that they have whole armies they can send after us."

"If they want us that bad. . . . Oh my."

"What?"

"Elmo. If he didn't get killed. He knows enough to put the whole empire on our trail. Maybe not so much for us as in hopes we'll lead them to Darling."

"What're we going to do?"

"Why're you looking at me?"

"You're the one seems to know what's going on, Croaker."

"Okay. I guess. First we find out about Raven and Darling. Especially Darling. And we ought to catch Shed and Asa again, in case they know something useful.

We got to move fast and get out of town before the empire closes in. Without upsetting the locals. We better have a sit-down with the Lieutenant. Get everything on the table for everybody, then decide exactly what we'll do.''

# Chapter Forty-One: MEADENVIL: THE SHIP

Ours, apparently, was the last ship out of Juniper. We kept waiting for a later vessel to bring news. None came. The crew of our vessel did us no favor, either. They yammered all over town. We were buried by nosy locals, people concerned about relatives in Juniper, and the city government, concerned that a group of tough refugees might cause trouble. Candy and the Lieutenant dealt with all that. The struggle for survival devolved on the rest of us.

The three wizards, Otto, Kingpin and Pawnbroker, and I stole through the shadowed Meadenvil waterfront district after midnight. There were strong police patrols to dodge. We evaded them with help from One-Eye, Goblin and Silent. Goblin was especially useful. He possessed a spell capable of putting men to sleep.

"There she is," Kingpin whispered, indicating Raven's ship. Earlier I'd tried to find out how her docking fees were being paid. I'd had no luck.

She was a fine, big ship with a look of newness the darkness could not conceal. Only the normal lights burned aboard her: bow, stern masthead, port and starboard, and one at the head of the gangway, where a single bored sailor stood watch.

"One-Eye?"

He shook his head. "Can't tell."

I polled the others. Neither Silent nor Goblin detected anything remarkable, either.

"Okay, Goblin. Do your stuff. That'll be the acid test, won't it?"

He nodded. If Darling was aboard, his spell would not affect the watch.

Now that everyone had accepted my suspicions about Raven being alive, I'd begun to question them. I could see no sense in his not having slipped away by now, taking his very expensive ship somewhere far away. Perhaps out to the islands.

Those islands intrigued me. I thought we might grab a ship and head out there. Had to take someone who knew the way, though. The islands were a long way out and there was no regular commerce. No way to get there by guesswork.

"Okay," Goblin said. "He's out."

The sailor on the quarterdeck had slumped onto a handy stool. He had his arms folded on the rail and his forehead on his arms.

"No Darling," I said.

"No Darling."

"Anybody else around?"

"No."

"Let's go, then. Keep low, move fast, all that."

We crossed the pier and scampered up the gangway. The sailor stirred. Goblin touched him and he went out like the dead. Goblin hustled forward, then aft, to the men on the rat guards. He returned nodding. "Another eight men below, all asleep. I'll put them under. You go ahead."

We started with the biggest cabin, assuming it would be the owner's. It was. It sat in the stern, where the master's cabin usually is, and was split into sections. I found things in one indicating that it had been occupied by Darling. On Raven's side we found soiled clothing discarded some time ago. There was enough dust to indicate that no one had visited the cabin for weeks.

We did not find the papers I sought.

We did find money. Quite a substantial amount. It was cunningly hidden, but One-Eye's sense for those things is infallible. Out came a chest brimming with silver.

"I don't reckon Raven is going to need that if he's dead," One-Eye said. "And if he ain't—well, tough. His old buddies are in need."

The coins were odd. After studying them, I recognized what that oddness was. They were the same as the coins Shed had received at the black castle. "Sniff these things," I told One-Eye. "They're black castle. See if there's anything wrong with them."

"Nope. Good as gold." He chuckled.

"Uhm." I hadn't any scruples about lifting the money. Raven had obtained it by foul means. That put it up for grabs. It had no provenance, as they say in Juniper. "Gather round here. I got an idea." I backed up to the stern lights, where I could watch the dock through the glass window.

They crowded in on me and the chest. "What?" Goblin demanded.

"Why settle for the money? Why not take the whole damned ship? If Raven's dead, or even faking he's dead, what's he going to say about it? We could make it our headquarters."

Goblin liked the idea. So One-Eye didn't. The more so because ships had to do with water. "What about the crew?" he asked. "What about the harbormaster and his people? They'd get the law down on us."

"Maybe. But I think we can handle it. We move in and lock the crew up, there's nobody to complain. Nobody complains, why should the harbormaster be interested?"

"The whole crew ain't aboard. Some's out on the town."

"We grab them when they come back. Hell, man, what better way to be ready to move out in a hurry? And what better place to wait for Raven to turn up?"

One-Eye gave up objecting. He is essentially lazy. Too, there was a gleam in his eye which said he was thinking ahead of me. "Better talk to the Lieutenant," he said. "He knows ships."

Goblin knew One-Eye well. "Don't look at me if you're thinking about going pirate. I've had all the adventure I want. I want to go home."

They got into it, and got loud about it, and had to be shut up.

"Let's worry about getting through the next few days," I growled. "What we do later we can worry about later. Look. We got clothes that belonged to Darling and Raven. Can you guys find them now?"

They put their heads together. After some discussion Goblin announced, "Silent thinks he can. Trouble is, he has to do it like a dog. Lock on the trail and follow around everywhere Raven went. Right up till he died. Or didn't. If he didn't, right on to where he is now."

"But that. . . . Hell. You're spotting him a couple months lead."

"People spend a lot of time not moving around, Croaker. Silent would skip over that."

"Still sounds slow."

"Best you can get. Unless he comes to us. Which maybe he can't."

"All right. All right. What about the ship?"

"Ask the Lieutenant. Let's see if we can find your damned papers."

There were no papers. One-Eye was able to detect nothing hidden anywhere. If I wanted to trace the papers, I'd have to start with the crew. Someone had to help Raven take them off.

We left the ship. Goblin and Pawnbroker found a good spot from which they could watch it. Silent and Otto took off on Raven's trail. The rest of us went back and wakened the Lieutenant. He thought taking the ship was a good idea.

He'd never liked Raven much. I think he was motivated by more than practical considerations.

# Chapter Forty-Two: MEADENVIL: THE REFUGEE

The rumors and incredible stories swept through Meadenvil rapidly. Shed heard about the ship from Juniper within hours of her arrival. He was stunned. The Black Company run out? Crushed by their masters? That made no sense. What the hell was going on up there?

His mother. Sal. His friends. What had become of them? If half the stories were true, Juniper was a desolation. The battle with the black castle had consumed the city.

He wanted desperately to go find somebody, ask about his people. He fought the urge. He had to forget his homeland. Knowing that Croaker and his bunch, the whole thing could be a trick to smoke him out.

For a day he remained in hiding, in his rented room, debating, till he convinced himself that he should do nothing. If the Company was on the run, it would be leaving again. Soon. Its former masters would be looking for it.

Would the Taken come after him, too? No. They had no quarrel with him. They did not care about his crimes. Only the Custodians wanted him. . . . He wondered about Bullock, rotting in prison, accused of Raven's murder. He did not understand that at all, but was too nervous to investigate. The answer was not significant in the equation of Marron Shed's survival.

After his day in isolation he decided to resume his quest for a place of business. He was looking for a partnership in a tavern, having decided to stick with what he knew.

It had to be a better place. One that would not lead him into financial difficulties the way the Lily had. Each time he recalled the Lily, he suffered moments of homesickness and nostalgia, of bottomless loneliness. He had been a loner all his life, but never alone. This exile was filled with pain.

He was walking a narrow, shadowed street, slogging uphill through mud left by a nighttime rain, when something in the corner of his eye sent chills to the deeps of his soul. He stopped and whirled so swiftly he knocked another pedestrian down. As he helped the man rise, apologizing profusely, he glared into the shadows of an alley.

"Conscience playing tricks on me, I guess," he murmured, after parting with his victim. But he knew better. He had seen it. Had heard his name called softly. He went to the mouth of the gap between buildings. But it had not waited for him.

A block later he laughed nervously, trying to convince himself it had been a trick of imagination after all. What the hell would the castle creatures be doing in Meadenvil? They'd been wiped out. . . . But the Company guys who had fled here didn't know that for sure, did they? They had run off before the fight was over. They just hoped their bosses had won, because the other side was even worse than theirs.

He was being silly. How could the creature have gotten here? No ship's master would sell passage to a thing like that.

"Shed, you're worrying yourself silly about nothing." He entered a tavern called The Ruby Glass, operated by a man named Selkirk. Shed's landlord had recommended both.

Their discussions were fruitful. Shed agreed to return the following afternoon.

Shed was sharing a beer with his prospective partner. His proposition seemed beneficial, for Selkirk had satisfied himself as to his character and now was trying to sell him on the Ruby Glass. "Night business will pick up once the scare is over."

"Scare?"

"Yeah. Some people have disappeared around the neighborhood. Five or six in the last week. After dark. Not the kind usually grabbed by the press gangs. So people have been staying inside. We aren't getting the usual night traffic."

The temperature seemed to drop forty degrees. Shed sat rigid as a board, eyes vacant, the old fear sliding through him like the passage of snakes. His fingers rose to the shape of the amulet hidden beneath his shirt.

"Hey, Marron, what's the matter?"

"That's how it started in Juniper," he said, unaware that he was speaking. "Only it was just the dead. But they wanted them living. If they could get them. I have to go."

"Shed? What the hell is wrong?"

He came out of it momentarily. "Oh. Sorry, Selkirk. Yeah. We have a deal. But there's something I have to do first. Something I need to check on."

"What?"

"Nothing to do with you. With us. We're ready to go. I'll bring my stuff up tomorrow and we can get together with the people we need to close the deal legally. I just have something else to do right now."

He went out of the place practically running, not sure what he could do or where he could start, not even if he was sane in his assumption. But he was sure that what had happened in Juniper would reoccur in Meadenvil. And a lot faster if the creatures were doing their own collecting.

He touched his amulet again, wondering how much protection it afforded. Was it puissant? Or just a promise?

He hurried to his rooming house, where people were patient with his questions, knowing he was from out of town. He asked about Raven. The murder had been the talk of the town, what with a foreign policeman having been charged on the accusation of his own men. But nobody knew anything. There was no eyewitness to Raven's death except Asa. And Asa was in Juniper. Probably dead.

The Black Company would not have wanted him turning witness against them.

He shed an impulse to contact the survivors. They might want him out of the way, too.

He was on his own with this.

The place where Raven had died seemed a likely place to start. Who knew where that was? Asa. Asa was not available. Who else? How about Bullock?

His guts knotted. Bullock represented everything he feared back home. In a cage here, but still very much a symbol. Could he face the man?

Would the man tell him anything?

Finding Bullock was no problem. The main prison did not move. Finding the courage to face him, even from beyond bars, was another matter. But this entire city lay under a shadow.

Torment racked Shed. Guilt cut him apart. He had done things that left him unable to endure himself. He had committed crimes for which there was no way of making restitution. Yet here was something. . . .

"You're a fool, Marron Shed," he told himself. "Don't worry about it. Meadenvil can look out for itself. Just move on to another city."

But something deeper than cowardice told him he could not run. And not just from himself. A creature from the black castle had appeared in Meadenvil. Two men who had had dealings with the castle had come here. That could not be coincidence. Suppose he moved on? What was to keep the creatures from turning up again, wherever he went?

He had made a deal with a devil. On a gut level he sensed that the net in which he had been taken had to be unwoven strand by strand.

He moved the every-day, cowardly Shed to a throne far behind his eyes and brought forward the Shed who had hunted with Krage and eventually killed his tormentor.

He did not recall the cock-and-bull story he used to get past the wards, but did bullshit his way in to see Bullock.

The Inquisitor had lost none of his spirit. He came to the

bars spitting and cursing and promising Shed an excruciating death.

Shed countered, "You ain't never going to punish nobody but maybe a cockroach in there. Shut up and listen. Forget who you were and remember where you are. I'm the only hope you got of getting out." Shed was amazed. Could he have been half as firm without the intervening bars?

Bullock's face went blank. "Go ahead. Talk."

"I don't know how much you hear in here. Probably nothing. I'll run it down. After you left Juniper, the rest of the Black Company showed up. They took over. Their Lady and what-not came to town. They attacked the black castle. I don't know how that turned out. What word there is makes it sound like the city was wiped out. During the fighting some of the Company guys grabbed a ship and got out on account of their masters were going to turn on them. Why I don't know."

Bullock stared at him, considering. "That's the truth?"

"From what I've heard second-hand."

"It was those Black Company bastards got me in here. Framed me. I only had a fight with Raven. Hell, he almost killed *me*."

"He's dead now." Shed described what Asa had seen. "I have a notion what killed him and why. What I need to know is where it happened. So I can make sure. You tell me that and I'll try to get you out."

"I only know approximately. I know where I caught up with him and which way him and Asa went when they got away. That should pin it down pretty close. Why do you want to know?"

"I think the castle creatures planted something on Raven. Like a seed. I think that's why he died. Like the man who brought the original seed to Juniper."

Bullock frowned.

"Yeah. Sounds tall. But listen to this. The other day I saw one of the creatures near where I'm staying. Watching me. Wait! I know what they look like. I met them. Also, people are disappearing. Not too many yet. Not enough to cause a big stink. But enough to scare people."

Bullock moved to the back of his cell, settled on the floor, placed his back against the wall. He was quiet for more than a minute. Shed waited nervously.

"What's your interest, innkeeper?"

"Repayment of a debt. Bullock, the Black Company kept me prisoner for a while. I learned a lot about that castle. It was nastier than anybody guessed. It was a doorway of sorts. Through which a creature called the Dominator was trying to get into the world. I contributed to the growth of that thing. I helped it reach the point where it attracted the Black Company and its sorcerer friends. If Juniper has been destroyed, it's as much my fault as anybody's. Now the same fate threatens Meadenvil. I can do something to stop it. If I can find it."

Bullock sniggered. Sniggers turned into chuckles. Chuckles became laughter.

"Then rot here!" Shed shouted, and started to leave.

"Wait!"

Shed turned.

Bullock stifled his mirth. "Sorry. It's so incongruous. You, so righteous. I mean, I really believe you mean it. All right, Marron Shed. Give it a shot. And if you manage it and you get me out of here, I might not drag you back to Juniper."

"There's no Juniper to drag me to, Bullock. Rumor says the Lady planned to loot the Catacombs after she finished the black castle. You know what that means. All-out rebellion."

Bullock's humor vanished. "Straight down the Shaker Road, past the twelfth mile marker. Left on the first farm track, under a dead oak tree. You go at least six miles on that. Way past the farms. That's wild country. You better go armed."

"Armed?" Shed grinned a big, self-conscious grin. "Marron Shed never had guts enough to learn to use a weapon. Thanks."

"Don't forget me, Shed. My trial comes up first week next month."

"Right."

Shed dismounted and began leading the rented mule when he reached a point he estimated to be six miles from the Shaker Road. He went on another half-mile. The track was little more than a game trail, winding through rugged country densely covered with hardwood. He saw no evidence man ever traveled this way. Odd. What had Raven and Asa been doing out here? He could think of no reason that made sense. Asa had claimed they were running from Bullock. If so, why hadn't they kept on going down the Shaker Road?

His nerves tautened. He touched the amulet, the knife hidden up his sleeve. He had splurged and bought himself two good short weapons, one for his belt and one for his sleeve.

They did little to boost his confidence.

The trail turned downhill, toward a brook, ran beside that for several hundred yards, and debouched into a broad clearing. Shed almost walked into that. He was a city boy. Never before had he been into country more wild than the Enclosure.

Some innate sense of caution stopped him at the clearing's edge. He dropped to one knee, parted the undergrowth, cursed softly when the mule nudged him with its nose.

He had guessed right.

A great black lump stood out there. It was the size of a house already. Shed stared at faces frozen in screams of terror and agony.

A perfect place for it, out here. Growing this fast, it would become complete before anyone discovered it. Unless by accident. And the accidental discoverer would become one with it.

Shed's heart hammered. He wanted nothing more than to race back to Meadenvil and cry the city's danger in the streets. He had seen enough. He knew what he had come to learn. Time to get away.

He went forward, slowly. He dropped the mule's reins, but it followed, interested in the tall grass. Shed approached the black lump carefully, a few steps at a time. Nothing happened. He circled it.

The shape of the thing became more evident. It would be identical to the fortress overlooking Juniper, except for the way its foundations conformed to the earth. Its gate would face south. A well-beaten path led to a low hole there. Further confirmation of his suspicions.

Where had the creatures come from? Did they roam the world at will, hidden on the edge of night, seen only by those who bargained with them?

Returning to the side from which he had approached, he stumbled over something.

Bones. Human bones. A skeleton—head, arms, legs, with part of the chest missing. Still clad in tatters he'd seen Raven wear a hundred times. He knelt. "Raven. I hated you. But I loved you, too. You were the worst villain I ever knew. And as good a friend as I ever had. You made me start thinking like a man." Tears filled his eyes.

He searched childhood memories, finally found the prayer for the passage of the dead. He began to sing in a voice that had no notion how to carry a tune.

The grass swished only once, just on the edge of audibility. A hand closed on his shoulder. A voice said, "Marron Shed."

Shed shrieked and grabbed for his belt knife.

# Chapter Forty-Three: MEADENVIL: WARM TRAIL

I did not have a good night after visiting Raven's ship. It was a night of dreams. Of nightmares, if you will. Of terrors I dared not mention when I wakened, for the others had troubles and fears enough.

*She* came to me in my sleep, as she had not done since our grim retreats when the Rebel was closing in on Charm, so long ago. She came, a golden glow that might have been no dream at all, for it seemed to be there in the room I shared with five other men, illuminating them and the room while I lay with heart hammering, staring in disbelief. The others did not respond, and later I was not sure I had not imagined the whole thing. It had been that way with the visits in the way back when.

"Why did you abandon me, physician? Did I treat you less than well?"

Baffled, confused, I croaked out, "It was run or be killed. We would not have fled had there been a choice. We served you faithfully, through hazards and horrors greater than any in our Company's history. We marched to the ends of the earth for you, without complaint. And when we came to the city Juniper, and spent half our strength storming the black castle, we learned that we were to be rewarded by being destroyed."

That marvelous face formed in the golden cloud. That marvelous face drawn in sadness. "Whisper planned that. Whisper and Feather. For reasons of their own. But Feather is gone and Whisper has been disciplined. I would not have allowed such a crime in any case. You were my chosen instruments. I would permit no machination of the Taken to harm you. Come back."

"It's too late, Lady. The die is cast. Too many good men have been lost. Our heart is gone. We have grown old. Our only desire is to return to the South, to rest in the warm sun and forget."

"Come back. There is much to be done. You are my chosen instruments. I will reward you as no soldiers have ever been rewarded."

I could detect no hint of treachery. But what did that mean? She was ancient. She had deluded her husband, who was far harder to fuddle than I.

"It's too late, Lady."

"Come back, physician. You, if no one else. I need your pen."

I do not know why I said what I did next. It was not the wisest thing to do, if she was feeling the least benevolent toward us, the least disinclined to come howling after us. "We will do one more thing for you. Because we are old and tired and want to be done with war. We will not stand against you. If you do not stand against us."

Sadness radiated from the glow. "I am sorry. Truly sorry. You were one of my favorites. A mayfly who intrigued me. No, physician. That cannot be. You cannot remain neutral. You never could. You must stand with me or against me. There is no middle ground."

And with that the golden cloud faded, and I fell into a deep sleep—if ever I had been awake.

I woke feeling rested but worried, at first unable to recall the visit. Then it slammed back into consciousness. I dressed hurriedly, raced to the Lieutenant. "Lieutenant, we got to start moving faster. She won. She's going to come after us."

He looked startled. I told him about the night vision. He took it with a pound of salt till I told him that she had done the same before, during the long retreat and series of encounters that had brought the Rebel main forces to the gates of Charm. He did not want to believe me, but he dared not do otherwise. "Get out there and find that Asa, then," he said. "Candy, we move on that ship tonight. Croaker, you pass the word. We're pulling out in four days, whether you guys find Raven or not."

I sputtered a protest. The critical thing now was to find Darling. Darling was our hope. I asked, "Why four days?"

"It took us four days to sail here from Juniper. Good winds and seas all the way. If the Lady left when you turned her down, she couldn't get here any quicker. So I'll give you that long. Then we hit the sea. If we have to fight our way out."

"All right." I didn't like it, but he was the man who made the decisions. We had elected him to do that. "Hagop, find Kingpin. We're going looking for Asa."

Hagop hurried away like his tail was aflame. He brought Kingpin back in minutes, King crabbing because he hadn't yet eaten, hadn't yet gotten his eight hours of sleep.

"Shut up, King. Our ass is in a vise." I explained, though it wasn't necessary. "Grab something cold and eat on the run. We've got to find Asa."

Hagop, Kingpin, One-Eye and I hit the street. As always, we drew a lot of attention from morning marketers, not only because we had come from Juniper, but because One-Eye was an oddity. They'd never seen a black man in Meadenvil. Most people hadn't heard of blacks.

Kingpin led us a mile through twisting streets. "I figure he'll hole up in the same area as before. He knows it. He's not very bright, either, so it wouldn't occur to him to move because you guys came to town. Probably just plans to keep his head down till we pull out. He's got to figure we have to keep moving."

His reasoning seemed sound. And so it proved. He interviewed a few people he had met in the course of previous poking around, quickly discovered that Asa was, indeed, hiding out in the area. Nobody was sure where, though.

"We'll take care of that in a hurry," One-Eye said. He parked himself on a doorstep and performed a few cheap magic tricks that were all flash and show. That arrested the attention of the nearest urchins. Meadenvil's streets are choked with children all the time.

"Let's fade," I told the others. We had to be intimidating to small eyes. We moved up the street and let One-Eye draw his crowd.

He gave the kids their money's worth. Of course. And fifteen minutes later he rejoined us, trailed by an entourage of street mites. "Got it," he said. "My little buddies will show us where."

He amazes me sometimes. I would have bet he hated kids. I mean, when he mentions them at all, which is about once a year, it is in the context of whether they are tastier roasted or boiled.

Asa was holed up in a tenement typical of slums the world over. A real rat- and firetrap. I guess having come into money hadn't changed his habits. Unlike old Shed, who had gone crazy when he had money to spend.

There was but one way out, the way we went in. The children followed us. I did not like that, but what could I do?

We pushed into the room Asa called home. He was lying on a pallet in a corner. Another man, reeking of wine, lay nearby, in a pool of vomit. Asa was curled into a ball, snoring. "Time to get up, sweetheart." I shook him gently.

He stiffened under my hand. His eyes popped open. Terror filled them. I pressed down as he tried to jump up. "Caught you again," I said.

He gobbled air. No words came out.

"Take it easy, Asa. Nobody's going to get hurt. We just want you to show us where Raven went down." I withdrew my hand.

He rolled over slowly, watched us like a cat cornered by dogs. "You guys are always saying you just want something."

"Be nice, Asa. We don't want to play rough. But we will if we have to. We have four days before the Lady gets here. We're going to find Darling before then. You're going to help. What you do afterward is your own business."

One-Eye snorted softly. He had visions of Asa with a cut throat. He figured the little man deserved no better.

"You just go down the Shaker Road. Turn left on the first farm road past the twelfth milestone. Keep heading east till you get to the place. It's about seven miles. The road turns into a trail. Don't worry about that. Just keep going and you'll get there." He closed his eyes, rolled over, and pretended to snore.

I indicated Hagop and Kingpin. "Get him up."

"Hey!" Asa yelped. "I told you. What more do you want?"

"I want you to come along. Just in case."

"In case what?"

"In case you're lying and I want to lay hands on you fast."

One-Eye added, "We don't believe Raven died."

"I *saw* him."

"You saw something," I countered. "I don't think it was Raven. Let's go." We grabbed his arms. I told Hagop to see about rounding up horses and provisions. I sent Kingpin to tell the Lieutenant we wouldn't be back till tomorrow. Hagop I gave a fistful of silver from Raven's chest. Asa's eyes widened slightly. He recognized the mintage, if not the immediate source.

"You guys can't push me around here," he said. "You're not anything more than I am. We go out in the street, all I have to do is yell and . . ."

"And you'll wish you hadn't," One-Eye said. He did something with his hands. A soft violet glow webbed his fingers, coalesced into something serpent-like that slithered over and under his digits. "This little fellow here can crawl into your ear and eat out your eyes from behind. You can't yell loud enough or fast enough to keep me from siccing him on you."

Asa gulped and became amenable.

"All I want is for you to show me the place," I said. "Quickly. I don't have much time."

Asa surrendered. He expected the worst of us, of course. He had spent too much time in the company of villains nastier than us.

Hagop had the horses within half an hour. It took Kingpin another half-hour to rejoin us. Being Kingpin, he dawdled, and when he appeared, One-Eye gave him such a look he blanched and half drew his sword.

"Let's get moving," I growled. I did not like the way the Company was turning upon itself, like a wounded animal snapping at its own flank. I set a stiff pace, hoping to keep everybody too tired and busy to fuss.

Asa's directions proved sound and were easily followed. I was pleased, and when he saw that, he asked permission to turn back.

"How come you're so anxious to stay away from this place? What's out there that's got you scared?"

It took a little pressure, with One-Eye conjuring his violet snake again, to loosen Asa's jaw.

"I came out here right after I got back from Juniper. Because you guys didn't believe me about Raven. I thought maybe you were right and he'd fooled me somehow. So I wanted to see how he maybe did it. And. . . ."

"And?"

He checked us over, estimating our mood. "There's another of those *places* out there. It wasn't there when he died. But it is now."

"Places?" I asked. "What kind of places?"

"Like the black castle. There's one right where he died. Out in the middle of the clearing."

"Tricky," One-Eye snarled. "Trying to send us into that. I'm going to cut this guy, Croaker."

"No, you're not. You let him be." Over the next mile I questioned Asa closely. He told me nothing more of importance.

Hagop was riding point, being a superb scout. He threw up a hand. I joined him. He indicated droppings in the trail. "We're following somebody. Not far behind." He swung down, poked the droppings with a stick, duck-walked up the trail a way. "He was riding something big. Mule or plowhorse."

"Asa!"

"Eh?" the little man squeaked.

"What's up ahead? Where is this guy headed?"

"Nothing's up there. That I know of. Maybe it's a hunter. They sell a lot of game in the markets."

"Maybe."

"Sure," One-Eye said, sarcastic, playing with his violet snake.

"How about you put a little silence on the situation, One-Eye? No! I mean so nobody can hear us coming. Asa. How far to go?"

"Couple miles, anyway. Why don't you guys let me head back now? I can still get to town before dark."

"Nope. You go where we go." I glanced at One-Eye. He was doing as I had requested. We would be able to hear one another talk. That was all. "Saddle up, Hagop. He's only one guy."

"But which guy, eh, Croaker? Suppose it's one of them creepy things? I mean, if that place in Juniper had a whole battalion that came out of nowhere, why shouldn't this place have some?"

Asa made sounds that indicated he had been having similar thoughts. Which explained why he was anxious to get back to town.

"You see anything when you were there, Asa?"

"No. But I seen where the grass was trampled like something was coming and going."

"You pay attention when we get there, One-Eye. I don't want no surprises."

Twenty minutes later Asa told me, "Almost there. Maybe two hundred yards up the creek. Can I stay here?"

"Quit asking stupid questions." I glanced at Hagop, who pointed out tracks. Somebody was ahead of us still. "Dismount. And stow the chatter. Finger talk from here on in. You, Asa, don't open your mouth for nothing. Understand?"

We dismounted, drew our weapons, went forward under

cover of One-Eye's spell. Hagop and I reached the clearing first. I grinned, waved One-Eye forward, pointed. He grinned too. I waited a couple of minutes, for the right time, then strode out, stepped up behind the man, and grabbed his shoulder. "Marron Shed."

He shrieked and tried to pull a knife, tried to run at the same time. Kingpin and Hagop headed him off and herded him back. By that time I was kneeling where he had knelt, examining the scatter of bones.

# Chapter Forty-Four: MEADENVIL: THE CLEARING

I looked up at Shed. He looked resigned. "Caught up faster than you expected, eh?"

He babbled. I could make little sense of what he said because he was talking about several things at once. Raven. Black castle creatures. His chance to make a new life. What-not.

"Calm down and be quiet, Shed. We're on your side." I explained the situation, telling him we had four days to find Darling. He found it difficult to believe that the girl who had worked in the Iron Lily could be the Rebel's White Rose. I did not argue, just presented the facts. "Four days, Shed. Then the Lady and Taken could be here. And I guarantee you she'll be looking for you, too. By now they know we faked your death. By now they've probably questioned enough people to have an idea what was going on. We're fighting for our lives, Shed." I looked at the big black lump and said to no one in particular, "And that thing don't help one damned bit."

I looked at the bones again. "Hagop, see what you can make of this. One-Eye, you and Asa go over exactly what he saw that day. Walk through it. Kingpin, you play Raven for them. Shed, come here with me."

I was pleased. Both Asa and Shed did as they were told. Shed, though shaken by our return to the stage of his life, did not seem likely to panic. I watched him as Hagop examined the ground inch by inch. Shed seemed to have grown, to have found something in himself that had not had a chance in the sterile soil of Juniper.

He whispered, "Look, Croaker. I don't know about that stuff about the Lady coming and how you got to find Darling. I don't much care." He indicated the black lump. "What're you going to do about that?"

"Good question." He did not have to explain what it meant. It meant the Dominator had not endured final defeat in Juniper. He had hedged his bet beforehand. He had another gateway growing here, and growing fast. Asa was right to be afraid of castle creatures. The Dominator knew he had to hurry—though I doubted he had expected to be found out so soon. "There isn't much we *can* do, when you get down to it."

"You got to do something. Look, I know. I dealt with those things. What they did to me and Raven and Juniper. . . . Hell, Croaker, you can't let that happen again here."

"I didn't say I didn't want to do something. I said I can't. You don't ask a man with a penknife to chop down a forest and build a city. He doesn't have the tools."

"Who does?"

"The Lady."

"Then. . . ."

"I have my limits, friend. I'm not going to get myself killed for Meadenvil. I'm not going to get my outfit scrubbed for people I don't know. Maybe we owe a moral debt. But I don't think it's that big."

He grunted, understanding without accepting. I was surprised. Without his having said as much, I sensed that he had launched a crusade. A grand villain trying to buy redemption. I did not begrudge him in the least. But he could do it without the Company and me.

I watched One-Eye and Asa walk Kingpin through everything Raven had done the day he died. From where I sat I could see no flaw in Asa's story. I hoped One-Eye had a better view. He, if anyone, could find the angle. He was as good at stage magic as at true wizardry.

I recalled that Raven had been pretty good with tricks.

His biggie had been making knives appear out of thin air. But he had had other tricks with which he had entertained Darling.

Hagop said, "Look here, Croaker."

I looked. I did not see anything abnormal. "What?"

"Going through the grass toward the lump. It's almost gone now, but it's there. Like a trail." He held blades of grass parted.

It took me a while to see it. Just the faintest hint of a sheen, like an old snail track. A closer scrutiny showed that it should have started roughly where the corpse's heart would have lain. It took a little work to figure, because scavengers had torn the remains.

I examined a fleshless hand. Rings remained on the fingers. Various metal accoutrements and several knives also lay around.

One-Eye worked Kingpin over to the bones. "Well?" I asked.

"It's possible. With a little misdirection and stage magic. I couldn't tell you how he did it. If he did."

"We got a body," I said, indicating the bones.

"That's him," Asa insisted. "Look. He's still wearing his rings. And that's his belt buckle and sword and knives." But a shadow of doubt lingered in his voice. He was coming around to my way.

And I still wondered why the nice new ship had not been claimed.

"Hagop. Hunt around for signs somebody went off in another direction. Asa. You said you lit out as soon as you saw what was happening?"

"Yeah."

"So. Let's quit worrying about that and try to figure what happened here. Just to look at it, this dead man had something that became that." I indicated the lump. I was surprised I had so little trouble ignoring it. I guess you can get used to anything. I'd paraded around the big one in Juniper till I'd lost that cold dread that had moved me for a while. I mean, if men can get used to slaughterhouses, or my business—soldier *or* surgeon—they can get used to anything.

"Asa, you hung around with Raven. Shed, he lived at your place for a couple years, and you were his partner. What did he bring from Juniper that could have come to life and become that?"

They shook their heads and stared at the bones. I told them, "Think harder. Shed, it had to be something he had when you knew him. He stopped going up the hill a long time before he headed south."

A minute or two passed. Hagop had begun working his way along the edge of the clearing. I had little hope he would find traces this long after the fact. I was no woodsman, but I knew Raven.

Asa suddenly gasped.

"What?" I snapped.

"Everything is here. You know, all the metal. Even his buttons and stuff. But one thing."

"Well?"

"This necklace he wore. I only seen it a couple times. . . . What's the matter, Shed?"

I turned. Shed was gripping his chest over his heart. His face was marble white. He gobbled for words that would not come. He started trying to rip his shirt.

I thought he was having an attack. But as I reached him, to help, he opened his shirt and grabbed something he was wearing around his neck. Something on a chain. He tried to get it off by main force. The chain would not break.

I forced him to take it off over his head, pried it out of stiff fingers, held it out to Asa.

Asa looked a little pale. "Yeah. That's it."

"Silver," One-Eye said, and looked at Hagop meaningfully.

He would think that way. And he might be right. "Hagop! Come here."

One-Eye took the thing, held it to the light. "Some craftsmanship," he mused. . . . Then flung it down and dived like a frog off his lily pad. As he arced through the air, he barked like a jackal.

Light flashed. I whirled. Two castle creatures stood at the side of the black lump, frozen in midstep, in the act of rushing us. Shed cursed. Asa shrieked. Kingpin zipped past me and drove his blade deep into a chest. I did the same, so rattled I did not recall the difficulty I'd had during our previous encounter.

We both hit the same one. We both yanked out weapons free. "The neck," I gasped. "Go for the vein in the neck."

One-Eye was up again, ready for action. He told me later he had glimpsed motion in the corner of his eye, jumped just in time to evade something thrown. They had known who to take first. Who was most potent.

Hagop came up from behind as the things started moving, added his blade to the contest. As did Shed, to my surprise. He jumped in with a knife about a foot long, got low, went for a hamstring.

It was brief. One-Eye had given us the moment we needed. They were stubborn about it, but they died. The last to go looked up at Shed, smiled, and said, "Marron Shed. You will be remembered."

Shed started shaking.

Asa said, "He knew you, Shed."

"He's the one I delivered bodies to. Every time but one."

"Wait a minute," I countered. "Only one creature got away at Juniper. Don't seem likely it would be the one who knew you. . . ." I stopped. I had noticed something disturbing. The two creatures were identical. Even to a scar across the chest when I peeled back their dark clothing. The creature the Lieutenant and I had hauled down the hill, after having slain it before the castle gate, had had such a scar.

While everyone else was suffering post-combat shakes, One-Eye asked Hagop, "You see anything silver around Old Bones? When you were checking first?"

"Uh. . . ."

One-Eye held up Shed's necklace. "It might have looked something like this. It was what killed him."

Hagop gulped and dug into a pocket. He handed over a necklace identical to Shed's, except that the serpents had no eyes.

"Yeah," One-Eye said, and again held Shed's necklace to the light. "Yeah. The eyes it was. When the time was right. Time and place."

I was more interested in what else might come out of the black lump. I pulled Hagop around the side, found the entrance. It looked like the entrance to a mud hut. I supposed it wouldn't become a real gate till the place grew up. I indicated the tracks. "What do they tell you?"

"They tell me it's busy and we ought to get out of here. There's more of them."

"Yeah."

We rejoined the others. One-Eye was wrapping Shed's necklace in a piece of cloth. "We get back to town, I'm sealing this in something made of steel and sinking it in the harbor."

"Destroy it, One-Eye. Evil always finds its way back. The Dominator is a perfect example."

"Yeah. All right. If I can."

Elmo's rush into the black castle came to mind while I was getting everybody organized to get out of there. I had changed my mind about overnighting. We could get most of the way back before nightfall. Meadenvil, like Juniper, had neither walls nor gates. We would not be locked outside.

I let Elmo lie in the back of my mind till the thought ripened. When it did, I was aghast.

A tree ensures reproduction by shedding a million seeds. One certainly will survive, and a new tree will grow. I pictured a horde of fighters bursting into the guts of the black castle and finding silver amulets everywhere. I pictured them filling their pockets.

Had to be. That place was doomed. The Dominator would have known that even before the Lady.

My respect for the old devil rose. Crafty bastard.

It was not till we were back on the Shaker Road that I

thought to ask Hagop if he had seen any evidence that anyone had left the clearing by another route.

"Nope," he said. "But that don't mean anything."

"Let's not spend so much time yakking," One-Eye said. "Shed, can't you make that damned mule go any faster?"

He was scared. And if he was, I was more so.

# Chapter Forty-Five: MEADENVIL: HOT TRAIL

We made the city. But I swear I could sense something sniffing along our backtrail before we reached the safety of the lights. We returned to our lodgings only to find most of the men gone. Where were they? Off to take over Raven's ship, I learned.

I had forgotten about that. Yes. Raven's ship. . . . And Silent was on Raven's trail. Where was he now? Damn! Sooner or later Raven would lead him to the clearing. . . . A way to find out if Raven had left it, for sure. Also a way to lose Silent. "One-Eye. Can you get hold of Silent?"

He looked at me strangely. He was tired and wanted to sleep.

"Look, if he follows Raven's every move, he's going to head out to that clearing."

One-Eye groaned and went through several dramatic shows of disgust. Then he dug into his magic sack for something that looked like a desiccated finger. He took it to a corner and communed with it, then returned to say, "I got a line on him. I'll find him."

"Thanks."

"Yeah. You bastard. I ought to make you come with me."

I settled by the fire, with a big beer, and lost myself in thought. After a while, I told Shed: "We have to go back out there."

"Eh?"

"With Silent."

"Who's Silent?"

"Another guy from the Company. Wizard. Like One-Eye and Goblin. He's on Raven's trail, tracing every move he made from the minute he arrived. He figured he could track him down, or at least tell from his movements if he was planning to trick Asa."

Shed shrugged. "If we have to, we have to."

"Hunh. You amaze me, Shed. You've changed."

"I don't know. Maybe I could have done it all along. I just know that this thing can't happen again, to anybody else."

"Yeah." I did not mention my visions of hundreds of men looting amulets from the fortress at Juniper. He did not need that. He had a mission. I couldn't make it sound hopeless.

I went downstairs and asked the landlord for more beer. Beer makes me sleepy. I had a notion. A possibility. I did not share it with anyone. The others would not have been pleased.

After an hour I took a leak and dragged off to my room, more intimidated by the thought of returning to that clearing than by what I hoped to accomplish now.

Sleep was a time coming, beer or not. I could not relax. I kept trying to reach out and bring her to me. Which meant nothing at all.

It was a weak fool's hope that she would return so soon. I had put her off. Why should she? Why shouldn't she forget me till her minions caught up and could bring me to her in chains?

Maybe there *is* a connection on a level I do not understand. For I wakened from a drowse, thinking I needed to visit the head again, and found that golden glow hanging above me. Or maybe I did not waken, but only dreamed that I did. I can't get that straight. It always seems so dream-like in retrospect.

I did not wait for her to start. I started talking. I talked fast and told her everything she needed to know about the lump in Meadenvil and about the possibility the troops had carried hundreds of seeds out of the black castle.

"You tell me this when you are determined to be my enemy, physician?"

"I don't want to be your enemy. I'll be your enemy only if you leave me no option." I abandoned debate. "We can't handle this. And it has to be handled. All its like must be handled. There is evil enough in the world as it is." I told her we had found an amulet upon a citizen of Juniper. I named no name. I told her we would leave it where she could be sure to find it when she arrived.

"Arrive?"

"Aren't you on your way here?"

Thin smile, secretive, perfectly aware that I was fishing. No answer. Just a question. "Where will you be?"

"Gone. Long gone, and headed far away."

"Perhaps. We shall see." The golden glow faded.

There were things I wanted to say yet, but they had nothing to do with the problem at hand. Questions I wanted to ask. I did not.

The last golden mote left me with a whispered, "I owe you one, physician."

One-Eye rambled into the place shortly after sunrise, looking a lot worse for wear. Silent came along behind him, looking pretty beaten himself. He had been on Raven's trail without let-up. One-Eye said, "I caught him just in time. Another hour and he would have headed out. I conned him into waiting till daylight."

"Yeah. You want to wake the troops? We get an earlier start today, we ought to be able to get back before dark."

"What?"

"I thought I was pretty clear. We've got to go back out there. Now. We've used one of our days."

"Hey, man, I'm ripped. I'll die if you make me. . . ."

"Sleep in the saddle. That's always been one of your big talents. Sleep anywhere, any time."

"Oh, my aching butt."

An hour later I was headed down the Shaker Road

again, with Silent and Otto added to the crew. Shed insisted on coming along, though I was willing to excuse him. Asa decided he wanted in, too. Maybe because he thought Shed would extend an umbrella of protection. He had started talking mission like Shed, but a deaf man could hear its false ring.

We moved faster this time, pressed harder, and had Shed on a real horse. We got down to the clearing by noon. While Silent sniffed around, I worked myself up and took a closer look at the lump.

No change. Except the two dead creatures were gone. I did not need Hagop's eye to see that they had been dragged through the entry hole.

Silent worked his way around the clearing to a point almost identical with that where the creature trail entered the forest. Then he threw up an arm, beckoned. I hurried over, and did not have to read the dance of his fingers to know what he had found. His face revealed the answer.

"Found it, eh?" I asked more brightly than I felt. I had started to count on Raven being dead. I did not like what the skeleton implied.

Silent nodded.

"Yo!" I called. "We found it. Let's go. Bring the horses."

The others gathered. Asa looked a little peaked. He asked, "How did he do it?"

Nobody had an answer. Several of us wondered whose skeleton lay in the clearing and how it had come to wear Raven's necklace. I wondered how Raven's plot for vanishing had dovetailed so neatly with the Dominator's for seeding a new black castle.

Only One-Eye seemed in a mood to talk, and that all complaint. "We follow this and we're not going to get back to town before dark," he said. He said a lot more, mostly about how tired he was. Nobody paid attention. Even those of us who had rested were tired.

"Lead off, Silent," I said. "Otto, you want to take care of his horse? One-Eye, bring up the rear. So we don't get any surprises from behind."

The track was no track at all for a while, just a straight shot through the brush. We were winded by the time it intercepted a game trail. Raven, too, must have been exhausted, for he had turned onto that trail and followed it over a hill, along a creek, up another hill. Then he had turned onto a less traveled path which ran along a ridge, toward the Shaker Road. Over the next two hours we encountered several such forkings. Each time Raven had taken the one which tended more directly westward.

"Bastard was headed back to the high road," One-Eye said. "Could have figured that, gone the other way, and saved all this tramping through the brush."

Men growled at him. His complaints were grating. Even Asa tossed a nasty look over one shoulder.

Raven had taken the long way, no doubt about it. I would guess we walked at least ten miles before coming across a ridgeline and viewing cleared land which descended to the high road. A number of farms lay on our right. In the distance ahead lay the blue haze of the sea. The countryside was mostly brown, for autumn had come to Meadenvil. The leaves were turning. Asa indicated a stand of maples and said they would look real pretty in another week. Odd. You don't think of guys like him as having a sense of beauty.

"Down there." Otto indicated a cluster of buildings three-quarters of a mile south. It did not look like a farm. "Bet that's a roadside inn," he said. "What do you want to bet that was where he was headed?"

"Silent?"

He nodded, but hedged. He wanted to stick to the track to make sure. We mounted up, let him do what walking remained to be done. I, for one, had had enough tramping around.

"How about we stay over?" One-Eye asked.

I checked the sun. "I'm considering it. How safe you figure we'd be?"

He shrugged. "There's smoke coming up down there. Don't look like they had any trouble yet."

Mind-reader. I had been examining farmsteads as we

passed, seeking indications that the lump creatures were raiding the neighborhood. The farms had seemed peaceful and active. I suppose the creatures confined their predations to the city, where they would cause less excitement.

Raven's track hit the Shaker Road a half-mile above the buildings Otto thought an inn. I checked landmarks, could not guess how far south of the twelfth mile we were. Silent beckoned, pointed. Raven had indeed turned south. We followed and soon passed milestone sixteen.

"How far are you going to follow him, Croaker?" One-Eye asked. "Bet you he met Darling out here and just kept hiking."

"I suspect he did. How far to Shaker? Anybody know?"

"Two hundred forty-seven miles," Kingpin replied.

"Rough country? Likely to have trouble along the way. Bandits and such?"

King said, "Not that I ever heard of. There's mountains, though. Pretty rough ones. Take a while to get through them."

I did some calculating. Say three weeks to cover that distance, not pushing. Raven wouldn't push, what with Darling along, and the papers. "A wagon. He'd have to have a wagon."

Silent, too, was mounted now. We reached the buildings quickly. Otto proved right. Definitely an inn. A girl came outside as we dismounted, looked at us with wide eyes, raced inside. I guess we were a rough-looking lot. Those who did not show tough looked nasty.

A worried fat man came out strangling an apron. His face could not decide if it wanted to remain ruddy or to go pallid. "Afternoon," I said. "We get a meal and some fodder for the animals?"

"Wine," One-Eye called out as he loosened his cinch. "I need to dive into a gallon of wine. And a feather bed."

"I reckon," the man said. His speech proved difficult to follow. The language of Meadenvil is a dialect of that spoken in Juniper. In the city it wasn't hard to get along, what with the constant intercourse between Meadenvil and Juniper. But this fellow spoke a country dialect with an altered rhythm. "And you can afford it."

I produced two of Raven's silver pieces, handed them over. "Let me know when we're over that limit." I dropped my reins over the hitching rail, climbed the steps, patted his arm as I passed. "Not to worry. We're not bandits. Soldiers. Following somebody who passed this way a while back."

He rewarded me with a frown of disbelief. It was obvious we did not serve the Prince of Meadenvil.

The inn was pleasant, and though the fat man had several daughters, everyone stayed in line. After we had eaten and most had gone off to rest, the innkeeper began to relax. "You answer me some questions?" I asked. I placed a silver piece upon my table. "Might be worth something."

He settled opposite me, regarded me narrowly over a gigantic beer mug. He had drained the thing at least six times since our arrival, which explained his girth. "What do you want to know?"

"The tall man who can't talk. He's looking for his daughter."

"Eh?"

I indicated Silent, who had made himself at home near the fire, seated on the floor, folded forward in sleep. "A deaf and dumb girl who passed this way a while back. Probably driving a wagon. Met a guy here, maybe." I described Raven.

His face went blank. He remembered Raven. And did not want to talk about it.

"Silent!"

He snapped out of sleep as if stung. I sent a message with finger signs. He smiled nastily. I told the innkeeper, "He don't look like much, but he's a sorcerer. Here's how it stands. The man who was here maybe told you he'd come back and cut your throat if you said anything. That's a remote risk. On the other hand, Silent there can cast a few spells and make your cows go dry, your fields barren, and all your beer and wine go sour."

Silent did one of those nasty little tricks which amuse him, One-Eye and Goblin. A ball of light drifted around the common room like a curious puppy, poking into things.

The innkeeper believed me enough not to want to call my bluff. "All right. They was here. Like you said. I get a lot of people through in the summer, so I wouldn't have noticed except like you say, the girl was deaf and the guy was a hard case. She come in in the morning, like she traveled all night. On a wagon. He come in the evening, walking. They stayed off in the corner. They left next morning." He looked at my coin. "Paid in that same funny coin, come to think."

"Yeah."

"Come from a long way off, eh?"

"Yeah. Where'd they go?"

"South. Down the road. Questions I heard the guy ask, I figure they was headed for Chimney."

I raised an eyebrow. I'd never heard of any place called Chimney.

"Down the coast. Past Shaker. Take the Needle Road out of Shaker. The Tagline Road from Needle. Somewhere south of Tagline there's a crossroad where you head west. Chimney is on the Salada Peninsula. I don't know where for sure. Only what I heared from travelers."

"Uhm. Long hike. How far, you think?"

"See. Two hundred twenty-four miles to Shaker. Round two hundred more to Needle. Tagline is about one eighty on from Needle, I think. Or maybe it's two eighty. I don't rightly recollect. That crossroad must be another hundred down from Tagline, then out to Chimney. Don't know how far that would be. Least another hundred. Maybe two, three. Seen a map oncet, that a fellow showed me. Peninsula sticks way out like a thumb."

Silent joined us. He produced a scrap of paper and a tiny, steel-tipped pen. He had the innkeeper run through it again. He drew a crude map that he adjusted as the fat man said it did or did not resemble the map he had seen. Silent kept juggling a column of figures. He came up with an estimate in excess of nine hundred miles from Meadenvil. He knocked off the last digit, then wrote the word *days* and a plus sign. I nodded.

"Probably a four-month trip at least," I said. "Longer if they spend much time resting up in any of those cities."

Silent drew a straight line from Meadenvil to the tip of the Salada Peninsula, wrote, *est. 600 mi. a. 6 knots = 100 hrs.*

"Yeah," I said. "Yeah. That's why the ship never left. Had to give him a head start. Think we'll have a talk with the crew tomorrow. Thanks, innkeeper." I pushed the coin over. "Anything odd happened around here lately?"

A weak smiled stretched his lips. "Not till today."

"Right. No. I mean like neighbors disappearing, or what-not."

He shook his head. "Nope. Less you count Moleskin. Hain't seen him in a while. But that don't make no never-mind."

"Moleskin?"

"Hunter. Works the forest over east. Mainly for furs and hides, but brings me game when he needs salt or something. He don't come around regular, but I reckon he's overdue. Usually comes in come fall, to get staples for the winter. Thought it was him when your friend come through the door."

"Eh? Which friend?"

"The one you're hunting. That carried off this feller's daughter."

Silent and I exchanged glances. I said, "Better not count on seeing Moleskin again. I think he's dead."

"What brings you to say that?"

I told him a little about Raven faking his own death and leaving a body that had been confused for his.

"Bad thing, that. Yep. Bad thing, doing like that. Hope you catch him up." His eyes narrowed slightly, cunning. "You fellers wouldn't be part of that bunch come down from Juniper, would you? Everybody headed south talks about how. . . ." Silent's glower shut him up.

"I'm going to get some sleep," I said. "If none of my men are up yet, roust me out at first light."

"Yes, sir," the innkeeper said. "And a fine breakfast we'll fix you, sir."

# Chapter Forty-Six: MEADENVIL: TROUBLE

And a fine breakfast we had. I tipped the innkeeper another piece of silver. He must have thought me mad.

Half a mile up the road One-Eye called a halt. "You just going to leave them?" he asked.

"What?"

"Those people. First Taken comes down this way is going to find out everything we did."

My heart flip-flopped. I knew what he was getting at. I had thought about it earlier. But I could not order it. "No point," I said. "Everybody in Meadenvil is going to see us put out."

"Everybody in Meadenvil don't know where we're headed. I don't like the idea any better than you do, Croaker. But we have to cut the trail somewhere. Raven didn't. And we're on to him."

"Yeah. I know." I glanced at Asa and Shed. They were not taking it well. Asa, at least, figured he was next.

"Can't take them with us, Croaker."

"I know."

He swung around, started back. Alone. Not even Otto joined him, and Otto has very little conscience.

"What's he going to do?" Asa asked.

"Use his magic to make them forget," I lied. "Let's move along. He can catch up."

Shed kept giving me looks. Looks like he must have

given Raven when he first found out Raven was in the body business. He did not say anything.

One-Eye caught up an hour later. He busted out laughing. "They were gone," he said. "Every blessed one, with all their dogs and cattle. Into the woods. Damned peasants." He laughed again, almost hysterically. I suspect he was relieved.

"We got two days and some gone," I said. "Let's push it. The bigger head start we have, the better."

We reached the outskirts of Meadenvil five hours later, not having pressed as hard as I wanted. As we penetrated the city, our pace lagged. I think we all sensed it. Finally, I stopped. "King, you and Asa wander around and see what you hear. We'll wait at yonder fountain." There were no children in the streets. The adults I saw seemed dazed. Those who passed us moved by as widely as they could navigate.

King was back in two minutes. No lollygagging. "Big trouble, Croaker. The Taken got here this morning. Big blowout down at the waterfront."

I glanced in that direction. A ghost of smoke rose there, as if marking the aftermath of a major fire. The sky to the west, in the direction the wind was blowing, had a dirty look.

Asa returned a minute later with the same news and more. "They got in a big fight with the Prince. Not over yet, some say."

"Wouldn't be much of a fight," One-Eye said.

"I don't know," I countered. "Even the Lady can't be everywhere at once. How the hell did they get here so fast? They didn't have any carpets."

"Overland," Shed said.

"Overland? But . . ."

"It's shorter than the sea trip. Road cuts across. If you ride hard, day and night, you can make it in two days. When I was a kid, they used to have races. They stopped that when the new Duke took over."

"Guess it doesn't matter. So. What now?"

"Got to find out what happened," One-Eye said. He

muttered, "If that bastard Goblin got himself killed, I'll wring his neck."

"Right. But how do we do that? The Taken know us."

"I'll go," Shed volunteered.

Harder looks you cannot imagine than those we bent upon Marron Shed. He quailed for a moment. Then: "I won't let them catch me. Anyway, why should they bother me? They don't know me."

"Okay," I said. "Get moving."

"Croaker. . . ."

"Got to trust him, One-Eye. Unless you want to go yourself."

"Nope. Shed, you screw us over and I'll get you if I have to come back from the grave."

Shed smiled weakly, left us. On foot. Not many people rode through Meadenvil's streets. We found a tavern and made ourselves at home, two men staying in the street to watch. It was sundown before Shed returned.

"Well?" I said, signaling for another pitcher of beer.

"It's not good news. You guys are stuck. Your Lieutenant took the ship out. Twenty, twenty-five of your guys were killed. The rest went out on the ship. The Prince lost. . . ."

"Not all of them," One-Eye said, and tipped a pointing finger over the top of his mug. "Somebody followed you, Shed."

Shed whirled, terrified.

Goblin and Pawnbroker stood in the doorway. Pawn had been carved up some. He limped over and collapsed into a chair. I checked his wounds. Goblin and One-Eye exchanged looks that might have meant anything, but probably meant they were glad to see one another.

The tavern's other customers began to fade. Word who we were had gotten out. They knew some bad people were hunting us.

"Sit, Goblin," I said. "King, you and Otto go get some fresh horses." I gave them most of the money I had. "All the staples that will buy, too. I think we got a long ride ahead. Right, Goblin?"

He nodded.

"Let's hear it."

"Whisper and Limper turned up this morning. Came with fifty men. Company men. Looking for us. Made enough fuss we heard them coming. The Lieutenant sent word to everybody ashore. Some didn't get aboard in time. Whisper headed for the ship. The Lieutenant had to cut loose. We left nineteen men behind."

"What're you doing here?"

"I volunteered. Went over the side off the point, swam to shore, came back to wait for you guys. Supposed to tell you where to meet the ship. Ran into Pawn by accident. I was patching him up when I seen Shed poking around. We followed him back here."

I sighed. "They're headed for Chimney, right?"

He was surprised. "Yeah. How'd you know that?"

I explained briefly.

He said, "Pawn, better tell them what you know. Pawn was caught ashore. Only survivor I could find."

"This is a private adventure with the Taken," Pawn said. "They snuck down here. Supposed to be somewhere else. Figured it was a chance to get even, I guess, now we're not on the list of the Lady's favorites."

"She doesn't know they're here?"

"No."

I chuckled. Despite the gravity of the situation, I could not help that. "They're in for a surprise, then. The old bitch herself is going to turn up. We got another black castle growing here."

Several of them looked at me askance, wondering how I would know what the Lady was doing. I had not explained my dream to anyone but the Lieutenant. I finished patching Pawnbroker. "You'll be able to travel, but take it easy. How'd you find that out?"

"Shaky. We talked some before he tried to kill me."

"Shaky!" One-Eye snarled. "What the hell?"

"I don't know what the Taken told those guys. But they were cranked up. Wanted our asses bad. Suckers. Most of them got killed for their trouble."

"Killed?"

"Prince what's-it got righteous about the Taken walking in like they owned the place. There was a big fight with the Limper and our boys. Our guys practically got wiped out. Maybe they'd have done better if they could've rested first."

Funny. We talked it over like those men and we had not somehow become mortal enemies, sympathizing. And, in my case, feeling bitter toward the Taken for having turned and squandered them.

"Shaky say anything about Juniper?"

"Yeah. They had a real old-fashioned blood bath up there. Not much left of anything. Counting us, the Company was down six hundred guys when the Lady finished with the castle. Lot more guys was killed in the riots that came after, when she cleaned out the Catacombs. The whole damned city went crazy, with that Hargadon leading the rebellion. Had our guys trapped in Duretile. Then the Lady lost her temper. She wrecked what was left of the town."

I shook my head. "The Captain guessed right about the Catacombs."

"Journey took over what was left of the Company," Goblin said. "They was supposed to pull out with the plunder as soon as they got it all together. City is so wrecked there isn't no reason to stay around."

I looked at Shed. A bleaker face could not be imagined. Pain and questions twisted inside him. He wanted to know about his people. Did not want to speak for fear someone would accuse him. "Not your fault, man," I told him. "The Duke asked the Lady in before you got involved. It would have happened no matter what you did."

"How can people do stuff like that?"

Asa gave him the odd look. "Shed, that's dumb. How could you do all the stuff you did? Desperate, that's what. Everybody's desperate. They do crazy things."

One-Eye gave me a how-about-that? look. Even Asa could think sometimes.

"Pawn. Shaky say anything about Elmo?" Elmo remained my main regret.

"No. I didn't ask. We didn't have much time."

"What's the plan?" Goblin said.

"We'll head south when King and Otto get here with the horses and supplies." A sigh. "Going to be hard times. I got maybe two leva. How about you guys?"

We catalogued our resources. I said, "We're in trouble."

"The Lieutenant sent this." Goblin deposited a small sack on the table. It contained fifty silver castle coins from Raven's horde.

"That'll help. Still going to make it on prayer, though."

"I have some money," Shed volunteered. "Quite a bit. It's back where I was staying."

I eyeballed him. "You don't have to go. You're not part of this."

"Yes, I am."

"For as long as I've known you, you've been trying to run away. . . ."

"Got something to fight for now, Croaker. What they did to Juniper. I can't let that go."

"Me, too," Asa said. "I still got most of the money Raven gave me after we raided the Catacombs."

I polled the others silently. They did not respond. It was up to me. "All right. Get it. But don't dawdle. I want to pull out as soon as I can."

"I can catch you one the road," Shed said. "I don't see why Asa can't too." He rose. Shyly, he extended a hand. I hesitated only a moment.

"Welcome to the Black Company, Shed."

Asa did not make the same offer.

"Think they'll come back?" One-Eye asked after they left.

"What do you think?"

"Nope. I hope you know what you're doing, Croaker. They could get the Taken after us if they get caught."

"Yeah. They could." I was counting on it, in fact. A vicious notion had come to me. "Let's have another round here. Be our last for a long time."

# Chapter Forty-Seven: THE INN: ON THE RUN

*Very* much to my amazement, Shed overtook us ten miles south of Meadenvil. And he was not alone.

"Holy shit!" I heard One-Eye yell from the rear, and: "Croaker, come and look at this."

I turned back. And there was Shed. With a bedraggled Bullock. Shed said, "I promised to get him out if I could. Had to bribe some people, but it wasn't that hard. It's every man for himself up there right now."

I looked at Bullock. He looked at me. "Well?" I said.

"Shed gave me the word, Croaker. I guess I'm in with you guys. If you'll take me. I don't have anywhere else to go."

"Damn. Asa shows up, I'll lose my faith in human nature. Also blow an idea I have. Okay, Bullock. What the hell. Just remember we're not in Juniper. None of us. We're on the run from the Taken. And we don't have time to fuss over who did what to whom. You want a fight, save it for them."

"You're the boss. Just give me a shot at evening things up." He followed me back to the head of the column. "Not much difference between your Lady and somebody like Krage, is there?"

"Matter of proportion," I said. "Maybe you'll get your shot sooner than you think."

* * *

Silent and Otto came trotting out of the darkness. "You did good," I said. "Dogs never barked." I had sent Silent because he handled animals well.

"They're all back out of the woods and tucked in their beds," Otto reported.

"Good. Let's move in. Quietly. And I don't want anybody hurt. Understand? One-Eye?"

"I hear you."

"Goblin. Pawnbroker. Shed. You watch the horses. I'll signal with a lantern."

Occupying the inn was easier than planning it. We caught everyone asleep because Silent had fuddled their dogs. The innkeeper wakened puffing and blowing and terrified. I took him downstairs while One-Eye watched everybody else, including some northbound travelers who represented a complication, but who caused no trouble.

"Sit," I told the fat man. "You have tea or beer in the morning?"

"Tea," he croaked.

"It's making. So. We're back. We didn't expect to be, but circumstances dictated an overland trip. I want to use your place a couple days. You and me need to make an accommodation."

Hagop brought out tea so strong it reeked. The fat man drained a mug the size of that from which he drank his beer.

"I don't want to hurt anybody," I continued, after taking a sip myself. "And I'll pay my way. But if you want it that way, you'll have to cooperate."

He grunted.

"I don't want anybody to know we're here. That means no customers leave. People who come through have to see things looking normal. You get my drift?"

He was smarter than he looked. "You're waiting for somebody." None of the men had figured that out, I don't think.

"Yes. Somebody who will do unto you as you expect me to, just for being here. Unless my ambush works." I had a crazy idea. It would die if Asa turned up.

I think he believed me when I claimed no wicked plans for his family. Now. He asked, "That the same somebody who kicked up the ruckus in the city yesterday?"

"News travels fast."

"Bad news does."

"Yes. The same somebody. They killed about twenty of my people. Busted the city up pretty good, too."

"I heard. Like I said, bad news travels fast. My brother was one of the people they killed. He was in the Prince's guard. A sergeant. Only one of us ever amounted to anything. He was killed by something that ate him, I heared. Sorcerer sicced it on him."

"Yeah. He's a bad one. Nastier than my friend who can't talk." I did not know who would come after us. I was counting on someone doing so, with Asa to point the way. I also figured the pursuit would develop quickly. Asa would tell them the Lady was on her way to Meadenvil.

The fat man eyed me cautiously. Hatred smouldered behind his eyes. I tried to direct it. "I'm going to kill him."

"All right. Slow? Like my brother?"

"I don't think so. If it isn't fast and sneaky, he wins. Or she. There's two of them, actually. I don't know which one will come." I figured we could buy a lot of time if we could take out one of the Taken. The Lady would be damned busy with black castles for a while with only two pairs of hands to help her. Also, I had an emotional debt to pay, and a message to make clear.

"Let me send the wife and kids away," he said. "I'll stand in with you."

I let my gaze flick to Silent. He nodded slightly. "All right. What about your guests?"

"I know them. They'll sit tight."

"Good. Go take care of your part."

He left. Then I had it out with Silent and the others. I had not been elected to command. I was running on momentum as senior officer present. It got angry for a while. But I won my point.

Fear is a wonderful motivator. It moved Goblin and

One-Eye like nothing I've ever seen. Moved the men, too. They set up every gimmick they could imagine. Booby traps. Hiding places prepared from which an attack could be carried out, each glossed with a concealing spell. Weapons prepared with fanatical attention.

The Taken are not invulnerable. They're just hard to reach, and more so when they're ready for trouble. Whoever came would be.

Silent went into the woods with the fat man's family. He returned with a hawk that he tamed in record time, and cast it aloft to patrol the road between Meadenvil and the inn. We would be forewarned.

The landlord prepared dishes tainted with poison, though I advised him that the Taken seldom eat. He petitioned Silent for advice concerning his dogs. He had a whole pack of savage mastiffs and wanted them in on the action. Silent found them a spot in the plan. We did everything we could, and then settled in to wait. When my shift came, I took my turn getting some rest.

She came. Almost the moment my eyes closed, it seemed. I was in a panic for a moment, trying to banish my location and plan from my mind. But what was the point? She had found me already. The thing to conceal was the ambush.

"Have you reconsidered?" she asked. "You cannot outrun me. I want you, physician."

"That why you sent Whisper and the Limper? To return us to the fold? They killed half our men, lost most of theirs, wrecked the city, and didn't make a single friend. Is that how you win us back?"

She had not been party to that, of course. Pawnbroker had said the Taken were acting on their own. I wanted her angry and distracted. I wanted to know her reaction.

She said, "They're supposed to be headed back to the Barrowland."

"Sure they are. They just go off on their own any time they feel like it, to settle grudges ten years old."

"Do they know where you are?"

"Not yet." I now had the feeling she could not locate me precisely. "I'm outside the city, lying low."

"Where?"

I let an image seep through. "Near the place where the new castle is growing. It was the nearest place we could put up." I figured a strong thread of truth was in order. Anyway, I wanted her to find the gift I meant to leave.

"Stay where you are. Do not attract attention. I will be there soon."

"Thought so."

"Do not test my patience, physician. You amuse me, but you are not invulnerable. I am short of temper these days. Whisper and Limper have pressed their luck one time too many."

The door of the room opened. One-Eye said, "Who you talking to, Croaker?"

I shuddered. He stood on the far side of the glow without seeing it. I was awake. I replied, "My girlfriend," and giggled.

An instant later I endured a moment of intense vertigo. Something parted from me, leaving a flavor both of amusement and irritation. I recovered, found One-Eye kneeling, frowning. "What's the matter?" he demanded.

I shook my head. "Head feels like it's on backwards. Shouldn't have had that beer. What's up?"

He scowled suspiciously. "Silent's hawk came in. They're coming. Come on downstairs. We need to redo the plan."

"They?"

"The Limper and nine men. That's what I mean, we need to redo. Right now the odds look too good for the other side."

"Yeah." Those would be Company men. The inn wouldn't fool them. Inns are the axes of life in the hinterlands. The Captain used them frequently to draw the Rebel.

Silent did not have much to add, except that we had only as long as it would take our pursuers to cover six miles.

"Hey!" The old comes-the-dawn. Suddenly I *knew* why

the Taken had come to Meadenvil. "You got a wagon and team?" I asked the innkeeper. I still did not know his name.

"Yeah. Use it to haul supplies down from Meadenvil, from the miller's, from the brewer's. Why?"

"Because the Taken are looking for those papers I've been on about." I had to reveal their provenance.

"The same ones we dug up in the Forest of Cloud?" One-Eye asked.

"Yes. Look. Soulcatcher told me they have the Limper's true name in them. They also include the wizard Bomanz's secret papers, where the Lady's true name is supposedly encoded."

"Wow!" Goblin said.

"Right."

One-Eye demanded, "What's that got to do with us?"

"The Limper wants his name back. Suppose he sees a bunch of guys and a wagon light out of here? What's he going to figure? Asa gave him bum dope about them being with Raven. Asa doesn't know everything we've been up to."

Silent interjected, in sign, "Asa is with the Limper."

"Fine. He did what I wanted. Okay. The Limper figures that's us making a run for it with the papers. 'Specially if we let a few pieces go fluttering around."

"I get it," One-Eye said. "Only we don't have enough men to work it. Only Bullock and the landlord that Asa don't know about."

Goblin said, "I think you better stop talking and start doing. They're getting closer."

I called the fat man. "Your friends from the South have to do us a favor. Tell them it's their only chance of getting out of this alive."

# Chapter Forty-Eight: THE INN: AMBUSH

The four southerners were shaking and sweating. They did not know what was going on, did not like what they saw. But they had become convinced that cooperation was their only hope. "Goblin!" I shouted upstairs. "Can you see them yet?"

"Almost time. Count to fifty, then turn it loose."

I counted. Slowly, forcing myself to keep the pace down. I was as scared as the southerners.

"Now!"

Goblin came boiling downstairs. We all roared out to the barn, where the animals and wagon were waiting, whooped out of there, stormed into the road, and went howling off south like eight men very nearly taken by surprise. Behind us the Limper's party halted momentarily, talked it over, then came after us. I noted that the Limper was setting the pace. Good. His men were not eager to tangle with their old buddies.

I brought up the rear, behind Goblin and One-Eye and the wagon. One-Eye was driving. Goblin kept his mount right beside the wagon.

We roared into a rising curve where the road began climbing a wooded hill south of the inn. The innkeeper said the forest went on for miles. He had gone ahead with Silent and Bullock and the men the southerners were pretending to be.

"Yo!" someone shouted back. A scrap of red cloth

whipped past. One-Eye stood up on the wagon, clinging to the traces as he edged over. Goblin swung in close. One-Eye jumped.

For a moment I did not think he would make it. Goblin almost missed. One-Eye's feet trailed in the dust. Then he scrambled up, lay on his stomach behind his friend. He glared back at me, daring me to grin.

I grinned anyway.

The wagon hit the timber prepared, flung up, twisted. Horses screamed, fought, could not hold it. Wagon and team went thrashing off the road, crashed against trees, the animals screaming in pain and terror while the vehicle disintegrated. The men who had upset the wagon vanished immediately.

I spurred my mount forward, past Goblin and One-Eye and Pawnbroker, yelled at the southerners, gave them the sign to go on, keep riding, get the hell away.

A quarter mile father on I swung onto the track the fat man had told me about, got down into the woods far enough not to be seen, halted long enough for One-Eye to get himself seated. Then we moved on hurriedly, headed for the inn.

Above us, Limper and his bunch came pounding up to where the wrecked wagon lay, the animals still crying their distress.

It started.

Cries. Shrieks. Men dying. Hiss and howl of spells. I didn't think Silent stood a chance, but he had volunteered. The wagon was supposed to distract the limper long enough for the massed attack to reach him.

The clangor was still going on, muted by distance, when we reached open country. "Can't be going all wrong," I shouted. "Been going on a while."

I did not feel as optimistic as I pretended. I did not want it to go on. I'd wanted them to hit quick, hurt the Limper, and fade away, doing enough damage to make him retreat to the inn to lick his wounds.

We hustled the animals into the barn and headed for our hiding places. I muttered, "You know, we wouldn't be in this spot if Raven had killed him when he had a chance." Way back, when I had helped capture Whisper, when she was trying to bring Limper over to her side, Raven had had a fantastic opportunity to finish him off. He had not been able, though he had had grievances against the Taken. His mercy had come back to haunt us all.

Pawnbroker went into the pig shed, where we had installed a crude, light ballista built as part of our earlier plan. Goblin cast a weak spell that made him seem like just another hog. I wanted him to stay out of it if possible. I doubted the ballista would get used.

Goblin and I raced upstairs to watch the road and the ridgeline to the east. Once he broke off, which he had not done when he was supposed to, Silent would fake in the direction taken by the southerners, retreat through the wood to that ridge, watch what happened at the inn. It was my hope that some of the Limper's men would keep after the southerners. I hadn't told those guys that. I hoped they had sense enough to keep running.

"Ho!" Goblin said. "There's Silent. He made it."

The men appeared briefly. I could not tell who was who. "Only three of them," I muttered. That meant four had not made it. "Damn!"

"It had to work," Goblin said. "Else they wouldn't be up there."

I did not feel reassured. I hadn't had many shots at field command. I hadn't learned to deal with the feelings that come when you know men have been killed trying to carry out your orders.

"Here they come."

Riders left the woods, coming up the Shaker Road amidst lengthening shadows. "I make it six men," I said. "No. Seven. They must not have gone after those guys."

"Looks like they're all hurt."

"Element of surprise. The Limper with them? Can you tell?"

"No. That one. . . . That's Asa. Hell, that's old Shed on the third horse, and the innkeeper next to last."

A slight positive, then. They were half as strong as they had been. I'd lost only two of seven committed.

"What do we do if the Limper ain't with them?" Goblin asked.

"Take what comes to us." Silent had vanished off the far ridge.

"There he is, Croaker. In front of the innkeeper. Looks like he's unconscious."

That was too much to hope. Yet it did indeed look like the Taken was out. "Let's get downstairs."

I watched through a cracked shutter as they turned into the yard. The only member of the group uninjured was Asa. His hands were bound to his saddle, his feet to his stirrups. One of the injured men dismounted, released Asa, held a knife on him while he helped the others. A variety of injuries were evident. Shed looked like he shouldn't be alive at all. The innkeeper was in better shape. Just seemed to have been knocked around a lot.

They made Asa and the fat man get the Limper off his animal. I nearly gave myself away then. The Taken was missing most of his right arm. He had several additional wounds. But, of course, he would recover if he remained protected by his allies. The Taken are tough.

Asa and the fat man started toward the door. Limper sagged like a wet rope. The man who had covered Asa pushed the door open.

The Limper wakened. "No!" he squeaked. "Trap!"

Asa and the innkeeper dropped him. Asa began heeling and toeing it, eyes closed. The innkeeper whistled shrilly. His dogs came raging out of the barn.

Goblin and One-Eye cut loose. I jumped out and went for the Limper as he tried to gain his feet.

My blade bit into the Limper's shoulder above the stump of his right arm. His remaining fist came up and brushed me across the belly.

The air exploded out of me. I nearly passed out. I settled to the ground, heaving my guts out, only vaguely aware of my surroundings.

The dogs boiled over the Limper's men, mauling them

savagely. Several hit the Taken. He hammered them with his fist, each blow leaving an animal dead.

Goblin and One-Eye charged out, hit him with everything they had. He shed their spells like rainwater, punched One-Eye, turned on Goblin.

Goblin ran. The Limper trundled after him, weaving, the surviving mastiffs snapping at his back.

Goblin raced toward the pig shed. He went sprawling before he reached it, twitched feebly in the mire. Limper rolled up behind him, fist raised for the kill.

Pawnbroker's shaft split his breastbone, stood three feet out of his back. He stood there swaying, a ragged little man in brown picking at the shaft. His whole will seemed to focus upon that. Goblin wriggled away. Inside the shed Pawn cranked the ballista back and dropped another javelin into its trough.

*Whomp!* This one ripped all the way through the Limper. It knocked him off his feet. The dogs went for his throat.

I regained my breath. I looked for my sword. Vaguely, I was aware of screeching from a patch of blackberries along a ditch two hundred feet north. A lone dog trotted back and forth, snarling. Asa. He had ducked into the only cover available.

I got my feet under me. The fat man helped One-Eye get up, then snagged a fallen weapon. We three closed in on the Limper. He lay in the mire, twisted slightly sideways, his mask slipped so we could see the ruined face it had concealed. He could not believe what was happening. Feebly, he waved at the dogs.

"All for nothing," I told him. "The papers haven't been here for months."

And the fat man: "This is for my brother." He swung his weapon. He was so badly bruised, and getting so stiff, that he did not get much into it.

The Limper tried to strike back. He did not have anything left. He realized that he was going to die. After all those centuries. After having survived the White Roses, and the anger of the Lady after he had betrayed her in the battle at Roses and in the Forest of Cloud.

His eyes rolled up and he went away, and I knew he was yelling for Mama's help.

"Kill him quick," I said. "He's calling the Lady."

We hacked and slashed and chopped. The dogs snarled and bit. He would not die. Even when we ran out of energy, a spark of life remained.

"Let's drag him around front."

We did. And I saw Shed, lying on the ground with men who used to be brothers in the Black Company. I looked up at the waning light, saw Silent approaching, followed by Hagop and Otto. I felt a numb pleasure because those two had survived. They had been best friends for as long as I could recall. I could not picture one surviving without the other.

"Bullock's gone, eh?"

The fat man said, "Yeah. Him and this Shed. You should have seen them. They jumped into the road and pulled the sorcerer off his horse. Bullock chopped his arm off. Between them they killed four men."

"Bullock?"

"Somebody split his head open. Like hitting a melon with a cleaver."

"Kingpin?"

"Got trampled to death. But he got his licks in."

I levered myself down beside Shed. One-Eye did the same. "How'd they catch you?" I asked the innkeeper.

"Too fat to run fast." He managed a feeble smile. "Never was meant to be a soldier."

I smiled. "What do you think, One-Eye?" A glance told me there was nothing I could do for Shed.

One-Eye shook his head.

Goblin said, "Two of these guys are still alive, Croaker. What you want we should do?"

"Take them inside. I'll patch them up." They were brothers. That the Taken had twisted them and made them enemies did not make them less deserving of my help.

Silent came up, looming tall in the twilight. He signed, "A maneuver worthy of the Captain, Croaker."

"Right." I stared at Shed, moved more than I thought I should be.

A man lay before me. He had sunk as low as any I'd ever known. Then he had fought his way back, and back, and had become worthy. A man far better than I, for he had located his moral polestar and set his course by it, though it had cost his life. Maybe, just a little, he had repaid his debt.

He did another thing by getting himself killed in a fight I did not consider his. He became a sort of patron saint of mine, an example for days to come. He set a high standard in his last few days.

He opened his eyes before the end. He smiled. "Did we do it?" he asked.

"We did it, Shed. Thanks to you and Bullock."

"Good." Still smiling, he closed his eyes.

Hagop hollered, "Hey, Croaker. What you want to do about this Asa creep?"

Asa was still in the blackberries, yelling for help. The dogs had the patch surrounded.

"Put a couple javelins in him," One-Eye muttered.

"No," Shed said in a tiny whisper. "Let him be. He was my friend. He tried to get back, but they caught him. Let him go."

"All right, Shed. Hagop! Dig him out and turn him loose."

"What?"

"You heard me." I looked back at Shed. "Okay, Shed?"

He didn't say anything. He couldn't. But he was smiling.

I got up and said, "At least somebody died the way he wanted. Otto. Get a damned shovel."

"Aw, Croaker. . . ."

"Get a goddamned shovel and get to work. Silent, One-Eye, Goblin, inside. We got plans to make."

The light was nearly gone. By the Lieutenant's estimate it would be but hours before the Lady reached Meadenvil.

# Chapter Forty-Nine: ON THE MOVE

"We need rest," One-Eye protested.

"There won't be any rest till we're dead," I countered. "We're on the other side now, One-Eye. We did what the Rebel couldn't. We've done in the Limper, the last of the original Taken. She'll be after us hard as soon as she's cleaned up these black castle leavings. She has to. If she doesn't get us fast, every Rebel in five thousand miles will get worked up to try something. There are only two Taken left, and only Whisper worth much."

"Yeah. I know. Wishful thinking. Can't stop a man wishing, Croaker."

I stared at the necklace Shed had worn. I had to leave it for the Lady, yet the silver in it might become a lifesaver down the long road we had to travel. I screwed up my courage and began digging out the eyes.

"What the hell you doing?"

"Going to leave these with the Limper. Going to feed them to him. I figure they'll hatch."

"Ha!" Goblin said. "Ironic. Fitting."

"I thought it an interesting turn of justice. Give him back to the Dominator."

"And the Lady will have to destroy him. I like it."

Grudgingly, One-Eye agreed.

"Thought you guys would. Go see if they've got everybody buried."

"Only been ten minutes since they got back with the bodies."

"All right. Go help." I levered myself up and went to check on the men I had patched up. I don't know if everyone Hagop and Otto brought back from the ambush site was dead when they got there. They certainly were now. Kingpin had been dead for a long time, though they had brought him to me to examine.

My patients were doing fine. One was aware enough to be frightened. I patted his arm and limped outside.

They had King in the ground now, beside Shed and Bullock and the Limper's boy they had buried earlier. Only two corpses remained unburied. Asa was making the dirt fly. Everyone else stood and watched. Till they saw me glowering.

"What's the take?" I asked the fat man. I'd had him strip the dead of valuables.

"Not a lot." He showed me a hat filled with odds and ends.

"Take what you need to cover the damages."

"You guys will need it more than me."

"You're out a wagon and a team, not to mention the dogs. Take what you need. I can always rob somebody I don't like." No one knew that I had filched Shed's purse. Its weight had surprised me. It would be my secret reserve. "Take a couple horses, too."

He shook his head. "I'm not getting caught with somebody else's animals after the dust settles and the Prince starts looking for scapegoats." He selected a few silver coins. "I got what I wanted."

"Okay. You'd better hide in the woods for a while. The Lady will come here. She's nastier than the Limper."

"Will do."

"Hagop. If you're not going to dig, go get the horses ready. Move!" I beckoned Silent. He and I dragged the Limper to a shade tree out front. Silent tossed a rope over a limb. I forced the eyes of the serpents down the Taken's throat. We hoisted him up. He turned slowly in the chill moonlight. I rubbed my hands together and considered him. "Took a while, guy, but somebody finally got you." For ten years I had wanted to see him go down. He had been the most inhuman of the Taken.

Asa came to me. "All buried, Croaker."

"Good. Thanks for the help." I started toward the barn.

"Can I go with you guys?"

I laughed.

"Please, Croaker? Don't leave me here where. . . ."

"I don't give a damn, Asa. But don't expect me to look out for you. And don't try any slick tricks. I'd as soon kill you as look at you."

"Thanks, Croaker." He raced ahead, hastily saddled another horse. One-Eye looked at me and shook his head.

"Mount up, men. Let's go find Raven."

Though we pushed hard, we were not twenty miles south of the inn when something hit my mind like a fighter's fist. A golden cloud materialized, radiating anger. "You have exhausted my patience, physician."

"You exhausted mine a long time ago."

"You'll rue this murder."

"I'll exult in it. It's the first decent thing I've done this side of the Sea of Torments. Go find your castle eggs. Leave me alone. We're even."

"Oh, no. You will hear from me again. As soon as I close the last door on my husband."

"Don't press your luck, old witch. I'm ready to get out of the game. Push and I'll learn TelleKurre."

That caught her from the blind side.

"Ask Whisper what she lost in the Forest of Cloud and hoped to recover in Meadenvil. Then reflect upon what an angry Croaker could do with it if he knew where to find it."

There was a vertiginous moment as she withdrew.

I found my companions looking at me weirdly. "Just saying good-bye to my girl," I told them.

We lost Asa in Shaker. We took a day off there, to prepare for the next leg, and when it came time to leave,

Asa was not to be seen. Nobody bothered looking for him. On Shed's behalf I left him with a wish for luck. Judging from his past, he probably had it, and all bad.

My farewell to the Lady did not take. Three months to the day after the Limper's fall, as we were resting prior to hazarding the last range of hills between us and Chimney, the golden cloud visited me again. This time the Lady was less belligerent. In fact, she seemed mildly amused.

"Greetings, physician. I thought you might want to know, for the sake of your Annals, that the threat of the black castle no longer exists. Every seed has been located and destroyed." More amusement. "There is no way my husband can rise short of exhumation. He is cut off, totally incapable of communicating with his sympathizers. A permanent army occupies the Barrowland."

I could think of nothing to say. It was no less than I had expected, and had hoped she would accomplish, for she was the lesser evil, and, I suspect, remained possessed of a spark that had not committed itself to the darkness. She had shown restraint on several occasions when she could have indulged her cruelty. Maybe if she felt unchallenged, she would drift toward the light rather than farther toward the shadow.

"I interviewed Whisper. With the Eye. Stand clear, Croaker."

Never before had she called me by name. I sat up and took notice. There was no amusement in her now.

"Stand clear?"

"Of those papers. Of the girl."

"Girl? What girl?"

"Don't come the innocent. I know. You left a wider trail than you thought. And even dead men answer questions for one who knows how they must be asked. Such of your Company as remained when I returned to Juniper told most of the story. If you wish to live out your days in peace, kill her. If you don't, I will. Along with anyone near her."

"I don't know what you're talking about."

Amusement again, but a hard sort. A malignant sort. "Keep your Annals, physician. I will be in touch. I will keep you apprised of the advance of the empire."

Puzzled, I asked, "Why?"

"Because it amuses me. Behave yourself." She faded away.

We went down into Chimney, tired men three-quarters dead. We found the Lieutenant and the ship and—Lo! —Darling, who was living aboard with the Company. The Lieutenant had taken employment with the private constabulary of a mercantile factor. He added our names to the roll as soon as we recuperated.

We did not find Raven. Raven had evaded reconciliation or confrontation with his old comrades by cheating his way out.

Fate is a fickle bitch who dotes on irony. After all he had been through, all he had done, all he had survived, the very morning the Lieutenant arrived he slipped on a wet marble diving platform in a public bath, split his head open, fell into the pool, and drowned.

I refused to believe it. It could not be true, after what he had pulled up north. I dug around. I poked. I pried. But there were scores of people who had seen the body. The most reliable witness of all, Darling, was absolutely convinced. In the end, I had to give in. This time no one would hear my doubts.

The Lieutenant himself claimed to have seen and recognized the corpse as the flames of a pyre had risen about it the morning of his arrival. It was there he had encountered Darling and had brought her back into the keeping of the Black Company.

What could I say? If Darling believed, it must be true. Raven could never lie to her.

Nineteen days after our arrival in Chimney, there was another arrival, which explained the Lady's nebulous remark about interviewing only those she could find when she returned to Juniper.

Elmo rode into town with seventy men, many brethren

from the old days, whom he had spirited out of Juniper while all the Taken were absent but Journey, and Journey was in such a state of confusion due to conflicting orders from the Lady that he let slip the true state of affairs in Meadenvil. He followed me down the coast.

So, in two years, the Black Company had crossed the breadth of the world, from the nethermost east to the farthest west, close to four thousand miles, and in the process had come near destruction, and had found a new purpose, a new life. We were now the champions of the White Rose, a bedraggled joke of a nucleus for the force legend destined to bring the Lady down.

I did not believe a word of that. But Raven had told Darling what she was, and she, at least, was ready to play her part.

We could but try.

I hoisted a glass of wine in the master's cabin. Elmo, Silent, One-Eye, Goblin, the Lieutenant and Darling raised theirs. Above, men prepared to cast off. Elmo had brought the Company treasure chest. We had no need to work. I proposed my toast. "To the twenty-nine years."

Twenty-nine years. According to legend it would be that long before the Great Comet returned and fortune would smile upon the White Rose.

They responded, "The twenty-nine years."

I thought I detected the faintest hint of gold in the corner of my eye, felt the faintest hint of amusement.